Books by Cate Michels

<u>Generations of Hope Trilogy</u>
All That We Have—Book 1
Sorrow's Trace—Book 2
In The Fullness of Time—Book 3

GET YOUR FREE PREQUEL NOVELLA:
***In All Its Fury**—The blizzard of 1888*
Join my mailing list at *www.catemichels.com* to get the free ebook or PDF
in addition to updates on my books, projects, and events!

All That We Have

A Novel

Cate Michels

F.B. Henry Press

Cate Michels

www.catemichels.com

Printed in the United States of America

ISBN: 978-1-7345705-2-6

First Printing: 2023*

*ALL THAT WE HAVE IS A REVISED & EDITED VERSION OF THE NOVEL FORMERLY TITLED HOPE SHALL BRIGHTEN DAYS TO COME

F.B. Henry Press LLC

For Mic

GENERATIONS OF HOPE SERIES

Book One

PROLOGUE

March 1891 • **German Empire** • **Near the upper Rhine.** Gusty winds swirled through the cobblestone streets of Strasbourg, churning the air that hung heavy in the village nestled between the Vosges and Black Forest Mountains. Herr Kaiser glanced at the darkening clouds while thunder rumbled in the distance. He quickened his pace past the stalls of vendors peddling baskets of sausages, cheese, early spring flowers, and the like. Shop doorbells jingled up the lane as patrons hurried in and out. Horses' hooves clacked in unison with the wooden wheels of buggies and wagons as they hastened down the road running parallel with the Rhine. Smoke billowed from the train gliding down the tracks on the Baden side of the river, the dark wisps disappearing into the sky.

Humid air mixed with aromas of bread and cakes when he opened the bakery door. A small child with a bun tucked in her fist pushed out underneath his arm, and an elderly woman hobbled to the threshold, pausing to loosen her scarf. Herr Kaiser held in a sigh as he waited for her to move forward into the crowded space. He stood near the back where the air wasn't as stifling, waiting until the counter cleared before approaching.

"What can I get you, Herr Kaiser?" The matron's flat voice mirrored her hooded lids. She tucked stray hair beneath her scarf, bits of flour remaining behind.

Herr Kaiser pointed to the cake in the back of the case. "Bitte, Frau Beck."

Frau Beck boxed the cake and slid it toward him in exchange for his coins.

"A birthday." He smiled, wondering if it would cajole one in return.

"Ah." Frau Beck nodded absently——her mouth pinched as she glanced over his head to the activity outside.

"Anything else, Herr Kaiser?" She craned her neck, looking past him again.

"No, thank you." He tucked the box under his arm and turned toward the door, wondering what caught Frau Beck's attention.

Herr Kaiser scanned the skies, the thick clouds near bursting. He maneuvered through the harried crowd, stopping for a moment to remove his topcoat, setting it over the Kuchen. A drop of rain splashed on his arm as he hurried past the bakery, but a cry stopped him in his tracks. He glanced around, hearing angry voices bouncing off the brick walls in the narrow alley. The rain increased, and for a moment, Kaiser considered turning toward home, but instead, he crept down the cobblestone path toward the sound. Footsteps beat loudly on the pathway as he rounded the corner, the fleeing persons now out of sight.

Herr Beck lay on the cobbled path, his white smock askew, an empty pail and crates scattered about.

Herr Kaiser approached the baker. The man groaned, putting his hand on a wall to steady himself as he attempted to rise from his prone position. Herr Kaiser rushed to his aid, reaching for Beck's elbow. Blood flowed from Beck's nose, a gash slashed his arm, and a bruise marked his cheek——already deeply purpled from age.

"What happened?" Herr Kaiser held out a hand. "Let me help you inside."

"I'm fine. I'm fine." Beck waved him off. "Go. Please."

"But, sir, you're hurt. Who did this?"

"Go. It's not your business." The baker stumbled toward the back door of his shop, putting one hand against the brick wall to steady himself as he pulled open the heavy wooden door and went inside.

Kaiser crossed his arms and frowned. Both Frau and Herr Beck customarily offered cheery greetings. *What could have happened here today? First Frau Beck and now this.* Kaiser swiveled around the small space between the back alley and the building until his eyes stopped on the large black letters scrawled on the brick wall. Aus Juden! *Out Jews.* A bucket of spilled soapy water flowed into the cracks and crevices of the stones, a course brush still inside, the intensifying rain splitting the bubbles.

Kaiser shuddered and picked up the soapy brush, scrubbing the wall until the hateful words became a grayish blur. He stacked the crates neatly against the store wall before heading back up the alley toward his home. This was not the first time he'd seen similar words on Jewish homes and properties. *Who were these vile people?* His anger rose, and he pressed the box under his arm, denting the sides. Shaking his head, he repositioned the cake, picking up his pace out of the village.

His youngest son rushed out to greet him when he stepped inside the front gate less than an hour later. The boy smiled a toothy grin. "Is the cake for me?"

"Nein. Now get back inside and out of the rain." Kaiser shooed the youngster away.

Movement on the side of the house caught Kaiser's eye. He stopped and watched, realizing his oldest son was leaning against a large tree, its umbrella of leaves barely keeping the boy dry. Kaiser tipped his head, curious——his son was paging through a large book.

Herr Kaiser opened the front door, called to his wife, handed her the cake, and then crept toward the tree. As he rounded the tree, the lad quickly shut the book, its pages thumping hard on a tattered paper that protruded from the top. The boy's face reddened.

"What is this?" Herr Kaiser nodded his head toward the book.

"A book, Vati." The lad squinted and dropped his head.

Herr Kaiser reached over his son's form, snatched the paper from the book, and promptly dropped it as if it were on fire. The words, *The Greater*

German Solution for the Superior Aryan Race, emblazoned in large red letters, soaked up the rain.

1917

CHAPTER 1

Jacob Harvey's jaw clenched as he folded the newspaper and set it on the kitchen table. He sighed heavily and wrapped his hands around the mug of coffee that grew cold as he mulled over the report, thinking it wouldn't be long before Wilson's reelection slogan *He Kept Us Out of War* would fall to the wayside. President Wilson had proudly launched his new campaign on that pledge, a testament to his position of neutrality after war broke out in Europe in early 1914. He'd garnered enough support for his position to win reelection by a narrow margin in November 1916.

Jacob couldn't comprehend what seemed to be a denial of the facts by many people in this country. They seemed to have forgotten how, less than two years ago, a German U-boat torpedoed the Lusitania, sinking the passenger ship in British waters——American citizens accounting for over one hundred of the drowned travelers. Jacob snorted and shook his head, remembering the grocer's recent comment about the Great War in Europe seeming to be another world away. Distance and President Wilson would keep them safe, despite the tenuous and oft-disregarded agreement between Germany and the United States about neutral passenger and commercial vessels.

On the other side of the kitchen, Jacob's wife Helene covered the bread and set it to rise, the yeasty smell clinging to the sides of the large, buttered crockery bowl. She moved around in the small kitchen to the table nestled under the window and cleared the breakfast dishes. The morning was quiet, only the clanking of the plates and cups she washed occasionally breaking the silence. Her heavy wooden clogs plodded on the floor planks as she moved to Jacob with the steaming coffee pot, topping off his cup with the rich, dark liquid. The aroma pulled him from his reflections, and he glanced at his wife as she set the pot back on the stove.

He exhaled heavily once again, and Helene came to the table and sat, the chair creaking under her weight. "What is it?" She leaned forward and raised a brow.

"I don't know yet, but it's not good."

He ran his hand through his gray hair and then reached out, briefly touching her hand before rising. The chair's legs scraped on the wood floor with the sudden movement——sharp punctuation to his comment. He grabbed his lunch pail and overcoat and headed out the door without another word.

Helene watched her husband move down the alley, his shoulders slumping. Still, the dark mood in the kitchen quickly brightened as their daughter Melania slipped into the room. Melania's dark hair was pulled back in a tight bun at the nape of her neck, just barely touching the scalloped collar of her crisp white blouse. She glided past her mother and peeked at the breakfast offering, a waft of lavender filling the space.

"The cinnamon buns smell heavenly." The girl snatched her wool cardigan off the peg by the door, slipping it on as she glanced out the window. Winter snows had pushed their way through to March, and although it was sunny, a crispness still hung heavy in the morning air.

"With March here, we can finally say that school is almost over!" Melania chattered as she gathered her schoolbooks into a pile before sashaying across the floor and plunking down in her seat.

"That it is, dear," Helene said, her voice tinged with sadness. Her daughter was nearly done with school, set to graduate soon——change was in the air.

Melania put her stacked books in her schoolbag and set them near her feet as Helene slid a plate of two eggs and a warm bun in front of her. Melania curled one leg under herself while she gazed out the window, nibbling at the edges of the cinnamon bun.

"Come, Melania. Eat before it gets cold."

Her daughter turned from the window, breaking the yolks into a pool of yellow. After a few quick bites, the fork rattled to the plate. "I really must go. Mr. Dickinson said the applications for the Minneapolis Teaching School will be on hand today. I want to get one straight away." Melania sighed wistfully. "I *so* want to be in the first class of this program." She set her yellow-soaked plate gently in the washbasin and then retrieved her bag.

Helene smiled, enjoying her daughter's banter, knowing the days of her youngest living under their roof were waning.

Melania stepped into her clogs and threw her wool coat over her arm, pecking Helene's cheek. "Goodbye, Mutti."

Helene reopened the back door just as Melania stepped into the alley. "Come directly home after school," she called after her daughter. *We need to talk about some things.* Did they? It seemed time. She sighed, realizing her exhalation was as long and loud as Jacob's earlier that morning. She didn't want to stew over the unknown, but she couldn't shake her husband's demeanor and mood. Helene already sensed the impending storm. Since the beginning of the war, she had overheard many conversations between her husband and older son Frank. The battle may be in Europe *now*, but it had already come close to home. Earlier in the war, a German officer had been arrested for bombing a railroad bridge between the United States and Canada. And today's headlines brought Germany's evil plans to the southern borders of the United States. It was coming all right, and this storm was not one from which they could shelter their youngest daughter or themselves.

The Harveys' small home on North Pine Street was like many others in Holmesburg——constructed of the quality, cream-colored bricks made from the region's deep, rich clay deposits. Nearly twenty percent of the town's population worked at one of the six local brickyards, with many German and Scandinavian immigrants bringing their masonry skills to the region. Jacob crossed the street and stepped over the double railroad tracks toward his job at the Holmesburg Flour Mill. The railroad carried goods to and from the mill, the cannery, and the brickyard to Minneapolis, St. Paul, and beyond——rail replacing the barge and steamboat transport that had been the pathway in the last century.

It was a short walk to the mill, but Jacob needed time to think. He veered toward 3rd Street, and within minutes, he was in the hub of activity as the town awakened to this bright March morning. The steady din of carriages, occasional motorized vehicles, and shop and church bells floated above his thoughts. The newspaper article weighed heavily, and he knew he must clear his head before his shift began. While unions had brought many upgrades to the mill machines and working conditions, Jacob was keenly aware of the dangers of operating *any* machinery. The task necessitated his complete focus. With war looming——*he was sure of it*——keeping his job was paramount.

Over his ten years at the mill, Jacob had moved from a loader to a packer to a smutter. His sixty-four-year-old body was too old for hard labor, part of why his eldest sons had taken over the farm a decade and a half earlier. He welcomed the mill job and the move to the smaller house in town, but the work still taxed him physically. He had hoped to retire completely in the next couple of years, allowing the income from his rental cropland to suffice for his now small household. But war would change everything.

For now, Jacob pushed that issue aside, focusing his attention on to-day's news. The bulletin troubled him, but he cherished the privilege of receiving it——the American free press was something he didn't take for granted. He knew that many of the townspeople would brush off the Herald's headline, confident that Wilson would keep his promise, come what may. *Foolishness.* He had been there and seen what some German citizens were capable of——his countrymen once, countrymen of most of the town's residents. *Didn't they remember? Or would they not acknowledge it?*

Deep in his meditations over the morning news, Jacob nearly ran smack into Helmer Helmke as the business owner came out of his blacksmith shop on 3rd & Chestnut.

"What's got you looking at your shoes today, Harvey?" Helmer ribbed him. "Worried about the news?"

"Ja. For sure." Jacob nodded slightly, quickly moving around the bench Helmer set against his shop window.

As Jacob stepped into the intersection toward Walnut Street, Helmer's voice carried in the air. "I'm outraged that Father Rausch dubbed the spring church dance a St. Patrick's Day celebration. It's *always* been an event honoring our Parish's German heritage!"

"Ja and this is just the beginning," Jacob muttered, shaking his head at Helmer's comment. "But no one is paying any attention."

"What did you say, Harvey?" Helmer called out to him.

Jacob waved his hand dismissively and continued on his way toward work. It wasn't worth discussing with Helmer when his neighbor focused on the trivial.

Jacob turned the corner toward the Holmesburg Flour Mill, clarity rising to the surface of his thoughts. Others might be in denial or focused on the wrong things, but *he* wouldn't be caught unprepared. He began to formulate a plan.

After a ten-hour shift with his hands nimbly working his wheat-cleaning machine, Jacob hung his work apron on the hooks outside the grinding room door. He knew what he and his family must do. It was essential.

Helene left her husband to his thoughts when he returned from his shift that evening. He muttered while doing his chores and mainly stayed silent while eating supper. Jacob still had not said much to her two hours later, and Helene looked up from her needlework to see him absently poking at the logs in the hearth. Firelight flashed in bright spurts, and swirls of robust oak wafted through the room. Helene pushed the darning needle in and out of the wool sock while the rocker knocked and creaked in a steady rhythm.

She looked up from her work again when Melania joined them by the fire, settling on the sofa with a book. After finishing the sock, Helene went back to rocking, picking up knitting needles. The swishes of the needles banging together were punctuated by other random sounds——her daughter turning a page in her book, a log rolling from the pile, and the clicking of the clock hands. She heard Melania shift in her seat, and she guessed her daughter had sensed the tension in the room.

Finally, the silence was broken by Jacob's deep voice. "War is coming," he said at last.

Helene watched as Melania's eyes shot up from the pages of her book, her brow furrowing in question. Clearly, their daughter was surprised, but Helene felt a sudden heaviness come over her body at her husband's words.

Jacob continued, "The United States will be involved before long——of that, I am sure. We must plan. We must conserve. Who knows when our sons will be called to serve?" The words tumbled out in a monosyllabic fashion.

Melania leaned forward, her eyes wide. "Hasn't the president said he'll keep us out of war?"

Jacob turned to speak to Melania directly, barely pausing as if he hadn't heard her question. "Your future is as uncertain as it is for the rest of us."

"What do you mean, Vati?" Melania rose from the sofa and moved toward Helene, putting her hand on the back of the rocker. Helene knew Melania wanted her assurance—telling her everything would be fine. But, would it? Helene opened her mouth and then closed it, the soothing words not coming.

"It's difficult to say what will be asked of us in a time of war and what will change. Nothing is certain. Not even your plans for the university."

"But Vater," Melania protested.

Helene looked between her husband and her daughter, feeling sympathy for the girl but confident that Jacob's message, despite its brusque delivery, was essential. The years with her husband had given her comfort in Jacob's preparations.

Jacob held up his hand and shook his head. "I won't discuss this any further now. Events will reveal themselves soon enough." He crossed his arms in front of his broad chest, effectively dissuading discussion.

Melania let out a sob and ran from the room, rushing up the staircase.

Helene stopped rocking, hearing the door click shut in her daughter's room, followed by the squeak of the bedsprings. Melania was both optimistic and naïve. Helene sighed and set aside thoughts about her daughter. Melania would work through it in time—she'd have to. Helene glanced at her husband, searching his eyes for the unspoken, but seeing only the shadow of despair. Plainly, he'd said all he was going to for the time being, so she bent her focus back on her knitting, knowing nothing would ever be the same once the U.S. was in the war.

After a time, Jacob rose and glanced at her before leaving the room. She gave him a slight nod of acceptance and listened as he plodded through the kitchen, pausing briefly for his coat. The back door creaked open, and a cold evening wind whipped low through the kitchen, its tail making its way through the doorway to the front room.

After giving Melania a spell to let out her emotions, Helene put her handiwork aside and went upstairs. The planks creaked under her pace and weight, announcing her arrival at Melania's door. The girl's eyes were red, her cheeks blotched from crying. Helene sat on the edge of the bed, placing her hand over Melania's. "Your father is a wise man. We must respect him and come together as a family."

Melania pushed herself up, crossing her arms. "War isn't here, Mutti. It's in Europe. The president said we wouldn't go to war." Her voice rose with each word. "Being a teacher has been my dream for so long. College starts in the fall. I must go!"

Helene instinctively reached to push back the hair from her daughter's forehead but then pulled back her arm and rose, the springs of the mattress squeaking. "You're nearly a woman. Being sensible and responsible are important parts of growing up."

Helene stood for a moment, about to say something further, but turned and left the room. If her daughter were to behave like a woman, she must be treated as such and not coddled.

Melania leaned against the dark wooden headboard after her mother left, unfamiliar feelings swirling deep within her. She wasn't used to being chastised by her mother and didn't expect to have her carefully laid plans threatened. She replayed the conversation in her mind, unable to reconcile the news. She pulled the blanket tightly around herself as if she could hold in everything——her worries, anxieties, and emotions. She bent her knees under her chin and willed herself to calm.

Melania shuddered despite the warmth of the cover, unsure what to do next. If only her brother Peter were here. He'd understand her position. Or would he think she was being childish? The uncomfortable sensation stayed in the pit of her stomach, reminding her of the choice before her——*her dreams* or *her duty*. When tears threatened to undo her again, she shrugged off the blanket and got up from the bed, shaking her head to move the deliberations to the recesses of her mind. She'd just have to face the facts as they presented themselves and not rush ahead. At this moment, she was capable of nothing else.

Her schoolbag sat in the corner of the room, papers and books bulging out the sides. She knelt and opened it, setting the books in piles next to the bag and searching through the crush of loose papers on the bottom. At last, she found what she was searching for and pulled out the tri-folded pamphlet, smoothing out the piece to its full size. She had scanned it at school but reread it thoroughly now.

THE MINNESOTA CAMPUS AFFILIATED RURAL SCHOOL PROGRAM THE UNIVERSITY OF MINNESOTA WOULD LIKE TO INTRODUCE ITS NEWEST OFFERINGS IN THE SCHOOL OF EDUCATION. RECENT EVIDENCE COLLECTED BY THE SCHOOLMASTERS' STUDY CLUB IN MINNESOTA REVEALED THAT FARM BOYS AND GIRLS WHO ATTENDED ONE-TEACHER SCHOOLHOUSES ENTERED HIGH SCHOOL POORLY PREPARED TO COMPETE WITH THOSE WHO HAD RECEIVED THEIR ELEMENTARY TRAINING IN CITY SCHOOLS. THE CHIEF FACTOR IN SCHOOL SUCCESS IS THE TEACHERS.

Melania ruffled at the claim that she may be less able than those from city schools. She liked Mr. Dickinson; however, she did know of others who struggled under his instruction. She reminded herself that she learned a lot on her own from books her scholarly brother, Mathias, sent her.

She continued reading the pamphlet, each sentence confirming her call to teach.

CONSIDERING THESE FINDINGS, DR. THEODORE ARCHER SUGGESTED A NEW TYPE OF RURAL TEACHER, ONE WHO CAN AROUSE HER COMMUNITY FROM THE LETHARGY OF ITS EDUCATIONAL INFERIORITY COMPLEX AND HELP TO DEVELOP ALL ITS LATENT POTENTIALITIES. THEY MUST BE SELECTED FROM THE SUPERIOR STUDENTS AND MUST BE TRAINED IN RURAL SCHOOLWORK.

Melania uncapped the ink bottle and carefully dabbed in her pen. Slowly and meticulously, she completed the application form, carefully describing her education and knowledge, highlighting her academic awards and achievements to stand out as a *superior student*. She finished the form and set it on her mother's dressing table, hoping Mutti would sign it without further discussion. Despite the evening's conversations, Melania refused to consider the possibility of her plans being derailed. Teaching had been her ambition for so long. Surely neither her father nor the war would get in the way.

Melania spotted a scribbled note from her friend Lydia in the bottom of the book bag. *Are you going to the dance?* Melania had nearly forgotten about the spring church dance after the evening's proceedings. The church dance was always enjoyable, and there were plenty of decent boys from school to dance with, though, thankfully, none who would distract her from her plans. When she considered the schoolboys were the same ones who pulled her pigtails when she was seven or who still spit at age seventeen, it was hard to think of them as potential beaus. A loud and boisterous voice boomed from downstairs, pulling Melania out of her musings. *Peter.*

Melania bounded down the stairs to greet her brother. Peter pulled her in, leaning his cold cheek on her forehead.

"Peter! Don't! Your face is like ice!"

"I saved it just for you." Peter put his cold hands on her cheeks.

Melania wriggled out of his reach and laughed.

"Peter. Come and sit. Have some pie." Mutti scooped up a slice of mince pie and set the plate on the checkered tablecloth. "It's not fresh fruit, but it's the best we'll get at this late time in our winter provisions."

"Pie of any of your delectable varieties, Mutti, is most welcome." Her brother dove his fork into the pie and shoved it in his mouth with an "Mmm."

"Melania? Would you like a slice too?" Mutti raised her brow, likely alluding to Melania's stomping off to her room *before* pie earlier that evening.

Melania hesitated and then perched on a chair with one knee tucked. "Yes, thank you." Her eyes narrowed. "Is Vati home?"

"No. Not yet." Her mother set a small slice of pie before her. "Talk with Pete a bit before you finish your schoolwork. You've some studying to do before tomorrow?"

Melania nodded. "Yes, a little." She appreciated her mother giving her an out so she wouldn't have to participate in another war conversation——a likely event now that Peter was here. Her nineteen-year-old brother lived with them in Holmesburg, but his job as a drayman with the local cannery often took him across the state making deliveries and collecting payments. He'd always relished getting out of their small town and expanding his horizons.

"Yes, little sister," Peter said, slapping his hand over hers. "Tell me what's new around Holmesburg since I've been gone this past week. I'm sure the news is most stimulating in this hustle-bustle little town."

Melania chuckled and smiled as she took a forkful of pie. Peter was her closest sibling in age and affection, but she wondered now, as they sat together, if she should ask him his thoughts on the war. Who knew what he'd say at this moment *before* he heard Vati's commentary? She wasn't up for more doom and gloom tonight.

"I saw Anna when I was in St. Paul," Peter said to their mother just as she was heading out of the kitchen.

Helene stopped in the doorway and turned, tilting her head a bit. "How is she?"

Melania watched her mother. Was that worry she saw on Mutti's face?

"Fine. Good, in fact. She just came back from a long retreat with the nuns."

Melania thought back to the earlier conversation, how Mutti had sat and listened to Vati's observations. She'd never thought of it before this moment, but that's what her mother often did. Mutti observed and let circumstances play out as they would. Anna, her older sister, was considering a life in the convent. Melania couldn't tell what her mother thought of the possibility; however, she realized now that Mutti mulled things over——tolerantly or patiently? Melania wasn't sure.

Mutti sighed and left the room. Relieved or resigned? Melania wasn't sure about that either.

Peter turned back to face her. "Now, little one," he said, putting his palms on the table on either side of his empty plate. "What's new with the butcher, the baker, and the candlestick maker?" His mouth opened to a wide grin.

Chapter 2

The March day dawned cloudy and cool, the sky foretelling snow, but regardless of the weather, the church event promised a good time. Melania longed for the frivolity of a dance. Vater scoured every newspaper he could get his hands on for updates on the war in Europe——his mood bringing a pall over the house. Melania's eldest brother, Frank, spent many evenings at the kitchen table with Vati, talking in low, hushed voices, scribbling in a notebook. Days after their first such gathering, Frank brought lumber from the farm and installed shelving in the cellar. Large grain, sugar, and coffee bags were purchased and stored on those beams within a week. Mutti already had a small garden patch in the backyard, but Vati purchased fencing materials to enclose a larger plot. Frank's wife sent envelopes of seeds for Mutter to plant next month. Clearly, Mutti took Vati's call for conservation and planning to heart when the remaining fall apples were sauced and jarred for storage, and a dozen new chickens were added to the small backyard coop. But when Melania's school application form appeared on her bed, signed, she realized that her mother was endeavoring to balance life and had likely coaxed her father's signature.

She ran her hand down the pale green linen of her dress, recalling her mother's admonition to be sensible. Anna's old dress *was* beautiful, and Mutti had refashioned it with a higher empire waist around which she'd tied a beautiful silk scarf.

Even though the snow hadn't yet come, Melania appreciated Vati conveying her and her twin friends, Lydia and Louisa Haas, to the dance in his buggy. She glanced at the felt *Juliet* slippers peeking out from under the long dress hem, hoping she could hop clear to the curb in front of the church without soiling them. A hubbub of activity moved around the square as motor cars, buggies, wagons, and even a couple of bicycles carried revelers to the dance.

"Here, Vati! Stop right here." Melania pointed to the street corner at the edge of the churchyard.

Her father pulled on the reins, stopping the horse at the next corner, and Melania leaped out across the pooled water that gathered from the melting snow. She held out an outstretched hand. "Here. Take it."

Louisa reached out, and Melania pulled her friend to dry pavement.

"No, thank you," Lydia said skeptically. "I'd rather not risk getting my dress splattered." She looked both ways before stepping onto the dry cobblestones on the street side of the conveyance.

"Good evening, ladies," Vati said before clicking his tongue and pulling the reins to move the horse back around toward home.

The girls momentarily stood on the street corner to smooth down their skirts.

"You both look enchanting." Melania regarded her friends as they walked toward the church.

"Lydia spent almost an hour picking her hair ribbon," Louisa teased. "I think she's hoping Peter will notice."

"And what was the reason you had Mama curl your hair tonight?" Lydia shook her head at her sister as she tiptoed down the walkway, stepping around puddles.

"You two are something else." Melania's nose wrinkled. "That's my brother we're talking about. Let's not get all lovey-dovey."

"But he's so tall and so kind and so——"

"Ewww!" Melania playfully pushed Louisa's shoulder before sprinting the final length of the walk toward the church, her friends following behind.

The massive arched doors were flanked by a large banner with a bright green shamrock and the words, St. Patrick's Day Dance. "I don't know why everyone was making such a big deal about this being Irish-themed." Louisa shrugged. "That's a dilly of a sign."

"My father said some folks don't like the influence of Bishop Ireland." Melania shrugged as she glanced over at the beer tents set up on the side lawn, several men already planted comfortably at the tables——for the duration, it seemed. "Doesn't seem to be bothering them." She laughed as she and her friends slipped inside the church.

They glided across the shiny marble tiles to the large banquet hall. The space was festooned with more green banners and streamers, illuminated by gas lamps on the perimeter and candles on each table. High windows near the top of the twenty-foot ceilings were propped open, and a cool spring breeze floated through the big hall.

The band spread out in a back corner with fancy-dressed men warming up their instruments. Tables and chairs were pushed away from the corner, allowing ample space to dance. Once the music began, the acoustics in the large, high-ceilinged room floated pleasantly throughout.

Melania and her friends surveyed the room. "Let's sit here," Lydia suggested, setting her sweater and handbag on a chair.

"I see the advantages. We can see the door, the dance floor, and the refreshment table from here." Melania picked a chair next to Lydia, but her friend shooed her away.

"Don't be a goof! Spread out so the table will look full." Lydia moaned. "Remember what happened last year?"

"I'll never forget." Louisa put a hand to her chest. "We ended up dancing almost the entire evening with the Obermeyer twins."

Melania laughed. "Twins for twins! The boys said it all night long."

"That may be funny for you, friend, but I recall you alternating between dancing with Josiah Wagner and Robert Brown."

"They're nice boys, but I don't think they cleaned up much before they came that night." Melania waved her hand in front of her nose. "I swear straw was still sticking out of Robert's shirt collar."

"Why we thought sitting nearest the dance floor was the best plan, I'll never know. We were ambushed all night." Lydia snorted.

"I think this table near the wall is a fine choice. We can see who's coming. The last thing I need is a boy complicating my plans." Melania chuckled.

"And maybe someone's brother might want to sit with us." Louisa patted the seat between herself and her twin sister.

Melania rolled her eyes at her friends. "You two! I'm not even sure he's coming. Since Pete began traveling for the cannery, he seems bored with this small town. Sorry, girls."

"Well, we can hope." Lydia shrugged.

As the sky darkened, candlelight glowed, the music picked up, and the room filled with the young and old alike, swaying to the melodies of intermingling voices and instruments. Melania and her friends became more open to dancing, not wanting to squander the night sitting at a table. Thomas Keene, the farmer's son who lived next to her brother Frank's farm, seemed to be at Melania's every turn. *So much for the vantage point.*

"Thank you, Thomas," Melania said after the third dance, turning abruptly toward the food and drink table to break loose of him. But as she leaned in to grab a glass of punch, Thomas reached around her, offering one he had just picked up. "Thank you, Tom. That's kind." She turned away and sipped on the punch, struggling to develop a new plan to brush off Thomas, when she spied Peter sauntering in the door.

Melania rushed toward him, calling loudly, "Peter!"

She didn't turn around to see if Tom noticed the rebuff but continued her quick stride toward her brother. "I'm so glad you're here." She threw her arms around Peter.

"And I'm glad we're here as well."

Melania didn't recognize the voice. She pulled away from her brother, surprised to see a tall, gangly stranger standing behind him.

"This here's Jim," Peter said, tipping his head toward the man who'd spoken. "He just started at the cannery. Jim, my little sis, Melania."

Peter's friend dipped his exceedingly tall frame slightly into a bow while looking at Melania with his playful green eyes. "James Patrick Wirth, at your service," he said through a crooked smile. The movement caused a piece of his slicked jet-black hair to fall forward on his forehead.

Melania stifled a gasp as she realized she'd nearly reached up to put it back into place.

She gathered her senses and reached out her hand. "Nice to meet you, Mr. Wirth."

"No need to be so formal, Mel." Peter's words slurred a bit, and he chuckled.

"Lydia and Louisa must be wondering where I am," Melania said hastily. "I should go."

She turned away from the men and quickly walked back to the table, wondering at the strange warmness in her right hand.

"Why are your cheeks red and blotchy?" Lydia asked when Melania sat down.

"Surely it's all the dancing," Melania responded quickly. "I think I'll sit for a turn. By the way, Peter's here, but——"

Before Melania could finish her sentence, Louisa dashed off to search for Peter. Soon, she had Peter and Jim in tow, showing them to the table.

"We saved seats if you showed up," Lydia said breathlessly. She patted the chair next to her while Louisa sat down one over.

Jim chuckled, raising an eyebrow. "I think I'll sit right here." He pulled up a chair right next to Melania.

Melania stiffened and popped up. "Does anyone want a refreshment?"

"We're good, Mel. We've had enough, haven't we, Jim?" Peter winked at Jim. "Plus, I think I'd like to dance. Anyone?"

"Oh, yes! I'll dance!" Lydia popped up and grabbed Peter by the hand.

Peter shrugged and turned to Louisa. "You're next."

Jim shook his head and laughed.

"I'll go get refreshments, Mel. You dance with Peter's friend." Louisa stood and quickly moved toward the drink table.

Jim stood too and stretched out a flat palm toward Melania. She hesitated, troubled about the peculiar reaction she had to Jim. *What possessed me to very nearly brush his hair back?* She'd never even met him, much less had that bold a reaction to any other boy saying hello. But then, Jim wasn't a boy, was he? *Oh my!* She could not entertain thoughts like that. She dropped her chin, placed her hand in Jim's, and let him lead her to the dance floor.

Melania surreptitiously wiped her hands on her skirt, one clammy from nerves, the other warm from Jim's grasp. Jim put one hand gently on her waist while meeting her other hand in the air, with an appropriate space between them. Although tall herself, Melania's head barely reached Jim's chin, and she was grateful she wasn't looking straight at him. That would be more than she could bear—she was still discomfited at her reaction to meeting him.

Although she avoided his gaze now, the initial impression of him was fixed in her mind. He was even taller than her brother, with darker hair and contrasting green eyes——eyes that seemed to dance when he looked at her. Perhaps that was the reason for her unease. Thoughts swirled in her head as she and Jim moved around the floor. Just as the dance was about to end, Jim extended his arm, sending Melania in a backward twirl, and she nearly lost her footing until Jim gently pulled her back toward him, steadying her.

"Couldn't resist," he said with a small chortle.

Now she remembered the other thing that had unnerved her earlier. It was Jim's smile——crooked and mischievous.

"How about dancing to this number?" Jim asked, still holding her hand. The band was heating up as partners on the floor split apart and began to move to the lively, infectious Scott Joplin tune.

Melania fumbled for words. "Ah——no, thank you. Perhaps later." She yanked her hand from Jim's grasp and rushed through the room and out the front door. She took in a deep breath and moved around to the side of the building, not interested in making small talk with anyone. The cool bricks on her back calmed her, releasing her thoughts. *Jim was merely being friendly. He's Peter's friend. He did nothing more than politely ask me to dance. I need to stop making something out of nothing.* When her mind cleared, she went back inside, guessing Peter would come looking for her if she stayed out too long——or worse, perhaps Jim would. She smoothed the front of her dress and repositioned the satin ribbon woven through her pulled-up hair. She sighed deeply and walked in clipped steps straight toward their table, careful not to let her gaze veer from her target.

"Where were you?" asked Louisa when Melania sat down.

"Just outside, cooling off." Melania averted her eyes lest her friend read into her absence and response.

"Peter and Jim were both wondering where you went," Louisa continued, lifting her eyebrows at Melania.

Lydia grinned.

"He's just a friend of my brother's. That's all."

Her friends giggled. "The lady doth protest too much," Louisa teased.

"Ah . . . Shakespeare. Mr. Dickinson was right. *Everything we learn in school has a use,*" chuckled Lydia. "What's up, Melania?"

"Nothing," Melania responded more tartly than she intended. "I don't want to talk about it. Besides, there's *nothing* to discuss." She felt her face flush.

"No, no, we do but jest. Poison in jest. No offense i' th' world." Louisa laughed.

"Spare me the Hamlet." Melania pinched Louisa's arm playfully. "Oh! Here comes Thomas. I think I'll dance the last dances with him."

Melania sprang from her chair, moving swiftly toward the boy.

Melania crept down the staircase the next morning, hoping she could pass unnoticed by Peter and Vati in the front room. Her mother greeted her and set a plate of hotcakes on the table when Melania slipped into the kitchen. She sat and leaned forward on one elbow, turning her ear to catch the men's conversation, wondering if Pete would mention his new friend. A few moments later, she let out a yelp when her tabby jumped in her lap, digging her claws in. She sat back and pushed the cat onto the floor, feeling ashamed for eavesdropping.

The animal circled Melania's ankles, apparently trying to make amends, so she carefully put the cat back into a circle in her lap. It purred contentedly as she cut out a section of the pancake and peered out the kitchen window, stroking the cat's soft fur, deep in thought as she turned the last evening over in her mind.

"Peter said you were having a nice time at the dance when he and his friend showed up." Mutti broke the silence.

"Uh-huh." Melania kept her focus out the window, hoping she could avoid further questions.

"Peter mentioned you danced quite a bit with Thomas Keene. He's such a nice boy."

Melania set down her fork and turned toward her mother. "That he is, Mutti. But I've little time for boys. I have plans." *Be sensible,* Mutti had said, and if she was going to achieve her ambition of being a teacher——war or no war——she must stay focused on the aim.

Mutti smiled. "I'll need you to make a pie for dinner tonight. We have company coming. I've brought a jar of apples up from the cellar."

"Who?"

"Peter invited his new friend, Jim." Her mother turned back to the task of peeling potatoes, cutting and dropping the slices into the crock of water.

Melania's heart began beating rapidly. "Why? I mean, why did Peter invite him?"

Melania was startled when Mutti's head snapped around. "I hardly think a dinner guest requires an explanation."

"Of course, Mutter." Melania pushed around the hotcakes, soaking them in the maple syrup that puddled on the edges of the plate. Her father's solitary moods and pointed comments were a matter of course. Such sharpness was uncharacteristic for her mother but had become more frequent.

A knife clattered to the floor, and Mutti let out a cry. Melania sprang to her feet and grabbed a towel, wrapping it around her mother's thumb, blood soaking the white linen.

"Here." Melania moved her mother to the table. "Let the bleeding stop, and I'll get you a cup of tea."

Mutti sat only for a few moments. "There's much to do." She discarded the soiled towel and wrapped her thumb with a bit of fabric.

"I can finish." Melania glanced around the space. "The roast is in the oven, and you're nearly done preparing the vegetables. Please. Go sit in the front room to ensure that thumb doesn't start bleeding again." Melania ushered her mother toward the door.

Mutti sighed and smiled briefly. "It looks as if you're giving me no choice."

Melania gathered up her plate and the remaining breakfast dishes, depositing them in the washbasin before setting the kettle to boil. She swept her hand across the cutting board, dropped the potato peels in a compost basket, and then cleaned and cut the winter carrots before adding them to the crock of water. The kettle sputtered, and she withdrew it from the heat, pouring it over the dishes after sprinkling in sodium carbonate. She sunk her hands to the bottom of the basin, enjoying the warmth of the water, standing for a time, staring blankly out the window, lost again in her thoughts.

Melania mainly dismissed her father's prediction of war because it threatened her plans. Her mother though——she wasn't herself. That seemed obvious now. The uncomfortable realization that Melania had paid little attention to the effect of the news on others, her mother, in particular, weighed heavily. Melania vowed to heed her parents' concerns and burdens and not be so singularly focused on her own goals and agendas. Satisfied with her new pledge, she picked up a plate, scrubbed it thoroughly, and set it on a towel to dry. "There!" she said before pouring the remaining water over the teacup for her mother.

Later that day, Melania hurried from the kitchen when she spied Peter and Jim coming up the walkway. She listened at the door as the young men greeted her parents.

"Vati, Mutti, I'd like you to meet Jim Wirth. Jim, my mother is the best pie maker this side of the Mississippi."

"It's nice to meet you, Mr. Wirth." Mutti's voice carried through the door. "Peter, your sister deserves credit for the pie this evening."

Nuts! Melania rolled her eyes at the attention on her and wondered how she'd avoid it throughout the meal. She sighed, wishing she could stay out of the kitchen and then shook her head at the realization that she'd eavesdropped again. Lands! The effect Jim Wirth was having in her life was unnerving. She took a deep breath and went back into the kitchen.

"Thank you, ma'am and sir, for the dinner invitation." Jim smiled, and Melania felt her heart skip a beat.

"Dinner is just about ready to be served," Helene said. "Peter, show James where to wash up."

Melania laid the napkins on the table, set a fork on each one and a knife opposite, and reached for the bread basket and butter dish.

"Hello, Melania."

Melania plunked down the bread basket, her face warming as Peter and Jim already reentered the kitchen.

"Ah——" Her words failed her as she faced the young men, mouth agape.

"Cat got your tongue?" Peter chuckled.

Melania scowled at her brother. "Hello, Peter. Jim."

Jim cocked his head and gave a slight nod. "It's nice to see you again so soon."

She exhaled heavily, wondering how she'd make it through dinner.

The men seated themselves at the table while Melania and her mother dished up hearty plates.

Jim swooned when the feast was set before him. "I can't say when I've last had such a banquet laid before me, Mrs. Harvey."

Melania smiled when Peter rolled his eyes——her brother seemed to be on to Jim's charming ways.

"Then we best get to it. Let's bow our heads." Everyone dropped their heads as Vati's low voice recognized the Lord's provision, and when he finished, utensils clinked the sides of bowls and plates as they dove into the meal.

"Where are you from, Mr. Wirth?" Vati asked.

Jim nodded as he finished a mouthful. "Please, sir, call me Jim. I grew up on my grandparents' farm about fifteen miles northeast of here in Augusta."

Vati nodded. "Sure, I know it well. I've been up the river with the cannery years back."

"Your parents, Jim? Are they still there?" Mutti asked.

"No, ma'am. My parents both died when I was small. My older brother Thomas and I were raised by my mother's parents on their farm in Augusta. My grandparents have since passed, and now my brother farms the land."

"Oh, dear." Mutter reached over and put her hand briefly on Jim's forearm. "I know what it's like to lose your parents at a young age."

Melania raised her brow. Goodness! Even Mutti was taken in by this man.

"You're not farming with your brother?" Vati asked.

"I was never one much for farming. My grandfather taught me to work hard, but I could never quite commit to the solitary, confining life of farming." Jim's head tilted thoughtfully, and he laughed. "Daid mór, that's what we called my grandfather. He would be furious when I disappeared for hours some afternoons. But Mamó's pleasure at getting a stringer of fresh fish for dinner made up for it." Jim shrugged and sighed. "I guess I'm just a bit of a free spirit."

Peter slapped Jim's back. "That, my friend, is why we get along so well."

Jim nodded in agreement. "Yes, your friendship has benefits too." Jim glanced at Melania but swiftly added, "Like this delicious dinner, Mrs. Harvey."

Melania gulped and looked down at her plate, mixing the carrots with her peas.

"Dear, you're hardly eating. Are you feeling well? You've been out of sorts all day." Helene reached out to touch Melania's forehead, but Melania pulled away.

"I'm fine, Mutti." Melania straightened in her chair, crossing her ankles and tucking her legs. She sliced the beef and slid it next to a forkful of potatoes, re-engaging herself in the meal. Despite her attempts, she found her focus taxed by her efforts to appear unflustered by Jim's presence at the table. When the dinner plates were finally emptied, she welcomed her mother's request to cut and dish the apple pie. Jim grinned when she brushed his arm while setting the pie in front of him.

The men went outside for a smoke in the cool evening air after dessert while Helene and Melania washed and dried the dishes. Melania stacked the plates on the shelf and set the utensils in the drawer of the Hoosier cupboard, hoping to sneak up to her room soon.

"Bring this out to Jim." Mutti held out a bundle to her. "It's pie."

Melania hesitated but knew she had no valid reason to object. Resigned, she walked out the door with the pie, and as she neared the haze of smoke, her father and brother stepped away to greet a neighbor walking by. Hoping to fulfill her duty quickly, she thrust the parcel at Jim. "From Mother," she said.

"How nice. Please thank her for me. And thank you for delivering it," Jim said, catching her hand.

Melania pulled away, her hand tingling.

"When's the next dance?"

"Not for a long time." She turned back toward the house, her breathing increasing as she hurried away.

"Well, I guess I'll just have to accept your mother's next invitation for dinner."

Jim's chuckle floated behind Melania as she hastened back into the house. What was going on? No boy had ever caused this reaction in her. *He is not a boy——* The very notion disconcerted her.

Once in her bedroom, she lay on the quilt and crossed her arms over the butterflies in her stomach. Everything she thought was certain was transforming into the unrecognizable. She was unsure of herself and those around her, which was both unsettling and uncomfortable. *Focus. Be sensible. You have plans.* Melania added to her mounting list of resolutions. Tonight, she resolved not to let *a man* hinder her plans either.

CHAPTER 3

—— • ——

THE HERALD • APRIL 1917 • ATTACK! THE AMERICAN STEAMER AZTEC WAS TORPEDOED ON APRIL 1 WITHOUT WARNING BY A GERMAN U-BOAT AS IT ENTERED BRITISH WATERS. TEN AMERICAN LIVES WERE LOST.

Jacob walked home from his ten-hour shift at the mill, a newspaper tucked under his arm. The word *torpedoed* jumped from the front page in his quick perusal of the headlines. The article wasn't a lead feature but tucked instead in the bottom corner of the page, the newspaper editors endeavoring, it seemed, to hold fast to the belief that war with Germany could still be avoided. *War is so close.* Surely President Wilson couldn't deny it. Jacob quickened his pace.

Tulips pushed through the dark soil encircling the foundation of the brick home, greeting Jacob as he opened the gate from the alley. The prolonged blustery weather had finally given way to temperate April conditions——a blessing, as it meant gardening could be started earlier. *God's provision.* Jacob must remember to count on that when the war knocked on America's door in the days to come. *Surely, it is coming.*

Jacob opened the kitchen door and greeted his wife with a quick peck on her warm cheek. *Another gift.* At this moment, he was keenly aware of his *many* blessings. He hung his coat and hat on the peg and sat down at the table, spreading the newspaper before him.

"Aren't you going to wash for dinner?" Helene stirred the stew simmering in the cast-iron kettle. "It's almost ready."

"Soon." Jacob's thick palms flanked the edges of the newsprint as he buried his head in the pages. Sounds of his wife rang in the background, familiar and distant at the same time——his mind chewing on the day's events. Helene set a hot cloth next to him, and he absently wiped his hands, folding the paper to a quarter of its size and pulling the bowl of stew toward him after she'd set that down.

A chair scraped across the wooden planks, and Jacob looked up to see Helene seated across from him.

"Where is our daughter?" His words were more abrupt than he'd intended.

"She's at the Haas home for supper tonight. The girls are working on a school project afterward."

"Well, then." His mind was still on the edge of his heavy thoughts as he returned to the newspaper and his dinner.

"Let's have our cake in the front room, by the fire," Helene said several minutes later, rising to take their bowls to the sink.

He stared at her a moment, noticing the tension in her shoulders.

"Ja. Good." He rose from the table and moved into the living room, setting the barley twist table between his and Helene's chairs. It was early spring, and the nights were cool—the fire a perfect way to warm the room for the evening. He heard his wife enter the room as he bent in front of the hearth and threw a match on the kindling, standing and watching until the fire took hold. He turned and looked at Helene, who sat with a cup of coffee resting in her palm. The fire crackled behind him, and the light danced off the walls, the glow warming the space and the heat pushing at his back.

"War is at our doorstep. Germany sank an American steamship. Ten Americans are dead." Jacob looked right past Helene as he played the inevitable out in his mind. "President Wilson has no other choice now," he said, faintly shaking his head and moving to his chair, sitting down hard, the chair arm chafing the table's edge. He picked up his fork and poked at the cake.

Helene turned to him. "Now what?"

"Our family." He shook his head and turned to directly meet her eyes. "It will reach us all. Frank and August should be fine for a time. Frank has his family, and there's the farm to run. Surely they won't get drafted first."

"Drafted? Are you certain?" Helene's fork rattled to the plate.

"It's inevitable. The newspaper reported that our army has barely over one hundred thousand men and almost no heavy artillery pieces." He shook his head in dismay. "Hundreds of thousands, if not millions, of men will need to be drafted, especially if the war rages on." Jacob's head dropped toward his chest, and he heaved a sigh. Slowly he raised his eyes. "We'll *all* need to make sacrifices."

A tear rolled down Helene's cheek, and she reached out to Jacob, their hands clasping for a moment. Abruptly, Jacob rose from his chair, cake unfinished, coffee tepid. "I'm going to the farm," he said, leaving the room. He snatched his coat off the peg in the kitchen and headed out the back door.

Helene didn't bother questioning her husband's timing——the fact that the dark and damp of the spring evening had already settled. She remained seated, and when she heard the horse and buggy move past the house, she dug a fork into her cake and sipped the lukewarm coffee. The affairs her husband laid out were significant. She had read about the lack of everyday staples and the sacrifices made by the families in Europe——surely the United States would pay a similar cost. In the room's quietness, with the heaviness of the coming trouble, she reflected on her children.

Frank, their oldest son, was a strong and capable man with a resilient and efficient wife. She hoped Jacob was right in that the military would not draft men with such responsibilities as wives and children, at least not initially.

Helene thought of their second child, dear, sweet August——of sturdy stock but simple mind. His place was outside the schoolroom, working and helping at the farm. He thrived in an uncomplicated, straightforward life, and Helene prayed that he would be out of the military's reach, but then, which of her sons would she want to send to war?

Mathias, her next son, was twenty-two. He set out into the world the moment he turned eighteen as if something in this small town——the farm, the mill, or the cannery——would shackle him if he didn't leave quickly enough. Mathias was different from his brothers——fiercely inquisitive, always fascinated with new inventions and innovations. He was bigger than this small corner of the earth and had headed to Hamline University in St. Paul to pursue a degree in law in the fall of 1915. He'd not been back to Holmesburg since.

As Helene pondered the effects of war on Mathias, she recalled his mention of the university's preparations. She lifted the small wicker basket overflowing with letters, flipping through until she found Math's missive from a month ago. She slid the pages from the frayed envelope. "Yes. Here it is." She remembered the enthusiasm in her son's words.

The university recently started military drills and first aid training and is now offering a pre-flight training school as part of its extracurricular programs. I'm most hopeful I will be able to attend. Of course, we'll not be able to fly in an aircraft, but we'll learn about aerial gunnery and general warfare tactics. It should be a hoot!

Helene's hand covered her chest, and she felt the throbbing of her heart. "Oh, Lord." Was her husband right? Would there be a draft? She thought back to Jacob's recent conversation with Frank——she'd caught bits and pieces of the exchange as she moved in and out of the kitchen. The men mentioned the last draft this country had was during the Civil War. Wartime was all the same, they decided, regardless of the century.

Helene sank back in the chair, too fatigued to deliberate on her other children, apart from Melania, who'd not yet returned from the Haas house. She gripped the arms of her rocker and rose, her feet shuffling as she moved to the dark kitchen, the fading fire throwing smaller and smaller shards of light in her path. She leaned on the sink and gazed into the night, appreciating the large, nearly full moon's illumination of their back garden. The glow was soon filled with the outline of her youngest daughter skittering up the path from the alley. Helene opened the door and embraced Melania as if she had been gone for days, not hours.

"Well, hello, Mutti!"

"Good night is more appropriate. Would you like a piece of ginger cake before you turn in?" Helene didn't suppose she would at this late hour, but she suddenly longed for her daughter's company. Perhaps they could talk of frivolous things and clear Helene's mind.

"I don't think I could fit in another bite. Mrs. Haas made the most delicious chocolate cake. She sent a piece home with me." She thrust a parcel at her mother. "You enjoy it."

"Thank you, dear. Perhaps later." Helene took the cake and placed it in the Hoosier cupboard, glancing outside after Melania left the room.

No Jacob yet. Nor Peter. She blew out the kitchen lamp and trudged up the stairs——the heaviness of the world pressing in on her.

⸻ ℓℓ ⸻

Jacob's buggy was not expected at Frank's farm when the horse clip-clopped up the long driveway. Still, before he reached the barn, Frank emerged with a lantern, calling a greeting, then turned to his oldest son and shooed him off the porch to tend to Jacob's horse. "Take the lamp."

Jacob followed Frank into the house, and in short order, Jacob sat at the table with his two oldest sons, Frank and August. Ida, Frank's wife, brewed a pot of strong coffee and cut slices of apple cake, reminding Jacob of the piece left uneaten on his table back home. He winced slightly at the thought of dropping the news on his wife and then abruptly leaving her to mull it over alone.

Jacob sat silently as his thoughts settled. When the room cleared of children and Ida was upstairs tucking them in for the night, Jacob recounted the newspaper article and his discussion with their mother. "There is no other choice now for our country. War is all but declared," Jacob concluded.

Frank spoke first. "The draft is our most immediate concern."

"Hmmm," August said, and Jacob glanced at him, wondering if he understood.

"It will likely come in waves. We have an ill-equipped military at present." Jacob lifted a shoulder.

"Ja. True. They'll only be able to handle a small number of draftees at a time. Perhaps we'll be spared for now."

Jacob tilted his head at Frank's words, thinking about the slight accent he heard and the German words interspersed. He blinked his eyes and rolled them back in thought.

"We must take care. Take care to be fully American."

Frank's eyes scrunched. "We are, Vater. Citizens, all."

"Ja, true. But they'll start pointing out differences, small or not."

"Vat do you mean?" August frowned.

"Many from here, from Holmesburg, came from Deutschland, *from Germany*. Some, generations back; others, like us, in your lifetimes. Hairs will be split trying to root out the enemy." Jacob pressed his palms into the table and leaned forward, swiveling his head between his sons. "August, you were young then, but Frank, you may remember how villagers began to be divided into groups——not by themselves, but by the Pan-German Nationalists whose sole aim was to unify the German people, those they deemed pure. The rest were pushed aside."

Frank's head cocked. "More than anything, I remember the hostility that seemed to be everywhere——at the school, in the streets——as if a gray cloud settled over the village and never left."

"Ja. The league held strong positions on imperialism and anti-Semitism." Jacob shrugged. "War divides too. Each country's citizens look to, *need* to, name the enemy as a way of survival, so they can deal with the sacrifice that comes with war. When people can isolate the adversary, they feel some sort of power over a situation that is beyond their control."

"I don't understand your meaning, Vati," August said.

"We must prepare for the inevitable coming of the draft, of rations, and of sacrifice. However, we also must get ready for the unforeseen. We *are* Germans despite being American citizens. And Germany is the enemy."

Chapter 4

Jacob turned the corner onto Chestnut the following Monday morning when Hector Young ran out of his grocery store waving a newspaper. "War! We are at war!"

Jacob snatched the newspaper with both hands, exposing the large block-typed headline:

UNITED STATES DECLARES WAR ON GERMANY!

Within minutes, the streets buzzed with store owners rushing from their shops and residents gathering in the streets. *"Could it be true?"* *"But he promised——"* *"What will we do?"*

Exasperation bubbled up in Jacob's chest, and he shook his head in disbelief at his neighbors' ignorance and denial. *How had he been the only one who saw this coming? Surely there were others.* He held his tongue, seeing no purpose in telling them of his predictions——knowing from his days in Germany that it was not easy to convince others of things they didn't wish to acknowledge. Jacob folded the paper under his arm, gave Hector a nickel, and headed toward the mill, stopping outside the factory's entrance to read the news.

THE HERALD • SPECIAL EDITION • APRIL 1917 • UNITED STATES DECLARES WAR ON GERMANY! ON APRIL 2, PRESIDENT WILSON DELIVERED A WAR MESSAGE TO A JOINT SESSION OF THE HOUSE AND SENATE, IMPLORING THEM FOR A DECLARATION OF WAR. THE SINKING OF OUR AMERICAN STEAMER HAS TIPPED THE SCALES OF WAR FOR THE PRESIDENT AS HE DECLARED THE "WORLD MUST BE MADE SAFE FOR DEMOCRACY." ON APRIL 6, THE DAY AFTER AN OVERWHELMING SENATE VOTE FOR WAR, PRESIDENT WILSON SIGNED THE DECLARATION. AMERICA IS OFFICIALLY AT WAR WITH GERMANY! WE MUST MOBILIZE AS A COUNTRY TO FACE OUR ENEMY.

When his shift ended later that day, Jacob ambled down the well-lit hallway of the mill's first-floor office area where the company owner, his secretaries, and the plant managers worked. The hallways were clean, and the offices well-kept, in stark contrast to the dark and dingy upper-level shop floors, and it seemed to Jacob as if he were in another place entirely. He'd not been past the secretary's desk since he was hired a decade ago. He was taking a risk here, he ventured, but he saw today as an opportunity to show his loyalty to the mill and the country. After he made his request to Miss Meyer, the secretary led him into Mr. Conlin's office.

"Yes, Harvey? What is it?" The boss man leaned forward.

At least he knows my name.

"I want you to know, Mr. Conlin, how much I value my position at Holmesburg Mill. I would be willing to train any new workers should the need arise——or do whatever is necessary."

Conlin wrinkled his brow, his face questioning.

"Now, Mr. Conlin. Now that the war is here," Jacob clarified.

"Yes, fine." Conlin shuffled the papers on his desk and picked up a pen.

Jacob hesitated, waiting for——a comment, perhaps.

Mr. Conlin appeared as if he were about to write down this information but abruptly stopped and looked up at Jacob. "Noted, Harvey," he said, waving his hand in a sweeping motion, shooing Jacob toward the door. "Shut the door on your way out."

Jacob walked down the hall and out the factory door, bristling under Conlin's rebuff. Clearly, the man wasn't planning for the inevitable, or he had other things in mind than utilizing Jacob. Jacob respected the authority of his superiors but resisted putting his future in their hands. For now, he would bide his time.

Melania set her book bag down on a kitchen chair and craned her neck at the noise out the back window. She expected it may be Mutti puttering around in her garden but leaned closer to the window as she got a glimpse of the men outside. Voices floated toward her above the thud of the shovel.

"That should help, Mr. Harvey." Melania watched as Jim wiped his brow with his handkerchief and shoved it into his back pocket. He shadowed his eyes with his hand and glanced over the space.

Had Jim turned the soil for Mutti? Melania tilted her head. *Why would Jim do that?*

"Ja. Danke." Vati sat down on the garden bench and turned toward the house. "Bring us a cool drink, Melania."

Goodness—Vati knew she was there. Melania exhaled sharply at another reminder of her mortifying new habit of listening in on conversations, mainly those involving Jim Wirth. Her stomach fluttered, and she jerked her head from the backyard scene. It didn't matter how she felt about

Jim Wirth. *Did she feel something?* She snorted and walked toward the cupboard, setting glasses on a tray as she reminded herself that she had plans. Plans from which she would not let herself be distracted.

Melania poured water into the glasses and added slices of lemon. She set several of Mutti's cookies on a plate and carried them outside, setting the fare on the bench next to Vati.

"Hello, Melania." Jim smiled, and his eyes twinkled. *Did they do that all the time? For everyone?*

Melania nervously smoothed her skirt down and glanced back toward the house.

"Sit, girl," Vati said, and Jim immediately brought a pair of wicker chairs to the spot and offered one to Melania.

She hesitated and then sat on the edge of the seat as she glanced around the garden space—the soil turned over from edge to edge.

"Jim's handiwork." Vati nodded with a satisfied look.

"Why would you do that?" Melania's brow furrowed at her sharp tone.

"Why not?" Jim laughed, and Melania was relieved she hadn't offended him.

"Peter is gone for several days, and Jim had time." Vati raised a brow at her. "We're at war, in case you haven't heard."

Melania blinked at the sharpness of his response. Despite that, she was startled at Jim's reply.

"I'm sure that's not what she meant, sir. She probably was referring to my comment a while back about my disinterest in working the land—farming and such." Jim chuckled. "Gardening is both small-scale and more rewarding work, in my opinion, and I'd be happy to help you and Mrs. Harvey anytime."

Melania stood and considered this man——maybe he was more than a charmer. It didn't matter, though, she reminded herself. She wasn't interested. A bead of perspiration trickled down the back of her neck and she put her palm under her hairline and went into the house.

CATE MICHELS

Chapter 5

The Herald • April 1917 • **FACING OUR ENE-MY!** The Minnesota State Legislature created a group focusing on public safety in response to our war with Germany. The Minnesota Commission of Public Safety (MCPS) has the power to fight the war on the home front by rooting out disloyal elements. We cannot be too careful as we face our enemy. One can never be sure if those around us are friends or foes. Governor Burnquist calls on all citizens of Minnesota to do their part in this important national cause.

Jacob was sickened. Being loyal to one's country, new or not, was critical——radical nationalism, on the other hand, could lead to extremist activities. He'd seen it in Germany——the arrests, the imprisonment, the systematic dismantling of an individual. Jacob shuddered, folded the paper, and headed out the kitchen door, stopping beside his wife as she worked in the yard. The light of dusk rapidly faded. He bent and gathered the mound of dried leaves and shriveled flower heads, depositing it on the compost pile.

Helene brushed off her apron and rose stiffly and slowly. "Are you going out?"

"Ja." He turned from her without further explanation.

A gust of wind thrust the gate shut behind Jacob and sent remnants of Helene's pile blowing past her shoes. She watched her husband amble down the alley, sure it was the news in the weekly that drew him out this evening. Perhaps he would find some kinsmen, some like-minded men with whom he could share his burden. All men and all families would eventually face their own concerns. Still, she wondered if any would carry them as deeply as her husband. Perhaps it would come for the others when the fears hit closer to home.

Thank goodness for Frank——he helped Jacob and Helene shoulder the responsibility. Jacob had retained a hundred-acre parcel of land after giving up the family farm to Frank years ago. The tract was long-leased to the farmer whose land abutted the field. The man had sought to purchase the field many times and had been willing to do so recently when Frank approached him on behalf of Jacob. Perhaps that was where her husband was headed tonight. He'd told her that Frank had collected a price of $109 per acre——a value not likely to be sustained post-war. For now, Jacob had told her, America's farmers would reap an economic boon with the war devastation in the European farm fields. The whole American economy would be providing for the war machine——farms, mills, and the railroad.

The kitchen door clicked shut behind Helene as she entered the quiet room and lit the lamp, brightening the room to a cozy yellow. As she hung her apron on the peg, glass suddenly shattered in the front room. She went completely still, listening. *Did the breeze from an open window knock something down? Was Melania in the front room?* Thoughts circled in her head. *No.* Melania had left the house right after dinner to look at magazines with Lydia and Louisa.

Perhaps it was the cat. Yes, that was it. Helene grabbed the straw broom from its hook in the lean-to, preparing to find a mess to sweep up. In her other hand, she carried the kerosene lamp——its light illuminating a generous circle of the room. She gasped at the large rock lying in the middle of the space, a piece of paper tied around it. Helene bent to retrieve it and then looked up to see the damaged window near the front door. *What on earth?* She turned cold when she unfurled the note and read, **"Friend or Foe, Herr KAISER?"**

The pool hall was dimly lit and smoky, filled with the sound of glasses clinked together by thirsty and boisterous men. Jacob wrapped his hands around a full mug and headed for a table, the chair scraping as he sat down heavily. Blacksmith Helmke and Georg Haas raised their glasses to Jacob's in salute to a victory for the United States. Foam spilled over Jacob's fist from the gesture, and he wiped his hand on his pants after taking a long swallow of his beer. These men were not his friends, but he had known them for years. There was no one, save his relations, with whom Jacob was close. With such a large family, he had little time for social activities, preferring, instead, to spend his free hours puttering about the farm or working on small projects. The people of Holmesburg knew him, though. They knew he was a dedicated family man——honest and hardworking. Jacob also had the reputation of being a shrewd landowner. When he and Helene had come to America, Jacob had been captivated by the possibility of owning land. His maternal uncle, Christoph Althaus, had written to him about the prairies of endless flowing grass. His uncle lost his two sons in the blizzard of 1888 and hoped that Jacob and his sons would help farm his 160-acre farmstead. Eventually, the family immigrated, and Jacob expanded his land holdings after inheriting his uncle's farm, buying and selling over the years. He was not greedy nor wealthy but prudent in his plans to provide for his family.

The cacophony of sounds allowed Jacob to take in the mood and conversation before speaking. Battle cries of *down with the Huns*! and warnings of *watch out for the enemy*! and *loose lips might sink ships*! filled the air. Beer flowed, and each response intensified the emotion. Finally, Jacob leaned into Haas. "Are you worried?"

"About what, Harvey?"

"We are *all* German——from there, at any rate," Jacob reminded him. "Did you see the notice posted in the town center? The MCPS just did away with German language lessons in Minnesota schools."

"They didn't actually outlaw it. It was just a recommendation," countered Haas.

"And a newsman was arrested in New Ulm——accused of being anti-American for stories published in the German language."

"Harvey, you're worrying about nothing. That wouldn't——couldn't——happen in Holmesburg." Haas balked, waving his hand at Jacob.

"Whatcha fellas talkin' about?" Helmer turned to his serious comrades.

"Jacob's just fretting over the governor's new public safety group. I told him he was overreacting. It'll be easy to tell who's anti-American and who's not." Haas shook his head at the men and shrugged.

"Agreed!" Helmer patted Haas on the back. "Here, here! Let's stomp on those Huns!" Helmer lifted his glass, slurring his cheer.

Jacob's head dropped and shook. He downed the rest of his ale and rose. "Have a good night, gentleman," he said, tipping his hat.

As he surveyed the room on his way out, he tried to figure out how the town had gone from total denial of the coming war to a celebratory mood for the battles to come. It befuddled him that so many missed the storm brewing below the surface. Jacob felt alone in his concern about the overzealous efforts of the Minnesota Commission of Public Safety. The

MCPS would surely be as swift in their judgment as the governor had been in creating the agency.

His time at the pool hall confirmed for Jacob that, although he felt a strong allegiance to his new country, his battle would be a personal one, fought by and for his family. He prayed the others would eventually take heed.

Jacob walked down the dark alley, breathing in the damp newness of spring mingling with the woody smell swirling from chimneys. The darkness of his home puzzled him as he approached——Helene regularly left a lamp lit in the kitchen and one in the front room until everyone was safely home. The waning crescent moon barely lit the sky, but Jacob's steps followed the familiar path without issue. He opened the kitchen door, preparing to light the lamp. Instead, he knocked over the broom perilously set in his path. He reached for the light on the table, but as his eyes adjusted to the darkness, he was taken aback to see Helene sitting there. Her hands trembled as she pushed up from the chair.

Jacob sat and lit the lamp. "What is it?" he asked gently.

The soft light shone on her when she sat back down. His wife was strong, but her face exposed vulnerability. She pushed a crumpled paper toward him.

He smoothed it open and read it, bursting up from his seat, anger rising in his voice. "Where did this come from?"

"It was tied to a rock and hurled through the front window," she whispered. "Who would know this?"

"I don't know. I've never shared this with anyone." His fist pounded the table. "Who would try to taint our standing in this community?"

Jacob paced back and forth, his anger increasing with the room's length. He crumpled the paper in his palm, marched into the front room, and threw it in the hearth, ashes reigniting around the clump. He shook his head in despair when he saw the sheet tacked over the window, his head snapping around at the noise behind him, his lips pressing together at the sight of his wife. "Did Peter or Melania see this?"

"No," Helene replied quietly. "Peter is away for a few days on cannery business, and I ushered our daughter quickly to the stairs when she arrived home."

Jacob stood in the center of the room, his eyes darting around. "This is only the beginning, I'm afraid."

He turned abruptly and marched out the back door to his workshop. When he returned, Helene had gone to bed, but he still pounded the boards over the window, indifferent to his wife's and daughter's slumber. Jacob knew his fuming only added to Helene's worry, but this was a matter of honor——of a man's pride.

Chapter 6

The Herald • May 1917 • DRAFT NOTICE! The President signed the Selective Service Act last Thursday, May 18, allowing him to increase the military establishment in the United States. The office of the Provost Marshal General has established a board in each state that will be responsible for registering men, classifying them, and considering manpower needs in industry and agriculture. This state board will also deal with special family needs and considerations of registrations. Local county boards will assist with calling registrants, determining the medical fitness of individuals, and classification and entrainment of draftees. The Draft will be held in June for all men between twenty-one and thirty-one years old. In addition to a fitness assessment, the board will gather draftees' full names, date and place of birth, race, citizenship, occupation, personal description, and signature.

Melania hugged her friends in affection as they left the schoolroom for the last time——a bittersweet parting, affected in every way by the war. Their school's graduation celebration was reduced to a small affair with just cake and coffee after Mass. The church canceled all summer festivals and dances, not wanting to waste precious resources.

Her father had told Melania they'd be moving to Minneapolis in mid-June, providing no further explanation than that the move was best for the entire family. But her mother had explained that after his rebuff from Mr. Conlin, Vati had taken the train to Minneapolis to apply for employment at Whitney Mill. The larger mills ran at full capacity to meet the needs of feeding the soldiers, so Whitney could offer him job security as a *miller*, beginning at the end of June.

Melania's friends Lydia and Louisa, like many remaining in Holmesburg, had their plans altered too as the war's effects swept the home front. Both girls would begin employment at the Charles Bros. Cannery in June. Melania and her friends shed tears over summer picnics, dances, and time together that would no longer happen.

Melania walked past Young's Grocery on her way home, considering the propagandist posters tacked on walls and lampposts, wondering how Mr. Young felt about the signs.

Eat More Cornmeal • Rye Flour • Oatmeal and Barley. SAVE the wheat for the Fighters!

FOOD WILL WIN THE WAR. You came here seeking Freedom. You must now help to preserve it. WHEAT is needed for the allies. Waste nothing.

Perhaps Mr. Young had mustered a patriotic attitude like many who'd been encouraged by Mr. Herbert Hoover's new appointment as the head of the U.S. Food Administration. He'd called on all Americans to help the war effort and save food. Melania smiled, remembering when her father had read Hoover's words out loud at breakfast last week, something about each person putting the nation's interests above their own.

Melania paid more attention to her father's words and tone of late, especially since his predictions had come to pass. She'd sensed a bit of——what? Cynicism? No, just wariness from her father, perhaps, when he quoted Hoover, the man calling for *complete self-effacement*. Vati had harumphed and repeated that phrase. She wondered now, as she had then, what he worried about.

She entered the back door and set down her schoolbooks and other personal items she'd cleared from her desk. She looked around at the packed crates and boxes, still feeling the sting of lost summer days. Her mother's humming floated in from the other room. Mutti was likely cleaning and packing as she'd been doing for the past week——preparing to move ahead, following Vati as she had always done. Melania sighed as she passed her reflection in the glass of the Hoosier cupboard. She was a graduate now——headed for college in the fall. She, too, needed to face whatever came their way. And at this moment, it was their move to Minneapolis.

The freight train pulled into the Holmesburg depot, its wheels screeching and smoke pouring from its top. By the time the massive steel train completely halted, it was hundreds of feet from the brick station building, the car in which Peter and Jim rode a quarter of a mile back still. Their duties of managing the cannery's shipments occasionally meant train travel, and both men loved traveling the country and the freedom that came with it, despite a bedroll and a dry car serving as their only comforts.

Peter hopped from the empty freight car and waited until Jim threw down their bags. Peter was glad to be back in this little town, surprised at the sentiment, but he felt a change in the air and wanted to be near his family before they moved to the city. He swung his satchel over his shoulder and followed Jim to the station.

"Guessing the mood will have sobered a bit now that the draft has been announced." Jim glanced around the station.

"Maybe. My Vati often speaks of the realities of war——the truths that settle in after the hoopla." Peter shrugged and slapped Jim on the back. "But you and I don't need to worry about that——yet."

"The advantage of youth," Jim chortled.

"Until we're drafted, I say we take advantage of everything we can. Neumann's. My Mutti's pie. The leisurely life on the rails." Peter laughed.

"I could use some suds about now." Jim's brow went up. "Pie first, beer later?"

"Perfect. Meet me at my house. With any luck, there will be dinner *and* pie."

"That'd be great." Jim walked away from Peter, waving his hand above his head as he pushed out the station door.

As the depot door shut behind Jim, Peter noticed his friend's watch on the ground. He stooped to retrieve it, pushed open the door, and called out to Jim, but the howl of the train's whistle drowned out his bellow. Peter spied a notice plastered to the wall as he tucked the watch into his coat pocket.

The Milwaukee Road Depot in Minneapolis is seeking strong men between the ages of eighteen and twenty to fill many upcoming vacancies due to the draft. Good pay, food, and accommodations are included. Help us serve our troops by keeping valuable supplies moving. Apply——

Peter ripped the notice from the wall, shoved it in his pocket, and walked the few blocks home.

He gingerly opened the back door and slipped into the kitchen. "Looks like you've almost moved out of here. Crates are everywhere."

Helene jumped at Peter's voice, and he pulled her in for a hug. "Sorry, Mutti. I didn't mean to startle you."

"Just a couple more weeks." His mother looked around at the stacked crates.

Peter breathed in deeply. "Smells heavenly in here——as if you knew we were coming."

"We?" Helene raised a brow and glanced at Melania.

"None other than the man after your daughter's heart." Peter chuckled and moved over to his younger sister, squeezing her shoulders as she stood at the counter peeling potatoes.

Melania sighed and turned to her brother, dropping her chin and narrowing her eyes. "If you're talking about Jim Wirth, you can tell him I'm not interested." She exhaled sharply and turned back to her task.

Peter laughed. "I am, indeed, talking about the dashing Jim Wirth, and you'll have to tell him yourself, little sister. I can't be responsible for breaking another man's heart."

Mutti shook her head. "Wash your hands for dinner or make yourself useful somewhere else."

Peter washed up at the sink, dried his hands, and then plopped down in the kitchen chair. "Whew! Glad to be home a few days."

"Eventful trip?" Mutti lifted a brow.

Peter leaned on an elbow and shrugged. "No. Not really. Just a lot of talk about the war. And the draft. And rations. And propaganda." He chuckled wryly.

Mutti nodded and moved toward the front room. "I'm going to get your father for dinner. Can you take the chicken out of the oven in a few minutes, Mel?"

Peter squinted at his sister as she set the table. "Wouldn't hurt for you to take Jim up on his offer. He just wants to take you to dinner."

"He's never asked me any such thing." Melania frowned. "He's just *everywhere*. You'd think he didn't travel as a drayman for how many times I've run into him lately. Lands!"

Peter laughed. "Ah, youth. So naïve. That's called *wooing*."

Melania snorted. "If it is, it's not working. Hardly better than a schoolboy who thinks I'll be charmed by how far he can spit."

"What would it take to charm you then, Melania?"

Melania jumped and turned, and Peter laughed uproariously. Jim stood on the threshold, head tilted, eyes twinkling.

"Maybe taking the chicken out of the oven would be a start," Peter suggested, winking at his sister, who stood with her feet planted as if she couldn't move.

"I don't have time for boys or men," she said defiantly. "Both of you are beyond the pale." She crossed her arms and huffed out of the kitchen.

"Until next time," Jim called after her before turning to Peter. "Where's a towel? If I can't impress your sister, I may as well help your mother."

The house brightened as Peter and Jim filled the kitchen with boisterous laughter, regaling the family with tales of their adventures. It was evident that they were easy companions, and Jacob watched as Helene's face glowed, clearly enjoying the banter. On the other hand, Melania barely said a word, shifting uncomfortably for the entire meal.

"Are you unwell, daughter?" Jacob frowned as he regarded his youngest.

Helene nudged him under the table, likely an intentional prodding, but he hadn't the slightest idea what he'd missed, so instead of inquiring, he rose from the table and asked the men to join him outside for a smoke and drink. He could almost feel the relief wash over his wife and daughter as if they were both glad that table talk hadn't turned to war.

The evening was cool, and the men gathered around a small fire lit in a tin bucket. Jacob pulled out a small bottle of whisky tucked in his coat and poured three small glasses. They sat in easy company for a time, sipping on the amber liquid and lighting their pipes and cigarettes. Eventually, the young men relayed the war discourse from their travels with light and enlivened banter.

"You should have seen the posters plastered over the city buildings——Germans as big, ugly creatures with pointed helmets." Peter relayed the information with a casualness that unsettled Jacob.

"Yeah," Jim chimed in. "And then the draft poster with the gorilla as the mad German brute." The boys guffawed at the memory as Jim mimicked a solemn recitation of the poster's message——his head ticking back and forth with his staccato words. "Enlist, dear boy, and destroy this animal!" Jim slapped his knee.

"Soon, it'll be our turn to beat back the Huns." Peter put on as if he were aiming a gun at the enemy.

"It can seem like an exciting time now, to be sure," Jacob commented. "The call to war, to battle our enemy. It brings about the warrior in a man."

Jim and Peter nodded enthusiastically, with Peter pounding on his chest for effect. "Down with the Huns!"

Jacob shook his head and touched his son's forearm, taking a deep breath. "War is not a singular activity. It won't only be fought overseas."

Jim's face twisted in confusion. "Whaddya mean, sir? You don't think they'll make it all the way over here, do you?" Jim crossed his arms.

"They couldn't. It's too far, and we'll beat them back!" Pete pounded a fist on the table next to him.

Jacob held up his hand to the young men. "Son. Jim. Listen. I know talk of winning the war against Germany is all around us, but so is talk of a different kind of war against Germans. People, not the country. You must pay attention."

"Do you mean the new commission the governor formed? The MPS or something?" Peter's brow furrowed. "What are they going to be able to do?"

"We're Germans. Our family. Jim. Many others in our town and beyond. This state is full of German immigrants."

"But we're citizens——even you, Mutti, and the others in our family who immigrated here."

"My family has been in this country for generations. My grandparents are from Ireland, for gosh sakes!" Jim's chin lifted.

"What could we possibly have to worry about?" Peter's brow flattened, and he lifted a shoulder.

"I've seen it before, these nativist groups," Jacob began. "They often begin with motives that seem pure, but then they start the separating and the purging——handpicking which individual, which family, is worthy of being part of their community, space, and country."

"If there's a German spy here, I'd want to know it, by golly." Peter abruptly stood.

"As would I!" Jim echoed, standing too, his fist pounding his palm.

"How would you be able to tell if someone were a spy?" Jacob raised a brow.

"We'd know by their activities. Maybe they'd commit a crime, and it would be discovered."

"What kind of activities?" Jacob prodded.

"Non-American doings."

"What are those? And who should decide?"

"There are obvious ones, such as——" Peter paused and scratched his head. "Well, I'm not so sure."

"The poster in the town square says, *Don't be suspected. Use American Language. America is our home.* Have you seen it?"

Both young men nodded.

"Are you an enemy because you refer to your parents as Mutti and Vati?" Jacob raised an eyebrow at his son. "How about the Rausch family? They speak only German in their home. Are they the enemy?"

The younger men sat back down, each watching Jacob intently. Jim nodded. "I see your point, Mr. Harvey."

"Just today, I read about goings-on in New Ulm. The MCPS dealt with protests over the draft by removing people of German descent from various city positions, including the city's mayor and the Martin Luther College president."

"Hmm." Peter rubbed his chin. "Well, if it stopped the protests, maybe it's not such a bad thing."

"That may seem true, but what speech is acceptable? Only talk in support of the war? What if a person is a pacifist, not necessarily anti-American?"

Peter nodded slightly. "But isn't it important that we support the war? And the military and our country?"

"Certainly," Jacob replied. "But who should decide what is appropriate support? Is it sending our sons to war? Is it planting a Victory garden? Buying Liberty bonds?"

The young men leaned back in their chairs simultaneously as if Jacob's words were weighing heavily on them.

"The MCPS has been given near-dictatorial powers to support the war efforts at home." Jacob opened his hands, palms up, as he shrugged a shoulder.

"That's a good thing, isn't it?" Jim asked.

"In theory, yes, it's a good thing." Jacob paused. "Wait. I'll be back."

Jacob walked into the house as he heard Peter's comment to Jim. "I'm not sure where he's going with this." He appreciated the young men's indulgence and hoped he'd be able to make his point. A few minutes later, Jacob returned with a large rock in his palm.

Peter chuckled. "What? Is that your suggested weapon against the enemy?"

Jim smiled, but Jacob remained grave.

"Did you notice the boarded-up window in the front room?" Before Peter could even respond, Jacob continued. "This was hurled through it last month."

Peter's face crinkled in confusion. "What? Who? Some young hooligan, no doubt."

"We'll likely never know. What's most unsettling is the note that was tied to the rock."

"A note? What did it say?" Peter leaned forward, palms on his knees.

"It said, *Friend or foe, Herr Kaiser?*" Jacob paused as the men pondered.

Peter threw his hands up and shrugged. "Well, then, it's nothing. It was thrown at our house in error."

"It wasn't son. Names matter. They did then, and they do now."

"Our name is Harvey, not Kaiser," Peter said, clearly baffled.

Jacob reached over and took the whisky. "Our name is Harvey now. But it wasn't always," he said as he poured, not meeting their eyes.

Peter reached for the glass and gulped the whisky.

"Back in the '90s, when your Mutti and I, along with Frank and August, were still in Germany, unrest began to grow. Some people became bitter toward larger countries and empires——Great Britain, the United States, and the like, feeling as if their country had gotten the short stick, so to speak. The German and Prussian Emperor, Kaiser Wilhelm, hated all things British, even though his grandmother was Britain's Queen Victoria. He regularly spoke out against its people publicly, and his citizens responded."

The night became still, and it seemed as if even nature quieted as Jacob told his story.

"Many German citizens felt that the only way to establish a strong Germany was to empire-build and do it with *pure* German peoples. Certain groups, like the Pan-German League, engaged in extreme ultra-nationalist activities, starting with identifying people groups they felt didn't belong in the country, like Jews and Catholics. People were targeted with hateful crimes. Kaiser Wilhelm turned a blind eye to the nativist activities. He's a military man, and aggression is a frequent and accepted tactic to him."

Jacob paused, looking at the men, who leaned forward in their seats, appearing to listen to his discourse earnestly. Jim lifted his glass and downed the whisky.

Jacob poured back his drink too, shutting his eyes at the residual burn.

"There was a family in our village, the Becks. Jewish bakers. One day——I won't ever forget it. Herr Beck was beaten physically——then in his spirit. His wife too. I could see it, we all could, but there was nothing we could do about it." Jacob gazed past the men as if the scene played out beyond, etched as it was in his memory.

"When I arrived home that particular evening, your brother Frank had this, this . . . filth in his hand." Jacob's head shook slightly, his brows furrowed, and his hand opened and shook as if he was releasing the actual document. "It wasn't his. He had been given it. Someone on the street handed them out to the school children on the way home." Jacob turned and spit on the ground.

"The nativists worked very diligently to turn citizens against each other. The young——what did they know?"

Peter reached out and put a hand on his father's forearm. Jacob's eyes met his son's gaze, and he continued. "*Grossdeutschland's solution for the superior Aryan race.* That's what the paper said. It called for *pure* Germans to take action——to take their rightful place."

Jacob stopped and sat silent for a moment, his eyes closed and his chin lowered to his chest. Peter and Jim waited in silence.

"You see? We could not stay. We could not be part of that." Jacob looked past them as he spoke, not explaining but remembering. "We left. My uncle, Chris. He was here, so we came." One shoulder lifted briefly.

"Ja. Our farm was his farm," Peter stated. "A godsend."

"To be sure," Jacob agreed. "I learned a lot from him about farming and America." He turned and looked at Pete. "He, der Onkel, he was *Christoph Althaus* in Germany. Just a small change to his given name but one, he said, that made him feel more *American*."

Peter's face registered surprise and understanding as the story's purpose became more evident. "You changed our name."

"Ja. I couldn't abide using the surname of that . . . that man." He spat out the last word. "A ruler who allowed such atrocities and even encouraged them." Jacob's face scrunched in memory.

"When we boarded the *Scandia* in Hamburg in early 1892, I recorded our family name as *Harvey* on an impulse. But now, looking back, perhaps it was providence."

"As we waited in line to board the ocean liner, I glanced at the finely polished boots of a gentleman standing further up the plank. It reminded me of a French Cordonniere, a shoemaker named Harvey Marchand." Jacob drew out the man's name in two syllables, cutting out the first letter——'ar-vey. "He lived near—just across the French border from our home in Strasbourg. Herr Marchand had a reputation for being a skilled craftsman. When he finished making a pair of boots or shoes, he would make a big display of giving them to a customer. He'd say, *I am ar-vey. My name means* strong *and* worthy. *My work is strong and worthy too.* And then he would place the footwear in the customer's hands as if they were receiving pure gold." Jacob chuckled.

"Sometimes, a pair of his boots wouldn't wear out for years, but it was no concern to Herr Marchand. He knew his reputation was what mattered." Jacob smiled to himself and then looked directly into his son's eyes.

"When I thought of him, I knew. Harvey would be our family's new sur-name. We are strong and worthy too. Worthy of being American citizens." Jacob sat back in the chair and crossed his hand over his lap.

The young men sat back too, both releasing their breath. The night sounds crept back into the space——the wind in the trees, the sounds of horse hooves on the street, the clanging of dishes from the slightly open kitchen window. Each man sat comfortably as the story settled in. Jacob reached down for a stick and poked at the fire.

In a low voice, barely audible, he said, "Your name and your honor. Two of the most important things to a man." Then he looked up, his glance going from face to face. "Watch. Pay attention. Don't forget we are at war on the home front too." He paused, rubbing his chin in thought. "Now that I think about it, our former surname could be on some of the documents filed with the city when uncle's land was transferred to me." He snorted. "That someone in an official position would stoop so low as to toss a rock through our window..."

He snorted again and rose to leave, but Peter stood and put a hand on his arm. "Vati, I have something to show you." He pulled the railroad brochure from his pocket and smoothed it flat on the table for Jim and his father to see. "I think we should do this, Jim. Now, before we're drafted."

Jacob and Jim scanned the paper. "What are the jobs?"

"There's several vacancies, but we could easily manage the freight han-dler positions." Peter grinned and flexed his muscles. "Strong and strap-ping as we are."

"There's no time like the present." Jim's brow went up.

"Speaking of," Peter said, pulling a watch from his pocket. "I'd almost forgotten to give this to you, Jim. You dropped it at the station earlier."

"That's a nice piece. Family?" Jacob nodded to the ornately engraved timepiece.

Jim wrapped his fist around the watch. "Ah, yes. My father's. I wondered where this was."

Peter placed his hand on Jacob's arm. "What do you think about the job, Vater?"

"Go. Now is the time."

Jim dropped the watch into his pocket. "I agree. Let's go travel the country. There's nothing keeping me here."

He's leaving? Nothing to keep him here? Melania stood in the kitchen doorway. She hadn't meant to eavesdrop on the men again. Mutti had simply sent her to collect their glasses. But their voices had stopped her in the doorway. She hadn't heard where exactly Jim and Pete were going. Only that Jim didn't feel there was any reason to stay.

She ducked behind the door as the men turned toward the house. There was no reason she should take offense to Jim's statement. After all, she'd done nothing to encourage him and everything to dissuade him. Why then, she wondered, did she have a sinking feeling in her stomach at the thought of him going away?

Chapter 7

The sun shone brightly in the warm afternoon sky, and Jacob shielded his eyes until he and Peter made their way toward the historic event—the first draft in generations. Helene had decided to stay home, and Jacob understood—being here validated the draft in some way, and he wasn't sure if his wife was ready for that reality. Many citizens did gather, however, in Holmesburg City Park to cheer and support the men approaching the military draft board, the process buoyed by a small military ensemble in the gazebo. During the band's breaks, the draft board played a disc recording of *Over There* on an Edison Company phonograph. The dark oak cabinet was festooned with an American Flag draped over its hinged lid——clearly an honored possession.

"Let's sit over there." Peter pointed to a cluster of benches near the back of the gazebo.

"Ja." Jacob followed his youngest son and plunked down on the seat, craning his neck past the movement of the musicians and instruments. Despite the merriment, the day was somber, the cheer and noise a temporary shield.

"There." Peter pointed. "Frank and August. See them, Vati?"

"Ja." Jacob nodded slightly, clasping his hands as if in prayer. He thought he was prepared for this day—knew it was coming—but being here, seeing his sons approach the draft board—*that* was something different altogether.

Peter rested a palm over his father's hands a moment. "Do you want to go over to them?"

"No." Jacob chuckled wryly. "It's a throng of women." Several ladies moved in circles around their menfolk——straightening collars, brushing dust off shoulders, clinging to their man's arm as if he were leaving for training this very day instead of just completing draft registration.

Peter laughed too and sat back, folding his arms over his middle.

The registration process moved along in an orderly fashion, and soon Frank and August joined Peter and Jacob. Jacob had followed the process as best he could, and Frank's description of the events offered clarity. One by one, the men slipped behind a screened area for a medical examination and then moved to the long side tables to complete and sign the registration cards. Medical examiners scribbled appraisals and assessments, and the draftees carried the cards to the next station, seemingly unfazed in the momentary blessedness of the unknown.

Then the draftees moved to the final registration tables, forming lines with cards in their grasp——the medical examiner's "P" or "F" boldly stamped on the front. When a man reached the table, draft employees, for uniformity and efficiency's sake, completed the cards, sometimes scribbling out mistakes made due to misunderstandings. The workers noted hair and eye color, general size——stocky, slim, average——and birthplace, citizenship, and general observations.

While it was not an official deferment, Jacob welcomed the information on August's card: "F" for *fail* and the phrase, *feeble-minded.* The words did not offend in their simplicity nor in their sentiment——Jacob was not concerned about explaining August to strangers. These words could keep August at home where he belonged.

Frank's card noted that he had a "dependent wife and children," likely a temporary deferment.

In many respects, the draft board seemed to be winging it with its inexperienced staff and untested process, but at the end of the day, they had a solid group of newly enlisted men.

Jacob and Peter walked home after Frank and August left for the farm in the wagon.

"Mathias?" Peter turned to Jacob.

Jacob nodded. Of all his sons, Mathias was the only one of age without a legitimate reason for deferment. "Registering in Minneapolis." Jacob's chest tightened briefly—the relief he'd felt for Frank and August replaced by the certainty of Mathias's deployment.

"Ah."

Peter rubbed shoulders with Jacob as they ambled down the street toward home, where Helene was waiting. *When would they come for this son—their youngest?* Jacob hoped his wife would be content in the unknown.

The relocation to Minneapolis was fast approaching. Jacob resigned from the Holmesburg Mill at the beginning of June, allowing ample time to make the transition. Many household items were stored at the farm, leaving basic pieces for the new tenants——two young women recently hired at the cannery.

The Harvey men discussed productive measures to deal with the nativist efforts. They would be careful about using German words in public and of offering commentary on nearly *anything* related to the war or the efforts on the home front. Navigating the propaganda machine, at full churn in the United States, would require conscious thought——of that, they were all aware. Correspondence must be carefully worded, they realized, and hoped they could send much of it with Peter during his rail travel.

"Mutti," Melania called downstairs. "I'm running out of packing crates."

Jacob came to the bottom of the stairs and looked up at his daughter. "Are you packing Anna's things too? I'll take them to the farm in my next load if they're ready."

"Yes. I did that first. They're pushed to the back of the hall, out of the way."

Jacob trudged up the stairs. "I'll bring them down now. You can help if you want. It's awfully hot up here."

Melania nodded and wiped her brow. "It's stifling." She chuckled. "Maybe a lemonade break before I finish up." She picked up one of the smaller boxes and moved aside as her father hoisted a larger one. "Will I have my own room at Mrs. Pritchard's?"

"Yes. It's just Emily Pritchard and her young daughter. Elizabeth, I think is her name."

"Really?"

"Her husband was drafted. He was in management at the mill in Minneapolis. It's how I heard about the accommodations. Many grass widows are bringing in lodgers."

"That's an awfully strange name." His daughter pushed out the back door and walked down the path to the wagon, setting the box on the edge of the bed.

Jacob set his next to hers and pushed them both toward the back of the wagon bed. "A term used in the old country." He leaned in conspiratorially. "Just meant a woman whose husband had gone——usually off to war." He chuckled. "Suppose we shouldn't say that either."

"It's going to be difficult, isn't it, Vati?" Melania's brow furrowed.

He patted her on the shoulder. "We'll manage." He was about to turn back toward the house for more boxes but stopped, figuring his youngest should be spoken to like an adult. She was headed off to college in the fall, God willing. And she, too, was moving to the cities, where there would likely be more propaganda targeted at Germans. "Frank, Ida, and August will manage the farm well. It should be some time before Frank's drafted, and August won't likely go at all. Mathias, though. He'll be going first."

He saw Melania grimace and touched her forearm. "Someone has to go. You understand that, don't you?"

She closed her eyes briefly and nodded. "It's sad that Mathias has to leave college. He's an intellectual, not a fighter."

"That's the way of things, daughter."

"Anna will be near us in the city since she's at the convent."

"For now."

"For now?"

"War can change everyone's plans." Jacob lifted a shoulder. "But Peter and Jim——they have time to wander a bit."

Melania exhaled heavily. "And, you, Mama, and I will hold down the fort, as they say." She smiled faintly. "See? I didn't say *Mutti*," she whispered.

Jacob smiled. "That will not be easy." He turned. "Let's get the rest and then I'll join you for some lemonade before I head out."

"Where's Vati?" Melania jumped at Peter's voice, the tray of lemonade and glasses clattering in her hands.

"Goodness, Pete. You startled me! Vati just took another load to the farm." She smiled and turned toward Peter.

"Oh, hello, Jim." He was leaving soon and so were they—she may as well be cordial.

Jim smiled, and she noticed the characteristic twinkle was gone. Was something amiss? Maybe he had given up on *wooing* her, as Peter had called it.

She set the tray back on the table. "I can bring out more lemonade if you two want some."

Peter nodded. "You bet. We just finished bringing Jim's things to his brother's farm."

Jim shrugged and sat down. "Not that I have much."

Melania's brow furrowed. *Was that what was bothering him?* "I think we have too much if you ask me. Goodness. We've stored loads at the farm already."

Melania paused with her hand on the doorknob. "Where will you two stay when you're not on the rails?" She laughed. "That sounds so funny—*on the rails*." She watched as Jim smiled again. Surprisingly, she realized, a genuine conversation with Jim and her brother was much more enjoyable than she'd imagined.

Peter sat on the bistro chair and leaned on the table. "Vati said there's room to sleep in the attic in the Minneapolis house."

Melania's eyes opened wide, and Jim laughed, the sparkle in his eye returning.

"Nothing to worry about, Melania. I'll be at a boardinghouse."

"Oh, that's not—" Melania grinned and shrugged. "Well, maybe, it did seem a bit—"

Jim laughed again. "Inappropriate." He lifted a brow. "If you've got more packing to do, I'd be more than happy to help you after we have some lemonade."

She hesitated. "Thanks." She paused again. What would it hurt for him to help? "That would be dandy." Melania stepped inside the house but then quickly turned back. "Goodness. I forgot the pitcher."

Once in the kitchen, she refilled the pitcher with water, squeezed in lemons and added sugar, stirring while she mused about the unexpected conversation. She felt more settled now that she knew where her brother and Jim would be. Surely, it wouldn't be the same in Mrs. Pritchard's home as it was here—they'd all be guests there. Maybe, just maybe, though, Jim would come with Peter sometime for dinner. *Seeing* Jim would not be the same as *encouraging* him, she decided.

Jacob pulled the reins and led the horses to the end of the block, where he gathered discarded crates in the alleys along Main Street. Next, he stopped at the lumber mill to pick up wood planks to build additional boxes. Finally, he swung by Young's store, snatching a paper from the rack and tossing a coin on the counter before he went back to his wagon. He unhitched the horse from the post, paused a moment with his foot on the running board, and unfolded the newspaper for a quick glance at the headlines. Without fail, attention-grabbing war features dotted the front page, but one article about the draft jumped off the sheet at him.

JUNE 1917 • THE HERALD • COUNTY SLACKER LIST • FULLER COUNTY'S MILITARY DRAFT WAS HELD LAST WEEK IN HOLMESBURG'S CITY SQUARE. TEN ALLEGED FULLER COUNTY DRAFT DODGERS WERE ANNOUNCED BY THE WAR DEPARTMENT YESTERDAY AFTER THE LIST OF SLACKERS FROM LOCAL REGISTRATION BOARD NO. 2 WAS MADE PUBLIC. THE REGISTRATION BOARD WAS GOING OFF DRAFT NUMBERS ASSIGNED TO OUR COUNTY BY THE DRAFT COMMITTEE. SLACKERS **BEWARE!** AS FULLER COUNTY SHERIFF SENDS THIS DIRE WARNING: **READ AND OBEY OR SUFFER THE CONSEQUENCES!** THIS MEANS YOU! THE U.S. GOVT. CANNOT BE TRIFLED WITH! IF YOU ARE BETWEEN THE AGES OF 21 AND 31 AS DESCRIBED IN THE ORIGINAL DRAFT NOTICE AND YOU HAVE NOT YET REGISTERED, YOU <u>MUST</u> COME

TO THE FULLER COUNTY CITY OFFICES IN HOLMESBURG BY JUNE 19, 1917, TO COMPLETE YOUR REGISTRATION! NO EXCUSE WILL BE TAKEN! IF YOU ARE SICK, SEND FOR THE REGISTRAR. IF YOU MUST BE AWAY, REGISTER BEFORE YOU GO. FOR FURTHER INFORMATION, CALL AT MY OFFICE. FAIL AT YOUR OWN **PERIL**! THE GOVT. AGENTS WILL FIND YOU AND YOUR MINIMUM PUNISHMENT FOR NOT REGISTERING WILL BE ONE YEAR OF HARD LABOR IN THE U.S. PENITENTIARY. **ALL CITIZENS!** HELP FIND OUR COUNTY'S SLACKERS AND PRESS THEM TO DO THEIR DUTY! HERE IS THE LIST FROM REGISTRATION BOARD NO. 2, BATTERY "B" 113TH FIELD ARTILLERY: PVT. THOMAS S. COFFEY, PVT. JOHN L. LINDQUIST, PVT. HENLEY C. LANGSDORF, PVT. EDWARD K. ELLINGTON, AND PVT. MATHIAS J. HARVEY.

Jacob slammed his hand on the wagon bed, cursing under his breath. "Damn them!" He knew full well that Mathias had registered at his college campus, as was required. Jacob shook his head and continued his muttering, concerned for what this could mean for his son. He looked around, suddenly aware that others had seen his outburst. He quickly hopped up onto the wagon seat, its springs bouncing under the movement as he hurried back home to unload the boxes and planks.

"Helene!" he called from the kitchen lean-to after he had unpacked his cargo. "I'm headed to see the sheriff."

CHAPTER 8

Jacob wiped his brow with his handkerchief and shoved it in his back pocket before shutting down his roller mill. It was hot on the floor, despite the windows open to the cool September air. He glanced around at the other workers finishing their shifts and the next laborers ready to take their positions. The Minneapolis Whitney Mill production ran eighteen hours a day, six days a week. The force worked alternate weeks of ten- and eight-hour periods.

Jacob's job as a miller had quickly expanded to areas he'd never anticipated. Being a man——an experienced man, and one in advanced years——lent an air of authority to him. The mill management took advantage of this, giving Jacob extra supervisory and training duties. While it pushed Jacob's endurance to its limits, he was grateful for a job——a well-paying, steady job——and gladly accepted whatever responsibilities were placed on him. Most in his charge were young, inexperienced women or newly transplanted southern blacks. The lot seemed eager to learn and do well—Jacob was aware many of the women's husbands had gone off to war, and he'd heard the harsh segregationist laws had driven many blacks north once the war began.

Helene, too, began work at the mill soon after they'd settled in Minneapolis, responding to the urgent call for women to fill the positions of drafted men. She took a packer position, working four eight-hour days, as did many of the older women.

Jacob welcomed the advancements at the Whitney Mill. Newer roller mills operated more efficiently than the old millstones, making it easier to separate out the bran rather than crushing it as they had in Holmesburg. Jacob took pride in knowing that the word *Minneapolis* on the head of a flour barrel guaranteed the excellence of its contents. The Minneapolis millers sought out the best inventions, avoided cheap processes, and were aided by the superb waterpower of the Mississippi River at the Falls of St. Anthony. War production flour was darker than premium flour as the government required mills to produce a lesser grade during the war. The war's demands on Whitney Mill were great: the mill sent out nearly two hundred train boxcars filled with flour each day.

Jacob hung his apron on a peg and moved down the enclosed steel stairway to the first-floor packing level to retrieve his wife. Helene's face was red from exertion, and her steps dragged slowly as she moved toward him. He wrapped his hand gently around hers and softly squeezed. In the three months since they'd started work at the mill, Jacob noticed the way his wife's back stooped and her step slowed. She bore her burden with the same fortitude she always had——doing what was necessary with no complaints.

"Let's stop for ice cream on our way home," Jacob suggested.

Helene paused, glancing at her husband. "I'm fine, dear."

"Of course. Ice cream would just be nice." He lifted a brow, knowing she wasn't fooled.

The Grand-Monroe streetcar line ran near the Whitney Mill, and it took the couple over the Mississippi River toward their home on the other side.

Jacob held his hand out to his wife as she stepped off the streetcar and onto the curb. The evening was warm and pleasant——the humidity had subsided with the end of August. They walked a block off their path to Selma's Ice Cream Parlor.

"Let's bring ice cream home for Emily and Melania," Helene suggested.

"We'd best eat ours here, then." Jacob chuckled. "I don't mind eating a sweet treat before supper."

Helene was settled at a small table in the corner when he returned with the ice cream, setting the dishes down and pulling a chair close to Helene's. They ate in silence until Jacob was finished. He reached his hand across and laid it over hers. "Are you sure you're fine?"

"I'm just tired," Helene assured. "But this ice cream has been a considerable pick-me-up." She smiled and rose from her seat. "We'd best get the girls' ice cream and head home. They'll start to worry about us."

Melania went to the front porch when she spied her parents coming down the sidewalk. She grinned when Mutti's brows shot up at the raucous laughter floating from the windows.

"You've no doubt who's here," she said to her parents as they came up the porch steps.

Her father chuckled. "Goodness. They'll call the MCPS to our door."

Melania moved aside to let her parents in, and the noise settled when her brother greeted Mutti.

"Liebe Mutter! How I have missed you!" Peter planted kisses on both of her cheeks, and their mother pushed him back in feigned embarrassment. "And you brought me ice cream."

"No. This is for the girls." Vati shook his head and moved past Peter toward the kitchen. "It's melted some, so I'll set it in the icebox."

"Or we could drink it now," Peter teased.

Melania rolled her eyes and sat down on the sofa. She loved her brother and was happy to see him. Peter and Jim had been gone since early June, their new job with the railroad taking them much farther and for longer periods than had their job with the cannery. Now they traveled from one end of the country to the other, often working for a spell in different cities. The pair filled Emily Pritchard's front room, their presence and banter transforming the space. They'd only arrived an hour ago, and so far, the men had filled the entire time with lively tales of their travels. If this conversation was anything like the day in June, when they'd talked over lemonade, Melania would make an effort to enjoy it. Maybe Jim had gotten her message—realized that she, frankly *they*, had no time for courting.

Mutti sat in the rocker and smiled at the young men. "How long are you in the cities?"

"Just for a couple of days, ma'am." Jim leaned casually in the arched doorway between the front hall and the living room. "I was just about to ask Melania if she'd go to the picture show with me one evening this week." Jim turned and winked at Melania.

Heat crept up her neck, and she popped up from the sofa—clearly very wrong in her assessment of Jim's intentions. "Let's have that ice cream now, Emily." She ducked past Jim into the kitchen.

Emily followed with the baby tucked in the crook of her arm. "It seems Jim is smitten with you."

"He's not. He's just teasing me. He's older and——" Melania stammered. "I have things to do. I have plans." She crossed her arms.

"It wouldn't hurt for you to go to the pictures with him." Emily's chin dropped. "Who knows how long it'll be before he's drafted. Have fun while you can."

Melania turned away to get bowls and spoons. She'd never thought of it that way before. Things were, indeed, changing——faster than she'd ever imagined. More and more of her friends from Holmesburg had been drafted or had brothers and boyfriends sent off to war. Victory gardens popped up everywhere——even in empty city lots and on the university campus. Rallies for war bonds and other military efforts happened all over the city. Nothing was static. Maybe it wouldn't be the worst thing to enjoy an evening with the plucky Jim Wirth. She felt a tingling sensation at the base of her neck and pressed her hand over it before turning and looking back at Emily through narrow eyes. Emily grinned, and Melania walked out of the kitchen without taking a bite of the ice cream.

Jim sat on the sofa talking with her father, and when the young man looked up, Melania's words rushed out. "The pictures would be nice." She spun around and hurried up the stairs as her heart pounded in her chest.

Jim called to her from the bottom of the stairs. "I'll be by tomorrow evening at seven o'clock!"

Melania slipped the cotton dress with the tiny purple flowers over her head the next evening, careful not to squash the curls in her hair. She tied the sash and hung a cream sweater over the crook of her arm before heading downstairs. It was still near sixty degrees this early autumn evening, but the nights were growing cooler.

Sitting upright in the chair, she waited on the porch, her small bag resting between trembling hands. *Why am I so nervous?* She knew Jim. He'd been coming around her home for months now. He was almost like another brother. *Except.* Except his presence caused her palms to sweat. She wiped her hands on her skirt and stood when she saw Jim come around the corner.

"Well, hello there!" Jim called as Melania skipped down the front steps. "You must be excited to see *Cleopatra*——or me," he teased.

"Yes——the movie." Melania strode up the walkway toward Jim, anxious to be out of sight of the front window.

Jim crooked his elbow, looping Melania's arm through. She let it stay there, feeling oddly comfortable.

Mercifully, Jim did most of the talking on the way to the theater, regaling her with tales of his childhood. It lightened the mood significantly, and for that, Melania was grateful. Perhaps this would be a more enjoyable evening than she'd anticipated. Once they had a box of popcorn and two Cokes, they headed to their seats in the dimly lit theater. The cinema was crowded for this much-anticipated production. They settled into their seats four rows back from the front, smack in the middle. Melania could barely see Jim, but warmth emanated from him, and she could hear the steady in and out of his breathing. She straightened her back and set her arms in her lap, reminding herself not to touch the armrest where Jim's arm lay. His long, bent legs had nowhere to go but to lean slightly one way or the other, and he shifted them away from her seat. Melania discreetly leaned her own legs away. Managing to keep their long legs from touching throughout the entire feature would take some doing.

The hall darkened completely, and the click-click sound of the projector preceded the sudden flash of light on the screen. Two war shorts, *Uncle Sam at Work* and *The War Waif*, played back-to-back before the feature.

Melania shot Jim a quizzical look when the projector abruptly stopped halfway through *Cleopatra*. "More war promotion," he said with a shrug.

"Haven't we already gotten enough with the first two shorts?"

Jim chuckled and leaned in to whisper. "This is about selling war bonds." He turned toward her. "In the bigger cities, we'd possibly see Mary Pickford, Charlie Chaplin, or Douglas Fairbanks."

"Really? Have you seen them?" She was very curious now, much more interested than she wanted to be.

"Can't say I've seen them, but I did see the top of Chaplin's hat in a parade when Pete and I were last in Chicago." He chortled. "Or maybe it was Douglas Fairbanks."

Melania gasped and swatted his arm. "Douglas Fairbanks is much too handsome to be confused for Chaplin."

"So you know a thing or two about handsome men, then?" Jim laughed and then touched her lightly on the arm. "We're about to see who'll be hawking war bonds this time."

The promotional film clicked and sputtered, and then Mary Pickford's name flashed on the screen, followed by the title, ***100% American.*** Melania sighed.

"No Fairbanks and only Mary's picture." Jim chuckled. "Darn."

The sky was dark as the couple made their way through the crowd outside the theater an hour later. Boisterous banter filled the air as customers talked about the films——*Cleopatra* and the hoopla from the war shorts.

Jim put his hand on the small of her back and led Melania across the street. "A lot is going on these days," he said.

She looked at him, unsure what he meant, but tipped her head and nodded as he continued.

"Did you hear about the women suffragists protesting at the White House a few weeks back?"

"Mmm hmm. Arrested, right?" Melania raised a brow. School kept her busy, but she endeavored to keep up on current events, especially those that may impact her one day.

"Yep, although that seemed a bit much." Jim sighed. "I keep thinking of your father's talk with Peter and me last summer. He warned us to watch out for——" Jim stopped. "Gosh, I don't know what to be on the lookout for. Unusual things, I guess."

"Seems strange to arrest women who merely want to vote."

Jim laughed. "I agree. I happen to know several smart and capable women." He stepped toward her and bumped her shoulder as they continued walking, and she smiled at his gesture.

"The Red Cross chapters are new too." Melania shrugged. "Seems odd that a chapter here will help the war across the ocean. But I guess they'll be sending medical supplies and such."

"A good cause," Jim said.

They walked on a bit longer in silence until they came to a newsstand——the front-page reporting on the recently deployed American soldiers. Already, lists of the missing, the injured, and the dead were reported weekly. Jim exhaled loudly. "These lists are only going to get longer."

Melania shivered, and Jim took her hand.

"Let's warm up with some hot chocolate at Woolworths."

She let him wrap his warmth around her slender fingers, and they walked without speaking toward Woolworths. Melania's hand felt comfortable in Jim's hold. The glow from the streetlights provided just enough illumination for the sidewalk, allowing her to enjoy the ease of Jim's company without scrutiny. In the shadows of the night, her hand in Jim's, the war seemed distant, and they were untouchable——for a time, anyway.

The brightly lit Woolworths restaurant on the corner of Hennepin and 6th shined like a beacon in the night. Couples walked in and out of the door as Melania and Jim approached. Melania pulled her hand from Jim's grasp, and he opened the door, ushering her inside. She looked around, unsure if they should sit at the counter or at a booth. Jim grabbed her hand again and led her to the counter. She sat on the round cushioned stool and rested her feet on the bar, holding her handbag in her lap, waiting for Jim's lead.

He elbowed her gently in the ribs after he sat on the stool next to her. "I'd order for you, but you may be one of those suffragettes." He winked and reached for the two menus tucked between the sugar and cream dispensers.

"I appreciate having a vote on what pie I eat," Melania joked back, welcoming the light banter. "Blueberry sounds delightful. And coffee." Coffee sounded much more grown-up than hot chocolate.

The pair enjoyed the light, easy chitchat and dessert, agreeing it paled woefully to Helene's pies. The restaurant slowly cleared, and the waitress gathered their empty plates and cups. Jim tossed coins on the counter and stood. Melania twirled in her seat, setting her feet on the ground, suddenly feeling awkward. She inhaled deeply, attempting to calm herself and remain in control of her feelings. There was no reason not to be enjoying the evening.

She looped her handbag and crossed her arms as thoughts rushed through her head. This get-together was enjoyable. But what now? Nothing had changed. She still wasn't interested in having a steady beau. There was school. And Jim would be drafted eventually. She averted her eyes and stepped behind him, letting him lead the way out the door and into the night.

"There should be one more streetcar this evening," he commented, putting his hand on her elbow and turning her toward the station. They walked silently——the light mood of the diner replaced with private reveries.

The horn of the approaching trolley sounded, breaking the silence. Jim stopped suddenly, turning to Melania, and reaching for her hands. He was so close she could feel the warmth emanating from his chest. Her body wanted to lean in, but her wits prevailed. She planted her feet and looked down, struggling not to yank her hands from his grasp.

"Melania."

She slowly raised her eyes to his.

"I know things around us are changing so fast. Everything is unpredictable. The war. The world. I may be drafted. *Soon*. But——I——I would really like us——" His stammering stopped for a moment, and in that hesitation, Melania pulled her hands out of his and turned to run.

She stopped after a few strides and turned back briefly. "I'm sorry." She bolted down the sidewalk.

Jim called out to her, but she didn't look back, instead turning the corner toward the streetcar stop.

Melania pushed the Tuec electric vacuum across the front room carpet the following day, grateful for the cleaner's droning. She'd never used such a contraption before but was thankful for the distraction and the isolation it allowed as her mind reeled. She ran the hose brush along the room's baseboard, lost in her thoughts about the night before. *What had Jim been about to say? Why didn't I listen? Oh, but how could I have stayed?* The thoughts swirled around and around in her head. She switched off the machine. It was no use——she was never going to figure out what to do. It was only a matter of time before that gangly man with the crooked smile and twinkling green eyes showed up at her doorstep again. She needed to get out of here. "That's it," she said aloud, calling to mind a Red Cross poster she'd seen plastered in the university's commons.

"What's it?" Mutti came from the kitchen, wiping her hands on a towel.

"Ahh——nothing I can fully explain right now. I need to go to school."

"But it's Sunday, and dinner will be ready soon."

"Don't wait for me." Melania grabbed her handbag and sweater, heading out the front door without further explanation.

Melania returned several hours later to find her parents and Emily sitting on the front porch, Elizabeth asleep in Mutti's lap.

"I'm sorry I hurried off and missed dinner."

"It must have been important for you to have missed Mutti's roast." Vati's tone was flat. *Goodness.* Was he upset? She'd told Mutti not to wait for her.

"There's plenty left, dear." Her mother stood and handed the child to Emily. "I can make up a plate."

Melania shook her head. "I had dinner with friends. We had so much to discuss."

Vati's gray eyebrow arched. "Such as?"

"This." Melania thrust a piece of paper toward her parents——a promotion for the new Minnesota Chapter of the American Red Cross. "With the war, the need, and the able student body, the university is the perfect place for them to look for help. I want to do *something*. I *have* to do something." She hesitated. "And I would like to live on campus."

"Slow down, daughter, and sit." Vati pulled a chair close.

Emily stood. "Time to put this one to bed." She and her daughter went inside the house.

The stars twinkled in the darkened sky, and Melania could feel the cold night air rolling in. She ran her hands over the goosebumps on her arms. Should she jump right in with her reasons for wanting to move to campus or let her father speak? Surely, he'd be the one voicing the most concern.

"I want to be near the activities," she started, deciding to lay it all out. "My schedule will be jam-packed with classes, schoolwork, training."

Vati cleared his throat. "There have already been several stories in the newspaper of the nativist activities. German textbooks have been banned——German language instruction forbidden."

"Has that happened at the university?" Mutti's voice surprised Melania, and she turned toward her mother. Usually, Mutti listened, letting Vati ask the questions.

"I don't know, Mutti," she said evenly, trying desperately not to sound flippant. What was the point of these comments? "I don't take any such classes." She smiled slightly. "I think those courses would be for the students who aren't of German descent."

"Clever as you are," her father said, with an obvious bit of reprimand in his voice, "*anyone* can be targeted by the MCPS. I just read of a school teacher in Stearns County who lost her teaching certificate after allegedly making pro-German comments."

Melania shrugged casually, grateful that the darkness would likely keep her father from seeing the dismissive action. She took a deep breath. "If she was talking about the war, then maybe the MCPS's action was warranted."

Vati slapped his leg, and Melania startled. "Listen, girl. *Allegedly* made pro-German comments. It wasn't proven, and pro-German does not mean against America."

He exhaled loudly as if he were trying to regain some lost patience. "With this flimsy approach, the MCPS is dangerous. I worry about you. You have to be careful about everything you say. Do you understand that?"

Melania nodded, trying desperately to figure out what her father was getting at. She was gone most of the hours on any given day—already out in the world her father seemed to be trying to protect her from. Was he trying to shelter her, or was it something else? She remembered the surprising conversation they'd had right before they moved from Holmesburg. Her father had spoken to her as he'd done with her brothers. Maybe he felt she could only understand the seriousness of the war if she was under their influence, living under their roof——if *he* could ensure she knew what was going on. Suddenly, she remembered something—something that would show her father that she was paying attention. "I saw what happened to the Germania Life Insurance building last week when I went to St. Paul with a friend."

Her father's chin dropped, and he nodded. She wondered if he already knew. "They removed the statue," she continued. "I imagine it was because it personified the nation of Germany. They changed the name to the *Guardian Life Insurance Company of America.*"

Vati let out a low chortle. "I see you *do* understand."

Melania heard her mother's deep exhalation, and she chuckled. "It's hard not to when your father keeps his finger to the pulse of the entire world's events."

Moving to Minneapolis and attending the university had given Melania a taste of independence and exposure to world affairs. "I'm almost eighteen," she reminded her parents at last. "Anna left home by my age and is nearly *married* to Jesus by now. Everyone is making their way, and so must I."

Her parents were partially lit by the glow from inside, and she saw Mutti set her hand on Vati's forearm. "Why, Melania? Why do you think now is the time to live in the dormitory?"

Melania took in a deep breath. She'd evaded Mutti's questions about her time with Jim last night, and she knew her mother was asking her if she was running away from something she didn't want to face. Was she? *No,* she told herself. She was doing the next logical thing for a college girl——living on campus and getting involved.

"I want to be near the activities. I'll be busy with school and the training." Melania bit her bottom lip and then looked at her mother with a smile. "Remember Jane? She and I will room together. Her other roommate recently left school to work in a factory in her hometown. It's perfect timing."

Mutti nodded. "Is there any other reason?"

Melania knew her mother was giving her one more opportunity to explain about Jim, but what could she say? She'd had a fine time with Jim at the movies and wasn't even sure herself why she'd pulled away from him and ran. Maybe it was that he'd seemed so serious suddenly——as if he was about to ask for her to wait for him if he got drafted. She'd heard about many fellows doing such things—proposing marriage, even! "No, Mutter." She stood and looked at Vati. "May I go?"

"Ja." He sighed deeply and his shoulders sagged a bit. He loved her and worried about her. She could see that now.

"Thank you. Both." Melania kissed Vati's forehead, embraced her mother, and then opened the door. "I must gather my things. I'm moving in with Jane tomorrow!"

The evening faded with the conversation, the chill of the night settling over them. "It was bound to happen," Helene said as she stood and moved toward the house.

"A cause is a good thing." Jacob held the door and then came into the living room after her.

He turned on the electric light and plunked down in the upholstered chair, pulling the newspaper from its tucked position within the cushion.

Helene sank into the rocker next to him and listened to the sounds coming from upstairs——Emily singing her daughter to sleep and Melania's footsteps on the wooden planks as she moved in her room, packing to leave. Helene exhaled heavily and grabbed the envelope sitting on the small table beside her chair. "I'll read the letter from Anna to you."

Jacob set the paper in his lap.

"Goodness," Helene said as her eyes scanned the page, silently reading it first. "Anna's joining the Red Cross." She looked up at Jacob and then back again to the letter. "To be a nurse overseas."

She looked up again at her husband, her eyes wide.

Jacob chuckled. "Is there anything else worth reading aloud, or does that cover it?"

Helene rolled her eyes. "Sorry. After tonight's talk with Melania, the words just jumped out at me."

She laid the letter in her lap with a deep exhalation. "It won't be just Mathias who's headed overseas." She'd mostly pushed thoughts of Mathias's service to the back of her mind as he was still in the United States, training and preparing. Soon, though, he'd deploy, and now so would their eldest daughter.

Jacob snorted. "They're lucky to have him after the mishap with the Draft Board."

"Well, dear, it's better than Mathias serving a year of hard labor in the U.S. Penitentiary, isn't it?" Lord, she hoped that was true.

"Of course," Jacob grunted. "I just hope the military has a better grip on matters when they send boys overseas next month."

Helene nodded, flipped Anna's letter over again, and finished the last paragraph. "She'll begin her training in November and plans to visit us later this week." Helene sighed heavily as the weight of the evening's news settled in on her. "Such a turn of events for Anna. But we cannot hold them back. Even Melania."

Jacob nodded and rose from his chair, sliding the newspaper back into its spot and grabbing his pipe instead. He ambled through the house, and Helene heard the back door open. She moved to peer down the length of the house, seeing her husband silhouetted in the night lights. A puff of smoke swirled over him while the slight shake of his head exposed thoughts aplenty swirling inside.

CHAPTER 9

—•—

Minneapolis mayor Walter von Esson rapped his fingers on the walnut desk, his patent leather shoes tapping the floor in unison. The staccato stopped, and he twirled his chair and glanced out the window, quickly turning back again. His head tilted, pulling out from the stiff collar. His palms rested momentarily on the rigid cover of the governor's latest communiqué. He had read it once, soon after it arrived. Still, he opened the document and sucked in a breath as he methodically reread every sentence. Governor Burnquist was on a mission——that was clear.

Since the Minnesota Commission on Public Safety had formed in the spring of that year, the MCPS had directed a laser-like focus on any group considered to be disloyal. Labor advocates, political dissenters from the *Nonpartisan League,* and the *Industrial Workers of the World* were currently in the Commission's crosshairs. The governor's latest directive called for the cities' mayors to root out labor and political dissenters in their jurisdiction. It would be a time-consuming task in a city the size of Minneapolis.

Walter laced his fingers together and pressed them closed as he reflected on these challenging days of war. He had a history with the labor movement that began as a child when his father, a coal miner, was shut out by management after stalled negotiations. The family suffered further when local merchants refused to extend credit to the striking men. Those early days had fixed Walter's vision of what *should* be versus what *was* and set him on his current path to the city offices——a place where he hoped to effect change for the working man. But now? With the governor's directives and labor advocates in his crosshairs, Walter would need to be careful, maybe even delay work for the unions until after the war. For now, he needed to carefully divert all attention away from himself and his labor leanings. It was a known fact that he'd run for office on a socialist platform——which was why he needed to do the governor's work with dedication and fervor.

The mayor exhaled heavily as he stood and moved to the window, looking out over the city. He must focus on being productive and the best mayor in the state——the man who would carry out every nativist effort set before him. He would shine the light on the *real* enemies of the country——the true anti-Americans. Maybe then, when the war was over, he could get back to the business of supporting the labor unions.

Walter shut the brown cover and set the document aside before removing the small red and white circular pin from his suitcoat, sealing it in an envelope, and dropping it in the back of his desk drawer. He plucked the red, white, and blue flag pin from the small dish near his lamp and plugged it into the lapel. *That should do*, he thought as he walked swiftly to the door, opening it just enough to stick out his balding head.

"Ruth. Call a meeting of all my staff. Immediately." Walter shut the door, tersely strode to his credenza, and poured a glass of water from the pitcher. The water sloshed up the insides of the clear slim glass, but not a drop spilled as his long legs stretched the three strides to the table. He snatched the folded handkerchief from his breast pocket and laid it down before depositing his glass on it, never having taken a sip. Within minutes, his door opened, and his staff trooped in, Ruth, notebook in hand, following at the rear.

"Gentlemen," he said when the four sat down. "We must shut down the dangerous menace to our great country! We will find those disloyal to the great U.S. of A.!" Walter pounded his fist on the table with each letter spoken.

Chapter 10

The eastbound train pulled into the Milwaukee Road Depot in Minneapolis right on time. "It's good to be back," Jim said. "I love the travel, but sometimes I'm just ready for a bit of home." He chuckled. "Not that I have one these days." He rented a local boardinghouse room, but it wasn't really home. *Home* had been the feeling he had when he was with the Harvey family and he hadn't been there in over a month. He missed that——missed the dinners in their company.

"I hear you," Peter said. "Travel in November doesn't have the same appeal." He laughed. "I'm going to continue on to St. Paul, though. Anna wanted me to attend a concert with her." He shrugged. "She was so bent on joining the convent that she's not had any boyfriends, so the available brother is the stand-in companion." His brow lifted. "Hopefully, I'll have time to clean up."

Jim felt a pang of envy at Peter's large and solicitous family. "I can stop by and let your folks know you'll be held up a bit," he offered, knowing it wasn't necessary, but he'd been looking for an excuse to see Melania ever since the evening at the theater.

"Sure. They'd be glad to see you." Peter threw Jim's bag out the door after Jim jumped.

Within minutes, the train's wheels rolled in their slow forward advancement toward St. Paul. Jim logged himself and Peter in and headed out of the station toward Second Street, the road bustling this busy late November afternoon. He flipped the collar of his woolen work coat against the crisp air, pulling the flat cap over the tops of his ears. The wind blew at his back, pushing him toward Central Avenue and the Grand-Monroe line. He hesitated but then quickly hopped the streetcar before he changed his mind. He hadn't seen Melania since she'd run away from their date. Though Peter had asked him to join the family for dinner more than once since then, Jim had turned down the invitations. He didn't suppose Melania wanted to see him. And he doubted she would be there waiting for him today, but, then, what did he expect? He wasn't even sure what words had almost spilled out of his mouth. But he'd said, "us." *No wonder she ran off.*

Jim contemplated stepping off at the next stop, but that wouldn't be until the car crossed the Mississippi. Grayish stratus clouds converged on the city, forewarning snow.

"There's no time like the present," Jim said, lifting his cap and raking his hands through his hair. He got to his feet and pressed his hat back on, sucking in a deep breath. The plain fact was that he needed to know—know what, if anything, Melania was thinking about him. Maybe she would be there this evening and they'd have a chance to talk without Peter present.

An elderly woman across the aisle clutched her purse and glared at him. He touched the top of his cap and smiled at her before walking toward the car door. Perhaps his head would clear as he walked the few blocks to the Harveys' home and the words, the *right words* would flow from his mouth. He chuckled wryly to himself as he approached the house. *If only.*

Jacob Harvey answered the door before Jim's hand reached the knocker. "Come in, son. I was just looking out to see if the snow had begun when I saw you approaching."

"Peter?" Mrs. Harvey's voice carried from the kitchen.

"No, it's just me, Mrs. Harvey."

"Jim. Hello dear. It's so good to see you. Peter's not with you?" She wiped her hands on the checked cotton towel.

"That's why I stopped by. I told Peter I'd let you know he was going on to St. Paul to see Anna." Jim tried to focus, but his eyes darted around for any sign of Melania.

"She's not here," Mr. Harvey said.

"Who?" Jim rubbed the back of his neck.

Mrs. Harvey quickly hooked his arm. "Come into the kitchen, dear. Let me warm some dinner for you."

"That's not necessary."

"Nonsense. Sit." The older woman pushed his shoulders down onto a chair. "I'm sure you've not had a proper meal in weeks."

Jim smiled gratefully, took off his cap and coat, and perched them on the back of the chair.

Mrs. Harvey portioned Jim's food, and once warmed, she set the plate in front of him, sitting down to talk.

An hour later, stuffed full of delicious food and Mrs. Harvey's conversation, Jim stepped out the door. "Thank you for the delicious meal."

As the door clicked shut behind him, he stood on the front porch, looking out over the street. His errand had been a foolish one. Melania was gone. She lived on campus, Mrs. Harvey had told him, fully dedicating herself to school and the Red Cross. Was that Mrs. Harvey's way of softening the blow for Jim? To make him think Melania's decision had nothing to do with him? He snorted and headed out, nearly stomping down the sidewalk. Maybe it was true that he wasn't a consideration. Whatever her reason for leaving home, the truth was that his chances of running into Melania were now almost nil.

A discarded newspaper in a wastebin on the corner reminded Jim of the stark headlines from today's Tribune. The first American soldiers had been killed overseas.

Surely Melania understood that Jim would be drafted soon, and who knew what would befall him after that? Any time they had together would be short at best. Clearly, this didn't matter to her——her actions spoke plainly. Jim had tried for months to entice her to no avail and then thought the evening at the movies had changed her. She had moved closer, physically and emotionally. Or at least it had seemed that way to him——until she'd fled as if he were a threat to her.

Jim trudged down the avenue toward the streetcar, no longer interested in going back to the boardinghouse. He'd stop at Leo's Pub tonight before deciding where to spend the night and perhaps with whom. The flickering light from the watering hole's window beckoned him. Snow swirled, coming down in clumps on his hat and shoulders, immediately turning to water once Jim entered the smoky establishment on North 6th. Hot, sweaty patrons crowded in with the rings of gray smoke, and a thick cloud filled the space——just the kind of place a man could disappear.

"Wirth! Over here!"

Jim squinted to see who was calling, removed his coat, and made his way through the crowd toward a man he knew from the railroad.

"O'Malley," he greeted his acquaintance. "You look like you've been here a while." Jim slapped the man on the back, chuckling at O'Malley's drooping eyes and crooked grin.

"My old lady's mother is moving in with us tomorrow——trying to establish herself before I go to war. I can't stand the hag." O'Malley raised his glass, sloshing the beer over the top and down his hand. "To my last night of freedom. I won't be able to do nothin' right with that wretch around."

Jim had hoped to be alone——disappear in the crowd, but now the thought of being distracted by someone else's problems seemed an attractive alternative.

"Barkeep! Beer. Whisky chaser. And keep 'em coming."

A frosty mug was set down in front of him moments later, and Jim wrapped his hand around it, draining it entirely before setting it down.

"Damn, Wirth! What's eatin' you?"

"Women. Old or not. Damn them all." Jim cringed at the thought of Mrs. Harvey's kindness as the curse left his lips but threw back the whisky, nevertheless.

The bar cleared as the night hours threatened to break to dawn. O'Malley lay passed out on the floor, jammed between the barstools and the bar—for hours, patrons sat right over his spent form. Jim barely fared better, a corned beef sandwich the only object between him and the same fate. The dawn's light began to angle in the small front entry window when the door flung open.

"Brendan O'Malley, you lazy, good-for-nothin' excuse for a man. Get yourself home right now!" Full up and angry, a woman marched toward the prone man, kicking his leg. "You disgust me. Get your sorry self up. Now!"

"Here, ma'am. I can help." Jim stumbled toward his companion.

"You look about as worthless as my husband." The woman snorted and bent down, hooking her arm in her husband's, attempting to pull him free of the stools. Her efforts yielded little result as O'Malley flopped back down, flat on the floor.

Jim didn't ask this time but grabbed the drunk by the back of his shirt and lifted him upright in one swift move, both men swaying at the motion, leaning into each other as props.

O'Malley's eyes fluttered open briefly. "Nora." His lids dropped heavy again, and he wobbled.

Jim propped O'Malley against the bar, wedged between two stools. "Leo," he called. "Help me come to this nice lady's aid."

The barkeep rolled his eyes and put his hands on his hips. "I've had just about enough of you two buffoons. Get him out the door, and I'll bring the three-wheeler 'round."

Jim put his strong arms under O'Malley's and dragged him out the front, Nora holding the door for the two juiced rats. They met Leo as he turned the corner of his bar with a wheelbarrow. "Get on your way before the neighborhood wakes up."

Jim dropped O'Malley into the wooden cart, his hands and legs hanging over the sides, his head bobbing up and down as Jim began to push him toward his home. Eventually, Nora rolled up her sweater and stuck it under her husband's head.

"Please," she pleaded with Jim as they neared her house. "Bring him 'round back, so the neighbors don't notice."

Jim nodded obligingly.

"It's bad enough he's gone for weeks on end. I don't need them talking about how he's drunk when he *is* home."

Nora opened the back door to the kitchen, and Jim dragged O'Malley up the stoop, set the man on a bench, and then stepped out the door without a word. His head throbbed, and he squinted at the bright sun as he picked up the handles to the wheelbarrow, noticing Nora's yellow sweater balled in the bottom. He grabbed it and turned smack into Nora, who'd stepped out to retrieve it herself. The encounter nearly knocked the woman to the ground, but Jim sobered at the realization and quickly steadied her, holding her arms until she was stable.

"Get your filthy hands off my wife, kraut."

Nora pulled back, rushing to her husband. "It wasn't like that," she explained, then smacked him in the arm. "Do you have any idea what he just did for you?"

"Yeah, I do. He made a pass at my wife."

"O'Malley. Come on," Jim said. "You know that wasn't happening."

"All I know is that you are a sorry excuse for a man and an American. I know what you Germans do. You change your name some so you can hide the truth. Get off my property, *Virth,* you Hun!"

Nora stormed into the house, and O'Malley held himself steady in the doorway, waving a fist at Jim.

Jim hung his head and turned toward the alley, walking away from the accusations. The door slammed, and Jim felt instantly sober. The shot from his friend——no, unmistakably *not* his friend——propelled him to a state of mental clarity. The country was at war, and *he* was considered the enemy. He had seen the posters plastered on the buildings warning citizens to watch for the enemy, the disloyal, the suspicious. Never once had he considered himself in any of those categories. His family had been here for generations. His mother had been Irish, not German. He and his brother had been raised by their Irish grandparents on Reilly farm. He had no connections with his German roots. Even though O'Malley called him out for his family *Americanizing* their name by changing the German V sound for the W in Wirth, Jim was an American, a proud and loyal one. Surely, Brendan O'Malley would come to his senses once he sobered.

The sun made its way above the five-story brownstone as Jim entered the boardinghouse door. His steps were as heavy as his heart when he turned his key in the lock of his room, realizing that he'd left his duffel on the Harveys' porch. He had nothing. He had no one. He pulled the shade, dropped onto the bed, and slept.

A sharp knock woke Jim from his slumber, and he opened an eye to see a sliver of light through the bottom of the shade. This time, the knock came louder, and his landlady's voice called, "Mr. Wirth? Are you in there? You owe me for two days."

Two days? Jim struggled to recall the preceding events, whatever day it was, but suddenly torrents of tortured thoughts rushed at him. "One minute, Mrs. Haggerty."

Jim's throat was dry and thick, and he took a swig out of the jug of stale water on his bedside commode before reaching into his front pocket for money. He moved to the door and opened it to his landlady, who stood squarely with her hands on her hips. "You know the rules. You pay by the day."

Jim thrust her a bill. "I came in so late. I thought I would be able to pay you today."

"You owe me for one more day. I knocked yesterday, and you didn't answer. I thought maybe you skipped out on me."

"My apologies, Mrs. Haggerty. I must have slept right through yesterday." Jim reached into his shirt pocket and smoothed out another bill before handing it to the woman. "I didn't mean to cause you any trouble." He swayed a bit as he said this, his stomach audibly grumbling. "I guess I missed dinner yesterday too." He chuckled ruefully.

"If you're going to stay tonight, I'd prefer you pay me right now," Mrs. Haggerty said sternly.

Thankfully, each pocket Jim tapped held currency, a miracle considering he'd spent hours at the bar. He shut the door and sat on the edge of his bed, dropping his head to his hands. *Well, this is a fine mess I've found myself in.* He counted the days back, grateful to realize he had not missed any work——his days off enough to cover this foolish venture. He washed up, about to head out for work, when Mrs. Haggerty called up the steps.

"I forgot to mention that someone dropped off your haversack yesterday."

Jim's head hung in shame. The Harveys were good and kind to him, and he'd lain dead to the world after a night of mayhem when they'd dropped off his forgotten possessions. No wonder their daughter rejected him.

Jim pounded down the steps and out the boardinghouse door. Maybe the railroad had a run that would send him miles away, perhaps permanently. He needed distance from everyone and everything.

Jim slogged through the mushy streets; the snow mostly melted, leaving mud in its wake. The sky was thick with low gray clouds, matching his mood. His eyes were fully opened this morning, not from two days' sleep, but from a keen awareness of the state of things——matters with Melania and events in the world. He skipped the trolley ride this morning, longing for time to clear the cobwebs from his mind. As he walked the block toward the corner of Hamburg Avenue, he stopped in his tracks. "Where is Hamburg Avenue?" he wondered out loud. The street sign read: Pershing Avenue. *Pershing?* Where had he heard that name? "That's right." Jim remembered reading about the General. *Didn't they call him Black Jack?* Jim rubbed his chin thoughtfully. *A bit hasty, isn't it? The war isn't even over.*

Another change came into full view farther down the street. The small German-owned market near the station had changed its name from Schmidt & Muller Grocery to *Smith & Miller Grocers*. Their window signs advertised *liberty cabbage* instead of sauerkraut and ground beef to make *liberty burgers* instead of hamburgers. *My God.* Jim was physically taken aback. "What is going on?" he whispered.

Chapter 11

The University of Minnesota, like Hamline College, launched an Army Training Corps for its male students, and the Red Cross chapter filled the extracurricular time for many females. The campus was a flurry of activity, with the military drills and Red Cross training adding another layer on top of the classroom and study time. War needs pushed the action to a frenzied state leading up to the Thanksgiving break.

Melania jumped when the bugle sounded, nearly dropping the Red Cross kit she'd been working on. "Lands! Whose idea was it to replace the class bell with the bugle?" She glanced at Jane, who studied a pamphlet on dietetics.

Jane laughed, shaking her head. "Gee. I didn't even hear it." She closed the multi-page guide and slid it over to Melania. "I don't think I'll ever remember all this stuff on good nutrition. How am I ever going to teach it?"

Melania smiled and nodded. "At first, I was a bit put out that we were merely rolling bandages and making surgical dressings while my sister Anna is headed overseas to *relieve human suffering.*" Melania snorted. "Of course I understand the importance of that mission but Anna never fails to remind me how much more important her Red Cross work is than mine. She can be so annoying."

Jane laughed. "I think all sisters annoy occasionally. And anyway, our bandages are important too. One of them could stop a soldier from bleeding to death! And think of all the men wearing one of the sweaters or socks we've knitted. Though heaven help whoever gets mine with their uneven stitches."

Melania smiled. "I know you're right. But I'm still glad we've been allowed to do more with the community training. Maybe the first aid and hygiene and home dietetics we share with the town will qualify as *relieving human suffering* too."

Jane reached for a pad of paper. "I've known a boy or two who could benefit from a lesson in cleanliness. That would spare many from suffering." She giggled and began scribbling on the paper. "On another matter completely, I need to find you a dance partner before leaving for the holiday break. Jasper says he has someone in mind, but I'm making a list if that plan goes south."

"For goodness' sake." Melania glanced at Jane's paper. "Is that what you're writing? Names of potential dates?" She pulled the piece from her friend. "I don't need a date. Plus, I need to focus if we're to beat the St. Paul chapter's fund drive numbers."

"Pshaw. Don't tell me the weight of the whole event is on *your* shoulders, Miss Harvey. If I didn't know any better, I'd think you were holding all other men at bay, waiting for your brother's friend to ask you out again."

"Ha!" Melania turned and felt a flush go up to her neck.

"You're turning crimson!"

"Some friend you are, Jane Vogel." She pressed her lips into a thin line and glared at her friend.

"These are our future soldiers. They *deserve* a good time." Jane's brow arched.

"Fine, I'll go with the fellow Jasper found for me." Melania moved to the door of the Red Cross room and stopped with her hand on the doorknob. "I'll see you after Thanksgiving. I want to check on one last detail for the fundraiser before heading home."

"Don't you want to meet the fellas? J thought we could meet up for drinks." Jane frowned and dropped her chin in feigned sadness.

"No thanks." Melania came back in and hugged Jane. "I do appreciate your effort, however. Next semester, you should consider the drama club." She chuckled as she headed out.

Melania grabbed her travel bag and coat from their dormitory and headed to the university commons where the dance preparation was underway. The dance-off was Jane's novel idea of beating the St. Paul chapter in their fundraising efforts. It was all in fun——the money raised would go to the valiant causes supported by the Red Cross. Melania reached for a dangling streamer and twirled it back around the post, then tilted her head to consider the banner posted across the entire top of the long window. "Crooked," she said to the room. Something to remember later.

She moved past the festooned space to the closet in the back——a locked and secure place to keep fundraising supplies and pledges. Melania served on the committee managing the fundraising details——*how* the money would be pledged, *who* would judge the competitors, and *how* the currency would be collected and distributed. Ensuring the particulars were in order would allow her to enjoy her holiday away. She pulled open the top drawer of the tall wooden filing cabinet and grabbed the thick brown packet, laying it on the desk, then sat and shuffled the papers, scanning the documents. A page slipped out from the bottom of the pile and floated to the ground. She picked it up, pausing to look at the Red Cross advertisement——different from those she'd seen posted around campus. She touched the note pinned to the top of the poster.

> **Note to staff**: We need to be careful not to recruit alien members unwittingly. Ask questions. What language are the volunteers speaking? Do they have a German surname? Watch and listen. Be aware.

A sickening feeling bubbled up from the pit of Melania's stomach, and she flipped up the note to view the poster in full. A beautiful woman draped in an American flag had the word JOIN and the Red Cross next to her. The bottom third of the poster warned:

Do not be suspected! Use American Language! America is our home!

Bile rose in her throat, and she dropped the document. It floated to the table's edge, tipped, and fell to the floor, an edge gliding under the cabinet. Were they talking about her? After all, her parents had immigrated from Germany, as had her older siblings. A thick accent sharply marked her parents' speech. She'd thought her father's request absurd when he'd insisted they be careful about using any German words outside their home. *Why the alarm*? Many people of German descent referred to their parents as Mutti and Vati. *And what did it matter*? Her entire family spoke English, and they were all American citizens. Thoughts whirled in her head with no sense. She shoved the papers back into the brown folder, secured it, and thrust it into the cabinet, slamming the door with a push.

Her eyes dropped to the floor——her loafer rested on the edge of the fallen poster. She pushed it entirely under the cabinet with the tip of her shoe and then turned, hurrying out of the building toward the streetcar stop.

The wind whipped around her ankles when she stood at the corner, and then moved up her body, nearly suspending her there. She closed her eyes and let her body sway in the wind channel and the impression of support it gave. She didn't even hear the trolley pull up.

"Miss? Are you getting on?" A young boy poked her back.

"Oh, yes, of course," Melania stammered. "Please, you first." She motioned to the boy, and he scrambled up the trolley steps, racing to the back seat. She followed and dropped into the first seat, leaning into the bar in front of her.

"Miss?"

What now? She raised her head.

"Are you unwell?" The driver's eyes assessed her.

"No. Sorry."

She wished she could just disappear. Did people know she was German just by looking at her? Did her speech belie an accent absorbed at the feet of her mother?

The streetcar ride, though less than an hour, seemed interminable as Melania peered out the window, noticing posters and signs as if they'd just been placed.

Defeat the Huns • Buy Liberty Bonds

She'd seen the fierce brute on these posters before but only now recognized he looked more like a man than a monster, a man of German descent——common in Minnesota. The propagandists were putting a face to the enemy, and that face was familiar.

Finally, she averted her gaze from outside the car, hoping to spare herself the sight of any more hoopla. The gentleman in the seat behind her shook his newspaper out with a loud snap. Melania turned around at the noise, catching the headline on the front page. She leaned in, squinting to read the small print.

NEW ULM MAYOR DEPOSED BY GOVERNOR BURNQUIST. NEW ULM MAYOR, DR. LOUIS FRITSCHE, HAD BEEN REMOVED FROM OFFICE IN MAY AFTER BEING CHARGED WITH SEDITION. CURRENTLY, A PANEL IS REVIEWING THE CASE TO DETERMINE IF THE EX-MAYOR'S MEDICAL CERTIFICATION SHOULD ALSO BE REVOKED.

Burnquist has interviewed Fritsche and conferred with the revocation board members, two of whom have competing medical practices nearby. The German doctor best beware.

Melania stepped onto the curb a quarter of an hour later, her hands shaking as she wrapped her coat tighter around her middle. The door slammed shut, and the car roared down the tracks to its next stop. She stood for a moment, feeling her body swaying, and steadied herself on the lamppost, pressing her eyes closed, hoping to gather her thoughts. *Mutti and Vati must not see tears*. Otherwise, they may discourage her return to school after break. She inhaled slowly, holding her breath deep within her chest, pushing her thoughts and fears down inside. She let go of the post and started down the block toward home, her feet crunching on the piles of dry leaves that littered the walk. Tree branches crackled and snapped together as the sharp winds moved swiftly through. Melania tightened her scarf and plunged her hands into her coat pockets after looping her satchel on her arm.

In the waning hours of daylight, she peered inside the lighted homes on her block. Families sat for dinner. Mothers moved about the houses in preparation, she supposed, for Thanksgiving. Other homes held solitary figures enjoying, perhaps, some time by the fire. *One would think all was well*. She sighed heavily. *Perceptions aren't always reality*. Suddenly a disturbing thought entered her mind. What if the neighbors watched *her* through their windows, making judgments about her comportment? Did she appear to be skulking around with ill-intent?

Melania hurried down the street and soon alighted the steps to her home, a pleasing orange glow casting off the parlor light. Swirls of smoke wisped from the chimney, sending the heady woodfire smell floating down.

Oh, it was good to be home.

Jim avoided O'Malley at the rail yard as best as he could, but he was stuck working on stalled locomotives in the freight yard. He'd much rather do the work of a freight handler, but he realized soon after he began his employment with the railroad every hand was necessary to avoid the government stepping in and taking over. The war effort significantly increased demand for rail service, and railroads struggled to keep up; consequently, Jim's mechanical adeptness, learned from years of farming, was suddenly more useful to the company than was his willingness to travel. His prospects of getting away seemed bleak.

Jim pulled his red handkerchief from his pocket, drawing it across his sweat-drenched brow. Despite the biting north wind, the work was grueling. The noon whistle blew across the yard just as he was about to turn back to his labor. Instead, he wiped his hands on his coveralls, grabbed his lunch pail, and walked, head down, toward an empty rail car on the far side of the property, hoping to eat without the grating war banter of the other men. It was easy for them, particularly for those without German surnames, to talk about the Huns. Ever since O'Malley had called him a *Hun*, Jim felt watched. He wasn't always sure if it was real or imagined, but the posters around the yard were genuine.

As Jim passed by a group of men gathering for a dinner break, O'Malley suddenly emerged from the middle of the crowd. He grabbed Jim and spun him around, pinning Jim's arm up and behind his back. O'Malley held Jim's wrist with one hand and poked his finger into the middle of Jim's chest with the other. "See, fellas? This here Hun is just like the one on the poster." A few men turned to view the sign to which O'Malley pointed.

"Wirth *says* he's American, but he toasts the Kaiser with German stout in private!"

O'Malley guffawed, and Jim yanked his arm away, shoving him back. "Shut your maw, O'Malley!" Jim turned to walk away.

The Irish man nearly fell off his feet but quickly recovered. "The guilty don't defend themselves, *Vvvirth,*" he jeered. "They just fight——vicious, like all German scum." He spat, and a scrap of the men joined in cursing and taunting Jim.

One man reached out as he passed Jim. "Ignore him, Wirth. O'Malley's a goon."

Jim tried to shake it off, but the accusations stung. He'd had his share of indictments over the years, but they'd generally been warranted—— brawls and bar fights, dancing with some other fella's girl, and the like. But never anything like this. *Hun.* Jim shuddered and made his way to the far side of the yard, leaning against the large boxcar wheel that nearly covered his entire frame, providing the solace he craved.

He released his grip on the lunch pail and then slowly unclenched his other fist, flipping the lid to examine the contents. He slammed the lid shut and tossed the pail aside, the bad taste in his mouth lingering. He slid down to a crouching position and closed his eyes, his breath evening as he considered his next move. *What can I do? I need this job.* He opened his eyes as the *chug, chug, chugging* sound drifted across the yard——a locomotive beginning its slow descent down the tracks, the line of hundreds of wheels rotating slowly, gradually picking up speed. The whistle sounded loud and piercing, floating above the work area, intermingling with the gray billowing smoke coming from its stack.

I'll have to keep out of sight, especially from that damn fool, O'Malley. Jim stretched his arms above his head and then pushed himself to his feet and grabbed his lunch pail, shoving bread and cheese in his mouth as he returned to work. *At least there's a day off tomorrow,* he thought, before realizing that he'd spend Thanksgiving alone.

The day stretched into the early evening when the ending bell finally sounded across the train yard. Jim managed to stay far away from most men while working on his locomotive's engine, making progress but still left with a week or more on this task. He hung back as the yard cleared, wiping his greasy hands on his handkerchief before shoving it in his pocket. He stepped inside as the last group of men left the station.

"Wirth!" A shout came from the office. "Come here. Now!"

Now what? Jim briefly pressed his eyes closed and then slowly walked the paces to the stationmaster's office, trying to gain some composure before he entered. He stood in the doorway, one hand on the frame.

"Yes, Mr. Hanson?" Jim asked in strained politeness.

Hanson looked up from his papers. "I hear you were involved in a scuffle today. I won't have any of that rubbish in my yard."

"I can explain," Jim started.

"Not *any* of that nonsense, or you're outta here." Hanson leaned forward and stuck out his chest, pointing to the large gold badge on his right lapel. "I'm a member of the American Protective League. Do you know what that is, Wirth?" Hanson didn't wait for an answer. "I've pledged to watch for and report disloyal Americans, especially German-Americans." The boss squinted, giving Jim a piercing glare.

"I never——" Jim attempted again to interject, but Hanson cut him off.

"Outta here, now. Just know that I have my eyes on you." Hanson crooked a finger and waved him out the door.

Jim shut the door behind him and threw his hands in the air, shaking his head. It seemed hopeless.

He looked around the station lobby, empty of workers now and with only a smattering of travelers fortunate enough to get a ticket on the limited passenger trains. With the demands for war supplies, the trains were used more for moving goods than moving people. Jim took a long, deep breath and let it out slowly as he walked toward the door, spying an elderly woman coming toward him. *Could it be?* For a moment, he thought it was Mrs. Harvey. Oh, how he longed to be in the bosom of their family. As the woman got closer, he realized she was a stranger, but she smiled as she passed, momentarily lifting his melancholy.

Jim arrived at Mrs. Haggerty's boardinghouse just as dinner was served. "Can you wait until I wash up, Mrs. Haggerty?" he asked.

As if she sensed the distress in his demeanor, she offered something out of character. "How 'bout if I put a plate together for you and set it outside your door?"

Jim nodded gratefully. "Yes. Please." He trudged upstairs, grabbed clean clothes, and headed to the washroom. He still felt dirty at the end, despite scrubbing grime from his face, neck, and hands. He met Mrs. Haggerty at his door.

"Here." She handed Jim the tray. "I'm making turkey with all the fixings tomorrow. Will you be here?"

"Yes. Thank you." Jim closed the door and set the plate on the small table, lying on his bed before touching the food. Sleep lulled him into its depths, and he didn't stir until dawn broke through his window.

Chapter 12

Melania nudged her mother toward the kitchen door. "Come, Mutti. Sit in the front room for a while." Despite the war rations, Helene and Emily had managed to create a feast. Peter had brought their older brother August from Holmesburg, along with vegetables and a turkey from the farm. A mince and an apple pie sat cooling on the counter while the turkey finished roasting.

"The rolls need to——" her mother started.

"Anna can help me." Melania led her mother to her rocker and pushed her shoulders down. "We've got this, Mutti. Besides, Emily will be back to help us after she puts Lizzie down for a nap."

"Oh, all right." Mutti leaned back and put her feet on the ottoman, settling in and smiling as she watched the lively banter between Vati and Peter.

"Anna?" Melania motioned. "Can you help me in the kitchen?"

Anna rose and followed her.

Melania moved to the far side of the kitchen and turned, leaning against the cupboard, her face becoming serious.

"Goodness, Mel. What is it? Afraid to take the turkey out?" Anna chuckled and moved toward the oven.

"No. Of course not. I just wanted to tell you something."

"Hmm. Sounds serious. Boy troubles?" Anna laughed. It was an unspoken joke between them since Anna had, until recently, intended to enter the convent. It was the one subject on which she conceded her younger sister knew more.

Melania exhaled sharply. "If it were only that minor."

"Gee. What is it?" Anna's brow furrowed.

"It was something I saw at the Red Cross." Melania's mouth pressed into a line. "It was so wrong. So horrible. I just can't believe it, and I don't know what to do."

Anna pulled her to the table. "Sit. Get yourself together and tell me what's wrong."

Melania hesitated, suddenly wondering the wisdom of telling Anna, who usually condescended to her more than helped. But Anna *did* train at the Red Cross. Her insight may be just what Melania needed.

Melania filled her sister in on the anti-German edict of the flyer she'd found and how absurd she thought it was that anyone would believe a German heritage would make someone anti-American. It mortified her. It angered her.

"Look," Anna replied, shrugging. "The world is changing. You just need to grow up."

"I know that! I'm not a child!" Melania rose and marched to the door.

"Wait! I didn't mean to upset you. It's difficult not to think of you as a young schoolgirl. Come on. Let's talk this through." Anna crossed her arms with an impatience that infuriated Melania, but she *needed* to tell someone.

Melania crossed her arms too and planted her feet as if she were taking a stand. She willed her voice to calm, using every bit of effort to tell a fact-based account, leaving out emotions. "I kicked the flyer under the cabinet and hoped it wouldn't resurface," she finished with a slight lift of her shoulder.

"That may stop it for now," Anna said. "But the Red Cross will surely just print a new one. It's war. Someone must always be at fault. It's the way things work."

"That's awfully cynical," Melania countered. "And not very helpful. Why would *you* want to work for an organization that hates you?" Her mouth pinched and she moved to the small oven, taking out the rolls and then opening the door to the larger oven, keeping her back to her sister the entire time. Melania basted the turkey, not even sure if she should, but determined to make Anna think she knew just what she was doing. Cooking was another area where she had a leg up on her sister since Anna had planned to enter the convent. Melania always wondered who Anna thought did the cooking and the cleaning at the convent. She doubted the nuns prayed *all* day.

She heard Anna take a deep breath as if she were waiting to respond, but Melania continued to ignore her, focusing on dinner preparations. She should have listened to her gut instinct. Anna was no help at all.

Jacob dropped down into the upholstered chair in the front room, putting his feet on the small stool and resting his hands on his full belly while surveying the bustle around him. Clattering and clanging sounded from the kitchen as the women worked to clean up from the grand meal. August sat on the floor next to baby Elizabeth, and Peter poked at the fire, throwing on another log. The fire sparked into fullness, sending shards of light into the darkening room. The house was warm and comforting, overflowing with those Jacob loved——a balm to his weary soul. It was the first Thanksgiving they'd spent without Frank's family, but he knew the demands of farming. And with his and Helene's job at the mill, traveling to and from Holmesburg didn't seem practical. Jacob was grateful for those who were here, reminded too of Mathias's absence. By now, Mathias would be at Fort Hamilton in New York City, Jacob guessed, soon to depart for Europe.

Jacob picked up the newspaper and scanned the headlines. What had been a pleasure was now an activity filled with trepidation. With the country's involvement in the war heating up, along with the activities of the nativist groups, the news was unsettling at best. A short article about the Red Cross in the *National News* section caught his eye.

"Helene, girls, come here," Jacob called when it seemed the work in the kitchen was at its end. Emily picked up her daughter to get her settled upstairs for bed, but the Harvey family gathered around Jacob's chair.

He folded the newspaper and handed it to Anna. "I thought you girls would find this interesting. Can you read it to us?" The room fell silent as Anna read.

LAST WEEK, IN AVOCA, PENNSYLVANIA, AUSTRIAN-AMERICAN LUKAS GRUBER WAS ACCUSED OF CRITICIZING THE RED CROSS. LUKAS'S DAUGHTER, EMMA GRUBER, TRAINS WITH THE RED CROSS TO SERVE OUR TROOPS OVERSEAS. GRUBER DECRIED THE CHARGE, CLAIMING HIS COMPLAINT WAS ABOUT LOSING HIS DAUGHTER'S HELP ON THE FAMILY FARM. THE PENNSYLVANIA COMMISSION ON PUBLIC SAFETY SAW IT DIFFERENTLY. COMMISSIONER ROBINSON PUT IT THIS WAY: "THE TEST OF LOYALTY IN WAR TIMES IS WHETHER A MAN IS WHOLEHEARTEDLY FOR THE WAR AND SUBORDINATES EVERYTHING ELSE TO ITS SUCCESSFUL PROSECUTION. LUKAS GRUBER PUTS HIS FARM'S NEEDS BEFORE HIS COUNTRY." SOME OF THE PENNSYLVANIA PUBLIC SAFETY COMMISSION SYMPATHIZED WITH GRUBER AND WARNED HIM TO "WATCH HIS LOYALTY." ON THE OTHER HAND, COMMISSIONER ROBINSON TURNED A BLIND EYE WHEN A GROUP OF CITIZENS LATER TIED GRUBER AND

HOISTED HIM THIRTY FEET IN THE AIR, BLASTING HIM WITH WATER FROM A FIRE HOSE FOR A FULL HOUR. THE ANSWERS ARE UNCLEAR ABOUT GRUBER'S FATE, BUT THE LARGER QUESTION IS HOW A GERMAN SUCH AS EMMA GRUBER CAN BE TRUSTED TO SERVE OUR BOYS.

Anna's voice fell off as she read the last sentence, and Melania's eyes filled with tears. "I told you, Anna," she whispered.

"What?" Peter's eyes darted between his sisters. "What's going on?"

"I saw a poster at my Red Cross chapter right before leaving Wednesday. It sickened me." Melania turned away briefly, wiped her eyes, and cleared her throat before filling her family in.

"Anna? Anything troubling in your training?" Jacob asked.

Anna shrugged and leaned back on the sofa, shaking her head slightly. "Nothing like that in my program."

Jacob turned to Peter. "What have you seen in your travels?"

Peter stood and moved to the hearth, putting his hand on the mantle and poking at the fire. "The posters and the name changes——it's happening everywhere." He turned around and shook his head. "Every time the train pulls into a community, there's several anti-German statements or a demonstration." He scoffed. "Our maps are so marked up they're hardly readable anymore. German-named cities have been crossed out and replaced——Germantown, Nebraska, is now Garland; New Germantown, Indiana, is now Pershing; and Berlin, Iowa, has been changed to Lincoln." Peter shrugged. "I figured it was mostly for show. Maybe not." His voice trailed off, a look of unease on his face.

"What about at the train yard?" Jacob glanced around the room and noticed that everyone, save August, was leaning forward in rapt attention. It was as he'd hoped in the beginning——that the Harvey family would weather the storm of war together, regardless of their physical location. He silently prayed for Mathias, the one family member who truly was alone.

"You know," Peter answered, "the bits going up everywhere——*Watch out for the Huns* posters and the like."

"What about Jim?" Helene frowned. "I'm surprised you didn't invite him to Thanksgiving dinner."

"Oh yeah, Wirth." Peter's eyebrows raised. "He's been out of sorts lately. I've barely seen him since a little scuffle he got into recently."

Melania's head snapped toward Peter. "Scuffle?"

"Some guy named O'Malley seems to have it in for Jim. The guy's stirring all kinds of trouble, accusing Jim of being anti-American. Who knows where *that* started?"

"That's nonsense!" Helene interjected with uncharacteristic fire, and Jacob nearly smiled at her fervor.

"I agree, Mutti, but you know how fellas are," Peter said with a shrug. "Someone does something to set the other off, and the whole thing blows up." Peter's mouth twisted, and his brow raised. "Oh yeah——and I heard some fellas mention that Stationmaster Hanson is hot on Wirth now."

"What does that mean?" Anna asked.

"Apparently, Hanson is all puffed up about being part of some citizen spy group. Wearing a badge and everything." Peter chuckled, shaking his head.

Jacob sat upright, his back straight. "This is no laughing matter. These nativist groups are serious." He narrowed his eyes at his youngest son. "Remember our discussion from earlier in the summer, Peter? The momentum is swelling."

All eyes shifted to Jacob.

Peter nodded. "You were right, Vati. I didn't doubt you then, yet it was difficult to imagine."

"What? What did you discuss in the summer?" Melania crossed her arms. "We all need to know."

Jacob's eyes scanned the room again. Even August's interest was kindled. "Do you recall when the rock was thrown through the front window in Holmesburg?"

Peter grabbed his brother's travel bag the Sunday after Thanksgiving and patted him on the back. "Are you ready to go, Gus? The train leaves within the hour."

"Ja," August replied as Mutti tucked a letter into his coat pocket.

"Don't forget to give this to Frank. It is very important."

August nodded. "Sure. I won't forget, Mutti." He smiled a big toothy grin, and she wrapped her arms around his broad frame.

"Are you certain you can make it back to Holmesburg yourself?" Mutti looked past Gus to Peter.

"He'll be fine, Mutti," Peter assured her. "Gus watched out the window the whole way here. I'll make sure he sits on the opposite side of the car on the return trip so he can see the same landmarks." Peter patted his older brother's back. "Besides, his ticket tells the conductor where to let him off. Frank promised to meet August when he arrives in Holmesburg."

Peter kissed his mother's cheek and open the back door, then stopped and turned back. "Would you rather I bring the letter to the post office?"

Mutti sighed. "No. Better not." She lifted a brow. "It's nothing serious. Just Vati giving Frank an update of what's going on in the city and beyond."

"But you never know how that may be misinterpreted if the letter gets read by someone other than family." Peter hated that his parents, especially his mother, had to worry about these matters. A family update. What was the danger in that?

Mutti nodded and shrugged. "Unsettling times."

Peter smiled, hoping to change the mood before he left. "It was a wonderful time together, even though not everyone was there."

"I can't actually remember many times when that was the case, and now Anna is heading off to Europe, and Mathias should be nearly there." Mutti's forehead creased, and Peter regretted reminding her of their distant family.

He'd utterly failed at changing the tone. "You're right, Mutti. Unsettling times." What was the point in pretending it was any different?

August stopped on the train steps and smiled at his brother.

"You good?" Peter asked.

"Ja, Ja," August said. "I'm a strong man." He laughed and pounded his chest.

Peter rolled his eyes. "Agreed, Gus. Don't forget to show the conductor your ticket."

August playfully pushed Peter back off the step. "Geh weg," he said with a twinkle in his eyes. *Go away.*

August made his way to a seat, stowing his small bag underneath and promptly opening the bundle of food his mother had sent, placing it on the empty seat next to him, nibbling on chocolate cake and biscuits as the train began to build its momentum. The swaying car and his full belly quickly dulled his senses, so he leaned back and shut his eyes.

He wasn't sure how much time had passed when he was jarred from slumber by two hands on his shirt, dragging him to the aisle. "Get outta here, you Hun!"

"Huh?" Sleep clouded his mind.

Gus attempted to remove the hands from his shirt when a foot met his backside and kicked him to the ground. Suddenly, boots were kicking his sides, his legs, his back. He covered his head with one hand while attempting to push himself up. "What?" he managed. "Whatcha want?" Angry faces glared at him. Fingers pointed.

"Only a dirty German Hun would eat chocolate cherry cake. Isn't that the national cake of you savages?" One of the men shoved the cake in August's face as the beating intensified.

"I. Not. Know. What. You're. Sayin'." August stuttered between blows. "Mein Kuchen? You vant mein Kuchen?" August was confused.

A man reached across his prone form and grabbed August's satchel. "I suppose you have other enemy food in there. Kraut, maybe? Schnitzel?" The men laughed uproariously.

What was happening? Why would they care about his food? "Meine Mutter packed this lunch for me," he sputtered, trying again to get up.

"Oh, your mother. I suppose she's a German Hexe," one brute snickered.

That was the spark that set August off. No one talked bad about Mutti. No one called her a witch. It didn't matter that he was outnumbered. He pushed himself up in one swift movement and started swinging. Punches first landed on the two men closest, and as they fell, he blasted the other. Just as two of the three men flopped in a heap on the floor, the car's doors burst open, and a railroad man rushed in.

"What's the meaning of this?" The red-faced man scowled at August.

"I dunno, sir," August offered. "Ich habe geschlafen. I vas sleeping——und——"

August's explanation was interrupted by one of his attackers. "This German Hun went after us for no reason. We was just mindin' our own business, and suddenly he starts attackin' us."

The guard looked around at the passengers pressed far into their seats. "Who can tell me what happened?" No one said a word, and several turned away. Blood from August's fists streamed down his forearm.

The railroad worker threw his arms in the air, and when the whistle sounded to announce the next stop, he swept his arms toward the door. "All of you. Out now!"

"But I don't get off here," August protested. "Mein Bruder. He's vaiting——"

"I don't care. Off. Now!" The train official pushed the attackers out but allowed August to gather his parcel and coat before leaving.

August stood on the platform, stunned and without a clue what to do next. The train's great wheels slowly began turning, continuing down the tracks, leaving him alone on the small platform.

Within minutes of the train's departure, the goons emerged from behind the station. "Now you're going to pay, Hun."

Chapter 13

P eter was surprised to see Jim's lanky frame amble into the Milwaukee Road station ahead of him. He doubted they'd be traveling together since Hanson had remarked that he'd be making the trip alone. Maybe plans had changed. He skipped to catch up to Jim and felt his pal startle when he touched his shoulder. "Geez, Jim. Didn't mean to scare you." He slung an arm over Jim's shoulder.

"Keep it down, Harvey." Jim shrugged Peter off and glanced around.

"What's with you?" Peter grinned. "The day is young, and you're already gloomy."

"Leave it to you to be cheery during a war," Jim muttered, shaking his head and moving ahead of Peter.

"Well, seize the day, pal. We're still free, aren't we?" Peter laughed.

"Save it." Jim frowned and kept walking.

Peter caught up again and hooked his arm around Jim's neck, pulling him in good-naturedly. "Lighten up."

"Seriously, Pete, back off." Jim twisted from his grasp and walked ahead. Peter skipped to catch up once more. "Is this about the business with O'Malley?"

"Yeah. Maybe. And other things. Just leave me be." Jim continued walking toward the railyard, quickening his step and outpacing Peter with his long strides.

Peter shrugged and turned to the station to find out where the railroad was sending him next. Maybe he could convince Hanson to let Jim join him after all. Seemed as if the distance would do his friend some good, and it wasn't as if the stalled engines wouldn't still be there when Jim returned. Peter glanced at the station log, confirming he was on the next flour shipment to Ohio.

He heard Hanson call to him. Maybe plans *were* changing. "Harvey! Get in here."

"Yes, Mr. Hanson?" Peter politely ignored the stationmaster's tone, keenly aware of Hanson's new badge.

Hanson had the telephone to his ear and a hand covered over the mouthpiece. "This here caller's looking for you. Some sort of mix-up. With your brother, I think?"

"What? My brother? I don't understand."

"Well, I ain't got all mornin' to be your operator." Hanson thrust the phone at Peter and headed out of his office. "I'll be back in a minute, so make it quick. My office isn't for conducting personal business."

Peter crooked his head and hesitated before putting the receiver up to his ear. They didn't have a telephone in Holmesburg nor at Mrs. Pritchard's. Sure, he'd used one before, but not often. "Yes?" he said into the mouthpiece, hoping he was doing it correctly.

"Pete! It's me, Frank. Where's Gus?"

"Whaddaya mean, where's Gus? Isn't he with you?"

"He never got off the train yesterday." Frank's voice was pitched and frenzied. "Did you put him on it?"

"Of course I did. Just as planned." Peter's palms began sweating, and he put a hand to his forehead. "Geez, Frank. I don't know where he is. Maybe he got off too soon. Damn him! I told him to show the ticket to the conductor."

"We gotta find him, Pete. Who *knows* where he is."

"Where are you calling from?"

"I'm at Meyer's Hardware. They let me use their phone. I gotta get off it. Tying up the line."

"Stay put a second, will you? At least at Meyer's. I need to talk to the stationmaster and get back to you. Soon. Don't go anywhere." Panic rose in his chest. *Where was August? That fool!*

Mr. Hanson returned to his office moments after Peter put the phone back. "Outta here, Harvey. You got a train to catch." Hanson made shooing motions.

"I've got a problem. My brother is missing."

"And how is that my concern?" Hanson crossed his arms and moved behind his desk.

"He's *simple*. Kind of slow in the head." Peter tapped his temple with one finger as he said it.

"So?" Hanson tapped his foot impatiently.

"I put him on the train back to Holmesburg on Sunday, and he never made it. That was my brother Frank on the telephone."

"Maybe he just stepped off to follow some pretty girl or got googly over the sight of a tavern." Hanson guffawed.

"No, sir. August's not like that. He's trusting——like a child, really. *Anything* could have happened to him."

"Well, I'll repeat it, Harvey. How is that my problem?" Hanson moved toward Peter, physically escorting him out the door.

"Please, sir. I need to go find him. Now. The weather——it's getting colder——he could be outside——anywhere. Please." Peter was cashing in all the favors he had. For a moment, a look of sympathy flashed in Hanson's eyes.

"Fine. Go. You have two days, and I'll expect you to work on the engine Wirth has been puttering with the last week when you return, as long as the repairs take."

"Thank you, sir. I won't forget your kindness." Peter turned toward the door, wondering how he'd ever fill in for Jim on the engine. Sure, he knew a thing or two about mechanics, but hardly as much as Jim did. He couldn't worry about that now. Right now, August was his priority.

Hanson called after Peter. "Tell Wirth on your way out to take over for you on the flour run to Ohio. Be quick about it. The train's about to pull out."

Jim looked up from his work as Peter came near, and he visibly tensed. Peter raised his hands and shook his head. "Jim! Quickly," he called in a serious tone. He couldn't risk Jim thinking he'd returned to razz him. "My brother August is missing." Peter panted as the words came out between breaths.

"What?" Jim stood and wiped his hands on his coveralls.

"He didn't arrive back in Holmesburg after I put him on the train yesterday. I need to find him. Now."

"All right," Jim said, brows furrowing.

Peter began tossing Jim's tools in the box and threw his travel bag in Jim's direction.

"Hanson wants you to take my trip to Ohio." He turned and pointed toward the long train that was beginning to pull out from the station. "Hurry. Go. I'll put these things away."

Jim grabbed the bag and darted off toward the moving train, leaving Peter at the broken locomotive. He stopped and glanced back at Peter, a look of near happiness on his face. Maybe Pete had been right that Jim needed some distance from this place. But that was a conversation for another day.

By the time Peter dropped Jim's things at the toolshed, Jim's train was no longer visible. Peter glanced toward the station but raced toward the departing express train, thinking the better of asking to use Hanson's telephone again. He boarded the train and sat on the edge of his seat, anxious for the express to hurry him to the Great Northern Depot.

August opened his eyes; the gritty blood stuck to his lids making the process painful. He squinted at the bright morning sun streaming sideways onto his face, sputtering out the grass and weeds that seemed fused to his dry lips. He propped himself up on one of his roughed-up hands and planted the other on the sloping ground, pushing himself to stand. He shielded his eyes from the brightness and scanned the horizon. *Where am I?* He didn't recognize either of the two small buildings on what seemed like the edge of the earth. No other living sign was nearby, save the mice running between his boots, in and out of their wintering holes.

August stepped up the steep bank and landed his last step on a train rail. Suddenly, the recent events——*of?* He couldn't exactly recall, but some of the particulars became clearer as the fog slowly lifted from his brain. He remembered being thrown off the train because——? *Hmm?* Could it truly have been because of his lunch? He scratched his head. That seemed ridiculous. He searched his mind for more details. Oh, his head throbbed——he reached up to find a sticky patch of blood covering an egg-sized bump. *The boots.* That memory surfaced. Then he remembered the hooligans surrounding him after they were all thrown off the train. A few punches——then the boots. That was all he could recall. *When was that?*

August stepped slowly across the thick iron rails to the other side of the tracks. Every inch of his body ached as if they had kicked him limb from limb. He tried to focus his mind on what he should do next. Far off in the distance, he saw a figure, a woman perhaps, walk out of the red brick square on the horizon toward a small cluster of scrawny trees. It looked like she was hanging clothes on the line. *Yes.* He nodded to himself, satisfied with the plan. He would go talk to her.

August brushed off his pants as best he could and glanced around for any of his belongings, finding only his coat. He groaned as he eased his arms in the sleeves and then trudged across the prairie toward the woman. He smiled and waved as he neared, hoping not to upset her, knowing his largeness frightened people, especially ladies and children. Ida always reminded him that his smile was his greatest gift, so when the woman dropped a shirt into her basket and turned to him with a stern expression, he smiled widely and called out.

"Guten tag!" He waved. "Hallo, I am no trouble." He stepped closer. "Ich brauche Hilfe. Help. Bitte. Please."

The woman took two steps backward while never taking her eyes off of him. As he got closer, he realized how nervous she was.

"Ich bin gut. Good." He held his hands out to show her that he had no plans to hurt her. "Ich brauche Hilfe. I need help. Bitte. Please." He stopped in his tracks. "Ich werde hier bleiben." He pointed. "Here, I stay." He felt his brow wrinkle but quickly smiled.

"What do you want?" she called, not frowning but not returning his smile.

"Just help, ma'am." He pointed down the railroad tracks. "Gone——my train." August frowned and hung his head.

"What do you mean, your train is gone? There hasn't been a train by here, one with passengers anyway, since yesterday."

"Sontag? Sunday?" Gus asked, his head cocked to one side.

She held up a hand. "That's blood." She pointed to his head. "Looks like you're the fighting kind. I don't want any trouble here. You need to get on your way." She pointed back the way he had come.

"Diese Manner. Those men." His forehead crinkled. "Sie nahmen meinen Kuchen. Meine Mutter." Gus's face screwed up in confusion. "*My cake. My mother.*" Water welled in his eyes. "They called her a *Hexe.*"

The woman seemed to soften, and she reached a hand toward Gus, inviting him to come nearer. "It's all right, dear. I'll help you."

August dropped his chin to his chest. "Danke."

It was nearly an hour later when Peter stepped off the express train into the busy Great Northern Depot, the hub of most of the city's business and personal travel and the place he'd dropped August yesterday. He sucked in his breath as he dodged the people on the crowded platform and found his way to a public telephone. There was a line waiting, and he tapped his foot nervously, wishing he'd just asked Hanson to use his office telephone again. A whistle sounded in the distance, and suddenly two people stepped out of the line and hurried away. Only one man remained ahead of him, and the elderly woman using it now fumbled with the earpiece, picking it up and setting it back down several times. Peter wanted desperately for her to either figure it out or leave. He turned around, peering across the expansive space to see if there was another telephone, and when he turned back, everyone had gone. Peter rushed to the wall, picked up the cone-shaped section, and put it to his ear, leaning toward the mouthpiece. "Hello. Hello. I'd like to be connected with Meyer's Hardware in Holmesburg, Minnesota." His heart raced, and the silence seemed to last for minutes even though it took mere seconds before he heard a clicking on the telephone and a voice that said, "I'll connect you now."

Frank was on the line within a moment, and the brothers came up with a plan to find August. Frank would take his wagon down the south side of the tracks, traveling east, and Peter would sit on the north side of the westbound train. With any luck, they'd come upon August, or, at the least, each other.

Peter quickly checked the schedule of westbound trains and saw he had two to choose from, leaving within ten minutes of each other, the first going in a quarter of an hour. He took a chance he could make the first one and dashed off to the ticket window. "Ma'am," he said urgently to the woman behind the counter. "Can you tell me if there's anything noteworthy from yesterday's westbound runs? In particular, those with a stop in Holmesburg?"

She frowned at him. "Sir. There are scores of trains each day. I can't possibly tell you what happened with any of them."

"Listen," he said, putting his palms on the counter and leaning in. "I work with the Milwaukee Railroad. I know very well how each run has a record. Delays, incidents, unexpected detours, breakdowns."

She sighed and pulled up the leather-bound book, running a finger quickly down the page before looking up. "There's nothing noteworthy." She shut the record book, and a note poked out from the pages. "Wait," she said, pulling up the paper.

"Goodness." She held up the note with the bold heading, *Security Alert!* "Hmm. Four thugs on a westbound train were thrown off yesterday in Excelsior."

Peter's brow furrowed. "It's only just my brother." He chuckled wryly. "And he's hardly a thug."

"It says *possible German malcontents.*"

"Really? It truly says that?" Now Peter was flabbergasted. Whether or not this was Gus, this was just the kind of labeling his father had warned them of. "Well." He made up his mind. "Perhaps I'll get off in Excelsior." He took the note from her and headed to catch the westbound train, making it minutes before the doors closed.

Peter leaned his elbow on the window's ledge, watching as the scenery flew by, the same view as August would have had——or should have had, *if* his brother was on the train. Peter knew there was no significant advantage to having the same view, but it comforted him, thinking he saw what August had viewed, at least until his brother left the train——if that was indeed what he'd done. Peter could hardly imagine Gus as one of the so-called malcontents, but anything was possible in this time of war. As the clouds gathered and darkened, signaling a potential for snow, Pete had little time to investigate a wrong lead.

The noise and rhythm of the train grated on Peter's nerves, the miles passed too slowly, and he found himself fatigued from his frantic search of the landscape. *Damn, Gus.* Pete went back and forth between thinking his brother had been irresponsible and genuine worry that danger had befallen his sibling. Finally, an hour into the trip, the train screeched to a stop at the Excelsior Depot. Peter exited, the gray plumes from the engine's smokestack concealing the small wooden building. When the gray dissipated and the engine had continued its travel, Peter stood on the platform and looked around.

"What first?" he wondered aloud, slowly letting out his breath as he considered his options. The depot had a small, tamboured window that opened facing Water Street. Passengers who had exited the train mingled with others already standing in line.

When the ticket line was reduced to one couple, Peter walked to the window and took his place behind the pair. When it was his turn, he tilted his head to lean in, keeping his voice low and his eyes fixed on the ticket agent. He wasn't sure what trouble had befallen his brother and decided it was unwise to broadcast his questions to the entire station.

"Whoa, mister! What are you doing? You trying to climb in here with me?" The ticket agent held up his hand.

"I just don't need my business heard all over the place, that's all."

"Didn't think buying a train ticket was such a private affair." The man chortled, patting his belly, apparently amused by his own cleverness.

"I'm not looking for a ticket. I'm looking for my lost brother." Peter willed himself to calm. He'd get nowhere if he upset the man.

"I don't have any youngsters sitting on the benches waiting to be claimed. Sorry, mister."

The man slammed the rolled window covering shut on Pete, nearly clipping his nose.

"Hey!" Peter shouted, rapping his knuckles on the wood. "That's not what I meant." He reached deep into his coat pocket for the crumpled piece of paper and slid the note under the crack in the window shutter. "Sir, please! Do you know anything about this?"

Peter heard the note rustle in the man's hands. Suddenly the ticket window rolled open. "Yes. I was here. No good thugs."

"What happened?" Peter reached out for the note.

"If you're part of their gangs, or some kind of German spy, I don't want any part of it or you."

The man pulled the window down again, succeeding in slamming Peter's outstretched fingers.

"Damn!" Peter dashed around the building to the back door, opening and entering before the ticket agent had a chance to lock him out. Peter held his hands in the air.

"I mean you no harm. I'm not a thug. As a matter of fact, I work for the railroad."

The man looked at him skeptically, and Peter took out his work badge and thrust it forward. "What happened?" Peter asked again, his eyes narrowing.

"I didn't see much——of the beginning, anyway. After a scuffle, the sheriff ushered the men down the road."

"If you didn't see the fracas, how do you know it happened?"

"I gathered that's what happened by the looks of the fellas. Blood, bruises." The man winced, and Peter found himself doing so as well. August was not a fighter. *Oh, Lord.*

"The note says the train official kicked four men off the train. Do you recollect how many men were marshaled out of here?" Peter forced himself to focus on gathering the facts——he couldn't afford to fret about the particulars now.

"Two. Maybe three." The man paused, his eyes rolling up to one side. "Yeah, three. I remember now because they were all tall and skinny as bean poles and stepped up in height, like a staircase, one being a head taller than the one before." The agent chuckled at the recollection. "They were gangly fellas, that's for sure."

"Well, my brother definitely doesn't fit that description. Gus is as big and broad as an ox and sometimes as simple as one." Pete's lips pursed in concern and thought. "What did you say happened to the fourth fella?"

"I didn't say. Never saw him," the ticket man said. "Perchance he got his hide thrashed in the fight?"

Peter struggled to conceive of that possibility but explaining Gus to a stranger was futile and a waste of precious time.

"Thank you, sir, for your help." Peter tipped his hat and turned, exiting out the door to the platform. He shielded his eyes from the sun that peeked out from the gathering clouds, shards of sharp light sending their beam down the tracks. Peter checked around the station——on and under benches, the washroom, and the back storage shed. *Nothing.* He exhaled in exasperation and started walking up and down the tracks within sight of the station, supposing it *was* possible that three fellas, skinny or not, could overtake his brother. Three against one, after all. Besides, Gus was a lover, not a fighter. *Oh, August. Where are you?*

The snow was just starting to fall when Peter came upon a spot on the side of the rails——grass and weeds crushed down as if something significant had lain there for some time. He skittered down the slope and looked up toward the tracks, noticing the compressed and muddied spots on the hill. A man, of that he was now sure, had lain here and climbed out. The boot treads stood out in the mud. This man surely could be his brother. Putting his hands and feet in the same spots, Peter climbed back up to the tracks. It was then he spotted the two smaller buildings on the horizon. The grass between the tracks and the buildings was quite long and blew back and forth in the wind-whipped snow, covering up any path, had there been one. Peter willed himself to think about what his brother would do. Seeing a light flickering in the structure on the right, he began striding toward the small buildings. As he neared the red brick house on the right, he saw a large figure emerge, followed by a smaller one. He stopped and squinted.

"Gus! Is that you?" Peter took a chance and called out as loudly as possible, his voice seeming to carry in the wind.

The large man stopped in his tracks and then broke into an awkward, stumbling run. "Peter!" August flung himself into Peter's arms.

As Peter assessed his brother's bruises, he listened to August's tale. It seemed surreal, but it was unlike his brother to speak untruths. In fact, quite the opposite. The more petite figure, a woman, caught up to the men now, handing a bundle of food to them. "I cleaned him up the best I could," she offered with a shrug of her shoulders. "He was quite a mess."

"You've been very kind." Peter reached his hand out, offering an introduction. "I'm Peter Harvey, August's brother. I'm sure he was a bit daunting at first sight, so I greatly appreciate your kindness."

The woman smiled knowingly at Peter. "You may want to find lodging——what with the weather. There's a small hotel on the edge of town."

Peter thanked her again and then set an arm around his brother's shoulder, turning and pointing him back toward the tracks. The sound of a wagon and horses could be heard in the distance——the snow making it nearly impossible to see the figure. It wasn't until the familiar ring of Frank's wagon bells sounded that they were sure it was him.

Under ordinary circumstances, the brothers would have bravely gone their own way, laughing in the face of any snowstorm. Today was different, however. Times were not normal. What was, anymore? Their brother had been beaten senseless and accused of being a German spy because their Mutter had packed him sausages and cake. *Lands.* What was the world coming to? The Harvey brothers bedded down in a double room with a fireplace in the Excelsior House, valuing the warmth of the glow and the comfort of kin.

"Frank?" August whispered in the quiet of the night. "Von Mutti." He handed Frank a crumpled envelope.

Chapter 14

— • —

Christmas came and went with little fanfare——rations, restrictions, and duty taking away much of the familiar——the Savior's birth the only unchanging element.

"Goodness," Melania said with a heavy sigh as she cut slices of apple and cranberry pie on the final day of December. "I can't believe what a year this has been."

Mutti smiled and nodded, heavily sighing herself. "Unlike any I can remember," she said, setting cups and saucers on a tray next to small cordial glasses.

"Do you think Peter will make it?" Melania frowned. On the one hand, she hoped to spend New Year's Eve with her brother, but on the other, she worried he'd bring Jim along with him, especially since Mutti kept asking after Jim. It wasn't that she disliked Jim—far from it, if the flutters in her stomach were any evidence. Frankly, she couldn't even think about Jim without her brain getting fuzzy. She'd realized, or maybe just acknowledged after that evening at the movies, that not only was Jim attractive, but he was also funny and kind, and she'd enjoyed her time with him very much. Still, nothing had changed. She needed to focus on school, and he would be drafted soon. *Goodness, it's too late now,* she thought to herself for what seemed like the millionth time. She drew in a long breath and held it. She'd not seen Jim since that evening anyway. And who knew when he'd come around again? She wondered if his friendship with her brother had gone cold after Peter had been forced to take a Christmas run with the railroad after Jim failed to show up for his shift. Jim had missed several shifts of late, her brother had said. She sighed heavily once more as she covered the pie and slid it toward the back of the counter. Maybe she'd been right to discourage Jim's advances——especially if he was so casual concerning his obligations.

Vati came into the kitchen on the heels of Melania's question. "Peter just came up the walk. He's shoveling off the steps. The snow is picking up."

"Good." Melania reached for the pie tin again, feeling a wave of sadness that her brother was alone. She shook her head in an attempt to dislodge any further thoughts of Jim Wirth. "He's just in time for dessert."

Peter and Vati were settled in the front room when Mutti and Melania came in from the kitchen with the dessert, coffee, and cordial glasses. "Hello, ladies." Peter stood to greet them. "Just like last winter," he said, putting his cold palms on Melania's cheeks, "except a lot has changed." Peter chuckled.

"That's an understatement." Melania sat down heavily on a chair and turned to her mother. "Is Emily joining us?"

"She said to start without her. Lizzie's been a bit more difficult to get down to bed with all the hubbub of Christmas." A look of contentment passed over her mother's face, and it gladdened Melania. A full house was one of the few bright spots for Mutti.

"Lizzie did seem to enjoy all the activity." Melania smiled and then turned to her brother. "I'm sorry you had to miss Frank's family——and Anna, of course." She rolled her eyes. "It *was* a lot of hubbub, as Mutti said."

"I can imagine——that's a lot of people in one space." Peter whistled. "I'm assuming August stayed on the farm?" He grimaced. "Can't see him boarding another train anytime soon."

Mutti nodded. "Doubt that. But it was good to see Frank and all, especially without you and Mathias home." Her face sagged. "Of course, days of us all together are behind us for more reasons than the war."

"Philosophical at the end of the year, wife?" Vati smiled slightly and picked up his pie plate, balancing it on his bent leg.

Mutti exhaled heavily, and Melania watched as a shadow crossed her mother's face. "It's been quite an eventful year."

"This pie is delicious, Mutti. Thankfully some things remain unchanged." Peter leaned over and squeezed Mutti's hand.

Melania frowned. "I made this pie, dear brother."

Peter laughed. "You'll make a good wife someday."

"I have plans, remember?" Melania narrowed her eyes at him. "Goodness, I've finished one semester of college already. And my Red Cross training has kept me quite busy."

"You were right, then." Peter grinned at her. "Not a moment for a beau."

"Will you see Anna before she goes overseas?" Mutti seemed to intentionally change the subject, and Melania appreciated it. Peter certainly knew how to provoke her.

"Hmm. I doubt it." Peter set his plate down. "She's somewhere on the east coast now, right?"

"Yes. They've sent the new nurses to various East Coast chapters until it's safe for them to travel overseas."

"Well, I may get to one of the ports," Peter said, "but of late, we almost immediately turn right back around once the shipments are unloaded. The life of a lowly freight handler."

Mutti sipped her coffee. "Anna's most eager to get started."

Melania looked at her mother again. Maybe she'd misread her face before. Mutti loved her children, clearly, but she was realistic *and* encouraging too. Her mother set an incredibly high bar, but that was no immediate concern for Melania. *She* was far away from the days of being a wife and mother.

Melania's shoulder lifted as she joined the conversation. "Anna told me three women from her group were let go after being accused of sabotaging bandages with poison and glass shards." She turned her palms up. "Who would do that?"

"What? The deed or the accusations?" Vati let out a low grunt. "They were likely women with German surnames. Their guilt was of no consideration." He paused and frowned, exhaling heavily. "It's nonsense and only getting worse. I just read that the U.S. government opened internment camps."

Peter leaned forward. "I've seen the one at Fort Douglas in Utah. And there's another in Georgia at Fort Oglethorpe."

"Seriously?" Melania's eyes went wide. She couldn't imagine such a thing. Who would need to be interned in this country?

"Yes," Vati said. "And rumors are they've detained a geneticist and nearly thirty players from the Boston Symphony Orchestra."

"Why would a scientist and musicians be under scrutiny? This is beyond all comprehension." Melania held her coffee cup between her palms, savoring the warmth as a chill ran through her.

Vati shrugged. "I suppose it's naïve to believe there are no traitors here, but it's unfathomable to suspect *every* German is a bad apple."

The room stayed silent for several minutes, and Melania was grateful. She wanted to be included in these serious conversations yet still found it difficult to completely accept events like this were really going on in the United States. She was grateful for her family's unity. *Some people don't have anyone*, she thought, and then, suddenly, Jim's face flashed across her mind. He'd enjoyed his time with the Harvey family. She could see it——his relaxed, good-natured banter with Peter, his genuine gratitude for Helene's care, and his willingness to help out with whatever was needed. *Lands!* she thought to herself. *Is there no way to get that man off my mind?*

Her father's voice drew her from her meditations. "Frank, August, and I had to complete a registration card because we were born in Germany. Wilson's newest order." He snorted. "Required to carry them at all times." He shook his head and dropped his chin.

"I don't understand it," Peter said, his brows furrowing. "It's so extreme."

Melania looked at her father, seeing the conflict between duty and logic. "Not Mutti? She was born in Germany too."

Vati let out a long ragged breath. "We've been in this country for nearly thirty years, and I've been classified as an *alien*." He stood and went to the hearth, poking at the fire, staring at the flames, something Melania had seen her father do many times when he seemed at a loss for words.

"That's a quarter of a million U.S. citizens being forced to comply with Wilson's nativist regulations," Vati said after a long pause, sarcasm edging his words. "I'm sure the women will be next. There seems to be no logic, so why not include the women?"

Peter cleared his throat and handed his mother and sister a glass of sherry. "To a better 1918."

Jim laughed aloud when he picked up the much-read Saturday edition of the discarded newspaper lying in the trash can on the street corner. Despite the paper's sullied condition, the bold words, **Prohibition Amendment**, shouted from the pages. "What incredible timing," Jim said sarcastically as he scanned the article. "Reason enough to buy whisky before it's outlawed."

He purchased two bottles, a block of cheese, sausage, and a loaf of bread from the corner store. "There. That should do nicely." He stepped out into the empty streets, the only activity spilling out from bars and taverns. He was sorely tempted to join the revelers but turned back down the sidewalk toward the boardinghouse. He didn't feel like company tonight and snuck past the festivities in the dining room, heading toward his room.

Mrs. Haggerty came forward and put her hand on his forearm when he'd reached the staircase. "Are you sure you don't want to join us, Mr. Wirth?"

"Naw. I'm happy to see 1917 go and none too happy to see what 1918 will bring." Out-of-town trips with the railroad were few and far between and never seemed to put enough distance between Jim and the trouble at the station. Problems dogged him at every turn——a snide comment, a rude remark, and most recently, sabotage of his progress on one of the locomotives. He longed to be free of it——the station, the job, everything.

Jim trudged up the stairs, the bottles clanking together in their brown paper bag. He chuckled darkly and twisted the bottle open between his teeth, taking a long, deep gulp, followed by a mouthful of bread, before plopping on the bed. He pushed himself up against the wall bedecked with yellowish-brown stained wallpaper and lifted the bottle in the air. "To the end of this miserable year." He closed his eyes as the burn of whisky spilled down his throat.

1918

CHAPTER 15

A frigid chill gripped Minnesota in the new year, extending across the entire state from its Canadian border to the Mississippi River valley near Iowa. Heavy icicles hung from the eaves of houses, dropping like swords into the crisp snow. Ponds and small creeks had a solid frozen layer, inviting skaters into the frosty air.

Powderhorn Park was a favorite place for Melania and her school-mates——the proximity to the campus and the lively crowds made it a recurrent destination to escape the melancholy of war. After exiting the streetcar, Melania and her friend Jane trudged through the snowy side-walks toward the small shelter on the edge of the skating rink, following carefully in the footprints of Jane's boyfriend Jasper and his friend Archie Addington——Arch, as his friends called him. Although their expanse was bigger, the boys' feet trampled a perfect place for the girls to step, and they giggled when they nearly tipped stretching from one footstep to the next. It felt so good to laugh and have something enjoyable to do. Ever since the Red Cross fundraiser dance, Arch had been coming around. Melania tried not to encourage him but enjoyed his company and the distraction. Yet her mind went to Jim. He hadn't been around in a long time, and Peter rarely mentioned him. It was almost as if he didn't exist anymore. Melania wasn't sure if something was amiss between Peter and Jim or if her family was intentionally sparing her discussion about a man with whom she clearly wanted nothing to do. At least, that's how she made it seem. Why then, she often wondered, couldn't she stop thinking about him?

The couples entered the park shelter and sat on benches, strapping on their blades. Melania swayed to one side when she stood, trying to accustom herself to walking on a single edge. Archie crooked his elbow as an invitation.

"Thank you." Melania hooked her arm in his.

Archie was unquestionably a gentleman and had beautiful deep bluish-gray eyes that were warm and kind but nothing like the sharp twinkle in a particular pair of green eyes. She brushed the thought off and unhooked from Arch's arm as soon as they reached the pond, looking back as she sped away. "Catch me if you can," she taunted.

"You watch out, sassy girl!" Arch started after her, seeming to keep a modest pace to prolong the game. The glow of the sharp wind and the heat from the exertion mixed on Melania's cheeks. She rounded the last curve of the pond and lost her footing, sliding on her side into the snowbank. She was unhurt, though slightly embarrassed, and welcomed Arch's extended hand to pluck her to her feet.

"Oh my!" She put a mittened hand to her mouth. "That was un-graceful."

"Think nothing of it," Arch said. "It was a race. No holds barred!" He wrapped his arm firmly around her shoulders and pulled her into himself for a hug. He let Melania go instantly, but the brief contact with his body unsettled her, and she pulled away from him, stepping in a tippy-toe manner onto the wooden planks that lined the lake's walk to the shelter. Archie was a friend—a good friend——and the last thing she wanted to do was to send him mixed messages.

She stopped and looked back at him, feeling a bit chagrined at her reaction. Surely he was aware they were just pals. "Let's get some hot chocolate."

Jane and Jasper made their way to the small table soon after Arch and Melania sat down with their warm mugs. Melania was relieved to be spared of small talk with only Archie. Jasper dropped his wet coat on the back of a chair and headed to get warm drinks for himself and Jane.

Immediately Jane's lively banter filled the space. "Wasn't that delightful?" She put her palms to the red patches on her cheeks. "It's so nice to be away from school having fun! I do hope Jasper remembers to grab a cookie too." Jane barely breathed between sentences. "Did you see the poster?" Her head swiveled between Arch and Melania, but she didn't stop long enough for either one to respond. "Lucille Holliday is leading a *Community Sing* at the Walker Chalet in two weeks. We should go, shouldn't we? Yes, let's plan on it!" Jane put her hand over Melania's, nodding at her friend in confirmation.

Jasper set down the steaming mugs. "Plan on what, Janie dear?" Melania chuckled at Jasper's success in silencing Jane. Her friend, indeed, was smitten. Jane tilted her head and batted her long eyelashes at the man.

"Well, J," Jane said. "There's a *Community Sing* at Walker Chalet in two weeks, and Lucille Holliday is leading it."

"Who?" Jasper asked.

"She's——oh——never mind. It doesn't matter if you know who she is. What matters is that I heard there were over three hundred people at the last event. We *must* go! All four of us. It'll be divine!" Jane clapped her hands together.

"Of course, dear." Jasper patted Jane's hand while rolling his eyes at Arch.

Melania smiled warmly at her friend. "It sounds like a plan." She appreciated Jane's gusto filling the space where she was more reserved. Having plans made for her saved Melania from having to commit to or outright decline requests from Archie. It was easier to just go along for the ride on Jane and Jasper's social train.

Jacob stretched his arms over his head, feeling his fatigued muscles pull. He brushed the layer of white flour from his shirt front and secured his suspenders, which had slipped off one shoulder, then put on his coat. It was stifling on the mill floor, but he knew the bitter cold would hit him when he stepped out the door. He trudged down the steps, happy to leave behind the ceaseless noise from the machines, enjoying the few moments on the quiet first floor before heading outside. He pressed his hat on his head and plunged his hands into his pockets as he pushed the door open with his forearm. His right thumb poked into the small hole in the corner of his pocket, and he sighed, thinking he may just sew it himself.

Helene was tired these days, and he wondered how long she could, or even should, endure at the mill. Maybe she'd done enough, tending family, farm, and home all these years. He wondered, too, how long he'd hold up with his duties extending to supervising and training the newer employees. For now, though, he reminded himself as he stepped out into the cold, he'd bear up, as would his wife.

Frosty air turned to ice on his eyebrows and beard as Jacob made his way to the newsstand. He purchased a paper and folded it underneath his arm, trotting to catch the waiting streetcar. He leaned against the seat as the trolley went down the boulevard. Light flashed in spurts from the streetlamps, reminding him of firelight——beautiful but not practical for reading by. He smoothed the paper on his lap, anxious to read it when he arrived home. Each week, it seemed, brought more extraordinary and heartbreaking news——American lives lost, shortages and sacrifice on the home front, the propagation of nationalist efforts. The chatter on to-day's milling floor was about the President's plan for peace——excitement blossomed into the hope that Wilson's scheme would make a difference. Jacob had been careful not to appear doubtful yet was unconvinced there was anything that could be accomplished by mere words at this juncture. He knew the German nationalists weren't likely to come to the negotiation table now. They were in too deep. To their minds, they were fighting for what was rightfully theirs. It was a battle to the end for Kaiser Wilhelm and many Germans——to the death.

Jacob stepped onto the icy street corner, steadying himself on the lamp-post as the streetcar ambled away down the street. Unable to resist any longer, he held the newspaper to the dim light and read the President's words to Congress.

> What we demand in this war is nothing peculiar to ourselves. It is that the world be made fit and safe to live in; and particularly that it be made safe for every peace-loving nation which, like our own, wishes to live its own life, determine its own institutions, be assured of justice and fair dealing by the other peoples of the world as against force and selfish aggression. The program of the world's peace, therefore, is our program.

Jacob's breath came out in clouds, disappearing around the edges of the newsprint. He angled the paper toward the light to read the conclusion.

> The peace plan includes independence for Poland, restoration of Belgian independence, the return of Alsace-Lorraine to France, an end to secret diplomacy, the autonomy of subject nationalities, and the formation of a League of Nations.

A grand plan, indeed. Jacob folded the paper, tucked it under his arm, and headed home.

Chapter 16

Walter von Esson slammed the phone on the receiver, then pounded his fist on his desk. Ruth heard it clearly from her reception desk, only paces from the mayor's door. It wasn't the first time he'd done that, nor likely the last. She exhaled heavily and crept to the threshold of his office just as he called her name.

"Ruth!" She jumped, startled even though she was expecting the summons. His hand swept across the desk, and papers scattered, floating to the floor. He rose from his chair, pushing it back, the wheels banging into the credenza.

She winced. "Is there anything I can do for you, Mr. Mayor?"

"Yes! Pick up these papers!" Walter's arm moved over the mess.

Ruth scurried in and began gathering the documents.

"Wait! Stop! Is there any correspondence from the governor?"

"I'm not sure," she said. "The mail was only just delivered."

"Then what are you doing in here? Go and open it! Mayor Irvin warned me something was on its way." His eyes utterly glowed as he spat out the order.

Ruth crept from the office, softly closing the door. She put her hand on the stack of mail and important papers and stared at the mayor's portrait hanging behind her desk. "He looks the part at any rate," she muttered, shuffling through the mail to retrieve the governor's official envelope, tucking it close to her chest and slowly creeping toward the mayor's office. She paused as sounds of Walter moving and clattering about seeped under the doorway. Her lips pursed as she moved down the row of portraits of other men who'd held this office. "It should still be you," she said to the image of Robert Nye.

"He didn't stand a chance." A voice spoke behind her, and she turned to see the janitor leaning on his broom, his mouth in a deep frown.

"What? Who?" Ruth's face crinkled.

"Nye. The financial scandal." The janitor's shoulder lifted almost imperceptibly. "Did you ever wonder if it was a set-up?"

Ruth took a deep breath and held it as she watched the janitor and his broom move down the hallway. She stepped quickly to the office door, meeting the mayor as he flung it open, snatched the envelope, and then slammed the door in her face.

Walter's eyes squeezed shut as he held the missive. "No doubt another damned distraction," he muttered. "First the MCPS, then the propaganda." He glanced at the posters on his wall——the same ones plastered all over the city——ominous pictures and warnings.

DON'T TALK! THE WEB IS SPUN FOR YOU WITH INVISIBLE THREADS! KEEP OUT OF IT. HELP TO DESTROY IT. SPIES ARE LISTENING! DON'T BE SUSPECTED! USE AMERICAN LANGUAGE! AMERICA IS OUR HOME!

Local businesses gladly hung the placards, and many others quickly and quietly changed their business names from German references to war heroes or other benign titles. Walter picked up a recent proclamation prohibiting Minneapolis schools from teaching the German language. The school year was nearly two-thirds done, for goodness sake. How would they change course so fast, he wondered and then asked himself why he was concerned. He had more important things to worry about and this was just one of the seemingly never-ending directives from the Governor's office. He opened a drawer and threw the notice in a file. He exhaled heavily and sat down, pulling his chair forward and sliding the latest message from the envelope. His eyes rolled, his face flushed, and he ran a finger under his collar before reaching for a glass of water. He took several long swallows and then stood, taking in and holding his breath as he moved to the door.

"Ruth, dear. Would you kindly call in Stempel and Deputy Hill?" Walter's mouth pinched into a semblance of a smile.

Moments later, the men hurried into the mayor's office and quickly sat at the table. "What is it, sir?" Stempel asked.

"This time." The corner of Hill's mouth turned up, and then he quickly turned away when Walter didn't smile.

"More of the same." Walter pressed his lips into a line and closed his eyes for a moment.

Then he looked at Stempel. "Where are we on the *Four Minute Men* events?"

Stempel cleared his throat. "Just as you asked. Every theater and movie production is interrupted with brief messages. The volunteers continue to speak at every draft board, war bond drive, college campus, and church. They talk about the draft, war bond, rationing——"

"Yes, yes, I'm aware. I just need to know that my, *our,* efforts are *noticed.*"

Stempel's brow furrowed. "Noticed?"

Walter cleared his throat and ran a finger under his collar again. "Well, I mean, we have work to do. Important work to keep the city running. And we'd hate to have that good work delayed. The workers——ahem, the voters——are counting on us." Walter clapped his hands together. "We don't need unnecessary distractions. The governor needs to know he can count on us."

Hill's bottom lip protruded as his head tilted, eyeing Walter. "What about the American Protective League, sir?"

"What about it?" A bead of sweat ran down Walter's forehead, and he quickly dabbed it with his folded pocket square.

Hill snorted. "They're not watching us if that's what you're worried about. Those amateur detectives won't make their way in here." The heavyset man slapped his knee and leaned forward conspiratorially, popping a button near his ample belly.

Walter took in a deep breath and held it while Hill continued. "We've handed out scores of badges and certificates, just as the attorney general wanted and have received hundreds of reports on German immigrants."

"Great, more paperwork to sort through." Walter shook his head and flapped the governor's envelope. "The latest. Take notes, Stempel."

Stempel flipped to a clean page and poised his pen tip.

Walter scanned the document and looked up from the pages, his face tight. "By the end of the month, the MCPS will begin registering unnaturalized non-natives to the United States." He shuffled the papers together and bounced them on the table between his hands until the stack was tight. "It'll be done at the MCPS St. Paul headquarters, but we should assist."

"Yes, sir. I'll set that up." Hill's mouth twisted, and his eyes narrowed. "Immigrants, non-natives, citizens with German surnames, political opponents. Seems no one's exempt." He let out a slow breath before turning to Walter. "Isn't von Esson a German name?"

Walter abruptly stood, leaving the question hanging in the air. "Get on with it, Stempel. Hill, wait."

He turned to the rotund man as soon as Stempel left the room. "Goodness, Hill, you're sweating. Are you unwell?" Walter's eyes narrowed. "Perhaps this job is too much for you."

CHAPTER 17

Jim ducked his head as he entered the rail yard, hoping to avoid attention from management. He was on thin ice after missing so much work——certain the railroad would have long ago fired him were they not desperate for men. He often wondered why he even kept working at the railroad, and every day he missed pulled at his conscience. Some days, he couldn't muster up the will to face the undeserving harassment, and other days, he couldn't get himself up after a night of drink. Either way, justified or not, his character had taken a big hit. Hadn't Mr. Harvey said your name and your honor were two of the most important things to a man? Jim scoffed. Both had been filched.

Jim had been watched like a hawk ever since O'Malley had stirred false rumors and innuendo about him——weeks before his recent absences. Men with whom Jim had once enjoyed a drink turned away when he walked by or watched him with eagle eyes, wary of his every action or word. The posters propagating extreme practices were everywhere——in the station, plastered to buildings, and nailed to posts. Fear of co-workers, neighbors, or even of being accused themselves caused many people to go to extremes. Some dressed in patriotic colors, waving American flags and whistling the national anthem. Others ducked low and tried to slink by unnoticed. Both, frankly, raised doubt, especially if a guy had a German surname. Jim wondered who he could trust. *Peter*. He was sure of that. But he hadn't seen Pete in a while. The incident with Melania had made Jim uncomfortable with the entire Harvey family. He felt like a heel, a cad, acting so presumptuously. They didn't need him around, especially with his tarnished reputation. He dropped his toolbox next to the locomotive and began his day.

Thankfully, the morning passed without incident, and Jim grabbed his lunch pail and walked in the shadows behind the line of stalled engines, heading for a small clearing where he hoped to eat in peace. Just as he stepped out in front of the last locomotive, two men grabbed him roughly, and a third dropped a sack over his head.

"Hey!" Jim tried to wriggle loose. "What the hell's going on?" His hot breath lingered by his face, seeming not to penetrate the burlap bag. Although ample, Jim's strength and stature were no match for three strong railroad workers. The men dragged Jim, thrashing, to the other side of the yard and dumped him. One of the men pulled the sack off Jim's head, and he gasped in a harsh breath. A circle of angry faces glared at him——sticks and other objects in their hands.

"Dance, you German!" They taunted him, jabbing at his feet. "Show us the vvvaltz!" Uproarious laughter ensued. "Give us the strudel you brought for lunch, you Hun!"

Jim vaulted to his feet and planted himself, fists in the air. "I'll take on any of you louts who dares to call me that again." Without waiting, Jim rushed forward and began swinging. He landed plenty of punches, some of them squarely on their intended targets, but his efforts were no match for the large group. Kicks and punches landed on his ribs, his nose, his stomach, until all mercifully went black.

When he finally came to, he nearly fell off the narrow station bench before realizing where he was, surprised that someone had even bothered moving him there. He tried to sit up, but intense pain shot through every part of his body. Next thing he knew, Hanson was striding toward him. Jim sprang to his feet despite the agony. He had to explain himself before the stationmaster made assumptions.

"I've had my eye on you, Wirth." Hanson poked his finger at the American Protective League badge pinned to his lapel. "By order of the United States government." Hanson's chest puffed when he spoke, and Jim struggled not to snicker at the sheer absurdity.

"The men tell me you went after them at lunch, daring anyone to call you a Hun."

"Sir, that's——"

"Silence!" Hanson grabbed Jim by the back of his coat, turning and pushing him toward the door. "You can show your loyalty to America right now."

Hanson shoved through the passengers milling about on the platform, steering Jim toward the semi-circle of railroad employees waiting as if for a planned event. "Go ahead, Wirth. Show us what a loyal American you are," Hanson commanded.

"I don't understand." Jim stared at the gaping and leering crowd.

"Sing the national anthem. Loud and clear!"

Some men chuckled. Others looked away.

"There," one man said, pointing to the American flag waving above the building.

"Kneel while you sing, Wirth." Hanson pushed him to the ground. "Show your loyalty to the red, white, and blue."

Humiliated and beaten, Jim squeezed his eyes shut, knelt, and opened his mouth to sing.

He didn't make it through the entire song, or maybe he did——it was as if he were no longer in his own body. He felt nothing. He heard nothing. When he finally opened his eyes, the crowd had mostly dispersed. A hand touched his shoulder, and he jerked, lifting his fists defensively.

"Whoa, Jim. Hold on. It's me." Peter's eyes narrowed. "What happened?"

Jim felt tears filling his eyes. Angry tears. He shook his head, words not coming.

"Come on," Pete said, grabbing his hand and pulling Jim to stand.

Helene heard Jacob's voice mixed with the muted sound of another male. *Peter?* She wasn't sure but expected she'd find out soon enough. She busied herself cleaning up from the night's supper, turning from the sink when the kitchen door opened. Peter's grave expression alarmed her.

"Son. What is it?"

"It's Jim."

"What happened?" Helene put a hand over her mouth.

"He won't say, but he's battered and bruised, physically and mentally too, I suspect. Crowds were scattering, and he was crouched low on the station platform when my train arrived this afternoon."

"What could that be about?" Her face wrinkled in concern.

"The fellas in the yard have been badgering Jim for months since he had that run-in with O'Malley. Seems like he's the scapegoat for something or someone."

"Where is he now? Is he hungry?" Helene wiped her hands on a towel and reached for two bowls.

"Vati is sitting with him in the front room. Jim wants to leave but may stay if you insist. I just don't feel right letting him go home———if you could call a boardinghouse a home."

"Set up the small table, will you? I'll bring in food for both of you. Perhaps a warm meal will do its part in clearing his head." After Peter left, Helene turned back to the stove, dishing two heaping servings of stew with biscuits. She pushed open the kitchen door with a tray in her hands.

The room was lit only by the fireplace———Jacob sat in the corner behind the two young men. Helene set the tray on the table between them and saw her husband's slight nod. She paused before Jim, pressing her hand over his and bending to eye level. "I'll prepare you a warm bath and a cot in Peter's room in the attic. You *will* go up after you eat. Do you understand?"

A tear formed in the corner of Jim's eye and escaped down his cheek, but he nodded. Helene turned before he saw her wet eyes———this man needed love more than sympathy.

Helene and Jacob sat by the fire late into the evening after Jim settled upstairs. Peter had been unable to relax and had finally gone out an hour earlier. Helene tried to keep busy with her sewing and needlework but found it too difficult to concentrate on this simple task. She dropped the socks in the basket beside her chair and stared at the dancing flames. She looked over at her husband as the sound of the crinkling newspaper broke the silence. As he straightened and folded the paper to read the next section, a small article on the back page caught Helene's eye. She leaned in and read.

A SOLDIER AT FORT RILEY, KANSAS, FELL ILL WITH AN ACUTE CASE OF INFLUENZA. LITTLE IS KNOWN ABOUT THE ORIGIN OF THE DISEASE THAT HAS BEFALLEN LT.

Stephen Jones. Did troops carry it home with them from overseas? Time will tell.

CHAPTER 18

Classes at the University of Minnesota ended in mid-May for Melania's rural teaching program. It had been a whirlwind school year for her with a full class schedule and many Red Cross trainings and events. She'd rarely seen her parents——their demanding work schedule mirrored her own harried life. They'd stayed in touch through weekly correspondence, each note getting shorter as the weeks passed. It troubled Melania to think of her mother and father working long hours, much more than their bodies could likely endure, but the sacrifices of war, she was beginning to realize, touched everyone. Even the wealthy ladies that used the Red Cross as a donation showcase for their causes rolled up their sleeves and worked tirelessly alongside the regular volunteers. As the month wound down, and before she headed home for the summer, the Red Cross chapter prepared for another fundraiser after President Wilson proclaimed mid-June as *Red Cross Week*, encouraging *Give Until It Hurts* campaigns across the country. Donations would be gathered for the war effort, collecting both men's war supplies and cash. Basic medical demonstrations and advice on avoiding and treating diseases would be provided. This would be the culmination of Melania's training, and she looked forward to wearing her crisp white apron adorned with the red cross.

She stepped cautiously down the dormitory staircase, arms so laden with personal belongings she could hardly see. The Red Cross campaign was only two weeks away, but she hoped to spend much of the time until then at home. She smiled as she thought of how she'd grown since first moving to campus. No longer was she a small-town rural girl. She had a year of university classes, Red Cross training, various new and exciting social experiences, and scores of new friends.

Melania shifted the box as she crossed campus toward the streetcar stop, her arms aching under the load.

"Whoa! Young lady! Just where do you think you're going? Are you sneaking off?" A hand touched her arm.

"Oh. Arch. No, not really. I mean, I was," she stuttered.

Arch chortled. "Relax, Melania. I was only ribbing you," he said as he pulled her in for a quick squeeze.

Melania grinned and looked at him around her box. Archie was friendly in a brotherly fashion, pleasant and fun to be around, not to mention a diversion from the somber events of the war. Archie didn't push her for a serious relationship, seeming to understand his time as a student and potential beau was limited at best, with the second draft round coming in June.

"Will I see you before the big Red Cross fundraiser?" Not waiting for a response, Archie continued, "How about inviting me over to your house for your mother's famous pie? It's wrong that I've heard tales yet never tasted one of the delights."

"Ah——sure. I guess." Melania was caught off guard and agreed without thinking.

"Sunday, week next? I'll be in your neighborhood. One of my sisters is part of the Red Cross chapter linked with St. Lawrence Parish. I promised my Ma that I'd show my support by doing some heavy work." Archie flexed his muscles and grinned.

"That's——kind." Melania blinked at him, confused by his uncharacteristic cheekiness.

"Sunday then." Archie took out a small notebook from his breast pocket and jotted down her address.

"See you then." Melania hurried on her way, suddenly feeling like their relationship had taken a new direction——one she'd not intentionally invited.

Jim had walked away from both the platform and railroad employment on that humiliating day in early March——no job was worth the degradation. When he'd awakened before dawn at the Harvey home the following day, his humiliation had driven him to slip quietly down the stairs and out the front door without a goodbye. He was ashamed to be seen in such a disgraced condition. The Harvey family didn't need him to sully their good name.

Jim knew Peter had come by the boardinghouse several times, but he'd avoided seeing him. Peter may be his only friend, but he was doing Pete a favor by keeping his distance——of that, he was sure.

Jim worked as a handyman now, thankful that skills learned on the farm in his youth had expanded his employable worth. "*Turn 'em in*" posters warning of "*enemies among us*" hung everywhere, in every major business. As a result, Jim mainly stuck to helping small business owners or women whose husbands had left lists of undone chores when they enlisted. This loose routine suited Jim——he could maintain his freedom and earn a steady income. Sometimes he bartered for food; other times, he worked to pay for his room and board. He was biding his time, as were many other young men who surely would be drafted in the next round.

Jim wasn't religious, but he didn't work Sundays as a matter of course. It just seemed like the right thing to do, he thought again as he dove into the hearty breakfast his landlady had laid out on the buffet. He remembered his grandparents talking about a day of rest, although he never recalled them sitting still on *any* day on the farm. They'd worked from dusk until dawn seven days a week. Maybe that was where his work ethic came from. And perhaps it was one reason the treatment he'd received at the railyard had been so infuriating. He didn't deserve it——he knew that. He was a good worker and a good man. He let out a ragged breath and pushed back thoughts of the railroad. It didn't matter anymore.

It was odd that thoughts of his grandparents had come to mind this morning. It had been some time since they'd died, and he often thought of himself as a true orphan, when in reality, he had experienced a relatively normal and stable childhood in their care. Still, his family was mostly gone now, and his relationships had never resembled what the Harvey family had. He shook off those thoughts too. He wasn't part of the Harvey family and never would be.

He forced himself to smile when Mrs. Haggerty came into the dining room. "Thank you. That was delicious."

"I was wondering, Jim, if I could ask you a favor?"

Jim stood and nodded. "Sure." A kindness to his landlady would lift his mood.

"The Red Cross chapter is preparing for a fundraising event today, and I've some donations, but new tenants are arriving this afternoon, so I can't drop them off. Could you do that for me?"

"Sure. Yes."

"Breakfast would be on the house next Sunday." She smiled at him.

"No need to provide breakfast, ma'am. I'm happy to oblige."

"Wonderful," she replied. "The event is at St. Lawrence's Parish on 7th Street."

Jim's heart dropped. That was just blocks from the Harvey home and possibly the parish they now attended. But it was too late to get out of the errand; Mrs. Haggerty was already gathering her donations. He sighed. He'd just keep his head down, complete the drop-off, and return home.

He glanced at the clock on the way out, hoping he'd arrive well after Mass, lessening his chance of running into the Harveys. He caught the streetcar on the corner, hopping out several blocks before the church. As the temperature rose on this late June morning, he unbuttoned his collar to let in air. Sweat beaded on his forehead as he rounded the corner toward the church. He swiped his brow with his sleeve before peering up and down the perpendicular blocks——empty, save for a few children playing hopscotch. He moved up the pathway toward the grassy area with a large open tent and smaller canopies. Several tables and stations filled the perimeter, and the place buzzed with activity, women in white aprons sweeping in and out like angels of mercy.

Suddenly Jim realized that Melania probably had the same uniform, working in her Red Cross chapter near the university. He pictured her tall figure bedecked in the crisp white garment, her dark hair tucked under the cap mounted atop her head, floating around as if she didn't have feet. He chuckled out loud, surprising himself. It had been so long since he'd laughed, and it felt good. He approached the table marked for donations and left his parcel there.

Relaxing a bit, Jim checked out each station, looking over the pamphlets and supplies, enjoying the chance to be just another person in a crowd without suspicion being cast on him. One table offered refreshments of lemonade and cookies. He threw a nickel in the donation jar and shoved the cookie in his mouth, immensely enjoying the rare sweet, chugging the beverage in intervals. He walked across the church lawn toward the sidewalk, feeling lighter than he had in a while. A young man crossed in front of him, heading in the same general direction. The man looked at a piece of paper before turning down the street toward Melania's home. When Jim reached the corner, the man was about two houses from the Harveys' place. Jim craned his neck and watched as the young man looked up at each house number and then abruptly stopped at the Harvey home, swiftly ascending the steps. Melania opened the door, reached for the man's hand, and ushered him inside.

Jim's mood instantly soured. *Had the man kissed her when he leaned in?* For a girl who didn't want a relationship, Melania certainly had a peculiar way of showing it. She'd held the man's hand! Jim had seen it clearly with his own two eyes. He wanted to march down the street and demand an explanation. *Who was this man? Why would she put* him *off only to welcome another man into her life?* The thought infuriated Jim. He forced himself to turn, heading in the opposite direction, walking in a daze for blocks, his mood shifting to bitterness.

He strode right past the boardinghouse on the return trip, took the next streetcar, and stopped off at the first open pub. He breathed in the smoky cloud that assaulted him at the entrance, welcoming the dingy atmosphere that matched his sullen mood. He drew up to the bar in the farthest dark corner, setting a stack of coins before him, beckoning the barkeep to keep the drinks coming.

The hours passed in a blur, the cookies and lemonade sitting in the pit of his stomach, soured by the quantities of beer he'd consumed. Mercifully, no one approached him, so he was left to wallow in his despair. Jim's mind churned out thoughts stewed in ale as the day wore on. *No woman is worth humiliation, just like no stinking job is worth dishonor. To hell with them all.*

He wandered out of the joint well into the evening, stumbling in the direction of the boardinghouse. He staggered past brick walls plastered with the mayor's newest push to rout out all the spies and political dissenters. Angry faces of the enemy glared at him from lampposts. Even in his drunkenness, the madness was clear. Friends turned on friends——neighbor on neighbor. The insanity of it all sloshed around in Jim's mind. If a person didn't buy war bonds, he was under suspicion, and his name was printed in the newspaper's weekly watch list. If a family failed to plant a Victory garden or donate to the Red Cross, their intentions were questioned, and the family was under threat of being exposed publicly. Across the entire country, former community leaders——lawyers, councilmen, and teachers——had been arrested and jailed. Orchestras stopped playing pieces by Beethoven and other German composers. It was lunacy.

Jim stumbled down the street as the dark thoughts swirled in his head, momentarily resting his hand on a brick wall. He removed it just as quickly as if he'd touched hot coal. The poster plastered there glared out at him with its propagandist message. It vexed him, and he ripped it off the wall without thought. Just as the paper floated in pieces at his feet, several police officers patrolling the area rounded the corner.

"Hey! What are you doing down there?" They raised their billy clubs in the air and charged down the walk toward him.

Jim stopped and put his hands in the air, swaying slightly from side to side. "Nothing, officers. Just heading home."

"What about the poster you just shredded? Don't ya know that's city property you're destroying?" The blue-uniformed men planted themselves firmly on either side of him.

"I didn't mean any harm. It ripped accidentally when I leaned against the wall. I didn't want to let a damaged notice adorn the walls of our fair city." Jim chuckled to himself at his clever response.

"You think this is funny?" One officer poked him in the chest, sending Jim swaying back. "You think rounding up spies is a joke?"

"No, no. I take it *very* seriously." Jim slurred, waving his arms in a big gesture. "All of this."

"Hey, he tried to swing at us!"

"No!" Jim protested, shaking his head. "I didn't."

"Cuff him, Ed. He's coming with us."

Before Jim could finish his sentence, the metal rings closed around his wrists. His drunkenness made his body seem to move in slow motion, the turning of his head barely catching up to the redirection when the police ushered him toward the station.

Once in the police headquarters, Jim was thrown into lockup with the evening's other rabble-rousers. He slumped against a corner of the cell, trying to keep one eye open for self-preservation. The dark cloud of liquor hung about him, battling him at every turn, and he eventually sank into a heap.

A police officer abruptly pulled him up. "Virth, huh? A German. A spy, maybe?" The officer glared, matching Jim's height but dwarfing him in size. Jim's eyes widened, taking in the comment and the massive girth of the man.

"Wha——?" Jim shook his head, trying to clear the sluggishness from his brain.

The officer pulled Jim out of the cell and led him to the interrogation room.

CHAPTER 19

—◆—

Jacob sat on the front porch with little Elizabeth at his feet. He stacked the blocks again as she tumbled them down.

"It's a never-ending task, Vati," Peter said as he came up the walkway. "Even I know that."

Jacob chuckled. "It is, but she's a good child." He gestured toward the chair. "Sit. I've been promised lemonade and a sandwich if I keep an eye on this one."

"What's the news this week?" Peter nodded toward the newspaper laying in Jacob's lap.

Jacob shrugged. "Americans are making a difference. They continue to hold Cantigny after the spring assault." He chuckled. "I still can't believe they pulled it off in broad daylight."

"Gutsy." Peter leaned down and restacked the blocks.

"A month-long campaign recently wrapped up in France. U.S. Marines joined Army engineers and infantry in Belleau Wood. They say it was one of the most important battles fought by U.S. forces since the Civil War."

"Hmm. Bluster?"

Jacob shrugged. "Time will tell, but I expect it's worth the hyperbole if it bolsters the men."

"Have you heard about Maning?" Peter leaned back and crossed his arms, letting out a low whistle. "News of him is all over the rails. They're talking about how he was severely wounded yet still managed to break up a counterattack with his spot-on marksmanship."

The corners of Jacob's mouth turned up. "Now *that* sounds like bluster." He shrugged. "Maybe some truth to it, though, as in most things. The newspapers are talking about the *American Fighting Spirit*." He nodded, considering. "So perhaps this Maning fellow did actually do this."

"Or something close. He's being awarded the Medal of Honor."

Jacob scratched his head and squinted in thought. "I think that was the same conflict that killed the poet, Joyce Kilmer."

Peter sighed. "The realities of war, I suppose."

"Over one hundred thousand American casualties so far."

"Have you heard from Mathias?"

"Not yet. Your Mutti holds fast to the only letter she received from him so far." Jacob shook his head slightly. "It won't be easy for him to write. Not like it is for Anna, relatively speaking."

"How will we know if he's well?"

"Have you heard the phrase, *no news is good news?*" Jacob's hands trembled at the thought, and he crossed his arms, tucking them to his sides.

Peter exhaled loudly. "I guess. I feel the same way about my draft notice. I haven't gotten one yet but expect it."

"It'll be the next round, likely. You and Frank missed this one too, but surely there's another round coming."

Emily brought out sandwiches and lemonade and took her daughter back into the house. Peter and Jacob sat in the silence of the news and their thoughts for some time.

Jacob's attention was drawn away by a man coming down the sidewalk. A military chaplain. He sucked in a breath and held it, keeping his eyes fixed on the uniformed man.

Peter turned too, and they both watched as the chaplain walked up the steps of the house next door. Jacob didn't have to hear the words to know the gist of what the man said. *With deep regrets, the U.S. Military wishes to tell you——*

Chapter 20

Minneapolis Tribune • July 1918 • INTERNATIONAL TRAGEDY! The spring and summer have been filled with both tragedy and triumph on the home front as reports of battles——successful and not——heroes and casualties——advances and retreats have dominated the national news. Today, however, troubling international news finds its way across the ocean. Former Russian Tsar Nicolas II was executed by order of the Ural Regional Council after they discovered a Czecho-Slovak threat against the capital of the Red Ural——a plot in which the former monarch was involved. The whereabouts of the remaining Romanov family are unclear.

The Red Cross chapter buzzed with the news of the mysterious disappearance of the Romanov family amid the Tsar's assassination. The women rolled bandages and packed care boxes, ruminating on the tsar's demise, from the collapse of his monarchy to his recent killing. It was tragic on many levels, as any death would be, but the mystery of the location of the Tsar's family added impending heartbreak. The Romanovs had five children, four daughters and one son. Melania recalled Vati mentioning that the family had been imprisoned in their home since early 1917 after the Tsar was deposed. In her naïveté, Melania initially had the impractical notion that the prince and princesses would be saved from their confinement in a fairytale ending.

As with all news bulletins this summer, the Tsar's death was a sobering reality. No longer did Melania have only a vague concept of war or its effects——its reach came closer every day. Two boys she knew from Holmesburg and nearly a half dozen fathers and husbands in Fuller County had died in overseas conflicts since the U.S. involvement. Friends and acquaintances from the university and the Red Cross had lost fathers, brothers, uncles, husbands, and friends. Both Mathias and Anna were in France, her brother fighting, and her sister with the International Red Cross. Thankfully, neither Frank nor Peter had been swept up in the latest military enlistments, but the next draft was coming——it was inevitable. There were no signs the war would end soon. It wouldn't be long before all the young men would be sent overseas——Jim and Archie too.

Melania set her basket, overflowing with bandages, on the table to be packaged and sent overseas. Taking a cue from her parents, she stayed on the periphery of war conversations, walking a line between interest and overzealousness. Too little attention to any aspect of the war could lead to accusations of supporting the German cause or spying. Melania found the work of the Red Cross to be noble, despite her early misgivings, and she cherished the opportunity to be involved. Still, walking the tightrope in conversations with the other volunteers left her mentally exhausted.

Melania glanced around the room. "Is there anything else I can do before my shift is over?" Her supervisor, Matron Jones, was typically quick to add small chores to the volunteers' queues, using up every minute of their shifts *for the cause*.

Matron hesitated. "Well. No," she conceded, scanning the tables teeming with items to be packaged and shipped. "There is one thing I'd like to speak with you about, however. Could you come with me to my office?" The older woman put her arm around Melania's shoulders and ushered her forward toward the small cubby on the other side of the room. Had Matron not done that, Melania may have turned and ran from the room, despite having done nothing to warrant suspicion.

Matron Jones must have sensed the tension in Melania's shoulders. "It's nothing to fret over. It's good news, I hope."

An hour later, Melania burst up the porch steps and dashed into the parlor. "Mutti! I have wonderful news!"

The house was silent save the rustle of curtains fluttering in and out of the window frames in the humid summer breeze. The smell of the morning's baked bread lingered, along with an unfamiliar but enticing aroma. Seeing no one around, she headed to the kitchen, hoping to satisfy her gnawing hunger. The voices of Emily and her mother commingled with the chortles and giggles from Elizabeth. Melania peered out the window to see the women bent over their Victory garden, harvesting the early lettuces. "Hello, Mutti. Emily. I have wonderful news!"

"Come out then and tell us what it is," her mother said. "But first, nick a cookie for yourself and another for Elizabeth."

"How did you manage to get the ingredients to make cookies?" Melania asked Emily as she stepped outside. "And sugar sprinkles too?" She popped a bite of cookie in her mouth with great satisfaction.

"I've found a vast bartering network in this city," Emily confessed. "Ration stamps cannot be traded, but goods certainly can. It's truly the most practical way to manage."

Mutti smiled and patted Emily's knee. "Different times, perhaps, but similar schemes. When I was raising my young family, I found bartering and sharing to be the most human endeavor. It brings people together."

Melania shielded her eyes as she scanned the garden plot. "It looks as if our Victory garden has yielded a bounty of lettuce and peas but little else."

"It's early yet, dear, plus I think we can trust Emily to be as fruitful in her gardening and market endeavors as she is in managing the entire household." Melania watched a look of melancholy pass over her mother's eyes and wondered again how long Mutti would have to endure working at the mill. Clearly, she missed being home.

"So, what's your news?" Mutti's eyes brightened as she looked at Melania.

"Matron Jones asked me to learn more advanced medical skills through the Red Cross. It would be similar to Anna's training."

"For what purpose?" Her mother rose from the bench. "Are you heading overseas as well?"

Emily gathered Elizabeth.

"We'll be in soon," Mutti said, touching Emily's arm as the pair left the garden. "I'll help make a light dinner with some vegetables and the fish Peter brought for us the other day."

"When was Pete here?" Melania asked.

Her mother held up a hand. "Let's finish this conversation first. How did this all come about?"

Melania was surprised that her mother seemed to be concerned about her news, almost as if she was worried.

"The Red Cross is partnering with the University Hospital to train more nurses' aides." Melania paused, her shoulders lifting. "With so many nurses and doctors in war service, they hope to fill the gap here."

"Did Matron ask for an overseas commitment from you?" Mutti's mouth flattened.

Oh, that's what she's worried about, Melania thought.

"Matron Jones didn't ask, and I didn't offer." Melania's lips twisted in thought. "I suspect the Red Cross is eager to link up with the university for future endeavors. Seems every volunteer is a student."

"Are you putting off your education?"

"Oh, dear me, no!" exclaimed Melania, surprised that Mutti seemed to be concerned about that too. "I love school, and while I do appreciate the more challenging medical tasks I've learned at the chapter, it hasn't changed my plans to become a teacher."

"Then why spend an entire month learning medical skills?"

"Well, I want a new challenge. Plus, all my friends will be doing it——Jane, Grace, Meg——even Archie and Jasper. And I'll be allowed to move back to campus earlier." Melania squeezed her hands together in delight. Life at Emily's house was quite dull compared to campus life.

"Archie too. Goodness." Mutti grinned and seemed to relax, perhaps realizing that Melania's plans hadn't really changed all that much.

"The fellas hope the training will give them a chance to be medics when they're drafted." Melania crossed her arms, tilting her head in thought. "I'm unsure what I'll ever do with more medical training." She chuckled. "Maybe there will be a day when one of my students needs me to bandage a cut."

She sat down next to her mother. "Are you worried about Anna, Mutti?" Melania knew the correspondence from her older sister had been sparse but didn't think Anna was in any danger.

Mutti took in a deep breath. "No, not really. It's just not knowing exactly where she is that's bothering me, I suppose. France and the U.S. Army jointly run over twenty hospitals and we haven't heard yet where she's been stationed."

"I'm sure Anna is terribly busy, Mutti. And mail is frightfully slow, isn't it?"

Mutti smiled and squeezed Melania's hand. "My wise daughter."

"Goodness!" Melania pulled away and sprang to her feet. "I need to pack! I hope to move back to campus tomorrow." She darted inside.

The family ate dinner on the porch that evening, the summer breeze thick with humidity.

Melania picked up her glass of lemonade, the fast-melting ice clinking on the sides. "You never did tell me about Peter's visit, Mutti," she said. "I seem to keep missing him." Of all her siblings, she missed Peter the most, especially after spending the entirety of her childhood with him in the house.

"He was here a couple of days ago when you were at the Red Cross packing donations. He waited until after dinner to see you, but you were late if I recall."

"Was anyone with him?" Melania asked casually. She tried not to think about Jim but continued to wonder about him.

"If you're referring to Jim, then no." Her father's frank response caused a warmth to creep up her neck.

"I wasn't necessarily."

"The news isn't good," her father said, ignoring her comment.

"What? What happened to Peter?" Melania leaned forward, desperate for details.

Her mother grabbed her hand. "It's Jim——he's missing."

Melania's face screwed up in confusion. "Missing? From where? The railroad?"

Her father briefly explained Jim's difficulties at the railyard and his eventual departure. Gone, they knew. Where was unknown.

"He and Peter remain good friends, don't they?" Melania's nose wrinkled. "It's not right for Jim to just go off without telling anyone where he is after all our family has done for him." She crossed her arms and frowned. "It seems awfully inconsiderate."

"Your brother regularly looks for Jim at his boardinghouse. Last week, Pete finally caught up with the landlady and discovered Jim's not been seen since mid-June."

"That's over a month! Has anyone looked for him?" Melania's throat went dry and she swallowed hard. "We have to——" She stopped mid-sentence. *What? Find him?* She exhaled heavily, her eyes pricking. Jim's behavior seemed selfish——missing work and disappearing without a word. But he wasn't really like that, was he? Maybe she didn't know him well at all. She shook her head as the thoughts swirled.

"Pete said the landlady told him that Jim just left his things."

"Oh no!" Melania's hand went to her mouth. "That can't be good." Her mind went over the details of Jim's run-ins with railroad coworkers. Maybe something *had* happened to him.

"Peter's checking every lead, asking around." Vati rose from his chair and moved toward the door. "That's all that really can be done."

"And pray," Mutti said as she stood, following Vati.

Melania moved to the porch swing and shut her eyes, letting the events of the day filter through her mind——it had been filled with such ups and downs. The execution of the Tsar and the disappearance of his family were tragic. It felt *personal* somehow, perhaps because the daughters were close to her own age.

The good news of the medical training with the Red Cross coupled with an early move back to campus had buoyed her spirits tremendously. But now, there was trouble in her own world. Jim was missing. Why did it worry her so much?

She sighed heavily and closed her eyes, feeling the evening air whisk the day's humidity away. The sky had darkened to a starry spectacle, and the half-moon shone brightly, bringing her comfort when she looked heavenward several minutes later. She blinked at the lunar lights, whispering quietly to the blanket of darkness around her. "The same moon and stars shine over my brother and sister in Europe and our family in Holmesburg. And the same moon is wherever Jim is." She felt a connection with them all until she realized this was only true if they were still alive and well.

She shivered, struggling to shake the darkness.

Chapter 21

Helene washed her hands at the back pump, the juice and seeds sliding to the ground. She loved the August harvest—the baskets overflowing with produce, and her mind sorted through plans for each variety. She'd can the beans and tomatoes after saving several fresh over the following weeks. Wash and share the second harvest of lettuce crops. Store the onions, potatoes, and carrots in crates in the cellar. She smiled——the ordinariness of a garden's bounty was such a welcome distraction.

The screen door slammed, bringing Helene out of her reverie. Elizabeth plodded out, her bare feet smacking in the water pooled on the brick walkway. The child wrapped her arms around Helene's legs and turned her face, squinting questioningly. "Cookie?"

Helene pulled Lizzie into her arms and deposited her on a nearby bench. "I believe, dear girl, your Mama would think it's too close to supper." Helene handed her a carrot. "How about this instead?"

Elizabeth scooted off the bench and banged the carrot on the wooden planks. Helene chuckled as she moved the baskets of vegetables, one by one, nearer to the back door. Elizabeth stayed near the bench, twirling around, carrot thrust high in the warm air. She sang parts of a song Helene knew Emily had sung to her child before. Elizabeth's voice rose and fell along with the tune, even though she didn't say most of the words. The carrot resumed its role as a drumstick in the child's hand as the song wound down.

"Well, that's one less carrot for the winter storage," Helene said, smiling. She turned toward the garden to gather Elizabeth. Behind her, the screen door creaked on its hinges.

"Perfect timing," she called to whoever was there. "You can help carry in the vegetables."

When she turned back around, Emily stood near the door, as white as a sheet and visibly shaking.

Helene stopped in her tracks, absently squeezing the child closer. "What is it?" Her barely audible words floated across the lawn. Elizabeth wriggled from the tightening grip and slid down Helene's side, padding toward her mother.

Helene noticed the envelope in Emily's hand. "Oh, Lord. What is it?"

"I'm not certain," Emily replied, slowly sitting on the top step. She placed Lizzie on her knee and slid over. "Come and sit. We'll read it together."

Helene felt like she was marching toward the edge of a cliff——unusual envelopes unsettled one like loud door knocks or visiting chaplains. She released the pulverized carrot when she sat, sending it rolling off the step. Elizabeth wriggled down from Emily's lap to retrieve it, and Helene leaned in to peer at the envelope. The return address read: ICRC, Geneva, Switzerland. It was addressed to Mr. & Mrs. Jacob Harvey.

"Whatever could this be? Switzerland?" Helene shook her head to clear the fog seeping into her consciousness. Her heart raced as terrifying thoughts circled in her mind.

Emily took in a deep breath and held it for a moment. "The ICRC is an international branch of the Red Cross. Phillip mentioned it in one of his recent letters. Maybe it's news from Anna. Shall I open it for you?"

"Please," Helene said, staring vacantly ahead, knowing the improbability of it being from Anna, who was in France, not Switzerland.

She turned toward Emily when she heard the missive sliding from its envelope. Helene reached over and ran her fingers over the official seal of the ICRC at the top of the envelope flap.

July 28, 1918. Dear Sir and Madam. It is our duty to inform you that your son, Mathias J. Harvey, has been taken as a prisoner of war in the Hun prison, Camp Rastatt.

Helene released a high-pitched gasp, her hand flying to cover her open mouth. Emily gently squeezed her other hand. "Shall I continue?" Helene nodded ever so slightly as a tear escaped her eye and slid slowly down her cheek.

He was wounded at the battle of Chateau-Thierry and taken prisoner. Be informed that the ICRC's commission is to be a neutral party between warring countries. Our duty is to ensure that prisoners are treated according to the 1907 Hague Regulations requiring that all Prisoners of War receive treatment the same as the detaining country's soldiers. We encourage you to write to your son at the address listed below. Please inform us if there is any service we can provide to your son while he is interned. Regards,

Helene grabbed the letter, crumpling it in her grip. Tears flowed down her face, and Emily embraced her. The pair sat until Jacob's heavy steps sounded in the kitchen nearly an hour later. "Stay," Emily said, standing.

"I'll send Jacob out." She scooped up Elizabeth, fully muddied from play in the garden, and went inside to fetch Jacob.

The couple sat on the back step, Helene's head resting on Jacob's shoulder. He read the letter several times, pursing his lips, not speaking. What could be said? Helene didn't need false reassurance and likely didn't expect it. Finally, Jacob stood, pulled his wife upright, and embraced her briefly before walking toward the produce baskets, picking them both up. He nodded toward the door, and Helene opened it, following in behind him.

"I've heard of this Swiss group," he finally said, setting the baskets on the kitchen table. "I can't say I understand a country remaining neutral in the face of such atrocities——but I commend their humanitarian efforts." Jacob spoke more to fill the space than to engage his wife. She was far from being capable——that he knew. He pushed open the swinging door between the rooms, and Helene shuffled to an upholstered chair, plopping down.

He regarded her from his position on the threshold——her stare was vacant. He caught Emily's eye as the younger woman descended the stairs.

"I've put Elizabeth down early tonight. Can I make you both tomato and cucumber sandwiches?"

"Please," Jacob answered, "but first, can you sit with Helene while I finish a couple of things in the garden?"

"Of course." Emily pulled up a straight-backed chair next to Helene's, taking up her wrinkled hand and holding it between her own.

"We will write him——there, in that place." Helene's voice floated toward him as Jacob went into the kitchen.

"Good," he said to himself. Helene was moving forward with a plan. Jacob knew there was little they could do, but he also knew they *must* do something. He flipped over the envelope from the ICRC. The Swiss letter had taken nearly three weeks to arrive, and he guessed it'd be no faster with correspondence originating here.

He knew a little of the 1907 Hague Convention and its efforts to establish an international code of warfare. The reality, he believed, was likely different, especially after a recent news story told of appalling conditions in some of the camps inspected by the Swiss agency. One of the results was the addition of more humanitarian efforts by the ICRC aimed directly at individual prisoners. "Hmm." He rubbed his chin in thought as the realities of his son's imprisonment sank in.

A moment later, he pushed back into the front room and stood in front of the women. "I've read the Swiss agency sends supplies directly to individual prisoners." He paused and furrowed his brow. "Do you think there's something——food, clothes, blankets, anything——we could send?"

"Send it directly to Mathias?" Emily nodded. "That would be ideal." She smiled at Helene, who had yet to comment. "What do you think, Helene?"

"It sounds impossible." Helene closed her eyes, leaned back in the chair, and was soon asleep.

Jacob moved back into the kitchen and gazed out into the yard at the garden. The harvest could wait, he thought. But then, maybe Helene needed a distraction—something to focus on while they figured out how best to help their son. Jacob ran a jerky hand through his hair and reached for the door handle, stepping out into the waning sunlight. He bent at the garden's edge, grabbed the small hoe sitting near, and began unearthing potatoes.

Helene wrote to Mathias almost weekly, agreeing that Jacob should send whatever money they could spare directly to the ICRC through the Western Union Telegraph office. It was unlikely that it would directly benefit their son——a long shot at best——but it gave both her and Jacob the illusion they were doing something for Mathias.

Jacob maintained a schedule of ten-hour days at the Whitney Mill as the summer heat finally dissipated into crisp, cooler temperatures. Generally, Helene journeyed home from work without Jacob, but Emily and Elizabeth strolled to the streetcar stop to greet her many afternoons.

Helene smiled and greeted the pair when she stepped off the trolley. "A change is coming," she said, waving her hand overhead. "Do you feel the layer of cool air?"

Elizabeth waved her hand over her head and giggled, then ran ahead, seemingly delighted with the crunch of fallen leaves beneath her feet.

Helene smiled and squeezed Emily's hand. "I'm grateful for you and Lizzie, dear."

"As we are for you and Jacob." Emily leaned in and put her arm around Helene's shoulder. "I don't know what we'd have done without you all in our home."

"The summer has brought so much news——the success of the Allied campaigns. But the cost——oh, so many. Then Jim missing——and Mathias . . ." Helene's voice trailed off——the unspoken was the constant worry each woman had for her own family.

"We'll remain hopeful," Emily said eagerly, reaching into her sweater pocket. "This came for you. Answered prayers."

Helene stopped and looked at the crumpled envelope, tears falling as she recognized Mathias's handwriting. The postmark was from weeks ago, but the sight was welcome, nonetheless. She wanted to open the letter straightaway, but Emily was already hurrying down the sidewalk after Elizabeth.

It wasn't unusual for Elizabeth to scamper down the walkway ahead of the women, but the girl knew to stop before the corner and wait for them.

Usually, she would turn and motion for the women to hurry because a cookie was generally the reward at the end of the walk.

Today, though, Elizabeth turned toward home. She pointed and waved at someone or something. Helene shook her head slightly and picked up her pace, nearly catching up to Emily.

"I wonder who she's waving at." Emily quickened her stride, pulling ahead of Helene again, and scooped up her daughter, peering down the street. Her hand flew to her mouth and a small "no" squeaked out.

Helene raced the last few steps toward the corner. Down the street, a uniformed man stood on their front porch, lifting his fist to knock on their door.

A moan escaped her lips as she put her arm around Emily's shoulder and moved them forward. They said nothing as they walked, seemingly in slow motion, toward the man, who continued to knock on their front door. After receiving no answer, he turned to look around and spotted them. He tipped his head in acknowledgment but didn't call out.

CHAPTER 22

Minneapolis Tribune • September 1918 • NO NEED TO WORRY! *"Spanish influenza does not exist in Minneapolis and never has, but it probably will reach here during the fall." ~ City Health Commissioner Dr. H. M. Guildford* The Spanish Influenza has made a ferocious sweep of the east coast. The illness earned its moniker due to its devastation in Spain. Hundreds of cases of sickness and death have been reported in nearly every New England city. Speculation abounds about the cause of the disease. The summer war news might have overshadowed reports of influenza in the military camps across the country, making one wonder if our soldiers carried more with them to Europe than the American fighting spirit. And now, authorities are speculating the military brought the disease back again to the United States. New York City's harbor has been a regular unloading spot for the ill soldiers and crew. When the Norwegian vessel, Bergensfjord, arrived in the harbor in late August, Port ambulances immediately whisked

ELEVEN SICK CREW AND PASSENGERS TO A CITY HOS-
PITAL. INFECTED PASSENGERS BECAME ILL WITH A NEW
AND PARTICULARLY AGGRESSIVE FORM OF INFLUEN-
ZA, WHILE MANY ILL SAILORS RECOVERED ENOUGH TO
BE PUT MERELY UNDER OBSERVATION BY THE NYC
HEALTH DEPARTMENT. OVER THE PAST SEVERAL WEEKS,
MORE SHIPS BEARING SICK SAILORS HAVE ARRIVED IN
NEW YORK HARBOR. THE STATE'S HEALTH COMMIS-
SIONER PLACED THE ENTIRE PORT OF NEW YORK UN-
DER QUARANTINE JUST DAYS AGO! WHILE SIMILAR STO-
RIES ABOUND AT OTHER EASTERN HARBORS, MINNEAPO-
LIS' HEALTH COMMISSIONER, GUILDFORD, HAS CONFI-
DENCE THAT OUR FAIR CITY IS INSULATED FROM SUCH
AN EPIDEMIC, STATING, "WE ARE SHIELDED HERE FROM
THE EXTREME SITUATION ON THE COAST."

Melania's heart swelled with pride. The Red Cross medical training had been an intense program——learning about common diseases, injuries, patient care, and means and methods of quick and practical assistance to the doctors and nurses. With many doctors serving in Europe and beyond, skilled medical assistants were essential. Melania, Jane, and the rest of the students had done it, and Matron Jones beamed as she gathered the graduates to her side near the university foyer. "The program's future is guaranteed with your talent and dedication," she said with a smile.

The group cheered and hugged, congratulating each other on their accomplishment. Matron Jones clapped her hands loudly. "Wrap your aprons tightly. There's no room for slovenly dress on the floor."

Melania smoothed down her apron after cinching it firmly in the back, leaning in to whisper to Jane. "I'm not sure how much we'll be able to do before the semester starts, but we certainly look smart."

The young women wore crisp white aprons, and the men had long white coats. While all Red Cross volunteers had the iconic red cross *somewhere* on their uniform, these graduates also wore armbands with a large red cross.

Matron Jones raised her hands above her head and clapped them again, this time more loudly, moving toward the front of the line of medical assistants. "Come! Line up. You'll be presented to the doctors and nurses through a promenade in the hospital's sick ward." Matron's body wiggled to a full-up, shoulders-back position as she began marching down the hall toward the hospital.

"Gosh, I feel like we're following the Pied Piper." Jane rolled her eyes. "I certainly won't miss Matron's clapping."

Melania giggled, nudging her friend forward. "Move, move!"

Matron pushed through the hospital doors and led the group in a zig-zag fashion through the rows of beds and patients, commenting loudly on various things, including patient care and process. She pointed out equipment and its uses along the way, stopping the group occasionally so they could see work in action. She directed the graduates to pay heed to the volunteer schedule clipped to a board on the wall, emphasizing the importance of being prompt and prepared for each shift, two of the three Ps instilled in them during training——*Pressed*, *Prompt*, and *Prepared*.

The ward buzzed with activity as the students moved through the space, their parade feeling a bit intrusive to Melania. "I feel like we shouldn't traipse through here." She looked past the group in front of her.

Suddenly, the heavy rear double doors swung open, loudly banging the wall in the process. "Move, move!" a voice called from behind them. Melania and Jane pushed themselves up against the wall as two men with a gurney rushed past them.

"He's so young," Jane whispered, eyes wide as she stared at the man on the stretcher. "I wonder——" She was interrupted by another pair of men rushing through with another young man on a gurney.

"They're cadets," Melania murmured back. "See the brown shirts and pants?"

The medical assistants scattered as the stretchers continued to arrive, leaving Matron Jones alone at the room's far end. She stood, arms crossed, seeming to survey the space as young, brown-bedecked men were placed in random beds throughout, in haste and, seemingly, without order. The patients soon outnumbered the medical staff. Once again, Matron Jones raised her hands and clapped, summoning the graduates to her side.

Jane sighed and elbowed Melania. "One more time, I guess." She jerked her head toward the Matron. "Let's go."

When most of the medical students had gathered, Matron spoke. "It seems it would be helpful if we remain on the floor right now. It's unclear what brings these cadets in——foodborne illness, likely. Regardless, this would be an opportune time to practice what you've learned." She raised an eyebrow and cocked her head toward the group.

Some begged off with one excuse or another, but neither Melania nor Jane had a compelling reason to leave. "I'll stay," they said in unison. Melania smiled at her friend, grateful they'd be together in this unexpected experience.

Matron Jones gathered the group of six remaining medical assistants and introduced them to the floor charge nurse. "It appears you're understaffed," she said as she looked down from her very tall frame at the short and stout woman standing behind the desk. The nurse's face wrinkled into a scowl, and Matron Jones quickly cleared her throat, continuing, "because of the unexpected arrival of the cadets."

"Oh yes——most unforeseen. Food illness, likely." The nurse nodded with conviction.

"What I predict as well," Matron Jones said. "I've six newly trained medical assistants as part of the Red Cross and University program."

The charge nurse shrugged. "Dandy," she replied flatly. "I really must get on." She looked past Matron Jones toward the clamor of activity.

"Dear me." Matron Jones put her hand to her chest. "I thought *everyone* was aware of the Red Cross's efforts with the university." She paused and then swept her hand past the group of starched assistants. Melania gulped, hoping Matron wouldn't ask them to speak to their training.

"These students have comprehensive medical assistant train-ing——*much* more than the typical Red Cross volunteer," Matron con-tinued, taking in a deep breath. "They can help. *Now*."

Melania's brows went up, embarrassed on Matron's behalf as she strug-gled to make her point.

"Tell me how I can help," Melania said to the nurse, the sentiment then echoed by the others.

The nurse scanned the room and then pointed to the far corner, where a man lay unattended. "There," she said to Melania. "Get him settled and ready for examination."

The nurse pointed to the next assistant. "You, there," and sent off each person accordingly before dismissing Matron Jones with a sharp nod.

Melania moved around the hectic space, weaving in and out of the rows of beds, settling patients, applying compresses, fetching supplies for doctors and nurses, cleaning up messes, and drawing partitions around several beds as the room filled. She stepped away from the sink in the back after rinsing out an enamel dish and pulled the chain around her neck, drawing up the small watch attached to it. *Eight o'clock. It couldn't be.* It'd been late morning when she'd first marched through, and now black darkness seeped through the cracks of the drawn shades. Her stomach rumbled, further evidence of the late hour——the coffee she'd managed to gulp down a few hours ago still sloshing in her empty belly.

By the last count, nearly two dozen cadets had been added to the mix of patients in the ward. Once she'd gotten her first cadet settled, she'd anticipated heading back to the dormitory, but the hospitals were sorely understaffed with the war——something she'd only understood in theory before today. The well-ordered patient intake process Matron had pointed out earlier had already broken down with the *unexpected arrivals*, as Matron had called them.

Certainly, emergencies were normal, weren't they? She watched as doctors and nurses moved from cadet to cadet, tending and conferring often, yet mayhem appeared to rule. The medical assistants would be called on for random things: "Fetch another cool compress." "Retake this man's temperature." "Run, quickly! Get a bucket." "Coffee. For me, if you please."

Matron had often lauded the *system* and *order* in the medical world. Melania shook her head. This was not what she'd expected. She sighed and scanned the room. It was blessedly calm now, with most of the young men sleeping. She walked toward the wall where the volunteer schedule was posted and flipped the pages, jotting down her assignments on a scrap of paper. She wasn't on the schedule for another two days. *Thank goodness.* She was so tired. The charge nurse appeared, touching her shoulder, and Melania jumped slightly and turned. "Yes, Nurse Bradley?" She dreaded the thought of another task.

"Nice work, Miss Harvey. Go get some rest now."

Melania found Jane sitting on a bench outside the double doors, looking greatly fatigued. "Oh, Mel," Jane whispered. "What did we get ourselves into?"

Jane hooked her arm in Melania's as the pair walked up the massive stone steps of the hospital later that week. "I'm not sure if I'm happy or relieved that the university has postponed the start of classes."

"I hear you." Melania nodded, her brow furrowed. "They said it was to allow the influenza situation to clear up, but then I read that the city's health commissioner is still saying that Spanish influenza hasn't reached Minneapolis yet."

Jane snorted. "That health expert needs to visit our hospital. Goodness! We're near to capacity with the Dunwoody Training Camp men being added to those already here from the university's Army program."

Melania pulled open the door, and the women climbed the stairs to the sick ward. "Well, here we go again." Melania regarded Jane. "Are you ready?"

Jane hung her coat on the peg outside the door and secured her apron. "As I'll ever be." She held open the door until Melania finished putting on her own garb.

"Who are those straight-backed men with the clipboards?"

Jane leaned in and whispered. "You mean those *boys* with the clipboards?" She tittered. "They barely look old enough to shave."

"Where's nurse Bradley?" Melania glanced around the room.

One of the boys sauntered toward her and Jane. "She's down for the count. I'm in charge now, and I've created a list." He flipped open the clean ledger marked with columns. "We'll record admittances——name, date, and status for each person entering or leaving the ward."

"Don't we do that already?" Jane's eyes narrowed.

The man harumphed. "Did you see the mess from the last several days? That system was not created to handle the unpredictable nature of this situation." He snapped his fingers several times. "It's rapid-fire decisions and actions most of the time." He exhaled in exasperation. "Is this your first day or something?"

"No, of course not," Melania replied indignantly, and then she glanced at the sheet. "I see. A column for symptoms and another for deaths."

Jane frowned. "Have we had any?"

"We will, and they'll be noted in red," the man said. "And we're likely to see many more admittances." He handed a stack of the sheets to Jane. "Post one at the end of every cot. Each patient's information will be added to the primary ledger at the end of the day. You," he said, turning to Melania, "slide a privacy curtain around the new beds."

The girls went their separate ways, and when Melania pulled the last curtain around the end cot, she spied the boy in charge paging through the ledger book at the nurse's station. She came toward him and dropped her chin. "Ahem."

He glanced up. "Yes?"

"Well, sir." She nearly giggled when his voice caught in his throat. "Your name might be helpful."

"Elvin Emerson." He narrowed his eyes at her and held up a list before tacking it to the wall behind him.

Melania leaned forward and glanced at the list of tasks divided into categories depending on the status. The list for medical aides was the longest and filled with the least desirable chores. "Hmm. I was just going to ask you what you'd like me to do next."

"Do you need direction?"

"No, of course not, but I didn't want to disrupt—the *system.*"

Elvin Emerson ran his long bony finger down the list. "Pick something," he said, moving from behind the desk with a self-important huff.

"What was that about?" Jane sidled up alongside Melania.

"Nothing." Melania sighed and giggled. "I was just checking the limits of the system." She pointed to Emerson's list. "Seems Elvin Emerson has it all mapped out—how tasks can get done amidst rapid-fire decisions."

Jane frowned. "Looks to me like the same things we've been doing for days now, before the young Mr. Emerson took charge. The only difference is that he wrote them down." She shrugged and lifted a brow. "Off to fill water pitchers."

"Gosh," Melania said as she and Jane left the hospital several hours later. "Elvin Emerson may have been on to something or he just got lucky. The day *did* seem to be a bit more organized."

"Or," Jane said as she pushed open the heavy doors to the outside, "everyone has just gotten into their stride."

"That may be. I almost felt like I was moving around in a trance for the last hour, moving from task to task." Melania sucked in a deep breath. "Goodness, something was needing to be done at every turn."

Several days later, sixteen University Hospital nurses were bedridden with the disease. More of the boys, who were third- and fourth-year medical students, were summoned to fill in for missing doctors and nurses. Within the same period, the hospital's standard hierarchy was turned on its head, and norms were set aside inside the medical facility——*everyone* was battling the same fierce enemy. They'd even organized bunk rooms within the hospital so medical staff would always be nearby. Emerson's list remained tacked on the wall, but lines quickly blurred as to who did what. The reality of the illness became apparent, and they largely disregarded the health commissioner's commentary on the virulence of the disease. They knew firsthand that it was exceptionally infectious and difficult to diagnose and control.

"I feel as if we're unconsciously trying to contain the disease with the windows and curtains pulled," Melania said to Jane before peeking out of a slit on the side of the tall, mullioned windows. "I wonder if it would help more to open them up and let the breeze and sunshine in."

Jane shrugged and nodded. "I agree. It's stifling in here." She began to walk down the narrow aisle between the beds before stopping and turning back. "Sneak out for lunch later?"

"Gosh, that'd be grand. *If* we'll even get a full break." Melania lifted a brow and then turned when she heard her name.

"Here, Harvey."

A medical student summoned Melania to a figure collapsed near where he was working. "Quickly!"

"Oh goodness." Melania rushed to the assistance of a young nurse who'd collapsed on the floor beside a patient she'd been treating.

"Let me help you up." Melania reached under the woman's arm. She still didn't understand how this disease could hit so suddenly——it seemed one moment someone was healthy, and the next they were struck down. It only took an instant for a doctor or nurse to go from caregiver to patient.

"Oh, my head," the nurse moaned, squeezing her eyes shut. She sat up, brushed the cap off, winced, and immediately lay back down. "I can't."

"Betsy! Help, please!" Melania called to the closest nurse. Betsy popped over and assisted in getting the fallen nurse into bed and conducting a brief assessment.

When Betsy had finished, she shrugged, shaking her head. "Get her comfortable. We'll just have to check back." She moved away and then turned back after a few steps. "Cool compress, aspirin, and a pile of blankets."

Melania pulled the privacy curtain around the bed and undressed the nurse, her hand touching the woman's scorching forehead. "Oh my, you're burning up."

The lethargic woman didn't respond, so Melania carefully nudged her arms into the holes of the gown——each movement effecting a moan. Once the patient was settled beneath the blanket, Melania left to fetch a cool cloth, returning to find the nurse sleeping, inhaling and exhaling slow and ragged breaths. Melania wished she had time to sit with the nurse, to be there when she woke up, but there was no luxury like that. Instead, she wrote the woman's name and symptoms on the chart and then glanced at the large industrial wall clock, her own watch buried underneath the layers of white. She scribbled down the date and time before moving out from behind the curtain. *One less nurse on the sick ward.* They could ill-afford it, with beds packed into every spare corner.

A loud noise burst from a bed across the room. Melania raced over, too late to catch the rush of vomit. The cadet moaned in pain, and she snatched his nearby bedpan, catching another ejection. She wiped his brow and then his mouth when it seemed he'd nothing left in his gut.

"Here, drink this," she offered, holding out a cup of water.

"My throat—— I don't——" He wrapped his hand around his neck.

"It'll be the best thing for your throat after getting washed in stomach acid." Melania held the cup to his lips. "Just a little, that's all."

"There," she said after he'd sipped a few drops. "Let's prop you up a bit." He winced in pain.

"What's your name?"

"Lawrence," he squeaked.

"Well, Lawrence," Melania smiled. "I imagine you'll be hungry, emptying your stomach as you did. I'll stop by later with something to eat." She patted his hand and pulled the blanket around him. Silly, she thought——such a matronly gesture considering they were around the same age. She looked out from the curtain at the quiet ward, a rare and likely temporary situation. The vital need for human connection washed over her, and she pulled a chair to Lawrence's bedside. "What would you like from the cafeteria?"

Lawrence put his hand to his throat and shook his head slightly.

"Oh my! Forgive me!" Melania again patted his hand. "The last thing you want to do is talk."

Lawrence's mouth turned up slightly at one corner. "Pudding, then. That's what I'll bring you." She rose and reached for a black leather-bound book sitting on the side table, pulling out a photo of a young woman. "Your wife? Girlfriend?" The man's head shook ever so slightly, and Melania quickly slipped the picture between the pages again, mortified. *What am I doing?* This was not helping the patient——the man clearly needed sleep. His eyes shut, and his breath became shallow as he drifted off. She quickly updated his chart and left, hoping Lawrence would forgive her silly indulgence.

Melania glanced at the clock again, fully registering the hours gone.

It was half-past six——she'd been on duty since mid-morning without a break——likely the reason for her foolish behavior. The lengthy roster of those under her care was added to frequently, giving her the sense of making little to no progress. She ran her finger down the names on the list. "Maybelle Anderson, Stephen Weber, George Smith," she said, mentally assessing her plan. The men's beds were next to each other——Maybelle was in the other room, near the exit to the back stairs. She decided to quickly check on the men before slipping down the back steps for a quick tuck. There was no one there, save herself, to make sure she got sustenance and rest, however slight. Her shoes clip-clopped along on the tile floor as she made her way to the last row of beds, the noise reminding her how her feet ached, swollen after the long hours without rest.

The whispered voices of the medical staff, consulting, diagnosing, and soothing, blended with moans from patients, causing a steady hum to vibrate across the space. Occasionally, a shout would shatter the droning sound, begging for notice. Days ago, Melania and the other aides had begun to respond only to the commands of the doctors, med students, and nurses, suppressing the urge to heed every distressing cry. The patients were in pain, their bodies aching mercilessly——some complaining of general aches and joint pain, while others cried out from severe headaches or sore throats. The staff focused on the most immediate and pressing needs, moment by moment, as they were pulled in many directions.

Melania smiled at each awake patient as she made her way down the row. She felt a deep need to acknowledge them as individuals, not merely sick patients, giving any human kindness she could provide.

"Well, Mr. Weber," she said brightly when she reached the bedside of the gaunt man stretched out under a gray blanket——his face remarkably similar in color to the coverlet. "I'm going to take your temperature."

She noticed that Stephen Weber was no more than twenty years old as she sat on the bed. *Another close to my age.* But then, they were on a college campus. Of course, they would be treating mostly young adults.

Stephen attempted to push himself up but cried out in pain at the undertaking. "I am——sorry," he sputtered.

"Please. Don't be. Lie back down." Melania gently pushed his chest toward the bed. She withdrew a small vial of powder from her pocket, poured a dose into a cup, and mixed it with water from the bedside pitcher before handing it to Stephen. "Here, take some of this."

Stephen blinked his eyes slowly and opened his mouth slightly, allowing Melania to pour the liquid down his throat. He writhed in pain, and she put her hand over his. "This should soon help ease the tenderness."

Just two days ago, only physicians, nurses, or medical students could administer any type of drug. But with the scores of new patients every day, every hour, the medical assistants had been given latitude to dispense aspirin or Salicin, both common pain-reducing medicines. Each dose needed to be correctly charted——not a perfect system, but it allowed the needs of patients to be more promptly met.

Melania pulled the thermometer from its protective case and inserted it under his tongue when Stephen calmed. The red line of mercury rapidly made its way up the scale, topping at 103 degrees Fahrenheit. She removed the thermometer and wiped it clean with an antiseptic-soaked cloth before stowing it back in its case.

"This should help you feel better until the medicine takes effect." She laid a cool cloth on his forehead. He shut his eyes and quickly succumbed to sleep or unconsciousness——she wasn't sure which. Melania rose and moved to Mr. Smith's bed.

After checking on Mr. Smith, Melania darted to the back stairway with plans to return straightaway to attend to Maybelle Anderson. Her steps pounded down the first three flights of stairs. She paused on the landing, leaned against the wall, and shut her eyes, taking deep, slow breaths. The day had been long, already an hour longer than the eight-hour shift she was assigned, and orderlies were bringing in more sick men nearly every hour. She opened her eyes and straightened, holding onto the railing and lifting one foot at a time to unbuckle the shoes that squeezed her weary feet. "Lord, give me strength," she prayed as she restarted her descent.

Melania paid for a bowl of chicken soup and a cup of coffee before moving to a table of other medical assistants and nurses. "Hello," she offered the group, setting her tray down and pulling up a chair.

"You look exhausted," one of the nurses noted. "Are those mighty medical students running you ragged?" Others chuckled. The ward was divided, essentially, with a kinship between the nurses and medical assistants.

"No. It's fine. Just a long day." Melania smiled slightly and then bent to her soup——the warm liquid soothing her but also making her think of the throat pain plaguing many on the ward. Two medical students, deep in conversation, sat across from her several minutes later as she finished the last dregs of her coffee.

"Yes, it *was* confirmed," one man declared. "A man at City Hospital, not even a soldier, became ill after returning from visiting his son at Camp Dix."

"Then it must be true." The other man slapped the tabletop. "Soldiers are bringing this damn influenza with them when they return to the U.S." He was nearly spitting the words.

"They couldn't have known, surely," a nurse piped in, turning from a nearby table. The men's heads snapped toward the woman, clearly annoyed at the unwelcome addition to their conversation. "It's really beside the point," the nurse continued, "the origin of the disease at this juncture. What with . . ."

One of the medical students stood up, cutting her off mid-sentence. "Don't be ridiculous! Of course the origin of the disease is important." The man confidently planted his hands on his hips. Melania pulled back as if preparing for a battle to ensue.

"Medical scholars teach the importance of identifying the source of illness to understand its spread, but nurses wouldn't be privy to *that* information." The man finished with a brusque grumble and turned away.

"Pompous fools. As if we have time for that now. We need to save lives, not gather research or lay blame." The nurse stomped from the cafeteria, with Melania quickly following.

At the top of the stairs, she stood in the doorway and looked over the space. The flickering lamps barely illuminated the room. She shivered. Despite the balmy autumn weather, a storm gathered inside and out. A dark cloud of uncertainty hung over the entire institution, obscuring hope.

CHAPTER 23

MINNEAPOLIS TRIBUNE • LATE SEPTEMBER 1918 • INFLUENZA IS HERE! CIVILIAN, MILITARY, AND SCHOOL OFFICIALS ANNOUNCED YESTERDAY THAT INFLUENZA HAS OFFICIALLY MADE ITS WAY TO MINNEAPOLIS. LEADERS IN ALL AREAS ARE DILIGENTLY WORKING TOGETHER TO DETERMINE APPROPRIATE STEPS TO MITIGATE THE SPREAD OF THE DISEASE. CITY LEADERS AND MILITARY AUTHORITIES ESTIMATE APPROXIMATELY 1,000 CASES, INCLUDING OVER 50 SICK ARMY SOLDIERS AT FORT SNELLING HOSPITAL AND SCORES OF OTHERS, INCLUDING NURSES, ILL WITH INFLUENZA AT THE UNIVERSITY HOSPITAL. AS HEALTH COMMISSIONER GUILDFORD EXPECTS MANY UNREPORTED CIVILIAN CASES, HE ADVISES ALL CITY RESIDENTS TO "TAKE CARE IF THEY BEGIN TO FEEL ILL."

Jim made his way through the crowded outdoor market in the Swede Hollow neighborhood on the edge of Phelan Creek in east St. Paul. It was just a short walk from his current lodgings——a boardinghouse in the Irish-settled Connemara neighborhood. Both areas were home to primarily poor and underemployed immigrant groups, yet the feeling of community was strong, even as newer immigrant groups merged with the established.

The market was a perfect example of camaraderie and a favorite destination for Jim——the smells and rhythms reminded him of time on the farm with his Irish grandparents. Vendors hawked the last of their summer produce, dried meat, and baked items. With the strict war rations, the hawkers formed a conglomerate, combining their goods and splitting profits——desperate times begetting ingenuity. *"Food will win the war,"* Herbert Hoover reminded the country with posters plastered on buildings and posts. Much of the flour in the market was a combination of nuts and ground legumes combined with a small amount of low-grade ration flour. No one could be sure what was in a cake or a cookie, but the longing for better days made many ignore what they didn't know.

Jim paused at one of his favorite spots and pointed to a generous square of cake, paying the woman for it and continuing on, enjoying both the treat and the din of the crowds.

Jim had made his way to the Connemara neighborhood when he'd finally been released from police custody in June——he'd had just enough coins in his pocket for a bed. He knew the police had nothing to link him to a German spy ring. It was an absurd notion, but it was evident the Minneapolis mayor's office pushed for *any* links to bolster their nativist efforts, regardless of how flimsy. Jim had been sure his fate was sealed——that he'd become one of the mayor's scapegoats. But he'd gotten off easy compared to a farmer in western Minnesota who had been whipped, tarred, and feathered by a group of men who had neither evidence against him nor authority over him. Shocking occurrences such as this littered the nation's newspapers, reminding Jim how difficult separating oneself from a German heritage was, especially if someone was gunning for you. He could only imagine the lengths to which the mayor would go to keep the spotlight off himself, especially since von Esson was a German *and* a socialist. *Power*, it seemed to Jim, had a random hierarchy, with the ranks and order determined by whoever happened to wear a badge, hold an office, or be most fervent in pursuit of the enemy.

As Jim bit off an edge of the spice cake, he shivered, though the October day held a trace of warmth. But he couldn't keep his mind from going back to his three days in police custody. That last night, he'd been tossed back in his cell after another hours-long attempt by the police *to get to the heart* of Jim's anti-American activities. Somehow, they knew he had worked at the railroad. Had a complaint been filed, or was the silly little badge the stationmaster wore real? Valid? Jim had thought it was mostly bluster.

Over and over again, Jim had professed his loyalty to America, discounting the railroad incidents as simply a misunderstanding with a coworker.

"I don't know what was eating O'Malley," Jim explained to the officers about his former workmate. "I helped him home that night."

"What about the stationmaster? He says you're a no-good scoundrel."

"Based on what evidence?" Jim fired back, straining to remain composed. "I worked hard and long hours for the railroad." He sat upright in the chair and looked directly into his questioners' eyes. "If you ask, there *are* people who will agree with that." *Who?* He was uncertain how far his condemnation reached. But surely Peter would vouch for him.

Finally, after three days of intermittent questioning, one officer asked Jim where he grew up. "You wouldn't likely know it," Jim responded. "A place called Augusta, west of here. Our farm is on Reilly Lake."

The officer had perked up. "I know that place! My cousin farms near there." His voice enlivened at the connection. "Edwin Peterson's my family. I've fished many a time on Reilly Lake. Good walleye, for sure." He slapped his knee at the recollection.

The sergeant in charge elbowed the chatty officer in the ribs, and Peterson ceased talking, rubbing his side, giving his partner a sideways look. The conversation soon wrapped up, and Officer Peterson led Jim back to his cell.

"I'll see what I can do for you," he offered as he ushered Jim inside the barred enclosure. "Imagine, a fella from Reilly Lake."

Jim shook his head. What were the chances that a perfect stranger, a policeman no less, would do anything for him merely on the nostalgia of a fishing hole? He laid back on his bunk and dozed.

Suddenly the cell door clanked open, and Officer Peterson was inside. "You're outta here, Wirth. Don't make me regret it."

Jim had left the 5th Street police station that summer morning and, with the sun barely over the horizon, hopped the first trolley car that came along. It had rolled past the boardinghouse, past the railyard, out of Minneapolis city limits, crossing over the Mississippi into St. Paul. As the sun had risen over the tall city buildings, peace and certainty had washed over him. His new home. Jim had disembarked at the first stop in St. Paul and made his way toward the east side of town, unsure of his destination but walking in the direction of the rising sun.

It had been a good choice.

Jim finished the last chunk of cake and shook off the memories. He strolled toward the apple peddler, but the smell of pork chops on an open fire drew him away. His mouth watered, and he dug for coins, a little splurge on his birthday——another, in truth, since the cake was meant to be his only treat. The smell of sizzling meat wafted through the air, punctuated by puffs of smoke rising as the man rotated the chops over the flame.

"I'll have one, please," Jim said, dropping a coin in the man's hand.

The man grabbed a hearty portion from the flames and handed it over. Jim took a bite, and the juices dribbled down his chin. He wiped it on his sleeve, accidentally elbowing a man next to him, sending beer foaming down the man's arm.

"Hey! Watch yourself!" The man's face showed more lightheartedness than anger.

"My apologies, sir." Jim held up his hand. "I didn't see you there. Can I buy you another?" Jim nodded toward the man's mug.

The man grinned. "Sure, fella. The beer man's over there." He pointed to the edge of the market.

"I don't recall beer at the market before."

"Damaged keg. The brewery sells them here by the glass."

"The brewery? Prager's?" Jim *had* noticed that before.

"You bet! I probably dented this one myself." The man guffawed, conspiratorially winking.

"You work there, then?"

"Yep. I'm the brewmaster. Been with Prager's fifteen years."

"Are they hiring?" Jim asked, suddenly feeling inspired to make a change.

"Whoa, buddy." The man held up his hand in jest. "With all these questions, I'll have this mug drained before you get me a new one."

"You're right. My apologies." Jim moved toward the beer tent, but the man caught him by the arm.

"Just jesting, pal. As a matter of fact, Prager's is hiring. Cellar rats."

"What?" Jim scrunched his face.

"Another question?" The man laughed heartily, slapping Jim on the back.

"Sorry." Jim shrugged.

"The cellar crew works on the lower floor, cleaning and taking care of the odd jobs for the fermenting and capping. It's physical work, but you look like a strapping young man. What's your name, son?" The older man stuck out his thick, calloused hand.

"Jim. Jim Reilly."

"Nice to meet ya, Reilly. Sven Olson." He put his large arm around Jim's shoulders and turned the younger man toward the beer vendor. "Now go get my beer!"

Jim dug the last coin out of his pocket and purchased a new mug for the man. After delivering it, he walked north toward the sprawling Prager Brewery, the property flanked by an imposing mansion. Jim had worked odd jobs since his arrival in St. Paul, planning to make do with limited funds until he was drafted. In early September, he'd registered under his legal name, James Patrick Wirth, but he'd been using his grandparents' surname around town. It was plain easier to be Irish than German these days, and he felt freedom from the shackles of his German heritage. He liked being out from under suspicion and felt a growing sense of community in this neighborhood.

Perhaps the brewery would take him short-term until his number was called——every employer eager for workers these days. A little extra scratch clanging around in his pockets wasn't a bad idea either. He opened the large gates and walked toward the massive stone building.

CHAPTER 24

Helene stepped off the trolley and breathed in the smell of drying leaves and smoke billowing from the chimneys. It had gone on with Emily long enough, she decided as she walked toward home. Winter was coming, and the cold, blustery days would do no better for bringing Emily from her dark state. In fact, they may cause her to burrow in more deeply. Emily had been grief-stricken since she'd learned her husband was missing in action that recent September afternoon when the uniformed man paid them a visit. Since then, inquiries into Phillip's status yielded the same unhelpful response. *It was an extensive and lengthy battle*, Emily had been told many times—*details beyond that are sketchy*. Helene had assured the young woman that Phillip was missing but presumed alive. It made little difference to Emily, and many days, Helene came home from work to find her sitting in a chair, staring blankly ahead while Elizabeth played at her feet. She struggled to focus on household work, leaving many daily tasks undone. The young woman was pale and thin, eating meagerly, and she and Lizzie stopped meeting Helene at the streetcar in the afternoons.

"Hello, Lizzie darling," Helene said brightly as she entered the house several minutes later. She hugged the toddler and looked around, finding Emily sitting in the exact spot she'd left her this morning. Helene went through to the kitchen and gathered a plate of iced buns she'd made yesterday, setting them on a tray, along with glasses of cider.

She carried them into the living room and smiled at Emily. "Let's talk before we get dinner started."

Emily turned, and a horrified look crossed her face. She stood. "I'm sorry, Helene. I'll get dinner."

Helene shook her head. "It'll wait. Sit, let's talk." She put a bun on a plate and slid it toward Emily. "I know you're in pain."

Emily blinked back tears.

"The waiting is most cruel. I know that," Helene added.

Emily dabbed an errant tear.

"Regardless of where Phillip is, you *must* carry on." Helene didn't want to be harsh but knew her words were necessary.

"I——I can't——what if?" Emily shrank into the chair.

"There's no use in borrowing trouble. There are no answers to the *what-if* questions. Today, we know Phillip is missing. Today, you must rise up and live with hope for his safe return." Helene stood, pulling the young woman to her feet, and looking straight into her eyes. "I'm here for you, and we'll continue praying for Phillip's safe return just as we pray for Mathias. The Lord will give us strength while we wait. We'll get through this together."

Emily nodded and sniffled.

"Let's make dinner together." Helene moved toward the kitchen, hoping she'd gotten through to Emily.

Peter came up the walkway later that evening. "Hello, Vati," he said as he joined his father on the porch.

Vati nodded a greeting as the smoke from his pipe swirled overhead. He patted his breast pocket. "Sorry. I don't have a smoke for you."

Peter shrugged, his breath coming out in vapors as he spoke. "It's all right." He pulled his coat closed and buttoned it, following his father's gaze to the bright stars in the clear dark sky.

"The ladies? Are they well?" Peter said after some time and then chuckled. "I'm referring to Mutti and Mrs. Pritchard, of course."

"Yes. They're both endeavoring to bear up under the shadow of worry."

"About Mr. Pritchard and Mathias?"

"Mostly. It's a difficult time for young Emily." His father exhaled heavily. "Your Mutti, though, she's sensible. It took her some time, but she understands the sorrow of war——a perspective that comes with age, perhaps."

"Any news on Mathias?"

Vati pressed his lips together and rubbed his chin. "Nothing other than confirmation from the International Red Cross that they've received our donations."

"Donations?"

Vati shrugged. "We've sent some money and supplies, but I wonder how much is put to helping Mathias. The ICRC told us we could supply *our* prisoner with things he may need——clothes, food, blankets, the like." He laughed dryly. "As if that were possible. Mail is slow, and a package is likely searched and pilfered many times throughout its journey." He crossed his arms over his chest and leaned back. "I guess it's supposed to make us feel like we're doing something meaningful for him."

"Mutti writes?"

"Yes, continually. I think it's what helps her the most——the effort to not forget her son in need."

Peter's brows went up, and he let out a long, slow sigh. "I wonder how Frank is faring. Have you received any word from him?"

"I did. He'll be at the St. Paul base soon if he's not there already."

"That's grand news." Peter was due on the base in a week. It would be terrific to see his brother before they went their separate ways. "Everyone's been called up now, save August."

"Duty." Vati coughed into the night air.

"Shall we go back inside?"

"No, just a tickle," Vati assured him. "Plus, war talk won't help either of them." He tilted his head toward the house and took in a deep breath.

"It's good, right? Allied successes and German retreats."

"Ja. Reports say German forces have become disorganized with the frequency of attacks." Jacob snorted. "Wait a few weeks, and they'll be changing another street name. *George S. Patton Avenue.*"

Peter chortled. "Likely. But Patton's efforts in France have been notable." He leaned on the porch railing and looked into the sky in thoughtful reflection. "I wonder where I'll end up. France too?"

"Training will take some time, so it's anybody's guess."

"A month or more, they tell me."

They stood in silence before his father spoke into the darkness. "You're a good man and will be a good soldier."

"I'll do my best, Vater," Peter answered just as his mother opened the door.

"Such a somber mood out here," she said with lightness in her voice. "Come in and join us for pie."

"Sure, Mutti." Peter knew Mutti's burdens weighed heavily on her, and his and Frank's impending enlistments would only add to her worry.

Vati snuffed his pipe, and Peter followed him inside. The men hung their coats and then settled in front of the fire.

"I'll be back with some pie in a few minutes." Mutti moved through the swinging door to the kitchen.

"Such service we get from that woman." Vati chuckled and then wagged his finger at his son. "Don't repeat that I called her '*that wo man.*"

Peter laughed, appreciating the lighter mood despite it lasting only a few moments.

"Apparently, St. Paul isn't suffering the number of influenza cases as is Minneapolis."

Peter glanced at his father and saw the lines of worry across his fore-head. Influenza seemed to be adding another complicated dimension to these days of war.

"Their mayor claims there's no epidemic in his city——the situation under control." Vati raised a brow. "It's been an interesting back and forth between the twin towns." He chuckled. "I've taken to getting a paper from each city to see the contrasting views."

Peter nodded. "A bit of a ruse?"

"Who knows?" Jacob stood and moved to the hearth, poking at the fire. "Minneapolis and St. Paul have very different views on the severity of Spanish influenza and how to deal with it. As with most things, time will tell which city is right."

"What about Melania? I heard the university canceled classes. Is she coming home?"

"She sent a telegram a few days ago with a myriad of reasons she wouldn't be home." Jacob threw another log on and returned to his chair. "The medical staff, Red Cross volunteers included, are working around the clock dealing with influenza. They're inundated with the ill."

Peter's expression became somber. "Do you think she'll be all right? She's just a girl, really."

Jacob chortled. "That's amusing coming from the young man who has been wandering the country without a care."

"Maybe. Once." Peter's expression remained serious. "What I've seen and heard." He shook his head. "Mr. Pritchard missing, Mathias in-terned. Truly, I understand the inevitable sacrifices of war." He let out an extended breath. "The home front, what's going on here——that's more troubling because it was less foreseeable." He looked back at his father. "I believed you, you know, that day back in the spring when you told Jim and me about the outcomes of extreme nativism." He ran a hand through his hair. "I guess it was just difficult to actually imagine."

His father nodded. "War changes everything and everyone. Thankfully sometimes it's for good. Melania is doing her duty, just as you will."

"I'm ready, Vati. Ready to do my part." Peter sat silent for a moment. "I just hope that it will make a difference."

His father answered with marked hoarseness in his voice, surprising Peter. "Scripture reminds us, *Faith is the substance of things hoped for; the evidence of things not seen.*" He paused and turned to his son. "We shall cling to hope."

The men sat in silence while the fire flickered brightly——the sounds of Helene in the kitchen and Emily and Elizabeth upstairs blended in the background. The kitchen door swung open, breaking them out of the quiet reverie, as Helene entered carrying a tray of pie and coffee. Peter rose and relieved his mother of her burden, setting a plate and cup before his father before putting down his own.

"I'll be back in with dessert for myself and Emily. Tell her if she comes down before I return. I may be a few minutes as the dishwater is near a boil."

"Ja. Eine gute Frau. *A good woman.*" Jacob dug into the pie.

Peter held his fork, hesitating as he pondered the heavy burden he'd been carrying for months, realizing now was his best chance to get his father's advice. "Vati. I still haven't found Jim. Do you think it'd be worthwhile to ask at the police station? Someone from the railyard said they saw Jim being roughed up by the police one summer night."

His father responded quickly and emphatically. "No! Not now. We all care for Jim, but we can't help him if we too are brought under suspicion. Can't predict what the police would do."

Peter sighed, nodding in agreement. "I thought you may say that. That's why I hesitated."

"Times are different with the state of affairs so unpredictable. Keep asking around and keep your eyes open. That's the best way to help your friend."

Emily came down the stairs when Mutti appeared with another tray of plated dessert. "Perfect timing," Mutti said, smiling at Emily. "I brought us some pie."

Peter stood, offering his chair to Emily. "Please, sit." He motioned to the empty seat.

Emily protested, but Vati encouraged her as well. "We'd love your company."

Emily sat and put a cloth napkin on her lap before taking the proffered pie. She poked her fork in the crust, pushing around the dessert more than eating it. The Harvey family chit-chatted, but Peter noticed his mother frequently glancing at Emily. Soon, Helene stood to gather the plates.

"Here, Mutti. Let me help you," Peter said, quickly rising.

"No, I can help." Emily stood——her face went instantly pale, and after one step, she buckled at the knees.

Peter lunged forward and caught Emily before she hit the ground.

"Here, lay her on the sofa." Peter laid Emily down, and then Mutti removed the young woman's shoes and covered her with a blanket.

Emily moaned. "Oh, my head hurts."

Mutti swept a hand across her forehead. "Peter, a cool towel. Quickly."

Chapter 25

October 1918 • University of Minnesota • NO-
TICE: The university will be further postponing
the start of the semester due to the ongoing influenza epidemic. The only students allowed on
campus will be those in the Student Army Training Corps (SATC). Female students and those male
students who are either unfit for military service or have not yet declared their intent to enter the Corp are prohibited from being on campus
until further notice.

Minneapolis Tribune • October 1918 • PUBLIC
BAN! Minneapolis Health Commissioner, Dr. D.
H. Guilford, ordered a temporary ban on all unnecessary public meetings until city and state
officials can meet to determine if more sweeping measures need to be implemented. As of today, University Hospital is off-limits to all visitors except those calling on patients on their
deathbeds. The entire hospital will be dedicated

TO INFLUENZA PATIENTS, AND OTHER HOSPITALS WITHIN THE CITY WILL SERVE ALL OTHER PATIENT NEEDS. HEALTH COMMISSIONER GUILFORD REQUESTED THAT ALL DOCTORS BEGIN ACCURATELY REPORTING CASES OF INFLUENZA.

ST. PAUL PIONEER PRESS • OCTOBER 1918 • WARNING: ST. PAUL HEALTH OFFICER DR. B. F. SIMON WARNS RESIDENTS TO TAKE CARE IF THEY FEEL ILL AS THE CITY IS LIKELY TO BE VISITED BY THE EPIDEMIC SOONER OR LATER. HOWEVER, MAYOR PAUL HODGSON TOLD REPORTERS YESTERDAY THAT "THERE IS NO EPIDEMIC HERE, PARTICULARLY AMONG THE CIVILIAN POPULATION, AND THE SITUATION APPEARS TO BE IN EXCELLENT CONTROL." HE FURTHER ASSURES US THAT "EVERY CORNER IS BEING WATCHED." CITIZENS OF ST. PAUL! BE VIGILANT, TAKE CARE, AND STAY WELL!

Melania scanned the room when she entered, as she did every time she arrived at the beginning of a shift. "Hmm." She searched the aisles of beds for Lawrence and Stephen, two of the first patients she'd attended. Last week? She'd lost track. Others now inhabited both the beds the men had occupied. "Stephen? Lawrence?" She asked the attending nurse. "Are they——"

"Mr. Weber is gone. Dead. Lawrence," the nurse started, flipping through the logbook. "Gone too. Back to the base, I'd imagine." She shut the leather-bound book and set it on the table before moving down the aisle of closely stacked beds.

"Oh, thank goodness!" Melania pressed her palm to her chest. "But a heartbreak about Mr. Weber." Her mouth pinched. He had his whole life ahead of him, and it was suddenly gone. There seemed no rhyme or reason to who walked out and who was carried out in a body bag. She scanned the book for other patients she'd recently attended. The logbook had become a memoir of sorts for the ward——its lined pages filled with names, dates, and status of each and every patient entering or leaving the hospital. One day, Melania thought, the book would chronicle the Spanish influenza epidemic——perhaps only for this region, but still, it seemed important. The log felt like a double-edged sword, similar to the military death notices posted about town. She looked at it through narrowed eyes, not truly wanting to discover the outcome for her patients who'd left. Ten more had gone home, and six had died in the same time frame. Perhaps it was a numbers game, and maybe the reprieve had come.

Melania bustled to work, spending the next hours giving countless doses of aspirin, applying scores of cool compresses, and cleaning up several messes from sick patients. She glanced up from her latest concern as an orderly pushed a rumbling cart past, gathering the soiled sheets and towels. Another followed behind him, restocking supplies. She observed them as they wove their way in and out of the beds, almost as if they moved in slow motion, the entire scene playing out like a Greek tragedy when the third and fourth men swept through at last, rolling the dead onto gurneys. *What was the point of all of this? Were they even making a difference?* Epinephrine, the injection that allowed for easier breathing, was seemingly the only mercy. Melania stood watching as the parade of orderlies filed out the doors. It seemed to be a never-ending cycle, and little could be done to relieve the misery. One minute a patient burned with fever only to throw blankets off the next moment, sweating profusely. Pain gripped patients' inflamed throats. Pneumonia often followed as a secondary influenza symptom, causing fits of bloody coughing and restricted windpipes.

Melania's stomach rumbled, and she tried remembering when she'd last eaten. She looked around at the relative calm—it seemed as if all needs were met for the time being. She hurried out the door and down the steps to grab a bite to eat.

She'd just gotten her food in the dimly lit cafeteria when a voice called out. "Over here, Ms. Harvey." She spied a man waving her to a table——a surprise, considering she was nearly unrecognizable in her head-to-toe white garb. She maneuvered her tray of food toward him.

"Oh, Arch! It's so good to see you!" She embraced him without hesitating, so happy to be with a friend. "What are you doing here?" She set her tray down, plopped in a chair, and then pushed her hair back from her forehead, tucking it under her cap. "I must look a mess."

"Not even a possibility." Archie smiled at her, briefly touching her hand.

"So? Tell me——why are you here?" Melania sat and began picking at her lunch.

"I just came from the St. Paul Army base. We've been training to ship out. I'll be an Army medic."

"Where? Where are they sending you?" Melania frowned. She knew it was inevitable, but it seemed like a personal loss each time someone she knew went overseas.

"That's just it. I don't know." Arch shrugged. "Today, my superiors sent the medically trained cadets here to help. The university and Fort Snelling programs have been hit hard with illnesses among the cadets, nurses, and returning soldiers. It's *all hands on deck,* so to speak."

"That's great news." Melania paused at the look on Archie's face. "Isn't it?"

"This isn't what I had planned," Arch conceded. "But it *is* good to see you."

"You too." Melania smiled. "What's your job?"

"Sounds like I'll be working with the influenza patients, same as you." He shook his head. "The disease is spreading like wildfire. It's madness."

"Oh, Archie, it is," Melania said, quickly losing her composure. "Nothing I learned in the Red Cross prepared me for what I've seen—— the agony, the death——" She stopped at the look of grave concern on Arch's face and forced herself to regain control.

"I'm okay, really," she said lightly, briefly patting his hand. "Are you taking a break before you even get started?"

"I don't think that's protocol, but they snatched us just before going into the mess hall. They likely figured we'd need to eat before we worked." He dipped a chunk of bread into his soup, sopped up the liquid, and shoved it in his mouth. "Sorry," he muttered apologetically through the mouthful of food. "I'm used to eating with a bunch of fellas."

Melania smiled and dipped her spoon into her soup bowl. It was nice to have another familiar face around, that was certain.

Chapter 26

Helene rushed up the stairs when she heard crying and snatched Elizabeth from her crib. "Hush, little one. We mustn't wake your mama." She brushed her lips across Lizzie's forehead, relieved there were no signs of fever. It'd been difficult, at best, keeping the girl from her mother these past several days, but Helene knew she must——typically, the young and old were the most vulnerable.

Her mouth pinched whenever this thought crossed her mind. How was it that neither she nor Jacob was ill, yet Emily——a young and vibrant woman——lay terribly sick? Helene hadn't seen an illness so dreadful since scarlet fever hit her household early in her marriage while her family was still in Germany. Her young children had been stricken with the illness but survived, save a few scars left behind by the itchy rash.

Jacob peaked into Elizabeth's room as Helene dressed the child. "I'm headed out now. Do you need anything before I go?"

Helene looked up, pins from the child's diaper pinched in her mouth. She shook her head and then released the pins into her hand. "The mill?"

"I've told them why you're not there." He lifted a shoulder. "You're not the only one. Influenza is hitting the mill hard too." He nodded. "This is where you belong."

Helene finished with Elizabeth, picked her up, and moved toward her husband, resting a hand on his forearm. "Are you . . . ?" Her eyes narrowed as she searched her husband's face.

"Well. Gut. Ja. Ja." He shrugged. "I just wonder if I should stay at the mill until Emily's well. I don't want to spread the disease nor bring anything else home." Jacob exhaled sharply. "Not sure what makes sense."

"I've spent many more hours than usual these past several days pray-ing——seeking answers, but none have come." Helene exhaled a heavy breath, and her eyes pricked. "I don't think there is a clear path right now——but rather moment to moment."

"Much of the news coming from the hospitals says as much. Seems no one has any idea of the answers. It'll be written in history, I suspect." Jacob leaned in and kissed Helene's cheek and Lizzie's forehead. "It's not warm, thankfully."

"Small mercies." She held out the girl to Jacob. "Could you get breakfast started for her? I'd like to check on Emily before I go downstairs."

"Ja." Jacob bounced Elizabeth on his hip, and the girl giggled as the pair descended the stairs.

The sun shone brightly through the high hall window, rising from its low position in the autumn sky. Helene hesitated outside Emily's door, listening. She'd heard nary a sound from the room since the middle of the night. Dread rose, and her heart pounded in her chest as the silence lingered. The door squeaked in protest when she turned the knob, pushed it open, and slipped in. She laid the back of her hand to Emily's fore-head——warm, not burning. *Good.* And not cold either. She sent a prayer of thanksgiving heavenward.

Surely this strong young woman would recover. Helene moved around the bed and opened the shutters, sending light streaming in and dust particles dancing.

Emily stirred and opened her eyes, blinking at the brightness. "Where? What?" She laid her fingers at the base of her neck and glanced around the room.

"Now, now. Let me help you sit up." Helene propped pillows around Emily. "You've been ill. Influenza, it seems."

"How long?" croaked Emily, sliding her hand up her throat. "Dry."

"Let me get you some water." Helene poured a glass from the pitcher on the bedside table. "Today is the third day. You fell so suddenly. We were eating pie. Do you remember?"

Emily sipped the water and then shook her head. "No. Not much."

Suddenly her eyes darted around the room. "Where's Elizabeth? Is she———"

"She's fine. Downstairs with Jacob having breakfast." Helene pulled up a chair. "I've kept her out of your room. Broke my heart, but it seemed best." She smoothed the blanket around Emily, tucking her in as if to keep the illness contained. "There were times when———" Helene stopped and smiled. "But look at you now! No fever. You're sitting up."

"I feel so much better." Emily folded back the covers. "I'd like to see Lizzie."

"No. You best not," Helene cautioned, holding up her hand. "You're likely weak after days with fever and little food." She pulled the covers around Emily again. "Stay put, and I'll bring you breakfast. Then we'll get the little one up to see her mama."

"You're right. Good." Emily laid her head back against the propped pillows and smiled. "Thank you, Helene."

Helene smiled———hopeful Emily had turned the corner on the illness. "Would you like me to help you lie down again before I go?"

"Oh, no, I'm content to be upright. And the view out the window is lovely."

CHAPTER 27

The street lamps had been lit for hours and the city tucked in early, abiding by the new Health Commission mandate. What day was it? Melania searched her mind, her eyes darting around the room glowing with reflected light. Friday? No——Thursday. She hoped to slip home and check on her parents. Death numbers had dropped in the last couple of days, so perhaps it was possible. Maybe, if the trend held, she could even catch an early Saturday matinee with Margarita Fisher starring in *Money Isn't Everything*. Oh, to do something ordinary.

She paused at the window, reflecting on the silent streets——so peaceful and tranquil——a stark contrast to what things had been like here in the hospital. There *were* stretches of calm——the soft breathing of exhausted patients, the hum of low voices conferring, the whoosh of a curtain pulled around a patient's bed, the click-clack of feet on the wooden floors, all of it creating an odd and soothing rhythm of sound. In those moments, it felt like they had a modicum of control over the illness as if *they* were winning the battle against the wretched disease. But the impulse to think they could rule this beast had been dispelled again and again——after every agonizing cry or regrettable death.

The clock struck the hour, and Melania glanced up. *Soon.* She was nearly done with her shift, and then she'd slip away, catching the streetcar home for a long weekend. She dared to hope that they'd actually beaten the beast back this time—they'd be victorious eventually, right? She sighed deeply and looked around the relatively tranquil room before picking up the water pitcher and refilling bedside glasses.

The water softly sloshed into the cups, adding to the soothing quiet of the evening. Abruptly, the calm was broken when a young woman rose from her prone position, grasping her throat. "I——cannnn——ttt breathe," she sputtered, her voice coming out in sharp splinters.

Both Melania and a nearby nurse rushed toward her. "Doctor! Quickly!" The nurse turned to Melania. "Hurry, get some water!"

Melania poured the last from her pitcher into a cup and handed it to the nurse. The patient's head swung back and forth, refusing the water and clinging to her throat, digging her nails in as if trying to rip open her skin. Melania gasped as the girl's lips and the area around her mouth turned blue.

"My God!" The nurse's hands dropped to her side as she stared at the patient.

The doctor approached just as the woman's hands loosened around her neck, and she flopped back on the bed, dead after that brief and futile struggle for air.

"Cyanosis," the doctor said matter-of-factly.

Melania crumpled to the ground in tears. This girl was so young and with so much life ahead of her. Within just three hours of being brought in, she had suffocated to death. Melania sobbed, unable to lift herself back up. The nurse hooked her arm through Melania's elbow and pulled her to her feet. "You *must* keep yourself composed," she whispered sharply in Melania's ear. "Get yourself a drink of water and continue your rounds." The nurse turned Melania by the shoulders, pushing her forward down the aisle.

"Orderly, here!" Melania heard the nurse call over her head, summoning the man to remove the young woman's body. Melania's feet felt like lead as she stepped toward——*what? The next dying patient?* She'd seen death on the ward before, but this had been more brutal and sudden. The girl was perhaps eighteen? Nineteen? Melania shivered and walked toward the hall's small break room. Archie stood at the counter, throwing back coffee and a biscuit. He pulled Melania into an embrace.

"What is it?" he whispered into her hair. "You look ashen."

"I——I——don't know——if I can do this anymore." The words spilled from her mouth, and tears streamed down her cheeks.

Archie released her and held her at arm's length, looking directly into her eyes. "We *must*. We're the only ones." He pulled her back into his chest, wrapping his arms around her tightly as he said softly, "The shift doctor said civilian illnesses are rising again——fifty new cases and seven deaths today in our hospital. Who knows what's happening elsewhere."

"But I thought the deaths were decreasing." Melania shook her head as if she were trying to shake off the inevitableness of defeat.

"That was yesterday," Archie said, loosening his hold on her. "They've put patients in every ward in the hospital, not just on this floor."

His brow furrowed and he wrapped his hands around her wrists as if he were bracing her. "It's bad, Melania. We need to do our part. We might be the only humanity between our patients and their illnesses." Arch's grip on her arms was gentle, but he shook her slightly, stirring her back to her wits.

Her shoulders sank as she gave up the idea of going home. They were essentially quarantined, with only the patients coming and going. She took in a deep breath. "All right. God-willing, I'll regain my focus." She dabbed her eyes with her handkerchief.

"Coffee will help too." Arch chuckled wryly, pouring her a cup.

"Thanks, Archie. Truly. You're a good friend."

Archie's mouth pressed flat, and he nodded, his brow curving. "Yep. Friends." He exhaled heavily and turned to go. "See you soon. Pal."

Melania wrapped her hands around the mug and watched him go. She knew he wanted more than friendship—he regularly suggested future events as if their togetherness was certain. She hadn't encouraged him, had she? She sighed. Archie was leaving with the Army soon, and she had school to finish. Then there was——

She shook her head and finished her coffee. Why couldn't she stop thinking about that exasperating man? Jim was the one who'd disappeared without letting anyone know his whereabouts. But then again, Jim was the man who helped her parents whenever he could. And wasn't he Peter's best friend? She harumphed. Goodness. She didn't know what to think about Jim!

She went to the hospital post station and wrote a quick note to her parents, explaining the situation at the hospital. She signed and folded it, paused, and smoothed out the page again, quickly scribbling, "Any information about Jim?" She creased the paper again and stuffed it in an envelope, paid for a stamp, and dropped the letter in the mailbox. Expressing concern over Jim was reasonable, wasn't it? He was a family friend, after all. She shook off further thoughts of him, pushing them to the back of her mind. She needed to focus on the tasks at hand.

Melania spent the rest of her shift changing compresses, feeding small snacks to alert patients, and administering doses of aspirin to those with severe body aches. She prayed silently for each person as she walked by their bed or tended to them. "Oh, Lord. Show yourself mightily." Maybe prayer was the only way to victory, she thought, remembering a similar sentiment spoken by her mother in the past.

Melania finally left the ward around three in the morning and walked up the back stairway to the bunk room, weary and eager for rest. She fell quickly into a deep sleep, awaking after what seemed like mere minutes to find the sun beaming in the tall paned windows, the rays of light dancing off the beveled glass, sprinkling a rainbow of color around the room.

She washed her face and put on a new dress and apron before pinning her hair back and setting on a cap. She slipped her still-swollen feet into her shoes, reached for the long white coat, and headed toward the stairs.

CHAPTER 28

—·—

Jim hung his apron on one of the hooks lining the wall near the cellar stairs. The brewery job was menial, but it allowed him a blessed quiet and anonymity he'd not had at the railroad. He'd been shocked to learn the extent of the brewery's operations despite Congress passing the 18th Amendment earlier in the year. The amendment had yet to be ratified, so Prager's still brewed beer, demand skyrocketing as folks stockpiled beer for future personal consumption. Jim had shuddered when Sven Olson told him how the ultra-nationalist efforts joined forces with the temperance folks, claiming the most menacing of German enemies within the country were Pabst, Schlitz, Blatz, and Miller. The sentiment seemed ridiculous, funny even, yet Jim knew the lengths people would go to rout out their enemies.

Prager's was nowhere near the size of those establishments, but it was still a German brewery, so Jonas Prager focused on contributing positively to the city. He publicly cut beer production to support the war effort's appeal to save grains for food production. The company also produced a malt syrup made of less than 0.5 percent alcohol——a concoction that most knew could easily be made into beer by adding water and yeast and allowing time for fermentation. It was a goodwill effort toward acknowledging the inevitability of Prohibition while meeting the needs of their customers in new and innovative ways. Whispered discussions floated throughout the floors about other plans when Prohibition was, in fact, law. Ice cream, soda, ceramics? It seemed ridiculous to Jim, but tough times called for drastic measures. He knew that well, and the irony was that his taste for beer had diminished since working around the strong smells at the brewery. Beer hadn't done him any favors, being at the root of most of his recent troubles. It was easier here, in St. Paul, yet Jim still walked the line of being solicitous and keeping to himself——eager to stay out of trouble.

"Hey, Reilly," a fellow cellar rat called to him before he was halfway up the stairs. "Headed to the pub later. Join us?"

Jim hesitated but couldn't think of a reason to decline. "Sure. For a bit."

The pub was in a building on the edge of the brewery facility. There, a tasting room held copious amounts of unfinished kegs——supplied as a perk for the employees. Jim had quickly mastered the appearance of imbibing——often dumping half-full mugs in the waste barrel. No one was the wiser, with each man generally paying no attention to anything other than the level of his own cup.

Jim headed to the brewing floor to chinwag with the brewmaster while the other cellar rats finished up. Sven Olson had taken Jim under his wing, throwing extra work his way, knowing Jim was saving all he could before his draft number was called. Jim squared up with the older man by working hard, staying loyal, and steering clear of rumors and scandal. Here, as with the railroad, there was a constant blather of gossip.

"Jim, ol' boy! How are ya?" Sven greeted Jim with a strong palm between his shoulder blades.

"Good. Good." Jim grinned and cocked his head, wondering what the man would say next. Sven had a droll sense of humor.

"So——the ladies? Have you been finding them? There are plenty lonely dames around without their man home." Sven chortled.

Jim held up his hand. "No, thank you. Not interested. And not in gals with fellas, for certain!"

Sven put his hands on his hips, facing Jim, his brow furrowed. "Got yourself a girl, then?"

"I hoped. Once." Jim hesitated. "Not now. Besides, I'll be sent overseas any day now, I suspect. Got no time for women."

"If you didn't come here so I could direct you to some fine ladies this Friday evening, what can I do for ya, Reilly?"

Jim shook his head. "Is there anything I can do for you before meeting some of the fellas in the pub? Got about an hour to pass."

"Sure. I always got jobs for a workhorse. Follow me." Olson led Jim to the other side of the floor, where a piece of equipment needed attention.

The hour passed quickly, and Jim cleaned the grease from his hands and headed to the pub. The drinking hole was stuffy, with the door being the only opening to fresh air. The room was dimly lit with the stench of sweaty men permeating any clean air that managed to find its way into the area. That alone was enough to motivate Jim to keep his time there short. The space was filled with barrels, many topped with wood planks as tabletops. As men would lean their elbows on them, the sparsely nailed planks occasionally loosened and flipped, causing mayhem as beer spilled and splashed on the men and the floor. The longer into the night the festivities went, the more chaos ensued. As Jim settled into a space between two boisterous workmates, he leaned both elbows on the width of one plank in a deliberate move to secure this portion of the table. He held his mug around its cool, sweating middle and sipped on the beer.

"Did you hear about the poppycock in Minneapolis?" A fellow shouted above the din, directing his question at no one in particular. "They got the whole damn place shut down."

"Whaddaya mean, the whole place is shut down?"

Jim listened with keen interest——the Harveys lived in Minneapolis.

"Seems they're worried about an epidemic," the first man explained. "The health department rolled up the whole town. Not one thing is open——churches, pubs, theaters, schools."

"Ah, too bad for them that they're not here in the better twin city!" The men clinked glasses in nonsensical superiority.

Jim had read the newspaper's headline this morning. St. Paul's health officer had, in one breath, banned public dances and meetings and, in another, dismissed the 1,400 cases of illness as *suspected* flu or *bad* colds. It seemed like folly to Jim. If Minneapolis had enough influenza cases to shut down the whole place, surely the disease would be equally as vicious in the neighboring St. Paul, if not now, eventually. The most essential lesson Jim had learned from Jacob Harvey was to pay attention to what was going on underneath the hubbub and to put stock in intuition and logic.

The room stank of spilt beer and foolhardiness. If the health officer banned public gatherings, this crowded room was surely a cesspool. Jim dumped his beer in the waste barrel. "That's all for me, fellas." If there was one thing Jim had learned, albeit the hard way, it was to avoid the company of fools.

He walked through the brewery gates just as dusk fell on the city. The street lamps were lit as he walked toward the Connemara boardinghouse. In recent weeks, he'd moved from an open space with many inhabitants to his own private room, flush from his brewery job. It didn't pay a lot, but he splurged on this indulgence instead of putting a portion into liquor. Who knew what kind of accommodations he'd get once in the military?

Jim nodded his head in greeting at the neighbors he passed on his way, appreciating the affable camaraderie. Here he was *Jim*. Jim Reilly. Presumably Irish——not a suspected German spy. The notion that he could be anything other than a fella just trying to make his way in the world was beyond comprehension. He shook off the momentary dark thought and breathed in the cool, crisp night air, a refreshing smell after the pub. Suddenly his breath caught, and the inhalation turned into a cough. An unexpected weakness overcame him, and he leaned his hand out to steady himself on the side of the brick building.

"Drunk." He heard someone accuse, disgust sounding in their voice.

"No," Jim started to counter but couldn't form a sentence. He crumpled, his lanky frame folding in on itself on the sidewalk.

Chapter 29

Helene paused at the stove with the kettle in her hand. "Would you like any more tea, dear?" Helene scrutinized Emily. Was her color better? Did she seem stronger?

"No, thank you." Emily smiled. "I'm still sipping on this cup." She reached over and brushed her daughter's hair from her face. "Goodness, this girl can make a mess of jam toast."

"That she can." Helene sat at the table with a cup of coffee and a plate of eggs and toast. Upon closer inspection, she saw a shadow lingering in Emily's eyes. She was much improved, but Helene could see she was not yet back to full form.

"I'm grateful you were here with me," Emily said, almost as if she knew Helene was assessing her. "Goodness, I don't know if Elizabeth and I could have received better care from my own mother."

Helene set down her fork and dabbed her face with the napkin. "I'm grateful I was here with you. God's providence, for sure."

"Phillip insisted I get boarders the moment he was drafted. Especially with a baby and my own parents so far away." Emily nodded. "It was a good decision. Plus, I'm most fortunate in my company."

Helene took a sip of her coffee and smiled over her cup. "As are we. You're like a daughter to me, and Elizabeth, like a grandchild."

Emily stood. "I'll get Lizzie cleaned up and dressed."

"Are you sure you're up for it?"

Emily smiled and nodded, picking up her daughter. "I really need to move around a bit——and be useful."

Helene nearly protested——insisted Emily rest more——but she understood the need to be helpful——to serve rather than be waited on. "I understand. I'll finish the dishes."

Later that afternoon, Helene sat in the living room with her knitting. She was making a sweater for Lizzie and hoped to measure the length of the arms after the girl's nap. Emily must have fallen asleep herself, Helene thought, since she didn't come back downstairs after bringing her daughter to her bedroom after lunch.

Helene finished one sleeve, then set her knitting in the basket and got up, hoping to get a start on dinner before Elizabeth woke up. A knock sounded on the front door, and Helene heard Emily's steps come to the top of the staircase. "I'll get it," Helene called, shuffling to the door.

Helene knew Emily dreaded visitors as much as she did and was certain the young woman stood expectantly at the top of the staircase. The war had considerably changed life on the home front, and visitors were rare, meaning a knock was generally a portent of an unwelcome message. Helene wondered whose lives this messenger would change. She swallowed the lump in her throat as her fears manifested. A young man, a boy really, stood in a khaki-colored uniform——the clothes hanging on his small frame. His face was solemn as he thrust out the envelope in his hand. "Ma'am," he simply stated and turned to trot down the front stoop.

Helene took the missive in her trembling hand. This delivery method was very different from the uniformed chaplain who'd greeted them a month ago with the news of Emily's husband. Helene's mind raced with possibilities in the short time it took her to walk to a chair in the living room. *Was this news of Mathias? Or of Anna or Frank? Or . . . new information on Emily's husband?* Foreboding pressed against her chest as she turned and saw Emily had descended the stairs, her face ghostly white.

"What——is——it?" Emily squeaked, barely audible.

"It could be anything," Helene said, "not necessarily bad news." She tried to smile but failed.

Emily set Lizzie down on the rug and came to sit on the sofa as Helene slid her thumb under the envelope's seal, pulling out the single half-page. She turned it over and read the string of words pasted on the paper:

```
MRS  P  PRITCHARD  35  7TH  STREET,  MIN-
NEAPOLIS,  MINNESOTA  11TH  OCT  REGRET  TO
INFORM  YOU  REPORT  RECEIVED  YOUR  HUSBAND
CPTN  PHILLIP  PRITCHARD  32ND  DIVISION
DIED  5  OCTOBER  IN  ALLIED  STATIONARY
HOSPITAL  NEAR  ST.  MIHIEL  FRANCE  HOURS
AFTER  BEING  RECOVERED  FROM  ENEMY  CAMP.
```

Helene had barely finished the document before Emily let out a ghastly scream and fainted against her shoulder. "Oh, Lord, help us," Helene prayed desperately as she rose and lifted Emily's feet to rest on the sofa. Lizzie watched her, wide-eyed. "It's all right, darling. Mama just needs to nap."

Elizabeth turned back to her play as Helene went to the kitchen to get a wet towel for Emily's forehead. She saw the welcome figure of her husband approaching out the kitchen window, wondering why he was home so early, yet grateful for the timing.

"What is it?" Jacob's eyes narrowed when he came through the back door.

Helene swiftly explained the telegram's contents to Jacob while she moistened a towel. The pair moved to the living room, and Jacob picked up the child.

Helene sat on the sofa's edge with Emily's hand in her own.

"Shall I bring Elizabeth upstairs for a nap?"

"Mmm. No. She just woke up." Helene turned the towel over and placed it back on Emily's forehead.

Suddenly, Emily burst into consciousness, sat up, and cried out, "No! It can't be true!"

Helene pulled Emily to her, holding her tightly as she cried uncontrollably. There were no words of comfort at a time like this, nothing that could be said to soothe or ease.

Jacob looked over the little girl's head at his wife. "I'll take her to the kitchen. Feed her an early dinner."

Helene and Jacob spent the evening in the dimly lit room while Emily alternated crying and sleeping until the hours finally passed into the night. Jacob eventually went upstairs after putting Elizabeth to bed, but Helene slept in a chair, wanting to be present should Emily call.

The morning sun made its way above the roofline, streaming into the front room and waking Helene. She stretched her stiff and aching body before standing upright. Emily lay motionless on the sofa, still asleep. Helene was glad of that, hoping the girl found some escape in the darkness of her slumber. Soon enough, she would wake to the realities of the day.

A chill filled the room, and Helene grabbed a sweater from the door hook, wrapping it around her housedress before slipping into the kitchen to make coffee and toast. She let the warmth from the stove envelop her as the bread browned on the toasting rack and the water boiled for the coffee. She buttered the slices and set them on a plate before pouring herself a cup of coffee. Outside, birds woke to the day, flitting from tree to tree, nibbling at the withering berries and seeds. She went to the window to get a better view, feeling a crinkle in her pocket as she leaned forward. She pulled out the letter from Mathias, which Emily had given her weeks ago on the day of the chaplain's visit. She'd never even opened it. *How could I have forgotten this?* She shook her head, realizing that each day since then had its unique demands, and while Mathias was always in her thoughts, he'd been pushed to the background with Emily's situation. Helene wasn't even sure she'd worn this sweater since then. *Goodness. The trials.*

Except for the past several weeks, Helene had written Mathias weekly since they'd first learned of his detention. Jacob warned her that any correspondence from their son would be slow coming and likely heavily marked from when the Germans reviewed it before approving it for the post. She set down her coffee, slid her finger under the envelope's seal, and pulled out the letter. The paper was torn and no more than a scrap, but surprisingly, there were no blacked-out lines. Perhaps the Germans didn't bother with this brief and benign message. The writing had smudged in transport, or maybe it was from the nubby pencil it appeared Mathias had used.

> *Dear Mother and Father, I imagine that you're both gravely concerned for my well-being, but I want to assure you——your prayers and letters suffice. I've heard from transferred prisoners that this camp's food is more abundant than others, so I'm grateful. Horse meat, soup, and tea have been supplemented by stale, although welcome, bread from the Swiss Red Cross. You'll be astonished to know that the small Bible I carried in my breast pocket took much of the shrapnel, leaving me with only a flesh wound that seems to be healing. I covet your continued prayers and letters. Your son, Math*

Helene set the letter on the counter, almost afraid that if she reread it, she'd crumble. Mathias was his father's son——strong and stoic. He'd given her and Jacob the specifics they'd both wanted without adding details that would cause worry or, perhaps, scrutiny. Helene knew the camp realities were likely far worse than Mathias let on. She squeezed her eyes shut, pushing out a few errant tears, and then left the kitchen with her toast and coffee in hand. She set a match to the fire Jacob had laid the night before and rocked in her chair, nibbling on her toast, sipping the strong coffee, and paging through the Psalms. God's promise of His comfort and care radiated from these pages, filling Helene's weary soul. She drank the last drop of her coffee and rose from her chair to get a refill. She hoped that Emily would be up and ready for a cup herself, so she paused at the sofa, noticing that the young woman had barely stirred since Helene began moving around the house. She laid a hand on Emily's forehead. She was burning up, and as Helene pulled the blanket back, she could see Emily's dress was soaked with perspiration.

"Oh, Lord . . . no!" Helene pressed her hand to her heart. Emily's condition presented just as it had last week. Helene leaned in, listening to the woman's shallow and ragged breath.

CHAPTER 30

Minneapolis Tribune • October 1918 • HEALTH DEPT. SHUTS DOWN THE CITY! The Mayor and the City Council unanimously endorsed the measure after nearly two thousand cases of influenza were reported in Minneapolis. Churches, schools, theaters, movie houses, dance, pool, and billiard halls are closed indefinitely, effective tomorrow.

After experiencing their own mini-epidemic as part of the city's surge, the university quarantined all cadets and medical personnel on campus, sick or otherwise.

"I guess we're in it for the duration," Melania said to Jane as her friend stepped from the stairwell into the sick ward one floor below where Melania worked. "Thank goodness we found time for a bit of breakfast this morning."

"Until we meet again," Jane said dramatically, putting the back of her hand to her forehead. "In the cafeteria or some other delightful destination."

Melania smiled. She didn't know how she'd manage this quarantine without Jane and Archie. She trudged up the remaining flight of stairs and slipped on a clean apron before moving to the farthest row of beds in the ward. She opened the curtains, bringing in welcome light and sun-shine——her intuition telling her the small gesture mattered. If she could only give each patient a glimpse of the other side of their illness——*hope.*

She took a deep breath and moved to the first bed, flipping up the chart. "Mr. Wilson. How are you this morning?" She laid her hand on his forehead. It blazed——he squeezed his eyes shut as if her hand added to the pain. She inserted the thermometer under his tongue, and he moaned as the mercury shot up the tube. She cleaned the glass and put it back in the case before reviewing his chart. Then she poured a dose of aspirin, stirring it into the water——astounded, still, by the tasks she'd been permitted to take on amid the combination of suffering and staff shortage. But this was their reality——the space where they dwelled twenty-four hours a day. *How long would it last?* She had wondered this to herself many times and had even spoken it aloud to Jane the other day. It had been weeks already, and the disease stretched on and on. If they were only giving antidotes to the symptoms and no cures or prevention, what would bring it to a close?

Melania passed by a cot where a patient hacked, sending bloody mucus from his lungs into a pan held by the attending nurse. Lands! It was Lawrence. He'd been released last week after his fever lifted. "Aide," the nurse called to Melania. "Take over here." She thrust the kidney-shaped dish at her, the bloody mucus swishing in the container, nearly causing Melania to vomit. "Rinse it out," the nurse directed as she hurried away from the bed.

Melania dashed to the washbasin in the corner of the room, not wanting to leave Lawrence unattended longer than necessary, using the short dis-tance to gather her wits.

"There," she said, sitting on the chair next to Lawrence's bed when she returned.

His coughing fit seemed to have subsided, and he was lying flat on his back, quiet for the moment. Melania reached to feel his forehead. *Hot.* She looked at the chart. The nurse had given him pain medicine just a half-hour prior, and it was likely he'd coughed it out, though nothing could be done about that now. She knew aspirin dosing was controversial, with some attributing influenza deaths to an overdose of acetylsalicylic acid. She shuddered every time she thought of that——the chance that what they all thought was helping could hurt more. She wanted to relinquish the duty of dispensing the medicine, but she couldn't in these desperate days.

She waited a few minutes as Lawrence dozed or perhaps even went unconscious. Many of the sick did that, falling into a seemingly blissful state of lifeless peace. Sleep was usually fitful, but still, it didn't require the medical staff to monitor the patient as closely. Comatose patients required vigilant nursing to ensure they hadn't slipped into the arms of death.

Melania filled glasses of water, mopped foreheads, and dosed aspirin up and down the lines of beds, watching for familiar faces. There were so many young people here——most close to her and her siblings' ages. While it seemed logical, given the university was full of young people, she expected to see at least one or two of the older university professors or physicians among the ill. She thought of her parents and prayed they were well.

A pair of hands landed on her shoulders from behind, and Melania jerked and turned around.

"Goodness, Melania. You're jumpy." Archie put his arm around her shoulders. "How are you holding up, old gal?" He squeezed her into himself and then released her.

"I'm fine, although I feel as if I am moving forward like a wind-up toy." She sighed and wiped her brow.

"I just saw Jane in the break room this morning," Archie said. "She's working on the floor below, helping with the recent influx of civilian patients."

"I know. We had breakfast together this morning. What about Jasper? Any word on him?"

"Seems he escaped university grounds before they quarantined us all." He chuckled. "He's headed to the St. Paul Army training base. Supposed to be shipped out soon."

"I think that's where my brothers are," Melania recalled. "I feel like we're stuck on an island without the ability to connect with the outside world." She thought for a moment, wondering how long ago she'd received the letter from her mother detailing Peter's and Frank's draft registrations. There was nothing in the note about Mathias——or Jim——making Melania wonder what her mother wasn't saying.

"Perhaps we can meet up with Jane for dinner later," Arch suggested, "especially since there will be no matinee in our future anytime soon." He turned back. "Dining in our lovely cafeteria, of course."

Melania smiled, appreciating having her friends around her, their presence an anchor in this storm——the only normal facet of this dreamlike state.

A sound reached her ears——so soft she barely heard it. She turned toward it, seeing the bent form of a small child leaning over a woman lying on a cot. The woman was stretched out long and stiff on the bed, clearly dead—the blue tinge of her lips and the pallor of her skin confirming it. Her eyes, however, remained wide open, staring at the heavens. Melania hurried over and shut the woman's eyes with a downward sweep of her hand, then knelt beside the small figure, embracing the girl as the grief for her mother spilled on the bedcovers.

CHAPTER 31

ST. PAUL PIONEER PRESS • OCTOBER 1918 • WELL IN HAND. THE SUPERINTENDENT OF THE CITY HOSPITAL HAS CONFIRMED THAT ONLY THIRTY-FOUR PEOPLE HAVE DIED FROM PNEUMONIA OR INFLUENZA SINCE THE END OF SEPTEMBER, THUS VALIDATING WHAT CITY OFFICIALS HAVE BEEN SAYING——A GENERAL CLOSURE ISN'T NECESSARY. ST. PAUL CITY AND HEALTH OFFICIALS ARE CONFIDENT THEY HAVE THIS DISEASE WELL IN HAND AND ARE ONLY BANNING PUBLIC DANCES AND SPECIAL MEETINGS DUE TO GENERALLY LARGE CROWDS. WHILE MINNEAPOLIS HAS SEEN WELL OVER THREE THOUSAND FLU CASES, LESS THAN HALF THAT MANY CASES HAVE BEEN REPORTED IN OUR CITY, MAINLY CHARACTERIZED AS "BAD COLDS" OR "SUSPECTED" FLU BY DR. B.F. SIMON. REST EASY, CITIZENS OF ST. PAUL, AND TAKE CARE.

Jim woke in his room, wondering what day it was and how he'd gotten there. Although the shutters were wide open, the cloudy gray sky sparsely lit the room. He tried to sit upright, but pain split his head, and he immediately fell back onto the pillow. He squeezed his eyes shut and breathed slowly in and out, trying to regain the strength to move again. He opened his eyes and pushed himself to sit, his body aching with every movement. He squinted through the agony, noticing he was fully clothed and that his boots sat on the floor near the door. He struggled to recall how and when he got here, but nothing came to mind except the dire need for water. He poured a glass from the bedside pitcher, surprisingly full of relatively fresh water. Who, if anyone, had been caring for him? How long had it been? Hours? Days? He wasn't sure, but he couldn't worry about it when the drink set fire to his inflamed throat, feeling more like kerosene than water. He clutched his neck and fell back in bed, squeezing his eyes shut.

Later—he wasn't sure how long—he sensed a presence hovering over him and then a hand pressing a cold compress to his forehead. Another hand supported his head and poured a small amount of grainy liquid that tasted like cinnamon milk down his tormented throat. The sting was unbearable, and he dropped his head back and fell into total oblivion.

Helene cracked open the window——the room seemed stifling with the despair of Emily's illness hanging heavy. Helene looked out into the world, watching clusters of leaves fall from the oaks and squirrels scrambling to gather nuts for winter storage. Life cycles carried on outside regardless of the circumstances behind closed doors. The cool autumn breeze slipped in under the window sash, fluttering against her apron and swirling into the front room. She heard children's voices in the yard next door.

She moved her rocker closer to the sofa, picked up Lizzie, and sat down, wondering if Emily could hear her daughter's voice in her seemingly lifeless state. Emily had lingered in a coma since her relapse several days ago. Thankfully, the child remained well.

"Your mother is sleeping, Elizabeth, but I think she'd enjoy your song."

Lizzie smiled and leaned forward, setting a chubby hand on Emily's arm.

Helene's voice wavered as she began the child's song, barely managing to continue when Elizabeth joined in. Once the girl got well into her song, Helene quit singing, and the girl continued with the willy-nilly words, gently patting her mother's arm. Helene teared up at the commingled sweetness and tragedy.

Suddenly, Emily's eyelids fluttered open, and she smiled weakly at her child and then reached for Elizabeth's tiny hand, holding it tightly in her own, clearly using every ounce of strength left in her body.

"Take care of her——please," Emily whispered.

Helene's brow furrowed in surprise. "No! You must——" Helene begged, shaking her head as understanding swept over her.

Before Helene could finish, Emily mumbled, "I love you," and closed her eyes for the last time.

Elizabeth continued her song until the end, patting her mother's arm, unknowing. Finally, Helene could bear it no longer, and she pulled the child in tightly, away from Emily's still form.

Helene's entire body bent over the small girl, cocooning her in her frame as the chair rocked back and forth on the wooden floor. Soon the rhythm was joined by the clip, clip, clip of a jumping rope on the sidewalk outside. The sounds, inside and out, swirled around each other before they mingled with eerie small voices chanting in time with the jump rope.

I had a little bird. Its name was Enza. I opened the window,
and in-flu-enza.

<h1 style="text-align:center">CHAPTER 32</h1>

The University Hospital had become an all-encompassing world as the weeks wore on——laundry, cafeteria, medicine dispensary, bunk rooms, and sick wards. The morgue was another reality in the hospital, and of late, more people were leaving through the grand hospital doors out front than heading to the undertaker's to be wheeled out later in a box. The shift in the disease's impact also meant Melania had enough time for a much-needed bath this morning rather than the usual basin-washing. She gathered her clean clothes and toiletries from the basket tucked under the bunk assigned to her in the women's sleeping quarters.

Another medical assistant handed her a small bottle of lavender oil when she headed out. "Put a few drops in your bath. It'll make you feel a little more human."

"Thank you, Alice." Melania's brows went up. "Heaven knows we could all use a bit of a boost." She hastened to the bathroom before anyone came to hurry her to the sick ward.

Melania slid down into the large bathtub, feeling the grit and grime wash away even though the water was more tepid than warm. She leaned back against the copper tub and closed her eyes, breathing in the lovely scent of lavender. The bold, heady smell brought back memories of the summer before her family moved to Minneapolis. Her mother often planted lavender around the edges of the garden, drying it in the autumn to make sachets, using it medicinally or for tea. Melania smiled at the sweet memories, lifted herself from the tub, wrapped her body in a towel, and quickly dried off.

As she stepped into her skirt, she suddenly swayed, reached for the windowsill to regain her balance, and continued dressing. She pulled on her stockings and then slipped into her shoes, the faint feeling a passing memory. She cinched the long white overcoat and then pulled the cap over her pinned-up hair before heading out, leaving the much-appreciated bottle of oil on Alice's bed.

Melania headed to the cafeteria and put together a simple breakfast of tea and toast. She nibbled on the toast, her stomach grumbling. She pushed the plate away and sipped the tea, the hot beverage soothing the rumble. She set her dishes in the receptacle and headed to the floor. All was tranquil as she entered the ward——equally welcome and worrisome. Sometimes the quiet was peaceful, and other times it meant grave illness and death. She reminded herself that the tables seemed to be turning for them. Maybe they'd finally beaten Spanish influenza, or at least contained it. She sighed. Would they ever really trust the shifts of this epidemic? *Ah, the hope of the mere human.* Maybe that was the silver lining in this mess—that despite the seeming never-ending ups and downs of Spanish influenza, she still held onto hope. Melania caught Archie's eye across the room and waved to him. He smiled brightly and nodded his head, returning his focus to the patient before him. It was nearly mid-morning but seemed as if the day had just begun, considering it had been almost four o'clock in the morning when she'd gone to bed.

Melania moved down the middle aisle, smiling at any awake patient while scanning for familiar faces, especially Lawrence's. She never knew if an absence was a blessing of health or a sign of death until she reached the table on which the logbook was placed. She quickly scanned the journal to see what had transpired in the hours since she'd gone to bed. Her main concern was Lawrence, who had recently relapsed and was especially vulnerable. His name was still on the list but without the dreaded red ink——the mark of death. "Thank goodness," she murmured to herself, wondering why she hadn't seen him on her walk down the row of beds.

Melania moved to the far end of the room and began refilling water pitchers and opening window curtains before glancing at each patient's chart to see who needed pain medication. Her stomach somersaulted, and she dashed to the corner, retching in a mop bucket.

"Goodness, Melania! What's up?" asked Alice, tending a patient nearby.

"I'm——I'm not sure." Melania wiped her mouth on a handkerchief. "My stomach *was* a bit off this morning, but I thought the tea had settled it." She folded the cloth and dabbed her brow. "I think I'll be fine now." She looked around to see if anyone else had noticed. It didn't appear so. "Please. Don't say anything," she said to Alice.

"But Melania," Alice protested, putting her hands on her hips.

"Everyone is needed here," Melania said. "I'm sure it was nothing."

"All right. But if you feel unwell again, you need to rest," Alice cautioned.

"Yes, I promise." Melania quickly moved down the row and out of earshot of Alice, not wanting to engage her any longer on the subject. She hated to do it but tossed the delicately embroidered handkerchief in the waste bin.

The hours ticked by, and before Melania knew it, it was mid-afternoon. She motioned to Archie across the room, letting him know she was headed to the cafeteria for a break. She was tired when she entered the dining hall, and not very hungry, but she took a bowl of soup and some bread to a table. She sat, spooning a bit of broth——still feeling a bit off-kilter despite having pushed through the morning and early afternoon. The soup, lightly dotted with chicken and vegetables, filled the emptiness in her stomach, but soon, a heaviness caused her to drop her head into her hands, the spoon rattling on the table as it clinked against the bowl.

"Melania?" Arch's hand rested gently on her forearm. "Aren't you feeling well?"

She lifted her head and immediately put her hand to the top of her hairline. "My head feels so heavy, and now, I have a fierce throbbing pain."

Quickly, Archie moved around to the back of her chair. "Here," he said, putting his arms on her shoulders to help her stand. "Let's get you to your room to lie down."

"I think it's only a stomach sickness. I heaved in a bucket on the floor earlier," she said sheepishly.

Melania gratefully let Archie escort her from the room——the smells not helping her queasy gut nor her pounding head.

"I hate to scold you, but *what* were you thinking? You should have left immediately once you felt ill." Arch whispered into her ear as he hastened to get her out of the cafeteria. "I hope no one noticed you."

"I know that now. It's just that we're so short-handed."

Melania weakened as they neared the stairs. "Lean on me," Archie said, putting his arm around her waist.

At the last landing, Melania swayed, and Arch immediately swooped her up, carrying her the rest of the way.

When Archie entered the women's sleeping ward, he glanced both ways, ensuring no one was in the room. Men weren't permitted in this area, but surely, under these circumstances, it would be fine. "We need to be quick." He looked down at Melania.

"That one," she said, pointing to the row of beds nearest the window. "Mine is on the far end." Her eyes shut, and a bead of sweat formed on her forehead.

"Hey! What's going on?"

Arch turned and faced the nurse striding toward them.

"It's my friend. She fell ill during lunch."

The nurse looked between Archie and Melania's prone form. "Influenza symptoms?" Her eyes narrowed.

"No, it doesn't seem so. Stomach."

The nurse put her hand on Melania's forehead. "No fever anyway," she said before turning to Archie, her expression grave. "She cannot stay here if she takes a turn. You know that——don't you? She'll need a bed in the sick ward."

"Yes. I know. I'll ask one of our friends to check in on her."

"Fine, then. Come." The nurse put an arm around Archie's shoulders and turned him toward the exit.

He stopped on the landing for the floor where Jane worked, stepped in the doorway, and glanced around the room, spotting Jane across the way. He walked toward her, calling out when he was in earshot, motioning her to come toward him.

She cocked her head, looking at him quizzically, holding up a finger indicating she'd be there soon.

She smiled when she reached him, hooking his arm. "What's up? A late lunch? I'm more than ready." She put her hand over her stomach. "Hear that rumble?"

"It's Melania," Arch said solemnly. "She fell ill at lunch an hour or so ago."

Jane's hand clamped over her mouth. "Oh no! Influenza?"

"I don't think so, but I'm not certain," Arch said. "I think it may just be something she ate. She said she vomited earlier."

"What else? What other symptoms?" Jane's eyes went wide.

"She's weak and tired but no fever. I left her sleeping up on her cot."

"How did you—— Oh, never mind. I'm sure you were resourceful or adamant enough to figure out a way to get her where she needed to go." Jane smiled slightly and shook her head. "Oh, Arch, I don't know, though. Vomiting isn't usually a symptom, but someone *did* present with that sign just yesterday on our floor."

"Well, we'll just have to keep our eye on her. You will, actually, Jane." Archie shrugged. "A very stern nurse appeared when I was getting Melania settled, and she made two things clear——I was not allowed back on the floor and Melania cannot stay if she develops influenza."

Chapter 33

—·—

Jacob pulled on the reins, leading the horse and wagon out of the alley toward the lumber yard. Dusk was upon him, and he moved to the side of the street with the gas lamps, one of the few boulevards where they'd not yet been replaced with electric. He glanced at the posts and buildings plastered with a new form of propaganda, sometimes tacked right over the war bulletins. *Don't share breath. Don't share drinking cups. Don't visit poorly ventilated places. Avoid worry, fear, and fatigue.* Jacob wondered if the warnings and closures would be enough. Emily had rarely left home with a young daughter to tend to, yet she lay dead on the sofa while his stricken wife sat nearby with Emily's child asleep in her lap. He hoped he could make it back home before the child woke.

The house was completely dark when he returned from his errand, and he quickly turned down the alley, leaving the horse and wagon right next to the gate while he ran inside. He lit a lamp and hastened into the front room, the noise and light waking Elizabeth.

"Here, child," he said, holding his arms out.

She climbed down from Helene's lap, the older woman barely noticing. Jacob carried Elizabeth into the kitchen, secured her in a chair, and set a slice of buttered bread in front of her.

"Are you hungry?" he asked his wife when he returned to the living room.

Helene shook her head almost imperceptibly. He left her there and returned with a cup of tea, setting it on the side table before hurrying back to the kitchen.

Jacob sat across from Elizabeth and drank his tea, gathering his thoughts. He slid the folded newspaper closer, flattened the front page, and scanned the headlines, snorting at an article suggesting children would be safer if looked after in schools. Thankfully, the powers that be had decided that the less movement and interaction, the better. He flipped to the back page, where a notice reminded him of the plan to sweep the city streets after the Retailer's Association became convinced that dust spread influenza. Jacob sighed. The cleaning would alter his travel plans, but he'd adjust, possibly getting an earlier start.

"I'll put her to bed," he said to his wife as he passed with the girl in his arms after Elizabeth had finished her snack. Helene didn't respond but continued to stare blankly ahead. Jacob turned and pulled Lizzie's head into his shoulder so she wouldn't ask about her mother——who was still on the sofa but covered by a blanket.

When he returned downstairs, Jacob reached for Helene's hand, pulling her to stand. "Come to bed."

"But?" Helene nodded toward the sofa.

"Later." He knew his wife had a fierce sense of duty, of loyalty and that she wouldn't want to leave Emily alone. But Helene needed rest, and she went willingly upstairs with him after his prodding—he wasn't sure if it was resignation or exhaustion that drove her.

He left the living room light on when he went through the kitchen and out the back to finally settle the horse and wagon. Jacob patted the horse's nose and nudged him forward so he could unload the wood near the carriage house. Jacob began his work once the planks were inside and the horse settled in for the evening. As dawn broke, he finished sanding the edges of the box, setting it in his wagon bed before returning to the house.

He found Helene in the front room, kneeling beside the sofa, humming softly as she tenderly washed Emily's body, performing the most personal and sorrowful task. Jacob realized it was one of Helene's favorite hymns. He stood for a time, watching his wife and marveling at the light that shone through these dark times. When Helene finished, she rose and turned——seeming to notice Jacob for the first time.

"I've made a casket," he said, breaking the silence. "I'll take Emily's body to the undertaker this morning, and then I'll be back to take Elizabeth to Holmesburg."

A tear ran down Helene's cheek, and she nodded in agreement. There was nothing more to say. Wakes and funerals were for different times——days that weren't dominated by war and disease.

CHAPTER 34

—·—

Walter von Esson rested his hands across his midsection as he looked out the office window toward the quiet streets, hoping to spot an incoming delivery. The back-and-forth directives between the city's health commissioner and the governor were ongoing——laser-focused on dealing with the influenza epidemic. Accordingly, messenger boys were a frequent sight. "Stempel," he called after turning away from the window. "Where are we with the newspapers?"

His new deputy stepped into the doorway, the man much more eager to please than had been his predecessor, Deputy Hill.

"Just as planned, sir. The last article about our work to round up dissenters will run this afternoon, followed by updates on efforts to stave off the epidemic."

"What's the word on the street?" Walter's brow raised as his lips pressed together.

"The streets are empty, sir." Stempel shrugged.

Walter sucked in a breath and let it out slowly, pressing his eyes shut for a few moments before responding. "I realize that. I meant, are we achieving the desired effect?" He threaded his fingers together and stretched his hands out, his knuckles popping in the brief silence that followed until the question's meaning dawned on Stempel.

"Oh, yes, sir." Stempel nodded enthusiastically. "Anti-war groups have all but disappeared. Streets are quiet, but then, of course, schools, bars, churches, theaters——pretty much everything is closed. Confidence in your leadership is high."

"And you know that how?" Walter fished for a response.

"Well, um, I just——well," Stempel mumbled. "No news is good news, right?" He chuckled nervously. "The governor is leaving us alone——trusting in our, ahem, *your* abilities to deal with the dissenters. And they're considering your grant, so one would assume——" Stempel stopped, sweat beading on his forehead.

Walter nodded in agreement. "Yes. Makes sense to me." He waved his hand above his head. "Lord knows I've gone above and beyond." He exhaled in exasperation. "What about the grant? I thought a response would have come by now. It's an ideal time to purchase art."

"You think so?" The deputy's brow furrowed.

Walter snorted. "Of course. It will be uplifting for our city's residents to see an American Folk Art display in the Minneapolis Society of Fine Arts. It'll raise spirits——once the epidemic has passed, of course. Plus, it shows my dedication to this country."

"And further distances you from your radical socialist past," Stempel said.

Walter stepped forward, swiftly shut the door, and pinned Stempel to the wall, whispering, "You take care of my business. You don't comment on it. Is that clear? Or would you prefer to go the way of Hill?"

Stempel nodded as a bead of sweat trickled down his face. Walter released the man and pushed him out the door. Stempel hastened down the hall.

Walter marched to the restroom and splashed water on his face before scrubbing his hands clean, washing off the perspiration from Stempel's neck, shuddering as the soap and water swirled through the drain. He stared at his face in the small oval mirror, straightened his bow tie, and pulled his cuffs down and straightened the cufflinks.

"Ruth," he said when he returned. "I need ink, paper, and a new blotter."

"For 1918 or . . . ?"

"1919, of course." Walter shook his head as he returned to his office. "Incompetence abounds."

He returned to the window and scanned the streets, finally spotting a messenger boy scurrying down the avenue with a bundle tucked under his arm. "Grand!" Walter grinned, satisfied. It was a parcel like those from the governor's office. Indeed, if this was grant approval, it had come rather quickly. He grinned and nodded, moving away from the window to clear a space on his table. Maybe he'd request a second grant on the heels of this one.

Moments later, on the street, the messenger boy moved the package to his other hand and then sneezed several times into the crook of his elbow. His nose dripped, and he wiped it on his sleeve before returning the parcel to its tucked position. In just a matter of steps, he arrived at the large arched entrance to the municipal building. He stopped to take in the imposing structure that took up an entire city block, craning his neck to see the grand clock tower, catching the subtle movements of its gigantic hands. He waited and then smiled as the bells chimed at the quarter-hour. Shading his eyes, he looked up at the towers jutting skyward from the red slate roof, quickly righting himself when his head began spinning. He pressed a palm into the granite blocks, feeling as if he was about to tip over, the cold sending a jolt of support through his body. He took a deep breath and then made his way through the middle arch and entered the building. He sucked in another deep breath, struggling to put one foot in front of the other and leaning on the walls for support as he made his way to the staircase. The boy nearly toppled when he finally stepped on the landing to the sixth-floor offices, leaning briefly against the double-paned doors to catch his breath before tugging them open.

Walter looked around, and not seeing Ruth, he impatiently waved the boy into his private office. The boy seemed to move at a tortoise's pace, so Walter strode toward him and snatched the parcel, turning back toward his desk.

"Sir," the boy said weakly.

Walter snapped back around and thrust a coin in the boy's hand just as the youth coughed.

"Oh, damn you!" Walter yanked back his hand and blotted it with his pocket square. "Off with you." He shooed the boy out the main office door and turned back to his private room, slamming the heavy wooden door behind him.

Walter set the package on his table and dropped the pocket square in the trash. He moved aside the first two pages of the governor's letter, noting it mainly was a jumble of *therefores* and *herewiths*.

As the mayor scanned the paragraphs, looking for the dollar amount of the grant, he heard Ruth re-enter the main office, calling out to him. He ignored her and continued reading.

"Sir," she called again, opening his door.

Walter looked up from his papers. "What?" he snapped.

"Sir. There's a boy. A dead boy in the hallway."

CHAPTER 35

Archie watched from the doorway as Jane reached Melania's bed. He wished he could be the one assisting Melania with her smock. He felt so helpless yet relieved at the same time. She'd been sick for several days, and he'd been able to do nothing except watch from a distance and convince the floor nurse that Melania didn't have influenza——an opinion he'd formed from information he'd gathered from Jane and Alice. He hoped he was right, yet there she stood——up from her sickbed and ready to go to work.

Jane and Melania finished settling their uniforms and headed to the doorway. Melania smiled at him when she came closer. His heart somersaulted.

"Hello," he said when the women reached him. "Are you feeling better?"

"I am."

Archie's eyes narrowed as he searched Melania's face. She squeezed his forearm. "I truly am fine."

"Here, Archie, old man," Jane said, unhooking her arm from Melania's. "She's all yours. I need to skedaddle!" Jane grinned and pecked Melania on the cheek. "Later."

"How long was I sick?" Melania kept her arm at her side, ignoring Archie's crooked elbow.

"Days." Archie's brows shot up. "Perilously close to being sent to the sick ward as a patient."

Melania took in a deep breath as they began their descent. "Gee. I'd much rather stay on the side of a hospital bed than in one." Her lips pursed.

"Breakfast first may be the ticket." Archie shrugged. "I'm guessing you've not eaten much."

"No," Melania agreed. "And I'm famished!"

Archie pulled her arm through his crooked elbow. "It's a long way down, Ms. Harvey. We'd hate for you to falter." He smiled.

"I suppose, and thank you, Arch. You're a good friend."

"Yep." Archie pressed his eyes shut a moment and shook his head. He knew the status of their *relationship*, but he didn't like to be reminded.

He led Melania to a table when they entered the cafeteria, then got her coffee and toast. He recounted the events from the days prior as she nibbled on the light meal.

"I really fainted in your arms? I don't remember much of anything."

"It's all true." He smiled and rose. "We should probably get a move on. You hardly ate a thing, though. Are you sure you're all right?"

Melania's eyebrows went up, and she smiled brightly and stood. "Great. Fine. Truly," she said as she handed him her tray.

He dumped their dishes in the bin and made his way back to Melania, trying not to scrutinize her too closely. He knew she wouldn't like that, and besides, what choice did he have but to take her word for it?

They made their way to the staircase, Arch resting his hand lightly on the small of her back as they began the ascent. "This up and down plan probably wasn't the best," he said with a nervous laugh. "I should have just brought you something to eat rather than taking you down to the cafeteria."

"You're not responsible for me, Archie," Melania said with a force that startled him.

Archie moved his hand from her back and exhaled heavily. "Well, now that we're clear on the parameters, I'll just leave you here."

"Archie," she said as he turned away.

He stopped and turned back, waiting.

"Ah, I really do appreciate——" Melania started and then pressed her hand to her head, closing her eyes. "Oh, goodness." She leaned into the wall, reaching back to grasp the handrail.

Arch lunged forward and grabbed her arms as she groaned and crumpled to the ground.

"It hurts," she said, pressing her hand down on her head again and then releasing it, her arm falling limply to her side.

Archie glanced quickly up and down the stairs before swooping her up into his arms. He pressed her into his chest and whispered in her ear. "I think you need to be admitted." She tensed in his arms. "I'm sorry," he said softly, "but what else can I do?"

"Home," she said, her eyes briefly fluttering open.

He glanced over his shoulder and then raced down the stairs, hearing voices coming behind them and other sounds from the cafeteria. He turned down the first deserted hallway and slipped out the door, leaning briefly against the cold brick façade, gently setting Melania on the ground as he removed his suit coat and put it over her. He picked her up and pulled her close again, pushing her hospital cap back, her brown waves matting against her burning skin. She shivered against him, and he pulled her in tighter as he darted to the streetcar stop.

"I hope this is the right decision," he said under his breath as he stepped into the trolley.

The driver grimaced. "Mister, you can't bring someone with influenza in the car. Come on! You know that!"

Archie sucked in a breath. "It's a stomach bug," he said as he dropped the coins in the slot and moved to a seat.

"I don't need anyone retching in the car!"

"Please, mister. Our stop is just a few blocks." Arch looked at him imploringly.

"Fine then. But you're cleaning up any messes." The driver waved a dismissive hand.

After shooting the pair looks of fear and disdain, passengers turned to the window. Archie slid into a seat and leaned Melania toward the side. He grabbed the gauze masks from their coat pockets and hooked them on each of them.

"Hope that's enough," an old woman commented as she shook her head and turned away.

This is not going as planned. Archie put his arm around Melania and watched out the window as the car slid down the streets, traveling several miles to her house, not the mere blocks he'd told the driver. Melania's eyes stayed shut, and he wondered if she was sleeping or unconscious. Finally, they reached their stop, and Archie lifted Melania up and scooched sideways down the aisle.

"You're damn lucky I didn't kick you both out a while ago, sonny." The driver pressed his lips together and made a *tsking* sound as Archie carried Melania off the trolley.

The house was dark and quiet as Archie stepped onto the porch. "Oh, Lord," he said to himself——a prayer and a petition. "I hope they're home." He gasped. "And not sick themselves."

Melania stirred at the sound of his voice but didn't wake. He lifted his hand to knock again just as the door opened. Mrs. Harvey stood in the doorway, and her eyes quickly moved from Archie's face to the limp body of her daughter.

"Nooo," she squeaked, her hand going to her mouth.

"No, no, Mrs. Harvey," Archie said. "She's sick, not——"

Mrs. Harvey's hand moved from her mouth to her heart, and she stepped back, letting Archie inside.

He set Melania on the couch and pulled a blanket over her before sliding his hand across her forehead. Still hot.

Melania's mother stood still, staring at her daughter but not moving. Archie felt uncomfortable, wondering if he should leave or stay and offer to help. "May I get a cool compress for her?"

Mrs. Harvey nodded and moved silently to a chair. Archie hurried to the kitchen to wet a towel, then returned and placed it on Melania's forehead.

He glanced around the room. "Shall I turn on a light or open the shade? Or . . ." He turned in circles, wondering what was wrong. He didn't remember Mrs. Harvey being so obtuse. "Would you like to know what happened?"

The older woman seemed to be nudged a bit from her stupor and placed her hands on the armrests as if she were about to stand.

"I'll get the light," Archie said when she didn't move.

He opened the window shade, turned on a light, and moved by the doorway. "I'll be going now."

"Tell me," she said, her voice tinged with desperation.

"Is Mr. Harvey around? I can wait and fill you both in at the same time."

"He took the child."

Archie moved back and forth from foot to foot and dropped his chin.

"Her mother."

"Oh, I see," Archie said, although he didn't. He reached for the doorknob.

"She died," Mrs. Harvey said, suddenly rising to her feet and looking at Archie.

"No, no, Mrs. Harvey. Melania's sick. She's not dying." He stepped forward and grasped the woman's forearm. "Would you like me to stay?" *Lord*, he prayed silently. *I hope she's not dying.*

Mrs. Harvey shook her head and pulled her arm from Archie's grasp. "Emily died."

Archie cleared his throat and put his hand on his chest, uncertain if the older woman was offering clarification or a statement that death can take anyone. "Melania——will——not——die."

"God willing," Mrs. Harvey said before turning away from Archie and pulling up a chair to her daughter's side.

He stood in the doorway for a few minutes before finally stepping out into the brisk autumn air, the rush of cold hitting his face like the reality of Spanish influenza. He sat on the porch steps and dropped his head into his hands.

CHAPTER 36

St. Paul Pioneer Press • October 1918 • Cloquet Fire Turns Everything on Its Head. Just as the cities' medical personnel and resources were taxed to their limit by the influenza pandemic, a massive fire broke out in northern Minnesota. The blaze in Cloquet was set when a passing train ignited nearby tinder-dry grasses. The fire quickly spread, burning the town to the ground, killing hundreds——injuring and displacing thousands. Doctors, nurses, and medical aides were called from surrounding areas, significantly burdening each already shorthanded community. This latest dearth of medical personnel requires Minneapolis and St. Paul to utilize the military, school nurses, and citizen volunteers to address Spanish Influenza's ongoing medical and social demands. The St. Paul Army base is a flurry of activity with troops mobilized to respond to war requests and the ever-increasing community needs.

Home Quarantines Drive Creation of Citizen's Committee. The messaging is jumbled. The Ramsey County Medical Society refuses to endorse the mayor's mandate for home quarantine for the actively ill and closure orders for public places. Health Inspector Bracken publicly avowed that St. Paul's epidemic had peaked, stating the city could expect an immediate decline in the number of new cases. Further, he urges the use of face masks and a six-foot safety zone around each person in a public space. However, how to implement or enforce a safety zone has not been specified. There is little data to support Bracken's views and more to suggest an imminent second peak is in St. Paul's future. Amidst the confusion and contradictions, one sign of unity has emerged with the creation of the Citizen's Committee to provide meals for families struggling due to the epidemic. A central kitchen has been set up at the Mechanic Arts High School, located at the south end of Central Park Avenue. Meals will be brought directly to the bedridden. Further, the Wilder Day Nursery has been organized to care for children whose parents are too ill. Hardships, dear citizens of St. Paul, are profound and ongoing.

Peter turned up his collar against the brisk wind that whistled through the trees lining the road to the entrance of the military camp. He slipped through the gate and shoved his hands in his pockets, starting down the street to the high school located a couple of blocks from the camp. He'd expected to be trained and sent overseas when he first arrived at camp, but the emergencies and dire community needs had turned that expectation on its head. As with many other recent recruits, he worked with the Citizen's Committee to feed the housebound and ill in St. Paul. He quickly realized it was his mother's example that inspired him to embrace this task——he thought often of how she'd tended Jim's physical wounds while also tending his heart.

When Peter called on the sick and weak, equally pathetic, whether rich or poor, he was reminded that in war, illness, and death, there was no difference. In ordinary times, the rich had better access to doctors and medical attention, but this epidemic didn't discriminate, knocking down whomever it chose, wherever it pleased. The deterioration of a family was often quick and brutal. Servants could be lying ill next to their masters. Small children could be found crying and hungry next to their unconscious, or sometimes dead, parent. Each home brought surprises, some sad, some joyful——but the human spirit astonished him.

Peter walked briskly down the sidewalk to the streetcar after he'd picked up a box of food from the central kitchen. He held the crate steady on the seat next to him as the car bumped along the tracks. He'd never been to this part of St. Paul. According to the woman from the Citizen's Committee, Connemara was the poor Irish section. She'd said that many residents worked at the brewery, commenting wryly on the Irish and their love of drink. Peter had winced——after a year of ducking anti-German rhetoric, he wasn't interested in disparaging another ethnic group.

He stepped off the streetcar and walked toward the community square. The building entrances bordered this space——clearly a site of activity in better days. Remnants of what appeared to be a market lay strewn in the middle of the square——tables turned, baskets and rotten apples scattered about. It was odd, as if the market had been hastily abandoned. Perhaps because poorer sections of towns were often uncharitably characterized as dirty and slovenly. But Peter understood from his travels across the country that generalizations were unfair and dangerous.

He held the food crate, glancing around for direction, noticing hints of what this neighborhood had been like before the war and the epidemic. Jump ropes lay against a building, resting next to an outline of hopscotch. A weathered baseball glove and twine ball sat on a bench. Autumn-dried flowers and vegetable plants withered in window boxes, and barrels tucked in corners caught rainwater from the building tops. Peter smiled, imagining the neighbors gathering for an evening of camaraderie——glad he'd taken a moment to look beyond the despondency to see what the neighborhood *was* and what it *could be* again when this damned disease had passed.

He was pulled from his thoughts by a woman waving and calling from a window. "Please, mister. Up here."

Peter scanned his list, noting two of the food baskets were to be delivered to her building. He left the crate on the landing and walked up to the third floor with a basket, judging that was the location of the woman who had called out to him. She waved him inside a dimly lit room with a grayish cloud coming from the smoking oil lamp. Once they adjusted to the sparse light, Peter's eyes darted around the space. A covered form lay in the corner. Peter's head cocked toward the woman with a questioning look. "Ma'am?"

"No, no," she said, weariness tinging her voice. "My husband, you see——"

"It's your husband?" Peter's voice rose.

"No. Just his things. He died——two or more weeks ago." She wiped her brow with the back of her hand and sighed. "First him, now them." Her hand swept across the four figures of her children, lying like cordwood on a straw mattress under a sparse blanket. "They fell ill, one by one." She exhaled a ragged breath. "There's been no way for me to get food." She took the basket from Peter and turned back to her children.

"Is there anything else I can get you? Do for you?" Peter wrung his hands and shuffled from foot to foot——the desolation was difficult to accept.

The woman said nothing, nor did she turn back toward him, and had Peter not been looking, he would've missed the slight movement of her head. He stepped out the door, shaking his own head in sorrow.

Within moments, Peter stood in the square again, looking at the list——a compilation of needy families provided by a neighborhood boy who'd brought the request to the Mechanics Art School yesterday. Peter wondered if the boy was around. The woman at the community kitchen had told him of the lad's story of *"rising from his deathbed"* well and eager to help those in need. Frankly, Peter could use enthusiasm and assistance from someone like that. He had not realized the distance from the food kitchen to Connemara.

He was studying his list when he felt a poke at his shoulder. A boy of about ten years old pointed at several names on the page. "Here, here, and here." He paused. "And the last one to the fella in 5B." The boy's voice lowered, and his face became grave.

Peter raised a brow. "But there's another family——four people who could use this last basket. Surely, the fellow can wait until later."

"Really, sir. The man's in rough shape. I don't think he's got anyone with him." The boy's face scrunched, and his mouth pressed into a thin line.

"How do you know this?" Pete wanted to trust the lad, but he also had to guard his precious time and resources. Maybe, though, this was the same boy who had made the list in the first place.

"My Ma saw the man when he came in a couple of weeks ago. He was bad off." The boy shook his head dramatically. "Our place is across from his. After no one came to check on him for days, my Ma finally went in to help him as best as possible."

"Well, all right. I'll go," Peter agreed. "But I need a favor from you. Come back with me to the kitchen to help carry back more food baskets."

"Yes, sir! I'll do that." The boy offered his hand to Pete, his chest puffed up a bit. "Name's Charlie."

"I think I'll skip the handshake this time, pal. Influenza and all." Peter chuckled, patting the lad on his back as the pair made their way back up the steps. "Go check with your mother first. Tell her we'll be taking the streetcar."

"Yippee!" Charlie yelped as the pair climbed the staircase.

"I'll go give this chap his food and then meet you downstairs before long." Peter turned and knocked quietly on the door of the man's dwelling after Charlie barged into his own apartment, calling out to his mother.

There was no answer, so Peter knocked harder and put his ear to the door, listening. A soft moaning floated toward him. He reached for the knob, found it unlocked, turned it, and slowly opened the door, calling out to the man inside.

"Sir. Sir. I've brought food." The room was pitch dark, save for slivers of light glowing in between the shutter slats——the odor so intense it nearly sent Peter stumbling backward. He held his breath and moved toward the window, opening the shutters to let in light and cracking the window to clear the air. He hoped to determine the man's condition and find a spot to leave the food before he moved on with his mission. It wasn't unusual for Peter to find the ill home alone, but typically someone had been caring for them. But it was clear that this man had gotten very little attention, likely only what he received from Charlie's mother.

The man's dark hair was matted, he was fully dressed except for his bare feet, and boots with woolen socks stuffed inside sat near the bed. A thin blanket twisted along the man's torso. He barely moved or acknowledged Peter's presence——even the light failed to stir him, the sporadic moans seeming to be an involuntary action, not an attempt to communicate.

Peter released his breath once he became accustomed to the smell in the room. Though the breeze had dissipated its intensity, the redolence was a mixture of cinnamon, sweat, and the pungent tang of illness——an odor

Peter had experienced many times recently. Thankfully, the smell of death was markedly different. Perhaps this man had a chance.

According to Charlie's mother, the man had been ill for nearly two weeks——a long time to have neither recovered nor died. Peter shook his head. What did he know? He didn't have any actual medical knowledge about the flu——he was only a delivery person. And he'd done that, he reminded himself. His duty was complete.

He turned toward the door to leave but couldn't set aside the nagging feeling that he shouldn't go just yet. He glanced around the room, spotting a small washbasin in the corner. He carried the pitcher outside the room and dumped the contents in the drain at the end of the hall. He called to Charlie, who'd just exited his own apartment, requesting the boy fill the pitcher with fresh water at the outside pump. Peter returned to the apartment and glanced at the man once more, noting he'd barely moved since Peter had been there. Peter found a cloth that appeared clean and an overturned cup. He set them on the small bedside table and pulled up a chair. Maybe he could get the man cleaned up before offering him some food.

Peter leaned slightly over the man's form and, hoping to turn him, gently touched his shoulder, careful not to startle the rather large man. The man moaned at the touch but didn't turn over at Peter's prodding. Peter was tempted to skip cleaning him up, leave the food, say a prayer, and hope the man ate his dinner. He moved a few steps away from the bed, but something nagged at him again, and he turned back once more——determined to try harder to make strides in caring for this man. Peter moved to the edge of the bed, put both hands on the man's upper arm, and yanked hard, turning the man over. When the man flopped on his back, Peter jumped back in shock. *Jim.*

Chapter 37

Peter was dumbfounded. "Well, I'll be switched!" After all his dead-end inquiries these past several months, *Jim was here*——*of all places*. From the look of it, his friend was on the edge of life——already a lanky fellow, but now? Clearly, it had been some time since he'd eaten. It was a miracle Jim was still alive——and that Peter had found him.

Peter looked around the room, gathering his thoughts about what to do next. His family would be relieved he'd found Jim——particularly Melania. The thought gave him an idea. He'd bring Jim to the University Hospital. Who better was there to give care than his sister? She'd protested her affection for Jim, but whether that was reality or stubbornness, Peter wasn't sure. Regardless, she'd tend Jim out of duty if for no other reason. Peter had no idea how to get Jim there but felt confident about the destination. They might be closer to St. Paul hospitals, but he knew recent events for Jim had been tainted with betrayal and loneliness. He couldn't see leaving his friend in a hospital where no one knew him, where no one cared if he lived or died.

Peter turned from the bed and quickly made his way to the door to catch Charlie, hearing the boy's footsteps plodding up the stairs. Pete leaned over the stairwell, calling for the boy to hurry. "I need to get the man to the hospital. Now."

"But——how?" Charlie took the remaining steps two at a time, the water sloshing out the pitcher.

"I know him. He's in a bad state. Find me a better blanket," Peter ordered.

"What? You know him?" Charlie didn't move.

Peter barked, "Go! Quickly."

While Charlie was gone, Peter uncovered Jim and propped him up before grabbing a coat and slipping it over his shoulders. Jim's eyes fluttered open momentarily, but he didn't seem to recognize Peter. Pete leaned his friend against the wall and filled the water glass——more or less pouring it down Jim's throat before he slid back down onto the mattress.

Finally, Charlie returned with a blanket and his mother.

"I'm sorry for my short fuse, Charlie." Peter shrugged and tipped his head to the woman. "I'm Peter. This is Jim, my friend," he said, pointing to the bed.

"By God's grace." Charlie's mother shook her head in disbelief. "I'm sorry I wasn't more help. We've had so much sickness and death. It's been——difficult." She grimaced.

"No worries, please, Mrs.?"

"Brennen."

"Mrs. Brennen. I'm grateful for you and your son. It's astonishing, really. All of it." Peter looked between Jim and the pair. "Is there a wagon or buggy or some other conveyance around here? I can't imagine getting Jim to the University Hospital on the streetcar."

"They likely wouldn't let you," Mrs. Brennan said.

"Don't you have an Army truck?" Charlie's brow lifted.

"Ah, I wish. Several are on base, but they're set to be shipped overseas. The pandemic caught us all by surprise, so this so-called *delivery* system for the Citizen's Committee is hardly without its blunders." Peter rolled his eyes and raised a brow at Mrs. Brennen. "And you're right about the streetcar." He inhaled deeply. "Figuring this out as I go."

"Why bring Jim all the way to the university?"

Peter patted Charlie on the head. "You ask a lot of questions, boy. Good ones, though." He chuckled. "My sister works there, so it seemed appropriate. Jim needs to be around——*family.*"

Mrs. Brennan nodded in agreement. "I truly think having someone around who knows him will make a difference." She smiled. "I'm glad to know his name."

"What about Mr. Cassidy's wagon?" Charlie touched his mother's arm.

"Yes, that's a fine idea."

"Are you certain it's no problem?" Peter started to lift Jim to sitting again.

"Mr. Cassidy is gone now. Wife too——they died a week apart."

"Cripes." Peter frowned. "Children?"

"They're at the community nursery." Mrs. Brennan came alongside Jim and held him upright. "Charlie, help prop Jim. Can you lift him over your shoulder?"

Peter nodded. "Yeah, though, shoot——I'll drag him down the stairs. Can't see a better plan."

"I'll go get the horse and wagon, Ma, while you hold the door," the boy said after Jim was hoisted over Peter's shoulder.

"I'll send Charlie back home on the streetcar, if that's all right with you," Pete commented as Mrs. Brennan tucked the clean blanket around Jim.

"Appreciated." She smiled. "Don't think my boy's ever been on the trolley." Mrs. Brennan watched in her doorway as Peter started down the stairs, calling after him, "Keep the wagon and horse if you have use for them. I'm sure Mr. Cassidy would want them put to good use."

After loading Jim in the wagon bed, Peter hopped in the driver's seat. "Can you sit in back with Jim——stop him from moving around too much?"

Charlie agreed and leaped up into the back.

Peter snapped the reins, sending the horse on its way. The streets were mostly deserted, what with the social gathering restrictions, but occasionally a figure skittered across the street, darting in and out of doors, anxious, it seemed, to be back in the perceived safety of enclosed private spaces. The distance to the Minneapolis University Hospital was great, and it took the horse and wagon over two hours to make the journey. The iconic *witch's hat* water tower was a welcome sight when it finally came into view, signaling they were near the University Hospital.

Unsure of the process for patient admittance, Peter asked Charlie to stay with Jim while he went inside to find his sister. A large "No Visitors" sign was posted near the unmanned front desk, but Peter sauntered past——confident his military uniform gave him the authority to walk the halls without question.

He stopped a passing nurse to inquire about the floor with the influenza patients. She snickered. "Where aren't they? Take your pick."

Pete moved from floor to floor, asking about Melania's whereabouts. Finally, after covering three levels, he came upon a medical student who pointed to a young woman down the row. "I don't know her," the man said, "but that medical assistant does, I think." The student nodded his head toward the woman and immediately returned to his task.

Peter looked around, *seeing* the intensity of the scene for perhaps the first time. There was a strange mood here——a concentration of sickness and death, smells, sounds, and patterns. It was overwhelming, and his sister dealt with it every day.

Peter walked toward the woman and softly tapped her shoulder. "Miss?"

She rose from her bent position over the patient and turned to face him, smiling slightly. "Yes, how can I help you, sir?"

"I'm told you know my sister. Melania?"

A hand flew to the woman's mouth. "Yes, I'm Jane. What's happened to Melania?"

Peter's brows furrowed. "What do you mean? Isn't she here?"

Jane grabbed Peter by the wrist, dragging him away. "Come. We need to talk." She turned to him the moment they were in the corner. "She's sick. Isn't that why you're here?"

He shook his head the tiniest bit. "No. I've not seen her. Where is she?"

"Home, isn't she?" Jane's eyes widened, and she pressed her hand on Pete's forearm.

"I didn't come from home." Peter took in a deep breath. "Why don't you start from the beginning, so we can stop talking in circles? She *was* sick or *is* sick?"

"Good idea," Jane said with a nervous laugh before filling Peter in on the last week and some fellow named Archie's decision to bring Melania home. "I thought you'd come to tell me she'd died."

Pete's shoulder lifted. "I don't know how she is. I haven't heard any news, but then," he said, chuckling nervously, "no news is good news, right?" He took a deep breath, wondering what was going on at home——with his sister, his parents, Emily. Had influenza spread to the entire household? He pressed his lips together to stop himself from demanding an explanation as to why this Archie fellow would bring his sick sister *home* instead of leaving her in the hospital.

As if Jane read his mind, she said, "I wonder if Melania should have stayed here." She shook her head a bit. "Why did you come here, then?"

"Nuts!" Peter smacked himself lightly on the forehead. "I got sidetracked. I have a sick friend——a family friend. I hoped Melania could look after him."

"Where is he?" Jane glanced around.

"He's outside, deathly ill." Peter rolled his eyes. "Not that I've any medical training."

"You'd be surprised how little of that there is around here." She motioned toward the desk and leaned in as they walked in that direction. "Bunch of warm bodies here doing their damnedest to help those burning up with a fever and deal with others who are cold with death."

"That's callous."

Jane let out a long sigh and then turned to Peter, shrugging. "I'm really not unkind, just scared——and overwhelmed——like most of us here." She flipped the calendar pages and ran her finger along the list of orderlies working. "Ask for Jack on the second floor. He'll bring your friend inside while I get a bed ready."

Peter returned to the wagon and flipped Charlie a couple of coins. "One for your help, the other for the streetcar," he said, pointing to the horse and wagon. "After these are dealt with, of course."

"Yes, sir," Charlie said, saluting Peter before grabbing the horse and leading it toward the post.

"Pull up a chair," Jane beckoned when Peter returned and Jim had been deposited on a bed. "I have a few questions to ask before you leave."

Peter scanned Jim's form splayed out on the narrow cot——the sick man had essentially been dumped on the bed like a sack of flour. He lifted Jim's arm over the edge, tucking it under the blanket before pulling the spread up.

"I would've done that." Jane squinted and then smiled. "He's a good friend."

Peter sat, not knowing whether that was a question or a statement. "Yes," he said, pressing his fingers into his forehead. It was a miracle he'd found Jim, and equally astonishing he'd gotten him here.

"Then it's my honor to care for him." Jane held the clipboard on her lap, pen poised. "Name?"

"Peter Harvey."

Jane chuckled. "Not yours. His."

Peter pushed back his hair. "Sorry. Long day."

"They get that way, don't they?"

"James Wirth."

Jane scribbled——the sound of the pencil sharp against the paper. "Address?"

"Gee. I don't know." Peter pondered it for a moment. "Put down my family's address."

She added that to the form and then flipped the pages, filling in bits of information here and there. "Do you know how long he's been sick?"

Peter shrugged. "I just came upon him today." He shook his head. "It's quite incredible. I've been looking for him for so long." He turned and gazed vacantly across the room. "I'd almost given up," he added. "There was a boy who helped me——he lives across from Jim. Said Jim had been sick for nearly two weeks."

"That's a long time." Jane's mouth twisted in thought. "Usually, they're either well by then, or they die." Jane briefly set her hand on Peter's knee. "I'm not usually so blunt either."

"These are peculiar times," Peter said, nodding his head in understanding. "There's value in the truth. What are his chances?"

"Oh, Mr. Harvey," Jane said regrettably. "I can't promise anything except that I will do everything I can for Jim."

"All right, then." Peter leaned in close to Jim. "Come on, pal. You're hard-boiled——and this flu is squat. Give it the kiss-off!" He patted Jim's arm and turned to see Jane's smirk. "Rallying cry."

"Whatever works. Hey, looks like Dr. Abbott's free. Can you hang on, and I'll get him over?"

Peter nodded and moved to the window, leaning into the broad stone sill, crossing his arms as he watched Jane approach the doctor, speak to him, and then come back to Jim's bedside.

"He should be over soon. Do you have time?"

Peter shrugged. "I suppose so." He shook his head. "Delivering food boxes isn't an Army job with a description or expectation——no one will be looking for me until later." He hoped that meant he'd have time to swing by his parents' house and make sure everyone was all right.

When the doctor finally examined Jim, he agreed it was remarkable that Jim was still alive if the duration of his illness was, indeed, valid.

"From what I understand," Jane explained, looking at Peter for confirmation, "the patient was alone, so perhaps he recovered and then fell ill again. You know how——"

Dr. Abbott interrupted Jane curtly. "Leave the doctoring to the professionals."

Jane took a deep breath and crossed her arms. "What, then, do you suppose, doctor? Mr. Harvey here is——family," she said, winking at Peter. "He'd like to tell his parents of Jim's condition."

Dr. Abbott cleared his throat and finished his examination. "A relapse seems probable, considering this virulent disease generally makes up its mind who it will take within a week or so." He rubbed the stubble on his chin and continued. "The only reasonable explanation for how this man is still alive is that he, perhaps, had a few days to regain some strength." The doctor shrugged and scribbled something on Jim's chart. "Fetch me if he regains consciousness."

Jane sighed heavily, raising her brow at Peter. "Nothing new or helpful."

The doctor turned after a few steps and said, "Get him cleaned up and watch his breathing. I heard a bit of a rumble in his lungs. May need a dose of epinephrine."

Jane shuddered. "Lung conditions are serious." She grabbed the washbasin and walked with Peter down the row. "You may want to come again tomorrow——maybe bring news of Melania?"

"Yes, of course. I'm headed there now——or soon. I need to bring the horse and wagon to the base first."

"Horse? Wagon?" Jane lifted a brow as she filled the basin with water and grabbed a stack of washcloths and towels. "I figured the Quartermaster Corp would have them all." She shrugged when Peter's eyes narrowed. "My boyfriend is in training with the Corp."

"Ah," Peter said and then rolled his eyes. "I acquired one after its owner died. You have no idea what it's like out there."

"I think I may, actually. Madness——just like in here."

CHAPTER 38

Jacob Harvey settled in the upholstered chair in the front room after stoking the fire. The small lamp flickered on the table next to him, and the fire sent shards of light dancing off the walls. The darkness of the evening carried in colder temperatures——the wind howled outside and leafless branches beat a rhythm on the windows. He closed his eyes and breathed in the robust scent of burning oak, taking in the rare feeling of tranquility. His journey to and from Holmesburg had been taxing, more emotionally than physically. It was difficult leaving his grief-stricken wife here while taking Elizabeth away from all she knew. Thankfully, the child settled in quickly with Ida and her children, and Jacob was able to catch a return train without delay——another rarity in this time of war. The memory of a fierce October blizzard two years ago hung in his mind during the journey——fortunately, this year, the snow had not yet come.

Jacob leaned forward into the warmth and mulled over his plans to return to the mill. *Tomorrow,* or soon. Whenever his daughter was back on her feet. He'd helped Helene move her to her room, and she'd slept for days since his return, no change since she'd first been brought home, his wife had informed him. Jacob regularly wondered if that was a good sign or a bad one.

Nothing seemed predictable——this time of war and intense disease was unlike anything he'd ever experienced. The mill had little choice but to adapt and accommodate, especially when it came to their employees——the draft had already strained the mill to its limits and the disease had nearly pushed it beyond.

Jacob grabbed the newspaper and leaned back into the cushion, folding and creasing the pages until it was a quarter of its size, savoring both the quiet and the news as he moved through the pages, folding and creasing each time. It was such a curious mix of stories——the news was no longer dominated by the war or nativist activities. There were reports about citizen appeals to reopen businesses, accounts of saloons defying closure orders by allowing patrons in through side doors, and statistics on the latest death toll from the epidemic. Center pages were covered with sketches and reports on the horrific fire in Cloquet——the death and destruction profound. War news included a circulating rumor that an armistice had been reached, but no military official backed that up.

As Jacob was about to set the paper down, he noticed an inconspicuous article in the lower corner of the back page. A familiar name and face stood out——Mayor von Esson. A small sketch of the buttoned-up, balding mayor was under a small type heading, "***Mayor Falls Ill; Recovery Imminent!***" Jacob discouraged his family from openly criticizing public officials, feeling respect was due to the office, if not the man. Von Esson, however, had gone out of his way to make life more than difficult for anyone in Minneapolis of German ancestry. It was a knotty issue to feel any goodwill for the man.

NEWS FROM THE CITY OFFICES STATES THAT MAYOR WALTER VON ESSON HAS FALLEN ILL WITH INFLUENZA. VON ESSON WAS RESTING COMFORTABLY IN HIS HOME UNTIL A RECENT TURN IN HIS CONDITION FORCED HIS ADMITTANCE TO UNIVERSITY HOSPITAL. HE IS BEING ATTENDED BY HIS VERY COMPETENT PERSONAL PHYSICIAN IN A PRIVATE HOSPITAL ROOM. THE MAYOR IS OF

STRONG STOCK, AND THE DOCTOR EXPECTS A FULL
AND SWIFT RECOVERY. DEPUTY MAYOR STEMPEL WILL
ATTEND TO THE CITY'S BUSINESS UNTIL THE MAYOR
RETURNS TO FULL HEALTH.

"Hmm." Jacob set the newspaper in his lap, considering the odd story——along with its strange placement on the back page and its peculiarly upbeat nature. He shrugged. Maybe a year of intense propaganda had made him callous.

Jacob reached for the mug of tea and nibbled on a crispy butter cookie. Unexpectedly, heavy steps sounded on the front porch, and he glanced at the mantle clock, wondering who'd call at this hour. Too late for the military. A neighbor, perhaps? He rose and ambled to the door, opening it just as the person on the other side released the heavy door knocker.

"Peter! What are you doing here?" Jacob searched his son's face for clues to the news he had brought. "Is it Frank?"

Peter crossed the threshold and embraced his father. "No, no. Melania? How is she?"

"She's unchanged. Not better nor worse, Mutti says."

Peter took off his coat and followed Jacob into the living room, plopping down in a chair with a heavy sigh.

"How did you know about your sister?" Jacob asked. "Did Mutti write?"

"I was at the hospital and met her friend, Jane." Peter leaned forward and stared at his father. "Vati. I found Jim."

Jacob watched as his son's face registered relief and fear.

"In the hospital? You happened upon him there? Is he sick too?"

"Yes," Peter said. "Jim is gravely ill." Peter released a jagged breath. "I found him in St. Paul during my food delivery rounds with the Army. By some miracle. I brought him to the University Hospital, thinking Melania could care for him."

Jacob nodded slowly. "Yes, a miracle." He shook his head in disbelief. He'd told his son to keep a lookout for Jim, and he and Helene prayed for the lost man, yet he marveled at the news.

Jacob moved to the fire and threw on another log, turning to see the flames light up his son's face.

"Astounding. Truly a miracle," Jacob said again. "I'd often wondered if Jim had gone to his family farm in Augusta."

The two men talked as the fire faded into ashes, Jacob updating Peter on the Pritchard family, Melania, and Helene.

"I really must go," Peter said, standing. "I'll come back soon——for news of Melania and hopefully with a report on Jim."

Jacob went upstairs after his son left and peered into the bedroom, seeing Helene's body rise up and down in a deep sleep. He went down the hall and into Melania's room, watching over her, touching her forehead. Cool. *Finally*. He listened as her breaths came and went in an even rhythm. Maybe she'd gotten to the other side. She stirred and turned over, the blanket twisting around her legs.

He pulled it loose and settled it evenly over her before pulling up a chair to her bedside. He leaned forward in prayer, resting his elbows on the bed and his forehead on his folded hands, running through a list of thanksgivings and petitions, barely able to form a lucid prayer by the time his thoughts turned to his children overseas. He slipped into a dreamless sleep.

Jacob's neck was stiff as he awakened the next day, the unfortunate position causing him to groan as he stood and stretched. He pushed the curtain open, the light streaming in bright beams across the space. Melania yawned and stretched, her eyes flittering open. "Vati?" She looked around. "How did I get here?" She tried to push herself to sit.

"Hold on. Hold on." He moved to her and swept back the hair from her forehead, grateful that it was still cool. "You were sick. Your friend Archie brought you home."

"Oh, yes." She paused, leaning on one elbow. "I remember now." She pushed herself up again.

"Are you sure you're ready for that?"

"Oh my." She put her hand to her head. "I'm still a tad woozy, but I just need to move a bit."

Jacob propped the pillows around her as she sat up.

"There," Melania said, nodding. "I feel slightly more right-sided." She reached for the glass of water at her bedside and took a sip. "Gee, my throat was so dry."

"Ja. Mutti struggled to get you to drink these past days."

Melania put her hand to her throat, her face wrinkling in memory. "I remember now. It hurt so much."

"She'll be pleased you're up and without fever." Jacob's eyes narrowed. "Rest——for your sake and for hers."

Jacob left his daughter and hurried downstairs, where he found Helene in the kitchen, making coffee and eggs. He placed his arms on her shoulders and kissed her cheek. "Melania is awake and well." He nodded when Helene turned. "No fever and sitting up."

Helene quickly put together a tray of toast and tea. "I'll take this up," she said brightly as she left the kitchen.

Jacob helped Melania down the stairs the following day, the girl still a bit weak but with more color in her cheeks. "Are relapses common?" he asked her as she sat down at the kitchen table. He looked over her head to Helene, knowing she likely wondered the same thing. It had happened with Emily, after all.

"I didn't have influenza before," Melania stated matter-of-factly. "I'm sure it was just something I ate." She dunked her toast in the egg yolk and took a bite. "I was probably just too eager to get back to work."

"I hope you're right." Helene narrowed her eyes.

"From what you've told me about Emily, my case isn't the same. *She* had a relapse. I didn't." Melania set her fork down and smiled at her mother. "Relapses *do* happen, but it's not a given." She shrugged casually. "Don't worry, Mutti. I'm fine. Really."

"Be that as it may, you won't help anyone if you get sick again." Jacob raised a brow, knowing the conversation was unlikely to end in total agreement. Thankfully, Peter's arrival at the back door changed the focus.

"Melania! So happy to see you up and well." Peter went straight to her and pulled her up, wrapping his arms around her.

Melania embraced him. "See? Even Pete sees that I'm well."

"You are, aren't you?" Peter's forehead creased as he pushed her out to arm's length and did the once over.

"Yes. *Finally.*" Melania exhaled heavily. "Why are you here? Aren't you supposed to be at the Army base?"

"You haven't told her?" Peter looked at his parents, and Jacob wondered about the wisdom of sharing this news with their daughter. Was she strong enough to handle it?

"Told me what?" Melania looked between the faces.

"Jim's in the hospital."

"You found him? Oh, thank goodness!" Her brow furrowed. "Hospital? Is that where he was?"

Peter sat and encouraged Melania to do the same as he gave her a much shorter and less-detailed version of what had transpired with Jim.

Jacob glanced at Helene and noticed that she, too, watched as Melania's expression changed from shock to genuine concern to conviction.

Melania stood. "I'm going back with you, Pete. Wait while I get my things." She hastened out the kitchen door without waiting to hear any resistance from her family.

"Is she truly better?" Peter's brows knit together.

"The girl's going to do what she thinks is best. Stubborn, that one." A smile flitted across Jacob's face.

"Just like most of the Harvey gang," Helene chortled, sitting down at the table after pouring herself a cup of coffee.

"Who's this Archie fella? Melania's friend Jane said he brought her home."

Helene shrugged. "I suspect he's smitten, but Melania's clearly not."

Peter shook his head. "Not about *that one*, anyway. I may be a bit thick when it comes to women, but she has *besotted* written all over her face." He laughed. "Did you notice her worry over Jim? She practically ran from the room to get packed for the hospital."

"Nothing like that with poor ol' Archie, I'm afraid." Helene leaned an elbow on the table. "How's Jim?"

"Still serious. He has a lung infection."

"Do you think he'll pull through?" Jacob knew the question was bleak, and he regretted it as soon as it left his lips. What could they do about it anyway? Thankfully, the question remained unaddressed when Melania burst into the kitchen.

"Let's get going, Pete. I've got a patient to attend." Melania quickly embraced her parents and then dragged her brother out the door.

Peter pulled open the large oak door to the University Hospital, ushering his sister inside. Melania stopped in the lobby and gazed up at the grand staircase, taking a deep breath.

"Are you sure you're up for this?"

"Yes." She pressed her hand to her heart. "It's just such a solemn place——now especially."

"I noticed that," Peter said, following his sister upstairs. "Beyond words, really, but there seems to be a force here. The human spirit, maybe."

"I know what you mean. It sometimes feels like our only weapon against this disease."

Peter stopped Melania on the landing before she moved through the doors of the sick ward. "You know that despite your best efforts, you may be unable to save him."

Melania shook her head slightly and opened the door. "I must," she said, slipping inside.

Peter paused inside the doorway, watching as his sister moved to Jim's bedside, brushed her hand across his forehead, shook her head, and put a cool cloth on him. The chair screeched loudly as Melania pulled it to the bedside and sat, taking Jim's hand between hers and bowing her head——in prayer, he guessed. Peter looked away, scanning the room for Jane, seeing her on the other side near the nurse's station. He also noticed a man intently watching Melania. The fellow, medium height and build, with blond hair sticking out of his white cap, seemed particularly interested in Melania's hand around Jim's. Peter wondered if the man was a doctor, maybe concerned at the special attention Melania was giving Jim when so many others needed assistance. Abruptly, the man brushed the cap from his head and gripped it tightly. *Curious.* Peter shrugged and went off to talk with Jane.

"Hello, Mr. Harvey!" Jane squeezed Peter's forearm. "I hope you have good news on Melania."

"I do. She's over there with Jim." Peter pointed across the room.

"Thank goodness!" Jane put her hand over her heart. "I was so worried. She's all right, isn't she? Arch wondered if he'd made a mistake bringing her home."

"Yes, she's well. I'm not sure it was the right decision, but she did recover, so perhaps it was."

"Archie said it was Melania's request."

Peter laughed. "That makes sense. She's a determined one." He laughed again. "I can imagine her, in the throes of her illness, demanding to be taken home." He grinned and shook his head. "There's little logic in being removed from a hospital when sick!"

Jane raised a brow. "Archie *would* do whatever she asked. He's a bit blinded with affection. He'll be glad to hear of her recovery."

Peter followed the direction of her gaze, realizing she was watching the same man who'd been observing Melania and Jim. Suddenly, the man turned and came quickly toward Jane and Peter, thrusting his hospital cap and coat into Jane's hands. "I need to get out of here."

"Why?" Jane called as the man hurried on.

"Him!" He turned and pointed across the room toward Melania. "*He* must be the reason she rebuffs me at every turn." He huffed and stalked out the door.

Jane called after him. "Archie! Wait!" She turned to Peter. "I'm sorry, I must go." She ran out the door.

"Archie. Poor fella." Peter exhaled deeply, shaking his head. He took one last glance at Jim and decided it best not to interrupt his sister, so he headed to the nurse's station and flipped through the ledger, swiftly paging until he found Jim's name. *Stable* was the last update logged earlier this morning. That would have to suffice for now.

Chapter 39

November 1918 • **THE WAR IS OVER! GERMANY SIGNS ARMISTICE!** On November 8, German delegates were escorted through a devastated French countryside to a railway car in the Compiegne Forest, Marshal Foch's Headquarters. They were presented with the terms of the Allied Armistice. The fighting ended on the Western Front, Paris time 11:00 a.m. on November 11, when Germany signed a truce with the Allied Powers. The terms are harsh, intended to show German acceptance of defeat and prevent any lengthy chance for Germany to regroup and start military action again.

Jim's eyes opened slowly, bringing an acute awareness of his stiff limbs. He looked up at the high ceilings, and his eyes scrunched in confusion, expecting to see his lodgings' stained and sparsely plastered ceiling. He turned to look around, but the pain forced him to squeeze his eyes shut, and a moan escaped.

The sound of his groan must have sailed above the din because suddenly, someone was at his side.

"Oh my! You're awake."

Jim rubbed his eyes, trying to focus through the bright lights and sort out why this voice sounded familiar. "Where am I?" he squeaked, putting his hand to his throat.

"Shhh. Don't talk until I get you some water."

"Melania?"

"Yes, here, drink——just a little now." She wiped his chin. "Thank God you're finally awake."

"Where?" Jim struggled to move again.

"Here, let me prop you." Melania pushed an extra pillow behind him and looped her hand under his arm, pulling him upright.

He squeezed his eyes shut.

"You've been lying flat for some time. Sores will lessen now that you're awake and can move more."

"How did I——" His head and thoughts were so jumbled.

Melania pulled up the chair and sat. "Goodness, it's a rather long story. Are you sure you're up for it?"

Jim nodded.

"For starters, you're at the University Hospital. Peter brought you here. He found you, by God's mercy, in Connemara."

Jim's brow furrowed as his mind struggled to piece together the events. He shook his head.

"Don't worry about putting it all together," Melania said, and he was surprised that she seemed to read his mind. "It's been several weeks."

He stared at her. "Weeks?" He flipped back the covers. He had to get back to work.

"Whoa. Hold still. What do you need to get back to?" Melania winced. "Sorry. I didn't mean it like that. I meant——you have to recover, *fully*, before you can think of anything else."

"Have I been here the entire time?"

"No. Only for a week now. Seems you were in your apartment before that."

"And Peter found me?" Jim's head shook slowly. It was just so difficult to believe.

"It's hard to fathom," Melania said, and Jim's eyes narrowed. Was he saying these things out loud?

"No one knew where you were." Her eyes became distant, and her forehead creased.

Jim watched her, searching her expression. What could he say? How could he possibly explain all that had led to him leaving Minneapolis? His mind was muddled, and he struggled to find the words. "I——I didn't mean to——" He looked directly at her, hoping she could see his sincerity, and then he turned away, frustrated that he couldn't encapsulate the past year in a few sentences. If anything, maybe he could clear the air. "I'm sorry——"

Melania abruptly stood and began attending to what Jim supposed were *nursing* duties. "Another time," she said, turning back briefly to face him. "Focus on regaining your strength for now." She refilled the water pitcher and cup, folded the blanket, and pulled the curtain open to the window.

He studied her as she worked, never looking at him but chattering about the epidemic and seemingly random things. Was she nervous? Or was she trying to change the subject? "It seems the worst has passed. Bans and restrictions are being lifted. The university will reopen on November 18. But there's a strike by local telephone operators now." Melania chuckled. "All kinds of new mayhem for the city."

"Were you here the entire time?"

She looked at him this time, her cheeks flushed.

"Yes. I mean, no, not initially." She stumbled over the words. "But yes, mostly."

Another medical aide sashayed into the space. "So this is Jim! Nice to see you awake." She stretched her arm and pulled Melania to her side. "This one has hardly left your side since you arrived. I'm Jane, Melania's dear friend." Jane leaned in. "Say, you *do* have piercing green eyes!" She winked at Melania and left.

Melania blushed. "I apologize for her. Some friend! Are you hungry?"

Jim was tempted to tease another blush out of Melania but thought the best of it, considering the tenuous state of their connection and the fact that he was famished. "I would greatly appreciate that," he said instead.

"I'll be back soon. The food isn't like my mother's, but——" Melania lifted a shoulder and then headed to the cafeteria.

Jim sat up and swung his legs around, sitting on the edge of the bed. His head spun, and he held the side table until it stopped. He sipped water and looked around, taking in the vast space, filled from wall to wall with beds. Two men carried a stretcher, set it down, and loaded a man on it, covering him fully with a sheet. Further away, a woman leaned over a child's bedside, her body shaking with obvious grief. Bit by bit, as he looked around——seeing and sometimes only hearing the agony and suffering——the miracle of his recovery washed over him. He closed his eyes and remembered the burning that had thrashed his throat, the intense body aches and raging fever that threw him from hot to cold. He rubbed his hands along his arms, remembering the pain that seemed worse than any beating he'd ever received. He drew in a deep breath and thought of those dark days in Minneapolis when he was rejected at every turn. But the Harvey family had never spurned him. He recalled the evening at the Harvey home after the horrific railroad incident——the family caring for him, body and soul, without judgment. He squeezed his eyes shut as shame and gratitude mixed together. Peter had found him——that thought surfaced. Had he been looking for Jim?

And then there was Melania. She plainly had spurned him. *Or had she?* He ran his hand through his greasy hair and released a long breath. He'd pursued her fervently since the first day they'd met at the dance, charming her, he'd imagined, with his wit and humor. He snorted. *Some ego.* Honestly, she had captivated him instantly——her self-possession was unlike anything he'd seen in a woman before. He knew he ruffled her——he could see it in her face. Typically, with other girls, it was easier. Many fawned over him——at least the girls in Augusta did, the main reason he'd high-tailed it out of there. Sure, they were friendly, those farmers' daughters, and they'd make fine wives, but they weren't Melania.

She wasn't silly or frivolous. She was serious-minded and had plans to become a teacher——dreams, he suddenly realized, he had never taken seriously, disregarding them entirely if he was being truthful. *What a fool.*

Melania had held him at arm's length, and though she'd seemed flustered by his presence, she'd stood her ground. It had felt like a challenge, he now realized, so he'd chased her with total disregard for what she may have wanted. In fact, he had never even asked, turning on the charm and backing her into a corner with his full-on pursuit. For months, she had pushed him back, and never once had Jim asked *why*. Instead, he'd continued laying on his charisma. *Oh lands! What a way to gum up the works!*

Then when she'd finally agreed to go to the theater with him, he'd ruined an enjoyable evening with a—— *With a what?* He wasn't even sure what he'd been planning to say. He only knew he'd been overcome that evening. The war, the propaganda, the draft. It had all seemed to be closing in on them that evening, and at that moment, he'd wanted——needed——to hold on to her. She had enjoyed their time together that night, though. He *knew* that for sure, though it appeared now that he'd been clueless about most everything else.

He exhaled heavily as these truths washed over him so powerfully that they nearly felt physical. He moved to stand, stretching out his lethargic muscles, taking several paces to the window. He looked out into the streets. Melania had been right. People were milling about——not as before the epidemic, but there was *life*. He turned and gingerly moved back to his bed, carefully sitting down to avoid planting himself face-first on the floor. He saw her as she came into the room with his food tray. Who was this girl? The same physical beauty that had first caught his eye, but so much more.

He could see that now——now that he was paying attention. She was here——at the university where she wanted to be. Maybe not pursuing her dreams of teaching at the moment, but soon. In the meantime, she was also *here*——in the midst of this ghastly epidemic, fighting the good fight for him and others.

Melania set the tray on a side table near the entrance, heeding a nearby doctor's call. Jim watched her as she nodded at the doctor's words and then proceeded, he assumed, to carry out the instructions. Jim had never seen her like this——in this light. He blinked back tears. *What in the world was going on?* He pushed himself back on the mattress as Melania came near him.

She set the tray on his lap. "Are you feeling unwell?"

"No. No." Jim shook his head. "I was just thinking, remembering." Despite his efforts to remain calm, the words tumbled out. "Melania. You don't know. You can't know." The feelings were coming out faster than he could string together coherent thoughts.

"What? What is it?" Melania's soft voice probed while she sat down.

"I was wrong, so wrong. Then so lost——alone." Jim struggled to remain composed. "After the railroad. After you. After the arrest." He stopped again, shaking his head. "No——it doesn't matter." He dug a fork in a mound of potatoes and shoved them in his mouth, turning his head away.

Melania stood and pushed the chair aside. Jim turned back. "Thank you for taking care of me, and thank you for the food." He stabbed at a piece of meat and moved his focus to the tray.

He listened as her footsteps clipped away and down the row, and he looked up when they abruptly stopped. She sat on the edge of a bed and dropped her head into her hands.

"Oh, lands," Jim said, dropping his fork on his plate. He hadn't meant to upset her——only spare her. He was surprised when she stood again and turned back, hastening toward him.

"Listen," Melania said, spilling out words nearly as frantically as he had. "So much time has passed. I've done things and seen things I never dreamed possible. I've faced death, loss, and joy——sometimes in the same hour. I've worried, I've prayed, I've been afraid, and I've grown. I'm not the same girl who walked away from you at the theater. And I am certainly not the girl you met at the dance." She huffed and snorted, pressing her lips together, sitting down hard in the chair and pulling it closer to Jim's bed.

He stared at her, not daring to interrupt. She took a breath and continued. "The war changed us, and this Spanish influenza is a brutal bookend to those horrific days. I don't know what the future holds——mine, or——" She stopped and snickered. "I've spent as much time in the medical world as in college. Who knows if I'll ever be a teacher?" She reached for his hand, and he nearly pulled it away, but she clamped both of hers over his. "I was wrong too. I did have feelings for you. I still do." A brow arched as she smirked. "I worried for you, prayed for you, and frankly, missed you." A tear trickled down her cheek, and Jim reached to brush it away.

Chapter 40

The St. Paul Army base was bursting with activity——soldiers trick-led in from posts abroad while others were just being deployed. Despite the Armistice with Germany, French, American, British, and Belgian troops would occupy the Rhineland indefinitely. Peter was released from his civilian service and prepared, along with scores of others, to keep watch on the Rhine.

Peter rolled his extra clothes, tucking them in his knapsack along with a few personal belongings while his thoughts wandered to his brothers and sister. He wondered which one would make it home first. Frank's short time in the service had been spent in France under the command of General Pershing. *Doggone,* Peter thought. It was a miracle that Frank hadn't been killed in the battle the General had led on the morning the Armistice was signed. Anna would need to be released from her Red Cross duties, but with the staggering number of American casualties flooding the hospital after the late battle, who knew when that would be? Then there was Mathias, his only letter home reassuring them he was alive, at least *then*, but who knew about *now*? Vati had told Peter of a clause in the Armistice agreement that called for *the immediate* repatriation of American and British prisoners of war. Still, speed was a relative term——and releasing captives was likely a low priority to a defeated army.

It seemed surreal that *he* was leaving for Europe at the war's end when others were on their way home. Peter initially felt disappointed that his commission was the occupation of a territory instead of battling for it. But any notion of *missing out on the action* was quickly changed after more and more battle-weary troops returned home, some missing limbs, others with disfigured faces, and still others in body bags.

Peter swung the pack over his shoulder and made his way to the wagon that would take him and the others to the train station. The group would travel to the east coast via the railroad, where they'd board ships heading overseas. As the horses began to pull the large, loaded wagon down the base road, a man came running after it, about twenty feet back. "Wait, wait!" the man yelled, waving his arms.

Word traveled from soldier to soldier until it reached the front, and the driver pulled the horses to a stop, turning back and yelling, "Come on! We don't have all day!"

Peter extended his hand, helping the man up and onto the wagon. *Where have I seen him before?* Peter's mouth twisted in thought and then broke into a grin when the man held out his hand. "Thanks. I'm Archie Addington."

"I'm Peter." Peter shook his hand. "I thought we had a full squad. What's up?"

"I volunteered. I need to get out of here." Archie shook his head as if he was shaking off bad memories. "A change of surroundings is just the ticket."

Peter nodded. "Wise choice, then. You're soon to get a whole new outlook on the world."

CHAPTER 41

The air was crisp and cold——snow swirled down in big lofty flakes, wrapping in bunches around tree bases, only to be lifted up and around by the gusty north winds. Helene gazed out the windows, glazed in the corners with frosty etchings, lighting lamps as she moved through the rooms. Thoughts of her children overseas ran through her mind. Frank's wife had told them he'd been demobilized and was now en route back to the states. Returning home would take a while, even after he arrived in the United States. Helene doubted Frank would stop here before heading to Holmesburg but lit the welcoming lights anyway.

She smiled when she passed the mantle where Peter's postcard was perched——the cheery farewell he'd sent just before boarding the ship bound for Europe. His service was just beginning, and she was grateful it was a peacetime occupation that took her son to Germany. Surely Jacob would follow whatever news of the Rhineland made its way to the American newspapers.

What news had come recently was hopeful, if not still a bit unsettling for Mathias's sake. Reports stated that many prisoners were only now being released from camps across the globe. Perhaps the new year would bring updates, but her fervent wish was that it would convey Mathias himself.

She sighed heavily as she moved through the swinging door to the kitchen, the welcoming aromas of fresh-baked bread and simmering stew filling the space. She set the table for herself and Jacob as she thought of Anna. They'd learned recently that the French Red Cross hospitals were dealing with the injuries sustained in the final days of both Pershing's battle and the East African campaign. She didn't know if she was more relieved or worried that Anna was still in France rather than making the complicated journey home. She exhaled heavily again. It would be a difficult Christmas for the entire Harvey family but also one that foretold of the hope to come——not only the hope in Jesus but also the approaching days when everyone would be back where they belonged.

Helene's heart squeezed as she thought of Elizabeth. She missed the girl dearly and could not stop the ache from Emily's death. Sharp, painful memories mixed with sweet ones from earlier days. Helene had written to Emily's parents straightaway after Emily's death, but the pandemic prevented the Bartons from traveling from Boston to claim the body and their grandchild. At their request, Emily was buried in the local church cemetery. A memorial was planned for the spring——a time for the Bartons to mourn and collect their grandchild. Helene's mouth pinched at the thought of Elizabeth going so far away permanently, but the little girl belonged with her grandparents.

Helene took the cutting board from the shelf and began slicing the bread. She saw Jacob as she glanced out the window. He strolled down the alley and through the gate with surprising vigor——there was a lightness to his step since the war had ended. Of course, her husband was realistic, knowing they were still far from calm and goodwill if that would ever come. *Peacetime* was a misnomer, he always said, yet he was hopeful. Helene smiled, thinking of a verse from Hebrews——*Now faith is the substance of things hoped for, the evidence of things not seen.* Duty was foundational to Jacob, as was prayer, and he continued to work long hours at the mill and would carry on until the workload and demand relented——assuming they could go back to prewar days. Clearly, not as many men who'd left for war would return, and further injury and death took their toll from both the conflict and influenza. Helene hadn't returned to the factory after Emily's death, but Jacob would remain until he was no longer needed. She smiled at that thought, wondering when the mill wouldn't need her husband's skill and wisdom.

"Hello, my wife," Jacob said as he came through the door. "It smells delicious in here." He lifted the lid on the stew and breathed in deeply.

"You're a curious one," Helene said with a raised brow. "Just stew——again."

"Still," he said, pecking her on the cheek. "You made it, and I'm home." He reached in his pocket as he hung his coat on the peg. "I come bearing news from Anna." He handed her the envelope. "Read it while we eat."

"Yes," Helene said, smiling as she dished the stew. "I hope it's good news."

Jacob washed his hands and then sat at the table. "I'm optimistic."

Helene grinned as she sat and slid her finger under the envelope's seal, pulled out the letter, and flipped over the page. "It's fairly long, at any rate. The difference between letters from a son and a daughter."

Dear Mutti and Vati, Goodness! The war is over, but you wouldn't know it here! We're busier than ever, with injured troops from all over being delivered to the many Red Cross facilities to be cared for before returning home. It's heartbreaking that some come to us near death and don't survive to make the trip home. So close. But we do now, as in war, the best we can. There are amazingly talented doctors among us. I have learned much from being around them. Dr. Lachance, in particular, is a brilliant man, and we are all the better for his service. He's compassionate as well as skilled—more important than ever with the POWs making their way to us in droves. I find it amusing that my pull to do benevolent, meaningful work has been found amid the war rather than in a convent! God's plans are better than our own! I am not sure how much longer

I will be in France, but I predict it will be well into the new year. We have much work to do here, and as the good doctor Lachance says, "It only takes ordinary talent and uncommon persistence." Despite the slim likelihood that he'll end up under my care, I keep watching for Mathias. In the meantime, I eagerly await your return letter with updates on all my brothers and young Melania. I hope she found meaningful commissions for herself in the war effort. The fondest wishes for a Merry Christmas——or a Joyeux Noël, as they say in France! Your daughter, Anna

Helene cleared her throat, and Jacob let out a loud chortle. "Meaningful commissions! Ha! If Anna only knew what the young Melania has done of late."

Helene shook her head. "Sometimes, the older sister can't see the forest for the trees." She shrugged. "Melania did, however, surprise us all, if we're being honest."

Jacob nodded as he dipped his bread in the bowl, swiping up the remaining gravy. "It was in there, that spirit covered by stubbornness and a bit of youthfulness." He looked at Helene. "Time would have brought it about, but war and disease thrust Melania's strength of character to the forefront."

"Goodness." Helene finally dug into her stew, slowly chewing as she reflected. "I feel weary sometimes thinking of it all." She took a bite of her bread and then chuckled. "Seems our Anna has eyes for a French doctor."

Jacob held up his hand. "I know nothing of the whims of a woman. That's a discussion for you and Melania." He stood and moved to the sink, setting his bowl and spoon in the water. "I sent a telegram to Frank's wife today, suggesting she bring the children to the city for Christmas."

Helene brightened. "Oh my! What a gift that would be! What about Frank? Do you think he'll be home in time?"

"It's difficult to say," Jacob said, "but I told Ida I'd attempt to intercept him at the station before he headed home. I've heard they've been posting estimated arrival schedules at the train station."

"Considering the telephone operators are still on strike, I'm certain that's most helpful."

Helene's whole body lightened. Perhaps they had some bright days ahead after all.

Jacob got up and cleared his dishes, and then moved toward the front room, stopping in the doorway. "I asked Ida to bring Elizabeth and all her belongings along. I think the child should stay with us until her grandparents arrive in the spring."

"Oh yes!" Helene put her hand to her heart and smiled. "Thank you," she said, standing and pecking Jacob on the cheek. "Go stoke the fire, and I'll bring in cake and coffee."

Helene came into the front room as Jacob was reaching for the box of Diamond matches. She watched as he absently pulled one out and struck the side of the box, igniting the red head. He held it for a moment, watching the red phosphorous glow before tossing it into the dry kindling and paper. Helene set the tray of coffee and cake on the table and sat just as the flames grew and caught the larger logs. The curved iron screen banged on the hearth as her husband set it around the fire to prevent the logs from tumbling onto the floor.

"Such good news." Helene could hear the smile in her own voice. She took a forkful of cake. "What about Melania? Do you think she'll come home?"

"I thought I'd check on her Saturday after my shift." Jacob sat and sipped his coffee, the cup clinking in the saucer as he set it down. "Another influenza spike in both cities, so schools are closed until after the new year.

I don't know what that means for her work at the hospital, but I imagine it will extend it."

"Is it safe to bring Elizabeth here then?" As much as Helene longed to see the child, she wasn't willing to do so at the expense of endangering her.

"Ja. I think so. She'll stay mostly inside with you, and the recent spikes in illness seem to go quickly." Jacob shrugged.

"I'd like to invite Jim as well." Helene smiled broadly, the feelings of elation a sharp contrast to the melancholy from earlier. "Fill the house with joy."

Jacob laughed. "Not quite the same level of merriment without Peter here to banter with Jim, but I'm sure our daughter would be glad."

"So you do know some of the whims of a woman then?" She chortled and sipped her coffee.

"Well, dear, she did say in her short note the other day that Jim was fully healed and back working at Prager's." Jacob rose and moved to the fire. "So I assume she remains interested in the man's well-being if nothing else." He chuckled and threw a log on the fire.

Helene nodded in agreement. "You're a wise one."

Jacob poked at the fire and became serious. "You know that Gus will likely choose to stay in Holmesburg over Christmas again——what with his experience last year."

"Yes, I confess I agree." Helene stood and wrapped her arms around her middle, moving to the frosted panes of the window. No one knew how long it would take to shake the memories and consequences of war and Spanish influenza. She breathed in the cold air that hung on the edges of the glass, watching her exhaled breath fog and then turn the wet air into ice crystals. She spotted children next door, running around, catching the big snowflakes on their tongues——their sing-song voices floating through the crisp air. Helene shuddered at the memory of their same voices drifting to her window just a few months back.

"What is it?" Jacob asked as she moved away from the window.

"Nothing. Just a memory."

CHAPTER 42

The hospital reopened to the public in mid-December with little fanfare after the influenza patients were moved to one floor of the infirmary to clear the way for other cases. New patients only trickled in, with many citizens remaining close to home, unable to shake off their heightened vigilance. The public and medical communities breathed a sigh of relief after the latest influenza peak quickly subsided, with most of the affected recovering swiftly and returning home. Many people hesitantly reestablished routines, though they remained watchful for the unexpected that came with this disease.

Melania gratefully moved out of the hospital dormitory, along with the other medical personnel. The temporary confinement had been a necessary but grueling existence——little outside contact with the world, long and arduous work shifts, sparse sleep, and little time for food. It had been an experience unlike anything Melania——or most people——had ever encountered, and she was glad to at last get some physical separation from the disease.

"It seems like ages since we've been here," she said as she pushed into her dorm room behind Jane. She glanced around at the dust particles that floated through the air. "Smells a bit musty, but I guess that's what happens when you seal a room for weeks on end."

"I'm exhausted!" Jane plunked her case down on her bed. "Goodness," she said, flopping down next to it and reaching for her pillow. "I could sleep for days!"

Melania laughed as she dropped her satchel of belongings next to her bed, pulled up a chair, and rested her feet on the mattress. "I agree. I'm sitting only to stay awake." She eyed Jane stretched comfortably on the bed. "Maybe a quick nap before we go to the bookstore." She yawned. "Gosh, I thought the burden would lift——literally——when we left the hospital dormitories. You know, shaking off the experience."

Jane stretched her arms overhead and nodded sleepily in agreement. "I don't know how we did it, honestly." She swung her legs around and stood up. "You're right about the bookstore. We should go before we nap, though. They're closing soon." She pointed to the wall clock.

"I suppose." Melania got up from the chair and grabbed her coat, slipping it back on. "Hopefully, school really will start this time. Goodness, we missed an entire semester."

"Everyone did. That's the only relief. I'd hate to get behind."

Melania laughed as she closed and locked the apartment door behind them. "We must be wearied if we're looking forward to school."

Jane hooked Melania's arm and pulled her across the campus square toward the student center as the sun was dropping behind the buildings. A chilly wind blew in thick, dense clouds, foretelling imminent snow. Lights flickered in windows throughout the space——bringing life back to the school.

Half an hour later, swirls of white whipped around them as they left the bookstore with their purchases. "Oh, this snow!" Melania blinked as large flakes landed on her eyelashes, threatening to slide into her eyes.

"Seems we skipped from summer right into winter," Jane chuckled wryly. "We spent the whole of autumn sequestered in the hospital."

"Locked away! Is the year still 1918?" The light banter seemed a relief, a balm after the intense and unyielding pandemic, though realities always crept in.

"Did you hear that Lawrence died? Your Lawrence," Jane clarified.

Melania stopped in her tracks, turning to Jane. "Do you mean the man who was there weeks ago? Two different times?"

"Yes, him."

"It couldn't be. He was well. He recovered." Melania nearly shouted now in disbelief, tears filling her eyes.

"I'm sorry." Jane squeezed her hand. "I know you were fond of him." The snow fell harder, clumps forming on their shoulders as they stood on the whitening lawn.

"In the beginning——before things got so bad——I felt like I could make a difference. You know, connect with the patients." Melania's voice wandered off. "I promised him——"

"I know. I know." Jane pulled Melania by the hand, prodding her to keep walking as the snow increased.

"I remember that day when I first became ill," Melania reminisced. "It was the same time as Lawrence's relapse. I looked in the logbook, and his name didn't have the dreaded red line through it." She shook her head as tears continued to fall. "I had such hope."

"He did leave the hospital soon after you left for home," Jane recalled. "We were so busy, so full, and gravely understaffed. I think many patients left prematurely."

Melania stopped again, the snow gathering on her coat as she stood. "When? When did he come back?"

"It was yesterday after you'd left for a bite to eat. Lawrence's brother carried him in. He was barely conscious——died almost immediately."

Tears flowed, and Melania was unable to stop them. "I——I don't know why I'm crying. I didn't even know him. Not really." She sniffled and ran a mittened hand across her cheeks.

Jane put her arm around Melania's shoulder, pulling her in close. "General tears, I think. I've cried them myself——many times."

Melania sniffled and blinked the tears back. "Goodness. We'll turn into snowmen if we stay here any longer. Let's run."

They ran down the sidewalk, their boots sliding on the slick paths. "This reminds me of skating." Jane grinned. "We should go to the park once the ponds freeze."

"Grand idea. Something completely ordinary."

When they returned to their room, the girls stamped their feet on the rug and hung their coats on the pegs near the door. The melting snow pooled in clumps near the baseboards. Melania stacked her books on the table next to her bed and turned on the light. She sniffled and plopped down in the upholstered chair, a worn but comfortable piece, leaned back, and closed her eyes, working through her sadness. Her stomach grumbled, and she opened her eyes to see Jane foraging in the small cupboard. "You too?" Melania stood up. "Darn. We never thought about food." She sighed. "Do you think the school cafeteria is open?"

"Doubtful. Although it should be. We're not the only students back on campus." Jane thumped the cupboard closed. "Empty——or, more accurately, nothing edible." She giggled.

"I don't think the dining hall will be open until January when classes start." Melania sighed heavily again. "Guess we could head back to the hospital's cafeteria. Or the corner store?" She moved to fetch her coat.

"I'll go," Jane said. "You just recuperate. Regenerate. Wallow. Whatever you need, dear friend. We have a right to be sad and tired."

Jane slipped her soggy wet coat back on and rolled her eyes as water dripped from the sleeves. "It's times like these that I wish we had a man around!" She chuckled. "Jasper. Archie. Either one of them would have fetched us supper."

Melania's eyes narrowed. "Have you heard from Jasper yet?" She stood, moving toward Jane. "I'm sorry." She put her hand on Jane's forearm. "Here I am blubbering away, and you're the one without news on your boyfriend."

Jane shook her head, and her shoulders slumped. "Not yet," she said, her voice dropping to almost a whisper.

Melania embraced her friend and then pulled back. "You *are* soaked! Goodness!" She smiled hopefully. "I'm sure you'll hear from Jasper soon. He's probably on one of those interminable ocean voyages at this very moment. My father says many of our men are coming back on captured battleships." She raised her brows and stopped speaking. Jane may be optimistic, but she wasn't foolish. In this case, no news wasn't good news, and Melania couldn't think of any way to ease the pain.

"I haven't seen Archie around lately." Melania hoped the change of subject would lighten the mood. "First I was sick, then Jim, and then the last peak of the flu." She paused and shrugged. "Was he working on another floor?"

Her brow furrowed at Jane's expression. Maybe she'd been wrong to divert the conversation away from Jasper. "Gosh, Jane. What a heel I am—changing the subject when you probably need to talk about your boyfriend." Melania touched Jane's arm. "The food can wait. Sit. Let's talk."

She was surprised when Jane's mouth pinched, and she began buttoning up her coat without commenting.

"What is it? Are you angry with me? Or did something happen to Archie?"

Jane released a heavy sigh. "No, I'm not angry with you, and no, Archie's fine." Jane waved her hand dismissively.

"What is it then?"

"He saw you. With Jim."

"What do you mean?" Melania stared at Jane. It was only natural that Archie had seen her taking care of Jim. After all, they worked in the same hospital.

"He didn't seem too pleased with the care and attention you gave Jim. He seemed to think that must be why you rebuffed him."

"What does that mean? Rebuffed him?"

"Oh, come now." Jane put her hands on her hips. "Don't tell me you never noticed how smitten Arch was with you." Her face pinched, and she focused on tying her scarf.

"Well, I suppose," Melania admitted. "I tried not to encourage him. He knew how important school was, *is*, for me." Melania sighed deeply and sat back down.

"I understand that, and I think Arch did too," said Jane. "But it *was* different with Jim. Everyone noticed it."

"Noticed what?" Melania asked.

"Melania Harvey! You are exasperating! You know it, and we all saw it. You might as well admit it. We saw how worried you were about Jim and how tenderly you cared for him. You have feelings for Jim Wirth."

Melania's eyes narrowed, and she hesitated before whispering, "I certainly did everything I could to *not* feel anything for that man." She giggled, and Jane grinned.

"He *is* handsome. And those eyes. You're right——they twinkle!"

The smile left Melania's face. "I didn't mean to hurt Archie. He *is* dear to me." She stood and moved toward her coat. "Where is he? I should speak to him."

"He's truly gone, Mel. Watching the Rhineland."

Melania's hand went to her heart as her mouth formed an O. "What have I done?" she asked, not expecting an answer.

Jane reached out her hand as Melania moved toward her. "You couldn't have stopped him, Mel. Arch needed some distance, and this was an ideal opportunity." Jane's face brightened. "We can write to him. We'll let him know how we're praying for his safety." Jane dropped Melania's hand and moved toward the door. "I'll be back in a jiffy!" She reached for the doorknob, opened it, and almost walked straight into a tall block of a man framing the doorway.

"Hello, ladies!" Jim said, lifting both arms to reveal a large beer bottle in one hand and a brown bag in the other. "Care for some refreshments?"

Melania could scarcely believe Jim was standing in her doorway. She failed to respond before her friend wrapped her arms around Jim's waist. "Thank you, dear man!"

Jim guffawed at the response. "Well, I thought I may get a *thank you*, but I didn't expect affection!"

"Oh, pshaw." Jane waved her hand at Jim, moving back into the apartment. "You're an answer to our prayers for a man bearing food! Come in, please." Jane moved aside and brushed the snow from Jim's shoulders as he passed.

Melania watched, amused, smiling slightly, though she felt suddenly shy. Jim shot her glances while he interacted with the exuberant Jane. Sensing he wanted her permission, she nodded to the table. "Please, set your things down and come in." She smiled at him. "We're ravenous!"

The three enjoyed mugs of amber beer, compliments of Prager's Brewery, paired with a slab of cheese, a chunk of sausage, and a loaf of fresh bread. "The market in my little neighborhood seems to be coming back to life," Jim remarked between bites. "It has the grandest mixture of fare from the different village vendors." He reached for his mug and took a deep swallow. "The pandemic put down the merchants for a time, with everyone either ill, quarantined, or——" He didn't finish his sentence, nor did he need to. The ladies shifted in their seats. Jim chugged his mug of beer and slapped his knee. "But a new day has dawned, and things are looking up." His green eyes sparkled.

Melania's smile grew wide watching Jim's high spirits. It'd been some time since she'd seen this playful side of him, likely not since those days right after they'd met at the church dance. A great deal had changed since then. She was no longer the bright-eyed and innocent young girl——the one who had big dreams, convinced she couldn't let anything or anyone stand in her way. War and influenza had touched her, touched her family, touched Jim——and most everyone——in profound and unexpected ways. Plans had been forced aside, some temporarily and some forever.

She, and others, had been called upon to meet challenges far beyond their perceived abilities.

Frank was on his way home, but Peter, and now Archie, had just left for Europe, and it was uncertain when Mathias and Anna would return. Lives had been lost, here and on the battlefields. Melania leaned back in her chair, enjoying the revelry and banter between Jim and Jane. At Jane's encouragement, Jim described the various purveyors at his neighborhood market, detailing their fare and personalities.

"Melania, dear," Jane said dramatically, pressing her hand into Melania's knee. "We *must* take the trolley over to St. Paul soon! Wouldn't it be delightful to visit the market?"

Melania laughed, quite sure of her friend's schemes. "I would like that. Yes."

Melania looked at Jim directly as she spoke. She'd seen the depths into which this man had fallen——into despair and near death. She realized now that she didn't need to see him as an obstacle to pursuing her dreams. She had been cautious even after they'd cleared the air at the hospital, but the look he gave her went deep, the characteristically casual twinkle gone.

"Soon, I hope," Jim returned.

Chapter 43

Minneapolis Tribune • December 1918 • PEACE PARLEY! President Wilson made his way to Paris late this past week for preliminary peace negotiations before he headed to London to meet with British officials. These meetings precede the Allied Nations Paris Peace Conference, which is set to convene early in the new year. Paris citizens greeted our president enthusiastically, grateful to be in happier times. The city is bursting with activity as it's filled with French soldiers waiting to be demobilized.

Despite the cramped streetcar seat, Jacob snapped the paper's page, bending his arms to fold and crease it. He'd picked up the paper at the small market, along with a block of cheese and a few of the last fresh apples of the season. Helene had started the basket earlier with fresh buns, a jam jar, and a small pie. Jacob knew the offerings would not sustain Melania and her roommate, but they'd send the message of home and love——the gesture as much for Helene as it was for their daughter. He gazed out the window, reflecting on the bold heading about the President's European journey. Peace. Such a blessed relief. Jacob looked around, noticing the murmur of passengers that seemed to increase at each stop, unlike weeks past when strict passenger limits and gauze masks stifled interaction. Then, as with most public places, the streetcars seemed wrought with fear and trepidation, but today felt like a turning point. The war was finished, thank God, and all prayed the same would be true of the wretched influenza. While the general discourse was upbeat, a few passengers kept to themselves, with others wearing gauze masks yet.

The car slid along the tracks, the snow of recent days pushed to the side and piled against the curbs. It was a lovely picture——pines heavy with white, rooflines wearing frosty caps, the snow cleansing the city and making it new. Jacob turned back to the newsprint, paging through the articles——more positive and forward-looking pieces than in past months. Death notices were printed, but the section was smaller than previously and now placed in the middle rather than on the front page. Advertisements for new theater shows, church dances, and new retail products had started to fill up the space. Joyous items about social events popped up——*Salvation Army to Give Children's Christmas Party; Soldiers and Sailors Invited to Riverview Club Dance New Year's Eve;* and on and on. The city was winding the crank toward normalcy. Even the mill resumed production of *refined* flour, rather than the lesser quality produced during the war for use in *Victory Bread.*

Jacob folded the paper and tucked it in the basket to read later, hoping he'd remember to retrieve it before handing the goods to his daughter. His experience, from frequent streetcar trips, was that the newspaper not only filled an intellectual need but it also spared him of idle chit-chat. He slid on his seat toward the window and looked out absently as he thought about the impending changes at the mill. Soldiers would be returning to the city——and to the jobs now held by women, blacks, and older men. Some of the women, especially those with returning military husbands, might go back home, the single girls might stay, and many of the Southern transplants had settled in the job and state permanently. He wasn't concerned about his position at Whitney Mill, reasoning that if management saw fit to keep him where he was, he would stay. If not, whether demoted to a lower position or outright replaced at the mill, he'd also manage that situation. Worry was pointless. Preparation was not. Jacob had options, and perhaps it was time to retire.

He exhaled heavily and leaned back in his seat, considering the societal changes brought on by the war and influenza——especially for his daughters. Indeed, both girls were eager and driven. Still, he'd never imagined the events of their recent lives, and he shook his head in wonder, reflecting on the challenges both Anna and Melania had faced *and* overcome these past two years.

His musings ceased as the streetcar stopped at the curb, and he glanced at his pocket watch as he gathered his things, noting the driver seemed a bit behind schedule——not like last week when the sparsely-filled car had zipped past half of the stops. He hurried off and walked through the university gates.

The campus buzzed with activity despite the frigid weather——students moved back into the dormitories, professors lugged armfuls of materials into the classroom buildings, and the great wooden doors of the hospital swung open with more people leaving than entering. Jacob nodded and pressed his lips together as he scanned the space, heartened at the resiliency of the city and its people. He paused at the sidewalk corner, dug in his pockets for the scrap of paper with Melania's location, and gazed down the walkway to the large three-story red brick building with the dormitory windows dotting the steep roofline. *Pioneer Hall,* he supposed, moving into the sunny courtyard.

The space was bordered by brick-lined paths leading to various doorways and encircling sturdy oak trees. Although most were small, Jacob envisioned the canopy and shade that would come from these trees one day. Patches of leaves blew around the space, gathering in the corners, intermingling with snow. A third-floor window flung open, and Melania stuck her head out. "Vati! Up here through that door." She pointed directly below her window. "I'll be right down to meet you."

Jacob pulled open the single wooden door and waited on the landing, listening to his daughter's heavy footsteps descend, smiling as he recalled his and Helene's wonder about how a girl could virtually float while she walked yet pound on a staircase. Melania threw herself into his arms before he had a chance to say hello. "Oh, Vati! It's so good to see you."

Jacob smiled broadly. "You as well, daughter." He held out the basket. "From Mutti——with a few additions added along the way." He pulled back the towel to reveal the treats.

"Goodness! Thank you! Jane and I are so weary of hospital food. It'll be lovely to have some goodies." She pecked his cheek. "Would you like to come up, or should we have tea across campus? There's a lovely café in the library building."

"Tea would be nice." He raised a brow. "Three flights may do damage to this old man."

"Oh, Vati! You're not old." She patted his shoulder lovingly. "Wait here while I drop this basket in my room before we leave. I want to tell Jane where I'm going too."

"Invite her to join us," he suggested. "And wait." He snatched the newspaper from the basket and tucked it under his arm.

Melania paused a moment, looking intently at him. "I think I'd enjoy having your company to myself today." She squeezed his gloved hand before bounding up the stairs with the basket.

When she returned, Melania looped her arm in Jacob's elbow, leading him across campus to the massive stone and brick building with a colonnade portico. Jacob was grateful for her arm as he craned and swiveled his neck, peering around the stunning edifice, marveling at the ornamental ceilings and intricate woodwork.

Jacob sat at a table nestled close to a large window and glanced over the courtyard, enjoying the outside activity. He turned his attention when Melania sat after setting down a tray of tea and apple tarts.

"This is one of the most heavenly places on campus," Melania said as she broke off an edge of the tart. "Delicious treats and books around the corner." She tittered.

Jacob placed his hand over hers for a moment.

"It's been so long since I've been here," Melania continued. "I think the place closed down along with the rest of campus, save for the hospital." Her expression became grim, and she shook her head slightly as if trying to dislodge a memory. "I wouldn't know, though, since we were all quarantined," she added dryly.

"Trying times," Jacob said, matter-of-factly, not as a question. He hadn't faced the same situations, but he knew that widespread war and disease left no one untouched. It was senseless to scrutinize events for differences in severity or impact. All of it had a lasting effect, and it was more important to stand in unity in healing, helping each other forward.

"Indeed." Melania's eyes held a darkness that Jacob had never seen before. She shifted in her chair and leaned forward, placing her palms on his forearms. "But I am and will be fine."

"Of course," Jacob said. "Remember, it's not weakness to feel."

Melania pulled back, her brow furrowed, seemingly surprised at his words.

He smiled briefly, then became serious. "Courage is valiant during a crisis, but one must sort out the effects afterward. Otherwise——" He paused, searching for the right words. "There's a balance. There must be. To feel is to be human. And humanity is what a civilization needs to reconcile the aftermath of tragedy. I'm proud of you, Melania. You are a woman of honor." Jacob chuckled, adding, "Just like your mother."

"That's quite the compliment," Melania said solemnly and then smiled. "Now, on to brighter subjects. How's the tart?"

Jacob sipped the tea, knowing full well she was changing the subject. He gently set the cup in its saucer. "You're right. It's delicious." He smiled and then his eyes brightened. "I have news."

"News?"

Jacob grinned as he relayed the Christmas plans and visitors. "Will you be home for a few days?"

"I'm not certain, but I'll definitely request days off from the hospital. Classes will resume after the new year, and my time at the hospital will be ending soon in any case." Melania smiled wistfully. "I'm looking forward to going home, seeing some family." She stopped. "I'm ready for a bit of normalcy but hardly dare to even dream about it."

"I know," Jacob said, wanting to offer comfort but not completely certain how. "It's difficult to truly move past the events that were such a harsh reality for so long." He squinted, hesitating to ask the question on his mind. "Mutti and I——we're planning to invite Jim for Christmas. Are you——" He hadn't finished when Melania smiled and nodded.

"Of course. Of course, Jim should be there." Melania's face seemed to show more than just resigned acceptance, but Jacob felt ill-equipped to discern the female emotions. "Well then, I'll try to stop by the brewery soon to invite him," Jacob said. "Unless——"

"I can invite him." A blush crept up her face. "Jane and I are heading to St. Paul next week to visit the market in Jim's neighborhood. He told us about it recently."

"You've seen him then?" Jacob raised an eyebrow.

Her face was entirely red and blotchy now. "Yes. Jim stopped by. Unexpectedly."

"Hmm. He's well then?"

"Yes. Fully recovered."

Jacob set his napkin on his plate and began gathering the empty dishes on the tray. He rose, saying, "I must go now to catch the rail home in time for dinner. I wasn't expecting the bustle of activity on the streetcar today."

He set the tray on the shop counter and then held Melania's coat as she slipped her arms into the gray wool. "I've enjoyed our time today," he said as they walked through the foyer. He stood at the top of the marble steps outside the building, taking in the massive university square——this place where his daughter seemed happy, even after everything she'd been through. For that, Jacob was grateful. He descended the stairs, noting his daughter's strength and poise as she smiled to fellow students and colleagues as they made their way to the edge of campus. Melania had grown significantly——in maturity and in confidence. Jacob turned to his daughter with a small, satisfied smile. "You're quite a young woman."

"Oh, Vati." Melania scrunched her face. "Enough with the accolades." She laughed lightly.

"I see you here——in this place——so far from where you came." Jacob paused. "We can never know exactly what's coming our way, regardless of our plans and preparations. But you've done your part——met the challenges head-on. That's good." Jacob finished without flourish and turned to go. He stopped after about five paces and turned. "Mutti will be pleased about Christmas."

Jacob reached the trolley stop just as the car arrived. He stepped up and onto the streetcar, scanned the aisle for an empty seat, and plunked down about midway. He was surprised to see a young girl next to the window and smiled at her when she gave him a hesitant glance. *Oh well,* he thought to himself, turning slightly toward the aisle, stretching his legs underneath the seat in front of him before snatching the small back section of the newspaper he'd saved for reading on the homebound ride.

He held the paper to the fading light that flashed in spurts through the car as it hurried down the tracks.

MINNEAPOLIS MAYOR SUCCUMBS! NOT TO FRET LOY-
AL CITIZENS OF OUR FAIR CITY! THE MAYOR HAS NOT

DIED FROM INFLUENZA. HIS STAFF REPORTS THAT WAL-TER VON ESSON HAS RECENTLY RISEN FROM HIS SICKBED, FULLY RECOVERED FROM SPANISH INFLUENZA. HIS TERM AS MAYOR IS WHAT HAS PASSED AWAY, OR WILL, IN JAN-UARY OF THE NEW YEAR, AS HE HAS LOST HIS MAYORAL REELECTION BID. IT IS DIFFICULT TO SAY IF VON ESSON'S REELECTION CAMPAIGN WAS AFFECTED BY HIS ILLNESS OR BY HIS SOCIALIST LEANINGS, BUT NEVERTHELESS, J. E. MEYER, INSURANCE SALESMAN AND PHILANTHROPIST, WILL BE OUR CITY'S 27TH MAYOR. MEYER RAN ON A PA-TRIOTIC PLATFORM WITH THE NEWLY DUBBED *LOYALIST* PARTY. MEYER PROMISES TO ENSURE OUR RETURNING VETERANS FIND JOBS AND HOUSING.

"A Loyalist!" Jacob said to himself. "What next?"

CHAPTER 44

Frank's train was due any moment, and Jacob quickened his pace to meet it, his boots sliding on the snowy planks as he hastened across the platform. Smoke from the chimneys of the locomotives and the buildings billowed in clouds above the station, the space bursting with people gathering to welcome loved ones home from war. Thank goodness his son was tall, Jacob thought, or he wouldn't stand a chance of seeing him in this crowd. Frank would be anxious to get to Holmesburg, his final destination in a journey that had begun weeks ago in Europe. Jacob glanced at the timetable——the train to Holmesburg would depart in less than an hour, and the one Frank was expected on had already arrived, though it was still likely sitting far back on the track, the passenger cars near the end of the long train. Jacob pushed through the throngs and planted himself near the platform's edge. He gripped a lamppost to steady himself as he watched the train cars slowly creep their way to the station. One by one, the car doors opened, and the soldiers tumbled out, weary, no doubt, and likely crammed to the hilt inside. Jacob didn't see Frank among them. The last car rolled to a stop, and the door creaked open——as if it too was done in. He watched as women, children, and elderly men stepped out of the train——not one person resembling a soldier. Blast it! Had he missed him? Jacob craned his neck to see if another train was coming.

"Vati?"

Jacob turned, stunned. "Frank! Where did you come from?"

Frank laughed and tilted his head toward the final train car. "There was room, barely, but the company was much more——convivial." He laughed again. "I was just lucky." He took in a deep inhalation. "Sitting with the women and children made me miss my family even more, though." He looked around. "Glad you could meet me, Vati, but I'm most anxious to get home." Frank set a hand on his father's shoulder and guided him through the crowd to a clearing near the station. "I've got to catch that other train." He pointed to a smaller westbound train.

Jacob chortled. "Well, son. You're coming with me. Your family's here."

"What? Where?" Frank's head swiveled.

"With Mutti. They came for Christmas." Jacob swiped a glove across his eyes when he felt them well up. "Let's get you to them."

Melania and Helene moved past each other in the kitchen early Christmas afternoon, checking the roasting goose and ham and welcoming the wafting smells when the oven door opened. August had wrapped a large ham and sent it along with Frank's wife and children, saying it was his gift to his mother since he wouldn't be joining them. He'd included a brief note stating they could count on him to watch over the farm until Frank returned home.

Melania peeled and boiled potatoes for mashing, happily accepting the bag of potatoes that Frank's wife, Ida, had also managed to transport to the city, along with her children and Elizabeth. Melania paused for a moment, noting the strength of the women around her——perhaps for the first time. As she drained and mashed the potatoes in the large, heavy kettle, she mused about her prior notions of her own maturity. She and her schoolmates had been so sure of themselves when they'd finished high school, confident they deserved to be regarded as adults. She chuckled. What she knew now that she hadn't known then . . .

"What's so funny?" her mother asked as she gathered a stack of dinner plates from the shelf.

"I was just thinking about how much I've learned this past year and a half." Melania chuckled again. "And not just at school or in the Red Cross either. About life."

Mutti gave her a quick squeeze around the shoulders. "This is just the beginning, my dear. But you're off to a good start."

The hubbub in the front room floated into the kitchen in bursts. Frank's wife Ida peeked her head into the kitchen. "I'm about to shoo these rascals into the backyard to burn off some of their vim and verve before dinner. Then I can help you two in the kitchen."

"That seems most sensible." Mutti turned to Melania and smiled. "Why don't you set the dining room table? Then you'll be there to greet Jim."

"Oh, Mutti." Melania rolled her eyes. "He's not only my guest." She grabbed the stack of plates, napkins, and silverware and backed out of the kitchen.

She smoothed the linen cloth over the extended table and began setting out plates. The dining room was mostly quiet save the murmurs from her father and Frank in the front room. Melania tilted her head in interest at their conversation about Frank's short service and the miracle that he'd survived Pershing's late-in-the-game attack.

They spoke of Peter's *occupation* deployment and the most burdensome question about when Mathias would return——and in what condition. The topics seemed endless. It appeared to Melania that the men needed to touch on all of the loose ends and tie them up before moving on.

The living room grew silent for a few moments when the front door opened and closed loudly, followed by the even louder stamping of feet.

Jim. Melania felt herself flush, and she moved to the cased opening between the rooms. Jim filled the entrance with his stature and his jovial greeting. She was grateful he was here and noticed that his burdens seemed to have lifted. He winked at her over Jacob's head while shaking the older man's hand, thanking him for the invitation. Melania came forward, arms extended. "Here. Let me take your coat."

"That'd be appreciated," Jim replied, never taking his eyes off her.

A shiver went up Melania's spine——she was both flustered and warmed by the attention. Melania hung the coat in the hall closet and smiled when she turned back to Jim. "You look like you're melting."

Jim brushed the remaining snowflakes off his head, slicking his dark hair back with his fingers.

"Sit and warm yourself." Vati pointed to the chair near the fire. "You remember our son Frank, don't you?"

"Yes, sir." Jim reached a hand out to Frank before sitting in the proffered chair. "You have a nice farm in Holmesburg, I recall."

"Thank you. I look forward to returning to it soon."

"If you gentlemen will excuse me, I must go back and finish in the kitchen," Melania said, nodding to Jim before quickly exiting the room.

Ida pinched Melania's arm playfully when she returned, a big smile still on her face. "Smitten, little sister?"

Melania's lips raised effortlessly. "Perhaps."

1919

CHAPTER 45

Jim wiped his hands on the heavy apron before pulling it over his head and hanging it on a hook near the door. He climbed the steps to the main brewery floor, squinting at the brightness of the swinging overhead lightbulbs and the final shards of sunlight shooting through the paned windows. Some days, Jim felt like an actual rat, rising from the depths dirty, blinded, and greasy, yet he was grateful for the job. He wasn't quite to full stamina yet, but frequent dinners at the Harvey home would surely help——an open invitation had already been extended.

Jim smiled to himself, recalling the warm and inviting Christmas he'd spent with Melania and her family. He was ashamed of his behavior months before——disappearing without a word when the entire Harvey family had displayed nothing but love and care. Those days had been so dark——the trials Jim had endured had clouded his thinking. He hoped he could make amends with the entire family, especially Melania and this new year seemed full of hope. He smiled again, thinking of the turn of events with her——he'd never imagined it possible. A voice pulled him from his reverie.

"Jim! What's got you smiling like a daft duck? Some girl?" Sven called from the far side of the large room.

Jim grinned. "Something like that." He thought well of Sven Olson, the brewmaster who always made time for him even though the man had more pressing duties.

Sven cocked his head. "Come here a minute, would ya?" He often gave Jim extra jobs, knowing he was being under-utilized in the cellar. Jim appreciated the gesture and the extra coin in his pockets, but tonight he had plans, so he hoped Sven didn't have extra work for him.

"What's up?" Jim leaned over the vat and watched as Sven waved his hand over the amber liquid, took several deep breaths, and quickly dipped a long-handled ladle before pouring a taste down his throat.

Sven squinted and sneezed.

"The bubbles, surely," Jim chortled.

"Of course." Sven patted Jim hard on the back, causing *him* to cough. "Needs a bit more——*something*. Later, anyway." Sven perched the ladle back on its hook and leaned close to Jim's ear. "Got a bit of news you should know."

Jim startled——this was not Sven's usual boisterous manner. "What?" His brow furrowed, and dread began to rise. He hoped he wasn't getting laid off, but he had no seniority, and men had returned back from the war.

"You're a good worker, son," Sven began and paused. "I don't know the timing, but I know that with this damned Prohibition amendment looming, Prager is making changes."

"Laying people off?" It seemed only natural.

"No. Maybe. Difficult to say. Prager's needs to survive somehow when we're no longer brewing beer." Sven turned back to the vat and looked in again. "Find something else. Something where you can use your talents and have security. You'll not get that from this blasted place." He let out a grunt and turned back to Jim. "I don't really mean that. Beer is the nectar of the gods. And Prager's isn't so bad." He snorted. "Those damn temperance women should leave well enough alone."

Jim smiled despite the somber message. He'd miss Sven if nothing else. "Thanks. I appreciate the advice."

Sven waved his hand at Jim. "Oh, pshaw. It's nothing. I'm just an old rusty gut trying to send a young fellow like you off to find his way. It's too late for me. I'm hanging on until the bitter end when those church ladies drag me out of here." Sven guffawed and smacked Jim on the back again. "Off with you. I can see you've got a girl on your mind."

Jim grinned. "You guessed it!"

Jim walked to his apartment, appreciating its proximity to the brewery but wondering if he should move back across the river. *No. Not yet.* The last thing he wanted was to muddle up the fresh beginnings of his relationship with Melania. All signs from her showed a returning interest, but he wasn't taking any chances.

He chuckled as he headed up the stairs to his apartment——never had he put this much thought into a relationship. But then again, that may have been his problem. After washing up and changing his clothes, he headed out, catching a streetcar on its way across the Mississippi River.

He got off at the trolley stop a block from the university and made his way down the snowy sidewalk to the dormitory courtyard. The sounds of giggling and slamming doors floated down the stairway. He shook his head. These girls were louder than any fella he knew——and he nearly ran smack into one of them as he turned on the last landing.

"Oh my goodness!" Melania put a hand to her chest. "You startled me! I didn't expect you so soon."

Jim hesitated, holding in a teasing response. If he expected to make progress with this girl——*woman*, he reminded himself——he needed to treat her as such. He smiled. "I was able to catch the streetcar imme-diately and thought perhaps we could——I don't know——maybe fit in an adventure before the show."

Melania grinned and squeezed his forearm. "An adventure? That sounds delightful." She held out a book. "I was just on my way to return this, but we could stop at the library on our way out after I grab my handbag."

"Grand. I'll be waiting outside."

The night was pitch black and clear, with the stars spread like a carpet. Jim flipped his collar against the cold and shoved his hands deeper in his pockets while he waited, his breath floating around his face in frosty clouds.

"You should have waited inside," Melania said as she came out the door. "Lands! It's cold."

Jim took the book from her and tucked it under his arm before pulling her close to his side.

"We'll stay warmer this way," he said with a smile in his voice.

"Most certainly."

The pair fell into a comfortable camaraderie as they headed out the campus gates after dropping the book at the library. The sidewalk was made narrow by the snow, and Jim swiftly stepped behind Melania whenever necessary, never letting go of her hand. They mainly walked in silence to the streetcar stop——talking made difficult by the cold and the path. The trolley car pulled up soon after they reached the corner, and Jim ushered Melania forward and up the steps.

He sat across the aisle from Melania, and she chuckled.

He turned to face her when the streetcar began to move, stretching his limbs out into the aisle. "Believe me," he said in response to her laugh. "Sitting next to you is preferred, but our legs would have been mighty crowded. Remember the night at the theater?" He winked, reaching out his hands. "Here, slide forward in your seat. I want to tell you what I've planned for our evening."

Melania smiled as Jim shared his plans——unable to hold back his enthusiasm.

"I don't know if you're aware, but there's a terrific bell chime concert at City Hall on Friday evenings," he told her.

"Really? Bell chimes?" Melania leaned forward.

"Absolutely. A fella at the brewery, an older man, worked on the crew that built the darn thing. The clock tower makes City Hall the tallest building in the entire city and houses the world's largest four-faced chiming clock."

"Is that so?" Melania laughed.

"Why, yes, it is, young lady," Jim responded, patting her knee. "This will be no ordinary evening. The concert features fifteen bell chimes!" He grinned.

"I can hardly wait!" Melania smiled back.

The streetcar reached the corner closest to the government building, and the pair exited the car, the cold air frosting their breath in puffs. Melania wrapped her woolen muffler in another loop around her neck and pulled down her cap. Jim drew her mittened hand into his, taking out his pocket watch. "We're about an hour early for the bell concert, and it's almost two before the vaudeville show at the Pantages." Jim rubbed off the layer of condensation on the watch before dropping it back in his pocket. "Donaldson's Glass Block is close by. Let's stop there for some pie and coffee. Warm you up."

"That would be lovely," Melania agreed. "Jane and Jasper have been to Donaldson's——before the war, and . . ." Her voice trailed off.

Jim stopped and reached for Melania's hand. "I'm sorry about Jasper." He cleared his throat. "I didn't know him, of course, but Jane's a keen girl and she deserves . . ." His voice fell off. What could he say? He knew Jane was deeply saddened by the news that Jasper was among the casualties of the Armistice Day battle. She'd held out hope when his name wasn't on the initial lists but then discovered Jasper had two identification tags on him—one of a fallen comrade. So when the Army finally made the correct identification, the news was crushing. Melania had told him that Jane cried for days.

Jim squeezed Melania's hand, and they started to walk again, making their way past the massive city hall structure. The red-hued bricks and the jutting, green-tiled towers and rooflines made for a stunning display. They craned their necks to see the building as they walked past. "The mayor's office is in this building," Jim commented. "It's made entirely of rose granite quarried from Ortonville. That's a town on the border of South Dakota, in case you didn't know."

"My! You're a fount of knowledge." Melania elbowed him in the ribs.

"Well, a guy's got to fill his hours somehow when trying to stay out of trouble." He chuckled. "I spent a fair amount of time in the St. Paul Public Library when I first came to town after the trouble at the train station. Read a lot. Learned a lot." He paused before adding, "And couldn't get into too much trouble there."

Melania squeezed his hand. "Time well spent."

They walked in silence for a time, the hum of the city swirling around them——streetcars buzzing on the rails, the occasional sputtering of a Model T, and the clip-clop of horses' hooves, an intermingling of new and passing modes of transportation. Signs of a post-war era adorned the city. Fresh stiff awnings jutted out of new retail spaces with their windows covered in advertisements. Theater and music posters announcing vaudeville singing and magic acts were plastered on buildings and posts. Couples and groups mingled——coming and going from buildings up and down the block. The cold winter temperatures couldn't stifle the excitement of being on the other side of war and disease. Jim looked down at Melania, her eyes flitting around the streets, a relaxed smile on her lips. He was pleased he could offer her this diversion.

The multi-storied glass block Donaldson's building came into view, its inside lights illuminating it like a beacon. "We've shaken off the past two years, haven't we?" Melania squeezed his hand, and he heard the lightness in her voice.

"I think you're right," he said as they stepped off the sidewalk's edge to cross the street, Jim absently pulling Melania closer to his side.

Without warning, the ground shuddered violently, thrusting Jim's body forward. Instinctively, he pulled Melania into the curve of his chest, covering her as their bodies flew toward the street.

Chapter 46

Mathias grabbed his coat and threw it over his shoulder before picking up the small satchel at his feet. A crush of men poured out from every nook and cranny of the *Arcadia* when it finally docked at Fort Hamilton in New York City early in the new year.

The captured German ship, already beaten and weather-worn had squeaked loudly in protest during the long voyage. It had been unbearably cold for most of the journey, so many of the men aboard had stayed below deck despite the crowded quarters and smells that ripened with each passing day. Mathias had found a spot to call his own in a corner near the iron stairway below deck. It was an active area where men traipsed up and down frequently, but the rush of fresh air and the ability to see daylight had eased his state of mind.

He'd spent months at a German internment camp, where the food had been so scarce that many prisoners had died of starvation before Germany had finally released its POWs in late December. Like the others, Mathias had layered himself in every item of clothing he could find while at the prison——items sent by the Red Cross as well as shirts and coats off the backs of dead comrades. It had sickened him to do it, but survival called for desperate measures.

Mathias had barely been conscious when the train had transported him from Germany to the Swiss International Committee of the Red Cross, but he remembered the cacophony of coughing that had echoed through the cars. His own lungs had been riddled with infection, and the spasms of coughing had broken two ribs. It had been almost two weeks before he'd fully regained consciousness. Slowly his lungs had cleared, and he'd been discharged for the long journey home. His hair was still long and shaggy when he left the ICRC, but his face was cleanly shaven, his body scrubbed, and his clothes clean, albeit mismatched and much too large. His shoes, thankfully, were close to the correct size, and the scrap of wool stuffed in the toes had the added benefit of keeping his feet warmer.

Now, though, after the interminable ocean voyage, he was dirty, hungry, and full of lice again. Anxious as he was to get home, he couldn't bear traveling farther in this disheveled condition. He left Fort Hamilton, joining several others in a horse-drawn carriage that quickly trotted through Brooklyn and crossed the bridge into Lower Manhattan. He hopped out and parted ways with the others, patting the discharge papers he'd tucked in his breast pocket. *Release.* A magnificent thought. He closed his eyes a moment and breathed in the air, coughing slightly at the puff of smoke blown in his direction from a passing businessman. Mathias grinned and craned his neck, following the buildings until they disappeared into the clouds. He was home. Maybe not his final destination, but in America.

Mathias walked the streets of the immense city, heading into the depths of activity. He saw other military men weaving like individual threads down the city streets. Some *were* home in New York City. Others? Who knew? Probably headed all over this vast country, like he would be——eventually. He stopped at a telegram office, standing in line for some time behind the scores of other soldiers who were likely sending word to their loved ones too. He imagined Vati had closely followed the news of POWs but was sure his mother, especially, would like to know when he'd landed on American soil.

After he'd sent the message, he turned his focus to finding a barber. He scanned the shops, turning onto Cortelyou Road, where he spotted a red, white, and blue barber pole with a light glowing on the top like a beacon. As he approached, he read the sign.

Gaspiri Morisi • Barber • Cuts 25¢ • Cut & Shave • Returning Soldier Special • 40¢

Mathias dug in his pocket and felt the quarters jingling with the silver dollar. He'd have enough to get a shave and a haircut before using the money in his satchel to secure a room and a new set of clothing. He opened the glass door and stepped into the dimly lit shop. Men lined the row of unoccupied chairs, smoking large cigars and seeming to be holding court. They looked each new customer up and down, grunting and uttering hushed comments followed by nods. Mathias smiled sheepishly at the group, sure his appearance would earn a murmur or two.

A small, hunched man——Morisi, Mathias supposed——worked almost simultaneously on three patrons, lathering up a face before moving to another man to trim around his ears. The barber looked up briefly at the sound of the doorbell, nodding toward the last chair in the row. "Sit. My son, the other barber, will be back in a shake of a leg."

Mathias ambled past the row of judges, nodding a greeting to them. He sat, setting his bundle on his lap, then realizing it looked absurd to clutch it like a woman's handbag, put it on the ground between the chair and the mahogany wall. He'd been so conditioned to hold his belongings close while a prisoner and on the ship that it seemed strange to part from it. He felt more than one set of eyes on the bag, and he wondered if it was real or in his imagination.

"Who's next? Who's next?" A young man entered the room in a flurry——he had to be Morisi's son, given that he looked almost exactly like the older barber.

Mathias looked around, not wanting to push his way in front of someone. No one spoke until the elder barber hollered. "Down at the end. For Pete's sake!"

Young Morisi hurried to the end of the row, appraising Mathias, tapping his chin with a fingertip, his eyebrows cocked into points. "Quite a scruffy one. Military too."

Clearly. Mathias nodded almost imperceptibly in case the statement required confirmation.

"Well, let's start with a shampoo and a shave," Morisi stated, "and take it from there." He made a sound of disgust. "Get rid of these little beasts." He reached for a dark bottle from the shelf and the shaving paraphernalia.

Mathias closed his eyes as the barber whipped up a lather in his bowl before swathing Mathias's face with it and laying a warm cloth over his eyes. He breathed in the clean smell of shaving cream, wondering if the fresh scent was intended to cover the gasoline-like smell coming from the dark bottle. As the barber worked, he chattered, his words mixing with the banter from the lounging huddle across the room. Mathias paid little attention until the barber nudged him. "You might be interested in a bath, considering your state and all."

"Mmm." Mathias agreed as best he could, not wanting to take in a mouthful of hair as the long locks slid down his face.

"We have a small room around the back with a tub. Twenty-five cents for a full tub or a nickel for a water basin and washcloth." Young Morisi clipped vigorously while talking, ending with a satisfied grunt as he set his scissors down.

Mathias calculated the sums in his head again. "Bath. Yes." He dug in his pocket for the coins. He was so close to completely shedding the war's outer effects and his travels. He turned back to grab his satchel near the chair. It was gone!

"Sir!" He called after the younger Morisi, who'd already moved on to the next customer. "Where is my bag? I left it beside the chair."

"No idea." Morisi shrugged and turned back to his new customer, and Mathias marched to him, grabbing his arm. "Did you see someone take it?

That's all I have. I need that bag back!" His voice rose with each word, and heat traveled up his neck.

"If it was that important to you, it was a mistake to set it down so casually, wasn't it?"

Mathias shoved the man aside and frantically walked up and down the row of men, asking if anyone had seen or taken the bag. One by one, they shook their heads and shrugged.

Finally, the elder Morisi gripped Mathias's shoulder and pushed him toward the door. "It's gone. Move on." He threw Mathias a clean towel from the counter. "Go. Take your bath and be on your way. You've learned a lesson, a hard one, about this city."

Mathias stomped out the door and around to the narrow space between the buildings, finding the side door leading to the small bath area. A water pump was perched outside, and a large kettle sat on the top of a pot-bellied stove. The money paid for nothing but the privilege of using their tub——labor wasn't included. Mathias's head cleared some as he filled the kettle and set it to boil, allowing him to focus on what to do next. The coins had been in his pocket, but the bills from his Army pay were folded between the pages of a small Bible in his pack. *What a fool I've been!*

He frowned as he put on the dirty oversized clothes after his bath. Clearly, he'd not thought this through. But on the other hand, he reminded himself, any new clothes would have been in the now missing satchel. He sniggered bitterly and left the bathroom.

Mathias wandered the streets for some time before coming to a large brick structure filling the block between East 25th and 26th streets. He looked up at the words *69th Regiment* in large, raised brick letters and the massive eagle perched in the center of an arch that spanned the doorway. An American flag waved in the wind at its side. *The 69th Regiment?* "Hmm . . . That's right," he said out loud. The regiment was known as "The Fighting Irish." A shipmate had mentioned them the other day. Mathias was startled when a hand patted his back, and he turned to see another soldier's face, only this man was in his olive drab uniform and russet brown boots.

"Sorry to alarm you," the man said with a laugh. "I saw you staring up at our great raptor. You goin' in?"

"Nah." Mathias waved his hand dismissively. "Not a member of this regiment." He turned to leave.

"You'll be my guest, then. Looks like you could use a good meal and maybe a change of clothes." The man chuckled good-naturedly as he considered Mathias's sorry form.

Mathias hesitated briefly, but he'd already been a fool once, and frankly, the man was right. He was hungry and certainly needed fresh clothes.

He followed the man into the building and found himself almost immediately telling his tale of woe since setting foot on American soil. He instantly regretted being so forthcoming. The man was a decade or so older than Mathias, but he'd confided in him like he would his own father. The soldier seemed to sense it when he assured Mathias that stories like his happened in the metropolis almost hourly. "It comes with the territory of being the most famous city in all of the world," the man said. "Everyone wants to be in New York City——even the hooligans."

The man gathered a set of fresh and better-fitting clothes from the armory's collection and tossed them to Mathias. "Clothes end up here, donations, abandoned, and the like. They're here for the taking."

Mathias hesitated. "I'm not sure. Other fellas may need them."

"Give a set of clothes to the local armory when you get home. It all comes out in the end."

Mathias nodded and gratefully left to change his clothes, finally feeling like a whole man when he returned.

"Don't you look spiffy?" The man chuckled. "Why don't you join me for dinner in the Garryown Club? It's an officer's club on the lower level." He slapped Mathias on the back. "And it's your lucky day because I'm an officer." He held out his hand. "Major Smith."

"Mathias Harvey. Civilian," Mathias said with a chuckle, feeling more relaxed than he had in some time.

Mathias didn't know what he'd done to deserve the major's kindness, but he thoroughly enjoyed the hearty dinner in the dark, wood-paneled club. He glanced around the room as he ate, noticing a large coat of arms emblazoned with Irish Wolfhounds and the words, *"Gentle when stroked, fierce when provoked."* The camaraderie and lively banter in the room suggested all were satisfied this evening.

The night was late by the time they finished their meal and drink. Mathias wanted to resist when Major Smith suggested he stay in the bunk room and head out in the morning, but again he was persuaded. "Plenty of men like you are heading off the ships and toward home. I'm sure you won't be the only guest here tonight." He left Mathias at the threshold to the large dormitory, shaking his hand. "Good luck to you, and thanks for your service."

Mathias nodded off almost as soon as he laid down his head. He slept soundly for the first time in months, clean and with a full belly. He left the armory early morning, heading toward a large hotel he'd spotted yesterday. *The Knickerbocker.* Maybe they'd be hiring. He'd never worked in a hotel before but imagined he had some skill set they would need. Indeed, his years working on the farm and later obtaining his education made him well-rounded. He didn't yet have enough perspective to judge what the military stint had taught him besides raw fortitude and perseverance. Practical abilities, too, he trusted.

Mathias approached the formidable front of the massive hotel that towered over ten stories up to its green terracotta roof. He guessed he'd be shooed out if he entered the front lobby but spotted a door propped open at the end of the side alley. The sound of clanging pots and pans mingled with the delicious odors wafting through the crack. It was early, and he hoped the kitchen staff was in good spirits at this hour. He slowly opened the door and called in. "Excuse me. I'm looking for work."

A man in a long white apron looked up, glaring at him. "Get out of here. We don't hire people off the streets."

Mathias straightened. "I'm not off the streets but a ship, a military ship. I just came back from Europe. Army."

The man stopped stirring his sauce and gave Mathias the once over. "Army, you say. What regiment?"

"Not from here. Minnesota. My pack was stolen, so my time in this delightful city has been extended." Mathias smiled a bit, looking to see if the man caught his attempt at humor. "I need to work so I can get home. I'll do anything. Please."

"I had an uncle who went to Minnesota once, years ago. He said they were fine people there." The man in white returned to stirring and then moved to his cutting board. He nodded at Mathias. "Well, come on. Get in here and put on an apron!"

After putting in a full shift, Mathias found a small room to let for the night with the advance given to him by the chef, who was pleased with his knife abilities. Who knew farming skills would be his saving grace? He began a letter to his father and mother on a discarded piece of paper he'd grabbed from the hotel trash.

Dear Mutti and Vati, I have been detained by unfortunate circumstances in New York City. Not to worry—I am well, and I'll find my way home eventually. I'm working in the kitchen of the Knickerbocker Hotel. What a surprise that the know-how learned cutting up meat and vegetables in my childhood at the farm has been put to good use! Mathias

CHAPTER 47

The nurse steered Jim to an examination room, nearly closing the door on Melania's foot. "Sorry, dear. No un-marrieds together." Melania sighed, resigned. She knew the rules——she just wanted to make sure the pain in Jim's side was being taken seriously. She was certain he'd fractured a rib though they'd assured him after the bombing that nothing was broken. But that had been weeks ago, and still Jim was experiencing pain.

Melania peered through the small glass pane on the wooden door, raising an eyebrow at Jim. He nodded imperceptibly but managed to get off a quick wink before the nurse noticed. Melania plopped down in the chair next to the door with a sigh. When would all of this come to an end?

The police were still investigating the mysterious explosion outside City Hall that had blown everything to pieces for a square block. *Minimal damage* was what the newspaper had reported. The massive structure had withstood the blast well, its foundation remaining sturdy despite the obliteration of several blocks on its façade. Windows had shattered, light poles had bent and melted, and carriages and cars had been sent reeling like missiles. The two people who'd died had been in a passing motorcar. Thankfully, the early evening hour meant the sidewalk had been nearly empty——aside from her and Jim.

They were both lucky to be alive. Or maybe it went beyond luck and good fortune. So much of the event was outside her recollection. Jim had told her afterward how his only thought had been to protect her as he'd cocooned her with his entire body, shielding her from flying debris and cushioning her landing. She must've blacked out for a time, as she remembered nothing of the actual event. She'd been entirely befuddled when she'd regained consciousness, wrapped in a blanket, staring into the face of a police officer. Despite being bent over in pain, Jim was at her side as the police asked a series of questions, interjecting from time to time about how lucky they were to be alive. *A few steps back,* the policeman had repeated several times, and they'd have felt the full impact of the blast.

Melania's father had been following the police investigation closely, telling her and Jim about similar, unexplained bombings across the country. Some newspapers dubbed it the *Red Scare*, and government officials were tracking known socialists and anarchists.

Melania waited patiently outside the examination room, occasionally hearing muffled voices or low grunts she assumed were coming from Jim. Finally, after an excessive amount of time, Jim emerged from the room, walking stiffly, wincing slightly. He took Melania's hand and brought it to his rib cage. "Broken. They think." He winked at her as she shook her head. "Just what you suspected, Dr. Harvey."

"Hmm. Maybe the doctor could have used the X-ray machine to make certain." Melania shook her head. "That *is* what it's for, after all. I don't understand how they didn't realize you had fractured your ribs in the first place." She hmphed.

"They did suggest X-rays. The nurse mentioned that the department has two now that the mobile X-ray machines are back from Europe."

Melania stopped in her tracks. "Why didn't you do it then?"

Jim lifted his shirt so she could see the bandage wrapped tightly around his middle. "I opted for the quickest route to get back to my girl." He chuckled and gently pulled her hand.

"Really, Jim!" Melania lightly slapped his arm.

"I'm sure the X-ray would have said the same thing, and the doc would have ended up bandaging me up in the end." Jim shrugged. "Frankly, I just believed what you said from the get-go." He squeezed her hand and led her toward the door. "Let's get out of here. Something about this place."

"I completely understand." Melania shuddered.

CHAPTER 48

March came in like a lamb——calm, mild, and atypically warm——and Helene was cautiously optimistic, hoping the folklore wouldn't come to pass, spinning the end of March's weather out like a lion. Memories of the fierce and prolonged 1917 winter, which had lingered far into spring with record low temperatures and high snowfalls, hung in her mind. Helene smiled when she spied the snow shovel Jacob had hooked near the back door, *just in case*. Earlier today, he'd pulled the remains from last summer's harvest in preparation for this season's garden. Still, he'd also stacked firewood next to the pile of dried foliage, in anticipation of many more cold spring evenings.

Helene slipped into a sweater and went into the backyard to remove the garments she'd hung earlier in the day.

Inside, she put the clothes basket down next to the drying rack near the front room fire to dry the few items that were still damp, then gently lifted the newly altered pale blue dress that lay over the rack. She held the garment to full length and turned it back and forth. It was a lovely piece that Emily had hardly worn, it seemed. There were several comely outfits in her closet, as Emily and Phillip had lived a life full of social occasions before the war. Helene sighed deeply. She missed Emily immensely but was grateful to have time with Elizabeth again, though those days were waning too.

Helene frowned and hung the dress on a hanger, hooking it over the door. Melania would surely be pleased to wear it to the St. Patrick's

Day dance tomorrow evening. Helene's mood brightened. So much had changed for their daughter and Jim since they'd first met at the same church event two years ago. The young couple spent much time together between her university classes and his work at the brewery. Helene could see that her daughter was happy, and Jim seemed to have moved past his customarily mischievous repartee, becoming more serious and settled, beyond the troubling days of the war and influenza.

Noise from the kitchen slipped underneath the door. Elizabeth pushed through to the front room and wrapped her arms around Helene's legs, looking up at her.

"How was your time with Opa?"

Elizabeth grinned and nodded, pulling half of a cookie from her pocket. "Cookie." She giggled as the crumbs fell through her pudgy fingers.

"Sorry," Jacob said with a shrug as he entered the room. "They were handing them out at the bank."

Helene smiled, squeezing the girl to her side. "No matter. If grand-parents can't spoil——" She stopped and pressed her lips together.

"It may be by circumstance, not birth, but that doesn't make it any less true." Jacob patted Elizabeth's head and then sat down, pulling the envelope from his pocket. "This should suffice as a down payment, I would think. We can wire the Bartons the rest if they're in agreement."

Helene sat too and pulled Lizzie into her lap, the little girl leaning back and shutting her eyes. Helene smiled and absently smoothed back Lizzie's hair. "It would be easier for the Bartons than trying to sell the house on their own."

Jacob's head twitched just a bit, and his eyebrows flattened. "I can't see how they'd refuse. Trust me——a willing buyer is any man's dream." He waved the bank draft. "And this is more than a fair offer."

Helene shook her head. "They said they had legal business to discuss when they arrive."

Jacob rose, and his face became stern. "That's a broad term, and it's no use speculating about what's on their mind." He chuckled. "We have *legal matters* to discuss as well."

"I guess you're right." Helene rose, hoisting Lizzie so the girl's head rested on her shoulder.

"Remember, the Bartons insisted we live rent-free after Emily's and Phillip's deaths. Likely generosity, not just in payment for taking care of their granddaughter."

"Yes, I suppose."

"Here," Jacob said, holding out his arms. "I'll take Elizabeth up for a nap. Looks like Melania is home."

Jacob stoked the fire and looked out into the darkness, catching Jim's form the next evening as the young man strolled down the street from the trolley stop. "Jim's here," Jacob called out to his wife and daughter.

"Come in, son," he greeted Jim, who was dressed in a worsted wool suit with a striped shirt and wide tie. "You look snazzy." Jacob guffawed. "Young speak, right?"

Jim chuckled and removed his bowler hat, tucking it under his arm. "Sure, but I feel doggy," he said, unbuttoning his suit coat as he sat down. "Fancy clothes!"

Jacob chortled. "When you see my daughter, I'm sure you'll feel it was all worth it."

"No doubt, sir."

Within a few minutes, Melania descended the stairs, a vision in her pale blue dress, its color complementing her dark features. She smiled a warm greeting at Jim. He rose and extended his hand to her.

She set a hand in his, and he twirled her around. Melania giggled. "Oh my! Ready to dance, already!"

"My apologies. I couldn't resist," Jim said, smiling.

Jacob rose from his chair, sure the young couple wouldn't want to linger any longer than necessary.

Helene descended the stairs, bringing a belted wool coat with her. "Here," she said, handing it to Melania. "This was Emily's too. It will pair nicely with the dress and keep you warm as the evening chill comes."

Melania slipped her arms into the coat, buttoned and belted it, and grasped Jim's hand as the couple headed out the front door.

"It's good——this thing with Jim and Melania." Jacob nodded, dropping into his chair with a satisfied grunt.

Helene picked up her knitting basket and sat in her rocker, settling back and quickly setting about her work. The knitting needles clicked together in cadence with the rocker. "Yes," she said after some time. "It is."

Several minutes later, she stopped rocking and held up a small pair of red mittens. "Elizabeth will like these."

Jacob folded the newspaper and set it on the floor. He sipped his coffee and poked around for something else to read from the basket. "She will," he said after a few minutes, chuckling at the realization that both he and his wife seemed to have a lot on their minds. It would be good to have the house issue settled with the Bartons. He rose and went to his coat pocket, pulling out two letters. "These came today. I saved them so we could read them together." His mouth turned to a smile. "One from Mathias and one from Anna. I didn't expect Mathias to write after his telegram."

Helene set the mittens in her knitting basket and leaned back, resuming rocking. "I'm still getting used to enjoying letters instead of dreading them. With Frank home now and Peter just beginning his services, these two are our only——concerns." She pressed her lips together. "Although I can't say that Peter is out of my thoughts."

"Occupation is complicated," Jacob said. "But Peter's a bright young man, and the American Army is capable."

He slit Anna's envelope open with his pocket knife and turned to his wife. "Shall I read it?"

She nodded and sat back, closing her eyes as her husband began.

Dear Mother and Father, Do you recall the doctor I mentioned in my previous correspondence? I have the most glorious news! He has asked me to be his wife! I know this news must come as a shock, especially since I was seriously contemplating a life of service for the church. I'm so sure. You must know that. My time in the Red Cross hospital, working beside Henri has changed me forever. He's compassionate, brilliant, and caring. You both would love him. I regret to tell you that we'll likely already be married by the time you receive this letter. Henri has been asked to serve at the American Hospital of Paris, so our wedding was arranged quickly. My work at the U.S. Army Base 21 hospital also allowed me to gain employment at the American Hospital. When you get a chance to look at a map, you'll see that the lovely Seine River flows through our current home, Rouen, and our new home, Paris. I hope we can visit you in the States sometime in the future when, perhaps, events allow. In the meantime, I send my love and a small picture of Henri and myself. Your daughter, Mrs. Henri Lachance

Jacob dropped the letter, letting it float to the ground. His daughter, *their* daughter, was married. He looked at his wife, who'd sat up, wide-eyed. A tear rolled down her cheek. He kept his gaze on her——tears of sadness or joy? Finally, she turned to face him, and he released his breath.

"It's good. Our Anna is married." Helene's smile grew. "And happy." Another tear fell, and she whispered, "I wish I could have been with her on her wedding day."

Jacob reached across and squeezed his wife's hand, holding it for a moment. Then he stood, went to the kitchen, and returned with two small glasses of sherry, giving one to his wife and raising his. "To our daughter, Anna, and her new husband, Henri." They clinked the glasses together and sipped slowly on the amber liquid.

After some time, Jacob turned to her, holding up Mathias's letter. "Do we dare open this one?"

CHAPTER 49

The clock on the wall clicked loudly, echoing in the cavernous space. Jim was the only one left, the last rat, the others feeling little motivation to stay in the Prager's cellar making root beer or ice cream or whatever offerings the brewery would establish. With the Prohibition act coming into effect in the coming months, Prager's, like most breweries, was in full swing with its new products and outputs. Sven and the other brewmasters held tightly to their positions, readily agreeing to brew root beer if necessary. Jim's only purpose in staying was self-interest, as he needed the money while figuring out his next move. This post-war summer was a curious time——a mix of reconciliation, progress, and unrest. Jim, long recovered from his broken rib, worked daily to put not only the war days behind him but also the memories of the blast. It was a challenging task since the news regularly reported anarchist violence. Several bombs had been intercepted in April, and even the creation of the new General Intelligence Unit headed by J. Edgar Hoover hadn't prevented eight mail bombs from being sent to prominent figures across the country earlier this month.

Jim felt fiercely protective of Melania, just as he had when they were thrown across the street in the blast. He knew she struggled not only with the specific event but with the ongoing *Red Scare*. Fortunately, of late, she'd been heartened by Congress's approval of the 19th Amendment, giving women the right to vote in the 1920 elections. It was a step in the right direction, Jim estimated. He could imagine the strong Harvey women making a real difference with their votes.

Jim finished his tasks and hung his apron on the hook before ascending the stairs to the main floor. "Are you still here, Reilly?"

Jim nodded and strolled over to Sven. His eyes narrowed as he held out his hand. "It's a little late for this, but my name's Wirth. Jim Wirth." He laughed when Sven's eyes went wide. "Long story, but if you have time . . ."

Sven pulled up a stool next to one of the last vats of beer they'd be brewing for some time. He grabbed a couple of mugs and ladled in the drink. "Sit and tell me." He chuckled. "A man of mystery."

Jim sat and took a long gulp of his beer, wiping the foam from his upper lip. "Gonna miss this."

"And now we've given women the right to vote!" Sven shook his head. "What'll they do then?"

"Plenty of men behind the temperance movement too." Jim shrugged. "It'll be interesting to see how it all plays out."

"I've got my cellar stocked to the ceiling with hooch, though I can't see this thing lasting more than a year." Sven nodded to Jim. "Now tell your tale."

"I *am* a Reilly too. My mother's side." He pressed his lips together. "Suffice it to say, being a *Wirth*," he began, pronouncing it with the German V, "wasn't easy in a city whose mayor was looking for scapegoats. Some fella at the railroad——" Jim laughed. "Irish, as a matter of fact. He and I got into it one day. It was a misunderstanding, but O'Malley had it in for me after that. One thing led to another, and I became the German scapegoat for the place. And after a whole heap of trouble, I just got on the streetcar heading to St. Paul and ended up in Connemara."

Sven nodded, seeming to understand.

"I never thought of this until now, but Jacob Harvey—— He's Melania's father."

Sven chuckled. "The girl."

"Woman," Jim retorted with a chuckle. "I got in trouble when I treated her like a silly girl. Days in the past! Yes, though——her. Jacob Harvey saw what was coming. He's a wise man." Jim clinked his glass with Sven's. "Like you."

Sven waved his hand. "No need for compliments. You can have as much beer as you'd like."

"Anyway," Jim continued. "Jacob Harvey changed his surname on a whim when he left Germany in the troubled years at the end of the last century. He went from Kaiser to Harvey."

Sven whistled. "Good plan."

"I felt free when the streetcar crossed the river into St. Paul. No one would know me here, so when the first person asked my name, I said *Jim Reilly.*" His eyes twinkled, and he grinned at Sven. "That person was you."

Sven guffawed. "I don't know if I'm honored or annoyed."

Jim shrugged. "Survival."

Sven slapped him on the arm. "I get it. Damn! That explains why you like beer."

Jim set his glass down. "Runs deep in the Irish and the German sides, I'd say. But, in truth, I'm working on my future plans. Some wise man once told me I should get out of here——do something more suited for my talents."

"You're right. I am a wily one. What are your plans? Days at Prager's are waning unless you want to work churning ice cream."

"I've been looking——scanning the newspapers and notices for opportunities, and what keeps coming up is steel."

"The iron range? That's what they're calling the Lake Superior region now. The land is rich with ore." Sven stood and peered in the vat. "Many from here have gone that way."

"Mining is arduous and dirty work——underground or in the pits." Jim whistled. "I heard one of the fellas read a letter from his brother who'd headed that way before him." He chortled. "His descriptions of the long days and hard labor were daunting. I can't imagine why some men do it."

"I've heard that many immigrants have gone to the range. You know how it can be. No matter when you begin anew, there's a process of finding a place to make a living. I've heard it's a diverse group of people." Sven raised a shoulder. "That may make it appealing to a young man such as yourself who's just trying to mix in with the crowd."

"Gee. I'm not sure." Jim finished off his beer.

"Well, they ship the ore through the Great Lakes to ports in Chicago, Detroit, Cleveland——all the way to Erie and Buffalo. Maybe the rail is the place for you. After all, you know a thing or two about the railroads." Sven emptied his glass too and set about his other tasks.

"Don't think I can fathom doing that," Jim said, standing and running his hands through his hair, pushing the long strands off his face. "I can hardly stand to go near the station. But the iron range does have an appeal, I have to admit. I could just focus on the work and disappear into the crowd." He paused and rubbed his stubbly chin.

"But then there's the girl. A-hem, the woman." Sven raised a brow.

Jim grinned, nodding. "Yeah. I'm not sure she'd like the brutal winters or the laundry." Jim laughed heartily. "Of course, that's assuming an awful lot."

"Steel mill?" Sven asked. "Maybe the best choice?"

Jim nodded again. "Enticing. Starting over in a completely new state is tempting but leaving all I know is a knotty matter."

Sven laughed heartily. "Let me give you another piece of advice before I send you on your way. Women are a lot of work but generally worth it."

"That's some endorsement." Jim moved to the door, reaching for the handle. "Thanks for the beer and the sage advice," he said before heading out into the warm summer evening.

Outside, he rolled up his shirtsleeves and unbuttoned his collar, the coolness from the cellar gone after the beer and time on the brewing floor.

He headed to his apartment to clean up while the conversation with Sven swirled in his head. He had choices before him and not just those involving employment. He wanted to start his life—shake off the suspended nature of his days during the war, when he was just biding time before his enlistment. *The future is now,* he thought as he shut the door to his one-room apartment. The summer sun was still high in the sky when he hopped on the streetcar heading across the Mississippi.

"Hello! Welcome to our new home," Mrs. Harvey said brightly as Jim approached the porch later that evening.

"New?" Jim gave Mrs. Harvey a questioning look.

"She's being clever." Mr. Harvey stood and shook Jim's hand. "The home is ours now."

"You bought it?" Jim leaned back against the porch rail.

"Intended to. The Bartons gave it to us. Can you imagine?"

"As repayment for our generosity to their daughter and granddaughter, they said." Mrs. Harvey smiled, but it quickly disappeared. "We're grateful, but we miss them so."

"Elizabeth left with her grandparents," Mr. Harvey filled in.

"Ah," Jim said, feeling a bit uncomfortable.

"Sit, pull up a chair." Mr. Harvey rose from the swing and pulled a wicker chair around.

"We were just talking about Peter," Mrs. Harvey said.

"Ah. I've been thinking about him. How is he?"

Mr. Harvey chuckled dryly. "Post-war occupation isn't as easy as it would seem. The treaty was signed under German protest and now unrest is rampant. Several German politicians have been assassinated." He shrugged. "Needless to say, the Germans aren't too keen on American occupation, even though we didn't agree to the treaty either."

"Surely that would make a difference." Mrs. Harvey's comment sounded hopeful, and Jim understood her feeling. The same thought had crossed his mind.

Mr. Harvey turned to his wife. "The Americans are like every other occupier to the Germans. They're in Germany, taking control of land Germany feels is theirs, right or wrong. Several borders have been changed, much to Germany's clear disadvantage, making it even more difficult for them to pay the extensive war reparations." He sighed. "Not a good way to rebuild and move on."

"I'd like to write to Peter." Jim looked at Mrs. Harvey. "I'll send him my good wishes too."

She smiled. "You know Melania isn't here?"

Jim nodded. "I hoped to talk to Mr. Harvey."

Mrs. Harvey quickly got to her feet. "I'll leave you two alone, then. Don't leave before I bring out some pie."

The screen door to the front room shut, and the men waited until Mrs. Harvey's footsteps faded. Jim appreciated the older man's patience, as if he understood the seriousness of the topic. But then, Jim reminded himself, that was the reason he was here in the first place. He greatly valued Jacob Harvey's insight and wisdom, respecting him as a father figure.

Jim rubbed his hands together and reached for the glass of lemonade Mr. Harvey had poured and slid toward him. It crossed Jim's mind as peculiar that the Harveys would have an extra glass on the tray. But then Jim had been a part of many impromptu gatherings in the Harvey home. It was as if the couple always expected guests. Jim gulped several mouthfuls of lemonade and wiped his hand across his mouth, remembering his talk earlier with Sven.

"Sir. My job at the brewery. It's not for long." Jim shook his head slightly as he talked, his gaze fixed at a distant spot. "Prohibition has had a severe impact, obviously. Even with the changes and new products——" He shrugged. "Who knows if the company will survive." He chuckled. "Root beer and ice cream and, with any luck, packages for making home brew. I reckon that's about the only product that has a chance."

Mr. Harvey nodded and rubbed his chin. "I've read a lot about what the different breweries across the country are doing. Coors is taking advantage of Colorado's clay deposits to make ceramics. Yuengling's opened an ice cream and dairy plant. Pabst, in Wisconsin, switched to making cheese. Others will sell *near beer* and soft drinks." His shoulder lifted. "Survival. Not unlike during the war." He chuckled. "I give this prohibition idea five years, tops." He chortled. "Mind me. I'm not a man for heavy drink, but it seems to go against everything America stands for, to tell a business what they can and can't produce, and to tell a man what he can and can't drink." He snorted and then shrugged. "I've never actually spoken those words out loud, despite thinking them often enough. The days of the war—when we *couldn't* say what we thought are still fresh."

Jim laughed. "Tell me about it. Time, I guess. And distance, maybe."

"Are you leaving?"

Jim was surprised Mr. Harvey came to such an abrupt point but answered honestly. "Maybe. I've been thinking about steel."

The older man nodded. "There's a lot to steel. It's a good bet with the post-war advancements in industry."

"From what I see, I have three main options——the iron range near Superior, working with the railroad transporting the ore, or finding employment directly with a steel company." Jim paused.

"What are you thinking?" Mr. Harvey asked after several seconds.

"A steel company. I can't think of a way to work for the railroad again, at least anytime soon."

The older man nodded in understanding.

"And the iron range. It's mine work. Dirty and dangerous."

Again, Mr. Harvey nodded.

"I understand the steel is being produced mostly in Pennsylvania and Ohio," Jim said, hesitating to look up and face the obvious.

But Mr. Harvey didn't go down that road. "I've read a lot recently about Bethlehem Steel. A man name Schwab, who used to work for Carnegie, purchased the small firm over fifteen years ago. He's on the way to making it a contender." Jacob nodded at the prospect. "Schwab's focus has been on big government contracts——ships, naval armor, construction beams. Big plans." He rubbed his chin again. "Another point to consider is the value of Bethlehem's efforts to avoid the strikes plaguing so much of the industry. Paying good wages too, I hear."

Jim looked up, nodding, taking in what the man had said. "Makes sense." Jim pulled out his handkerchief and wiped his brow.

Mr. Harvey reached out and patted Jim's shoulder. "You're a good ma and a good worker. They'd be fortunate to have you."

Jim abruptly stood up as if intending to leave. Then he sat down again and began shaking his bent legs. Mr. Harvey looked at him. After a time, Jim stood again and planted himself firmly on both feet.

"Sir, your daughter. She means a lot to me. The world. I know I don't have a lot, nothing really. But I will. I'll work hard." He again wiped his brow, which had begun to drip profusely.

The old man's mouth turned up into a small smile.

"Sir. Mr. Harvey. I'd like to ask for your daughter's hand in marriage."

At that moment, Mrs. Harvey pushed the door open with a tray laden with pie and coffee. She hesitated and froze as Jacob rose and extended his hand to Jim. "Welcome into the family, son. You really should start calling us Helene and Jacob."

Mrs. Harvey set the tray down on the table and embraced him as tears streamed down her face. "We're family now."

EPILOGUE

The Herald: MISS MELANIA HARVEY IS BRIDE OF JAS. WIRTH. *Pretty Autumn Wedding Solemnized at the Blessed Sacrament Church in Holmesburg, Sept. 3, 1919* A QUIET BUT PRETTY WEDDING WAS SOLEMNIZED AT THE BLESSED SACRAMENT CHURCH IN THIS CITY ON WEDNESDAY MORNING, SEPT. 3RD, WHEN MISS MELANIA HARVEY, YOUNGEST DAUGHTER OF MR. AND MRS. JACOB HARVEY (FORMERLY OF HOLMESBURG), BECAME THE BRIDE OF JAMES WIRTH, ORIGINALLY OF AUGUSTA. THE NUPTIAL MASS WAS CELEBRATED BY REV. FATHER BERNARD. THE BRIDE WAS A VISION OF LOVELINESS, ATTIRED IN A HANDSOME DARK BROWN SUIT WITH A HAT TO MATCH, AND WAS ATTENDED BY MISS JANE VOGEL. THE GROOM WAS ATTENDED BY FRANK HARVEY, A BROTHER OF THE BRIDE. AFTER THE CHURCH SERVICES, A WEDDING BREAKFAST WAS SERVED AT THE HOME OF THE BRIDE'S BROTHER——THE BRIDAL PARTY AND A FEW IMMEDIATE RELATIVES BEING PRESENT. THE BRIDE IS WELL-KNOWN AND EXTREMELY POPULAR AMONG THE YOUNGER SET HERE. THE MAN OF HER CHOICE IS UNKNOWN TO US BUT IS SAID TO BE HIGHLY ESTEEMED IN HIS HOME COMMUNITY AND A

MAN OF PROMISING FUTURE. FOR THE PRESENT, THEY WILL RESIDE IN MINNEAPOLIS, ALTHOUGH THE GROOM HOLDS A POSITION IN BETHLEHEM, PENNSYLVANIA, BE-GINNING IN OCTOBER. HOLMESBURG AND THE HERALD JOIN THEIR HOST OF FRIENDS IN WISHING THE COUPLE UNBOUNDED SUCCESS AND HAPPINESS AS THEY START THEIR NEW ADVENTURE.

BOOK CLUB DISCUSSION GUIDE

1. Cate Michels brings to life the difficulties for citizens of German descent in Minnesota during the first world war. Were you aware of these nativist activities before you read this novel? How did you feel about the Governor's mandate and the authority of the Minnesota Commission on Public Safety?

2. Jacob is wise and discerning. Did you find this realistic? How did you think he developed his intuitive nature?

3. Melania matures significantly in a short period of time. What lessons does she learn during these tumultuous days that she may not have learned otherwise?

4. Cate Michels named the book *All That We Have* to reflect that people cling to certain feelings, beliefs, and principles during difficult times. What are some of these for the main characters and how did it help them?

5. Helene and Jacob have an abiding relationship. What are your thoughts on their interactions with each other and with others in their lives?

6. Melania and Jim took a long and winding road to becoming a couple. Did Melania choose the right man? What do you think their future holds?

7. Cate Michels wrote this book before the Covid pandemic. What similarities did you see between the characters' lives in the time of the Spanish Influenza and your own life during Covid?

8. St. Paul and Minneapolis took different approaches to the Spanish Influenza. Why do you think that was and did you feel that one way was better than the other?

9. What are your thoughts on Jacob changing the family surname? Was it an impetuous decision? Do you know of any surname changes in your family history?

10. How were Peter and Anna important to the story despite having minor roles in the book?

11. What did you know about this time period before reading the book? What did you learn that has stayed with you? Was it difficult to keep your own modern-day experiences from influencing the reading of a historical fiction tale?

— · —

AUTHOR'S NOTES

I have a picture of my grandparents on their wedding day—my grand-mother seated in a dark jacket and skirt with lace-up boots and my grandfather standing beside her. They looked serious, like most people in old photos, but a lively newspaper article is taped on the back of the picture that assures me they were happy that day. They met at a dance in 1917, the year the United States entered the war, and married in 1919, not long after the Great War ended. I wondered what those two years were like for them, a young couple setting out into the world in the early twentieth century, so I started to look into the *time* and *place* of their story. I learned about the 19th-century events that contributed to the beginning of the Great War. I read about the sinking of the Lusitania and the forms of German aggression that finally brought the United States into the war nearly three years after it began. I was stunned to learn of the ultra-nationalist efforts in Minnesota and the country to *root out the enemy*—many extreme and arbitrary. The days on the home front were marked with the obligations of war that many hoped would show their loyalty to America—sacrifice, volunteerism, war bonds, Victory gardens, and sons, husbands, and fathers drafted into service. And then the world was nearly pushed to the brink when the Spanish Influenza sped across the globe near the war's end, taking three times as many lives as did the fighting. Goodness! I can't believe my grandparents even survived to get married! The title, *All That We Have,* is inspired by the spirit of everyone who lived through these tumultuous years—clinging to hope, faith, integrity, and love.

My book is not about my grandparents but is inspired by them—a tribute to their fortitude. It's a work of fiction, but it's been carefully researched, which is much easier to do in this world of the internet. There are museum and university databases about both the war and Spanish influenza, and several other terrific sources that give insights from journals, newspapers, and military and hospital archives. Pictures, which there are surprisingly many from this era, were a great source of material and inspiration.

While Walter von Esson is a made-up character, Minneapolis did have a socialist mayor during this time, and the Minnesota Governor was very adamant about rooting out enemies within, so I envisioned the Mayor making every effort to shine the spotlight away from his office. The stories of nativist incidents were based on *real* stories across the country. For those of you familiar with the city of St. Paul, Minnesota, you'll recognize that I took liberties in describing Connemara. A group of Irish did come to Minnesota in the 1880s from the Connemara region in Ireland, many eventually settling in St. Paul. What I imagined for this community decades later was a rich and vibrant Irish neighborhood, just the place that the weary Jim Wirth needed.

Spanish influenza was challenging to encapsulate because much of what was known about it was drawn from data gathered in the aftermath. My goal wasn't to convey a perfect understanding of Spanish influenza but rather the intense and frantic nature of dealing with this virulent disease. Interestingly, I wrote this book *before* the COVID pandemic, and not surprisingly, I discovered a similar sense of just doing our best with the unknown.

I tried to be as accurate as possible with all things historical and avoided taking any unnecessary liberties with details. But this is a work of fiction, so chill and enjoy the story.

ACKNOWLEDGMENTS

A great big thank you to my family for their love and support. My husband, Mic, is incredibly patient and has been my biggest promoter. My son, John, has offered many helpful and creative insights during the writing process. My son, Jacob, is always encouraging and has excellent marketing ideas. My sister, Carolyn, is my right-hand girl—supportive, helpful, always ready to listen, and a rock star in cover design.

I am grateful for the support of my friends, especially those who were early readers of this book.

Thank you to Val Bodden, my editor, for her sharp eye and helping me grow as a writer.

Thank you to Cathy Williams of Hammer Gams Photography for the cover photo. She is a talented and visionary artist.

About The Author

Cate Michels grew up in the Twin Cities and loves to tell stories inspired by the extraordinary people who have made the Midwest their home. She is an avid history lover and hopes to inspire your love of history with her stories. Find more information about her books and future projects at:

https://www.catemichels.com

https://www.facebook.com/CateMichels.author

https://www.instagram.com/catemichelsauthor/

YOUR FREE BOOK IS WAITING!

In All Its Fury—A Novella Prequel to the Generations of Hope Series. Join my mailing list at *www.catemichels.com* to get a free ebook or PDF in addition to updates on my books, future projects, and events!